AS
SHE
ASCENDS

BOOK TWO
OF THE FALLEN ISLES TRILOGY

Also by
JODI MEADOWS

The Fallen Isles Trilogy
Before She Ignites
As She Ascends

The Orphan Queen Duology
The Orphan Queen
The Mirror King

The Incarnate Trilogy
Incarnate
Asunder
Infinite

The Lady Janies Series
Coauthored with Cynthia Hand and Brodi Ashton
My Lady Jane
My Plain Jane

AS
SHE
ASCENDS

BOOK TWO
OF THE FALLEN ISLES TRILOGY

JODI MEADOWS

 KATHERINE TEGEN BOOKS
An Imprint of HarperCollins Publishers

For everyone who's stumbled

Katherine Tegen Books is an imprint of HarperCollins Publishers.

As She Ascends
Copyright © 2018 by Jodi Meadows
All rights reserved. Printed in the United States of America.
No part of this book may be used or reproduced in any manner whatsoever
without written permission except in the case of brief quotations embodied
in critical articles and reviews. For information address HarperCollins
Children's Books, a division of HarperCollins Publishers, 195 Broadway,
New York, NY 10007.
www.epicreads.com

Library of Congress Control Number: 2018939882
ISBN 978-0-06-246943-4

Typography by Carla Weise
18 19 20 21 22   PC/LSCH   10 9 8 7 6 5 4 3 2 1
❖
First Edition

THE CREED OF SILENCE
the final day
of the Hallowed Restoration
in the first year of the Fallen Gods

Holy are the silent—
Men who move without sound
Men who speak without voice
Men who live without intrusion

Holy are the silent—
Men who listen to the land
Men who hear the hum of light
Men who perceive the world's power

Holy are the silent—
Men who confess their deeds
Men who obey without question
Men who follow the light

Holy are the silent—
Men who cast out the sinful
Men who abhor the wicked
Men who deny the dark

Strength through silence
Cela, cela.

Power demanded to be used.

And I had power.

AARU

Thirteen Years Ago

WHEN I WAS FOUR, I REALIZED THAT I WOULD NEVER be enough.

A strange man had come to my house all the way from Summerill, the capital of Idris. When the front door shut, blocking out only scraps of the storm's rush and clatter, Mother performed her duties: offering towels to wipe off the rain, tea to warm the body, and a new reed mat on which to place his wet shoes. All this she did quietly, speaking only with looks and gestures. Aloud, Father apologized for her slowness. The man said slowness was expected when a woman could give birth at any moment; his annoyed tone, however, outweighed his polite words.

After all the proper welcome rituals were finished, Father introduced me. Not my sister, although she stood at my side, as still and soundless as a held breath. I lifted my chin, as expected of the boy of the house. But of course I spoke not a word. Today, of all days, I was meant to be silent.

More than silent.

The man strode toward me, his footfalls hidden under the rain that pattered endlessly against the house. The Isle of Silence had two seasons: the dry season and the wet season, and the wet season was always, always loud.

As the man peered at me, I stuffed down a whimper. A choke of worry. A breath that might be too loud. I pushed it all deep inside my stomach, locked away in an imaginary box that resided there, because I was certain he would be able to hear any noise I made, even with the rain beating the walls.

Strength through silence, I prayed, but the man's scrutiny was like fingernails scraping my skin, harder when thoughts turned into words. So I put prayers in the box, too.

Perfect silence: unattainable by mortal men, but demanded nonetheless.

My heartbeat was thunder in my ears; he must have heard it, too, because abruptly he spun and his attention returned to Father. Freed of his sharp stare, I didn't dare make a sound in relief. I just faded into the background with Korinah and wondered if that was all, or if there would be another test.

With the expression of a most obedient son on my face,

and my hands twisted behind my back, I tapped ::**Strength through silence**:: over and over, as though Idris might look up from his bed in the sea and suddenly find me worthy.

Had the god of silence found the strange man's companion worthy?

The man had a boy with him, just a year or two older than me, though besides their light-brown skin, the pair didn't look anything alike. Where the man was round, the boy was narrow. And while the man's facial features were all spread out, the boy's were squished into the center.

Yes, I decided. The man must have gone to that boy's home, squinted at his face, and deemed him not just satisfactory, but *worthy*. Silent enough to be taken.

But silence had little to do with manners, at least as far as the boy was concerned, because he prowled the edges of the room until his brown eyes settled on Korinah, who was still very small for a two-year-old. Then he smiled, his boredom and apathy transforming into keen interest.

Korinah tensed, and I quickly shook my head at the boy, hoping to warn him off.

But he pinched her.

My sister flinched, closing her eyes and swallowing hard, but she didn't make a sound.

He pulled one of her curls.

She winced and sidled toward me, and I put myself between them, tapping in the quiet code for him to quit bothering her. But the other boy was bigger. He simply reached over me and tried to poke her left eye.

3

"Stop," I hissed, underneath the thrum of rain.

Until that point, the entire exchange had been sound-less. But at my word, all the adults looked over, deep frowns crossing their faces.

::He was trying to hurt her,:: I explained in hurried quiet code, but it was too late. I'd spoken aloud. In front of a guest. An adult guest.

It didn't matter that the other boy had been cruel to my sister, or that I'd used my voice to stand up for her. It mattered only that I'd broken the first high law of Idris:

Strength through silence.

FIRST IT WAS the basement. Later would come the beat-ing.

There, as close to Idris as I could possibly be, I learned about silence.

In a society that valued silence most of all, every book was next to holy. They possessed the ability to convey words and thoughts and meaning across time and space, with-out uttering a single sound. Books were for the wealthy, though, so my family had none—save *The Book of Silence*, of which every family owned at least one copy. The holi-est book of all. Idris's words, silently spread on sheets of paper so soft that they didn't so much as whisper against one another when the pages were turned. Every evening, Father read the book's stories and teachings aloud, while Mother tapped them in quiet code.

The Book of Silence, as expected, had a lot to say on the

subject of silence. Hand-copied pages were scattered on a table in the basement, with a pencil and pile of empty papers next to them. Waiting for me. Though I couldn't yet read well, I could copy letters, and I knew what these pages were about.

Primarily, they instructed on reflective silence. In traditional music, the silence of every instrument was meant to allow the listener time to reflect on the note that just ended—to be joyful or frightened or worried. This silence heightened tension.

And they instructed on submissive silence—only one or two instruments playing while the others sat at rest. It forced the listener to focus on what was truly important in the moment, rather than the unendurable crush of unnecessary voices.

I sat at the table and copied letters one by one. I should have reflected, as *The Book of Silence* instructed. I should have surrendered my voice to the adults in the room. To the grown men.

Above, I could hear the man speaking: "Thank you, but he clearly doesn't have the gift."

"Please reconsider," said my father.

"You embarrass yourself. But I should not be surprised. You have such a noisy little family." Scorn filled the man's tone. "I'll take my leave now."

I had shamed my family.

The sky went dark behind its ever-present shroud of storm clouds, and Mother came to get me. One hand curled around her belly, as though it had finally grown too big to stay up on its own.

"Are you finished praying?"

I hadn't been praying at all. I supposed that meant I was finished.

I put down the pencil and nodded.

"Then come up and apologize to your father for humiliating him." She turned and gripped the banister to haul herself back upstairs. Halfway there, she paused and looked back. Her voice was low, meant only for me. "I'm proud that you wanted to protect Korinah. But if you want a good life, learn how to do it silently, or don't do it at all."

PART ONE

WITHOUT SOUND

CHAPTER ONE

Mira

"RUN," I WHISPERED.

Ilina, Hristo, and Aaru grew still, excitement forgotten. We'd only just escaped the Pit, but already warriors pursued us. Sounds echoed across the sunbaked field:

1. *The cry of horns.*
2. *A clamor of shouts.*
3. *Boots beating the ground.*

We had only minutes before they rounded a bend in the cliffside. Mounds of rubble blown out from the explosion offered us a little more cover, but it wouldn't last long.

Escape did not mean freedom. We still had to fight for that.

"Run," I said again, but this time I took off toward the thin forest that bordered the western side of the field, its edge too neat to be natural. Gerel would likely have been able to tell me how they sent trainees to cut back the growth using dinner knives or letter openers, but she and Chenda were somewhere else, securing more supplies.

I wished they were here.

On my shoulder, LaLa coiled into a tight ball of tiny dragon, then pushed herself into the air as I picked up speed. Her wingsister—Crystal—followed. I trusted them to keep up, to keep track of us. All dragons were excellent hunters, but *Drakontos raptuses* were the best at chasing scents and following movements.

Hristo and Ilina ran with me, and Aaru not far behind. Our four pairs of footfalls drummed against the ground, too loud to go unnoticed. Pain, exhaustion, and hunger weighed us down. Whatever I'd done in the Pit—that explosion of heat and power—was taking its toll; not that I'd ever been much of a runner before this, but now I felt in particular danger of slowing the group.

Even Hristo lagged, though, and under other circumstances that might have made me feel better. But if he couldn't defend us, there was no hope of this escape lasting. We'd end up back in the Pit, our situations worse than ever. My identity was public now, and while some of my fellow first-level prisoners might not care, others did: a man called Hurrok had already made efforts to end me.

But he wasn't a concern right now. The warriors were.

We stumbled toward the trees, so close that their heavy shadows fell over us.

"There!" I didn't know the gruff voice, but I recognized the tone of a warrior. We'd been spotted.

I risked a glance over my shoulder to find three warriors closing in. We outnumbered them, and somewhere out here, there were at least four other escaped prisoners. But we were on Khulan, the Isle of Warriors, where the people's god granted them immense strength. We didn't stand a chance, even with three dragons.

Three dragons.

I stopped running. We were missing the third dragon: Kelsine.

When Ilina and Hristo came for Aaru and me, they'd said Kelsine was sleeping outside, waiting for us. But I'd been so consumed by seeing LaLa, *my* dragon, that I'd forgotten the *Drakontos ignitus*. And now we'd left her behind?

"What are you doing?" Ilina darted back toward me and grabbed my arm. "Let's *go.*"

Before I could speak, she dragged me toward the woods again. My toes caught on tufts of grass and clumps of dirt, but I picked up my feet and ran. Ilina was right: stopping, even for a moment, could get us killed.

We plunged into the trees. A green veil dimmed the world as we moved deeper into the shade. Brush and brambles tugged at my dress, while birds called and bugs droned, their voices somehow adding to the oppressive heat. The air was heavy with humidity, making sweat form along my hairline and bead down my face.

Inside the fire-resistant jacket I'd stolen, it was getting hard to breathe. Plus, this was my second flat-out sprint of the day. I couldn't keep this up. Not long enough to outrun a trio of *warriors*.

My legs burned as we careened through the woods, and pain stabbed at my side.

Fifty-seven, fifty-eight, fifty-nine.

I counted my strides, desperate to hold on to some measure of control.

My chest tightened, and even my hearing dulled to a low rush of air squeezing in and out of my lungs.

Seventy-five, seventy-six, seventy-seven.

My vision faded, and it was all I could do to keep Hristo in my sight as he navigated between tall, dark shapes. Trees, but they looked more like shadow beasts now.

One hundred and three, one hundred and four, one hundred and five—

My foot dragged over a root, and I stumbled. Fell. Twigs and leaves scraped at my palms, but it hardly mattered. I wasn't going to be able to get back up. Not if I had to keep running.

Aaru dropped next to me, his hand on my shoulder. He squeezed in a silent question. Was I hurt?

I couldn't catch my breath well enough to speak, either aloud or in the quiet code, so I just shook my head and stared hard at the ground, willing color back into my vision. Grainy shades of gray stained the world, no matter how much air I gulped. Surely this was what dying felt like.

Ilina and Hristo grabbed me under my arms and hauled me to my feet, dislodging Aaru. "No time for a nap." Her teasing words were forced, though, and also breathless. She glanced over my shoulder. "But you're right; this isn't going to work. We're creating a trail."

LaLa and Crystal landed on a huge branch, watching with wide eyes as they shifted their weight from side to side.

"The warriors know these woods," Hristo conceded, wiping threads of sweat from his brow. "They'll be able to track us."

"We have to do something different. And fast." Ilina kept her voice low and, when I signaled that she could release me, she stepped back. "They're walking. They know they have us. They know we're tired. There's no need for them to run."

A pitiful whimper escaped me.

Hristo put his arm around my shoulders, lending me strength. "Let's split up to confuse the trails. Then we'll meet at the cabin in three hours." With his free hand, he motioned—northward, I guessed, but I couldn't tell, thanks to all the trees. We'd taken so many twists and turns that I was completely lost.

Earlier, he'd said the cabin was about an hour's walk

northwest, toward a pair of mountain peaks. At least, those had been the directions from the ruins. From here, I had no idea. Navigating through heavy foliage and zigzagging a trail would be even more confusing.

Hristo continued, "I'll take Mira—"

"No." Ilina hooked her arm with mine. "I'm not separating from her. Not again."

Aaru stepped closer, too.

Hristo opened his mouth to argue, but Ilina had a history of winning, and the crash of warriors moving through the forest wasn't that far off. "Fine. We'll go together, but everyone must do as I say."

We nodded.

"They'll expect us to go downhill, toward the stream. We should create a false trail that way, but we don't have time."

Aaru lifted his hand. ::Will go.::

I interpreted.

Hristo nodded. "All right. The rest of us will head uphill, where we can hopefully get a better view of our surroundings."

"Where is the stream?" Ilina asked. "I don't hear anything but bugs."

Aaru cocked his head, then pointed to the left.

"Leave a trail," Hristo said, "but don't be too obvious. When you double back, make sure you take the exact same path as before, or they'll know."

Aaru gave a swift nod.

"We're going directly north. Up the mountain as far as we can. Are you sure you can find us? We can't leave a trail for you to follow."

This was starting to sound a lot like the original plan of separating, but instead of two and two, it was three and one. That was supremely unfair.

But before I could speak up, Aaru was slipping between the trees, toward the stream. He had the light step of a soft breeze, and he disappeared into the shadows quickly. It seemed unlikely that someone as quiet and careful as Aaru could leave enough of a trail for the warriors to follow. I should have volunteered.

"Come on." Hristo touched my elbow and started north. "We have to hurry. Step where I step. Move how I move."

I followed, with Ilina taking the rear. Obeying his instructions was harder than it sounded, because his strides were long and cautious. I had to clutch my dress up to my thighs to keep it from catching on brush, and that left my legs exposed for bugs and brambles.

This uncomfortable way of walking made counting steps difficult, but after five hundred paces and no sound of the warriors behind us, I chanced a question. "Why did you let Aaru go? What if he can't find us?"

"Aaru knows what he's doing." Hristo kept his voice low.

He couldn't possibly know that. Hristo had just met Aaru the day before, and that didn't count because they'd been separated by an entire cell and Aaru had stopped speaking after Altan tortured him.

Hristo glanced over his shoulder, his brown skin flushed dark with heat. "He offered to go to keep you safe. Because he knows I will not separate from you, and neither will Ilina."

And Aaru thought that since he was the newest of my friends, he was the most expendable.

Or . . .

Or he was using this as an opportunity to leave, now that I'd done my part in helping him escape the Pit.

He hadn't even said good-bye.

After picking our way through the woods another seven hundred steps, I asked, "What about Kelsine? We left her behind."

"She wasn't there," Ilina said. "When we came out again, she wasn't where she'd been sleeping before."

"You didn't say anything." Hurt bit into my tone. Kelsine had been used by the warriors. She was a victim. People came in and took her parents. Her family. And then she was thrust into a dark hall with strange humans. If she breathed fire at them, it was out of fear. She was a *child*, and Ilina should know that.

Ilina shook her head. "At first, I was so surprised to see Crystal and LaLa. And then the warriors came and we had to run."

I lowered my eyes. She was right. My thoughts had been uncharitable. Of all people, Ilina understood the importance of dragons.

"We might still see Kelsine again," she said as we climbed up a series of rocky shelves. "I don't imagine she got very far. Not in her condition."

"No more talking." Hristo's command came an instant before we heard a stray *crack* in the woods.

The three of us held absolutely still, waiting for another sound.

Above, LaLa trilled and wove between the trees. Perhaps the sound had come from her or Crystal. But no, both dragons had been up there all along. The noise had come from somewhere on the ground.

My heart pounded as I scanned the forest around us. Everything was brown and green, dripping with humidity. Birds called and red squirrels skittered from tree to tree. There was nothing unusual about the woods, at least as far as I could see. This place *was* different from the peaceful forests around Crescent Prominence, though.

Maybe I only felt that way because I'd never been hunted there.

After fifteen seconds, the tension in Hristo's shoulders loosened and he continued guiding us uphill.

Our journey was slow, mostly because we kept pausing to throw stepped-on twigs away from our path. Several times, Hristo had us all bend and drag our fingers through trampled grass, to help it stand again and erase evidence of our passing. Then we'd toss fallen leaves and other forest debris in our wake, to create the illusion that no one had come through this area for some time.

Four thousand steps.

Five thousand.

Six thousand.

I tried to stop counting, because the numbers were getting ridiculous, but my mind dutifully tracked every step as though my life depended on it.

The sun dipped toward the horizon, and the whole time, I waited for Aaru's return. It occurred to me that I knew so little of his upbringing—whether he could traverse strange woods without leaving a trail, or if he knew how to find clean water, or even if he was good at walking long distances.

What if he was hurt? Could he patch himself together well enough to find us?

I wanted to ask Hristo if we were almost to wherever he wanted to be—because we'd definitely been walking for more than an hour—or if we could go back for Aaru, but that tension had returned to his shoulders, and he kept checking our surroundings like he couldn't feel how utterly alone we were out here.

Abruptly, LaLa and Crystal peeled off from our group and flew south, as though they'd spotted a mouse or vole. It was hard to blame them for choosing dinner over following us; my stomach grumbled with hunger, too.

I'd long since managed to catch my breath, at least, and the agony of running through the woods was mostly behind us. Only my chest hurt now, still pinched from physical exertion. As though my lungs believed that sprinting meant I needed less air, not more.

Stillness touched the forest.

First the birds. Then the bugs. Even the wind seemed hushed, and my mind worked through half a dozen possible explanations for this unbidden quiet. Warriors. Predators. Aftershocks. Storms. Sudden deafness. Aaru?

But Aaru's silence would have been complete, and when Hristo paused to look around, I was fairly sure it wasn't just me noticing.

Hristo glanced over his shoulder, long strands of sunlight shining amber against his dark skin. His mouth opened, like he was about to say something, but behind him, a haggard man stepped onto our path.

A map of white tattoos glowed against deep-brown skin. His filthy, matted hair had been recently cut, likely chopped by the long knife that rested against his thigh. I'd rarely seen his face, but I knew the man immediately. His fierce scowl, aimed at me, was unmistakable.

I'd been wrong to fear the warriors or a predator or anything else. I should have kept watch for the other escaped inmates, particularly the one who'd been imprisoned for attempting to kill me.

Hurrok.

CHAPTER TWO

Sᴡᴇᴀᴛ ꜱʟɪᴛʜᴇʀᴇᴅ ᴅᴏᴡɴ ᴍʏ ꜰᴀᴄᴇ ᴀꜱ I ᴄᴏɴꜱɪᴅᴇʀᴇᴅ our situation.

Hurrok had the long knife.

We had: Hristo, the battered sword he'd carried from the Pit, Ilina's bow (but no arrows), and three knives—one each. We'd had more, but they'd been destroyed along with the Pit. Ten minutes ago, we'd had two dragons, but they'd abandoned us for voles.

"Mira Minkoba." Hurrok's voice hissed with the wind. "What happened to your face?"

Before I could stop myself, my fingers brushed the bumpy ridge on my cheek. Though it was a new injury, the noorestone power I'd wielded in the Pit had healed it, leaving behind a scar.

Hurrok laughed. "You made it out. Hard to believe a

pathetic thing like you could survive all that."

He wasn't the only one who was surprised. "That's no thanks to you." The presence of my friends made me stronger, and words I'd have never said alone came out when I was with them. "You almost ruined our escape. Why was killing me more important than freedom?"

"You wrecked everything. My work. My family. My whole life." His knife hand trembled with rage as he stepped closer. "Killing you is the only thing I have left."

"Stay back." Hristo drew and lifted his sword, a move that should have been intimidating, but his arm shook with strain. He'd already fought off Luminary Guards and warriors, and escaped the noorestone explosion I'd caused. It seemed unlikely he was truly up to fighting off another opponent, even one who'd spent the last year in the Pit, screaming every time the noorestones went dark.

"Or you'll have me arrested?" Hurrok's face twisted with amusement. "The Pit is gone, Fancy." That was Altan's name for me, not his, but it sounded the same from both men, dripping with derision. "The warriors are dead. I can do whatever I want."

And killing me was at the top of his list, apparently.

"There are plenty of warriors left," I said.

"We're still trying to get away from them. You should, too." Ilina stood right behind me, her arm touching mine. Beads of sweat formed between us.

"I don't care if they find me, as long as you're punished for what you've done."

I fought to keep my tone gentle. Calm. "You mean the

Mira Treaty? You're not the only one whose life changed because of it." If I could keep him talking, then he wasn't attacking. It seemed unlikely I could persuade him not to end my life—that would take someone with more Daminan skill than I had—but I had dealt with people who hated the Mira Treaty before.

Business owners who'd once made a living off transporting Hartan produce away from Harta, but were now destitute.

People who'd kept small dragons as pets and had to give them up to sanctuaries.

Dignitaries who were now required to respect the beliefs of other islands, rather than being allowed to dismiss them entirely.

But most of those people were able to separate the girl from the treaty and had no desire to hurt me. Until Hurrok revealed his attempt on my life, I'd had no idea there'd been more than one, and that first man had come when I was only seven; Hristo had saved me then, and apparently several times since.

Sweat trickled down Hurrok's face. "This has nothing to do with the Mira Treaty. It's all about what you said. You care for *creatures* more than you care for people." He stepped toward us. "You Daminans claim that love is the most important thing in the world, but you proved that wrong the day you supported closing the mill." Roaring, Hurrok surged forward with his knife, but Hristo lunged in front of me and blocked with his sword.

Metal clashed, sharp and bright and deadly. Hurrok whipped his knife around, and Hristo moved to counter. In the sinking sunlight, steel flashed and gleamed with every movement.

Ilina tugged my arm, drawing me backward—away from the fighting.

"We have to help." But what could I do? I wasn't a fighter, or a diplomat, and even if I'd had those skills, I was too exhausted; I couldn't trust my body to do what I asked.

"Where did our dragons go?" Ilina looked to the sky. "A little fire wouldn't hurt right now."

She wasn't wrong.

Desperately, I glanced around the forest, but only the lengthening sunshine fell through the trees. Twilight shadows grew across the ground, and for a heartbeat, I hoped Chenda was nearby; she wielded shadow skill like I'd never seen.

But these were normal shadows, not gifts from Bopha, and the fighting ahead took on a new fury as Hurrok pushed toward Ilina and me.

"We should run." Ilina squeezed my arm and tugged, but where would we go? This whole trek, I'd unthinkingly followed Hristo uphill, and if he had a destination in mind, he hadn't shared it. Yes, we'd been heading to the safe house, but obviously we hadn't been going *straight* there.

Every time Hurrok lunged, Hristo put himself between

the attacker and me, swinging his sword fast enough to blur.

Numbers rattled in the back of my head: beats of metal on metal, thumps of boots on dirt, and gasps from both men as their struggle progressed. Neither was at his peak, and the failing sunlight made it difficult to see.

But no matter how exhausted Hristo was, his pace never flagged. He met every strike with a parry, like he read intent in the other man's eyes.

"Do you think Hristo will kill him?" Ilina's hand was heavy on my shoulder. "Is that a dumb question?"

Hristo had killed people back in the Pit. Gerel, too. And maybe Ilina, though I'd seen her aiming for legs and shoulders, places that would injure but not eliminate. But what happened in the Pit had been desperation. We'd been trapped. Surrounded. And at least one group would have killed all of us; the other group would have killed most of us.

"I think Hristo will do whatever it takes to keep us safe." My throat felt dry as we watched the battle move through the narrow space, brushing against trees and ferns and fallen branches.

Hurrok had said something about a mill—that I supported closing it.

Lightning flared in my head, and I *knew*. I knew what I'd done to him and why he hated me.

"The Nightmeadows!" I stepped forward, away from Ilina. "You're talking about the Nightmeadows."

Hurrok loosed a roar, jamming his knife at Hristo's gut. My protector twisted his body, and the blade sailed safely past. In the same motion, Hristo lifted his knee, catching Hurrok's flank, and the would-be assassin went down, arms and legs flying. His knife clattered against a rock, just out of his reach.

Hristo's breath heaved as he planted his boot on Hurrok's chest, pinning him down. He slid his sword point toward his opponent's throat: a warning not to move.

"I remember the Nightmeadows." I paused three paces away from them. "The mill was struggling to produce enough grain, thanks to broken equipment. The owners wouldn't pay to have it fixed. The supervisors had started beating some of the workers to *inspire* them to reach their goals."

Shadows melted into darkness as the sun dipped below the horizon. Through the purple gloom, Hurrok sneered at me. "My family depended on the mill. On the money I brought home. And *you* had the mill shut down and destroyed. For *dragons.*"

The Stardowns—the local Bophan sanctuary—had acquired a new *Drakontos maior*, but the bordering properties were too populated to safely keep such a territorial dragon. So they'd sought to purchase the surrounding land, offering a more-than-fair compensation for the trouble of relocating families and businesses.

"The sale was going to happen whether or not I spoke about it," I said. "I'm Daminan, as you said. And I was only a voice, not a senator or councilor or judge. I read the speech I was given." I'd done a lot of that in my life. Until that new year's speech in the Shadowed City, the one supporting the deportation of Hartans, I hadn't ever questioned the words I'd been given. I hadn't ever *refused* until then.

But I had inquired about the fates of people before giving the Stardowns speech. Both the Bophan and Daminan governments had assured me everyone was being treated fairly in this agreement. And it was to help *dragons*. Of course I supported better accommodations for dragons.

"Your speech tipped the mill's owners." Hurrok's tattoos twisted with his scowl. "They sold because of what you said. You ruined everything. My family *starved* because of you."

Heedless of the sword at his throat, Hurrok kicked up and hooked Hristo's leg at the knee.

My protector dropped and rolled back to his feet, and the sword flashed in the waning twilight. But it was too late. Hurrok had retrieved his knife and footing, and somehow he'd managed to place himself between Hristo and Ilina and me.

Hristo shouted, "Run!"

Ilina grabbed my hand.

Hurrok lunged for me, knife gleaming.

I stumbled away, but not fast enough. Fiery pain lit my shoulder blade, slicing my dress and my skin. Warm blood dripped down my back.

Then, chaos.

Ilina screamed my name, and I was running with her—or at least trying. Darkness hid roots and brush, and suddenly the entire space was a death trap.

We didn't get far before Ilina pulled me behind a large rain tree. "Are you all right?" she whispered.

"I'll live." Between the trees, I could just see Hurrok and Hristo fighting. Hurrok thrust and twisted, suddenly inside Hristo's guard. He pushed forward, jamming his shoulder into Hristo's chest. My protector kicked the other man's knee, and even from here the sickening noise of crunching bone was audible. Hurrok didn't fall; though starved and weak from the Pit, he had a rage that gave him terrifying strength.

"Why did you say anything?" Next to me, Ilina was shaking. The whites of her eyes were bright in the purple gloom. "Upper Gods, Hristo should have killed him while he had him on the ground."

Shame spiked inside me. She was right. I shouldn't have said anything, but there'd been a part of me that hoped I could work the same magic my speeches did. That maybe the Daminan gifts of charm and persuasiveness would finally manifest. "I'm sorry," I rasped.

The blades slid off each other with a loud *shing*, and Hristo moved to block a new attack—

Maybe it was the dark.

Maybe he'd misjudged.

Maybe Hurrok was just cleverer than he'd expected.

The knife came inside Hristo's parry, cutting across the side of his hand. My protector screamed as both he and the sword dropped to the ground, and the sharp scent of blood pierced the air. An anguished howl rent the night.

Birds took flight, a flurry of squawks and feathers.

"Oh, Damyan. Darina." A sob choked out of Ilina, and its twin wrenched up my throat a moment later when understanding hit. "Hurrok cut his hand." She sank toward the ground, trembling with shock.

I dug my fingers into the rough tree bark, heart pounding and vision swimming with tears. Hristo had lost. The evidence was undeniable. Hristo slumped on the ground, his bleeding hand pressed against his chest as Hurrok seized the sword and drew it back.

"Watch your friend die, Hopebearer. Like I watched my family die."

The blade swung.

CHAPTER THREE

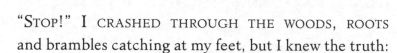

"Stop!" I crashed through the woods, roots and brambles catching at my feet, but I knew the truth:

I wasn't going to reach Hristo in time. The sword would slice through his neck, and I'd lose him forever.

"Hristo!"

But the blade swung and—

Noorestone light blazed through the forest; two pairs of footfalls beat the ground; a knife whistled through the air and struck Hurrok in the back of the neck.

The sword fell. Hurrok followed an instant later, and he didn't get up.

There was Hristo, bleeding next to a corpse and the blade that had almost taken his life. He'd doubled over, clutching his hand like the pain would cause him to explode if he didn't shield it with his body.

I skidded and dropped to the grass beside him. Wet warmth leaked through my dress: blood. Hristo's blood. It pumped from his hand with every beat of his heart, soaking the earth.

He listed to one side, and I caught him in my arms, ignoring the sharp pain in my shoulder blade as my cut tore wider. Hristo had always seemed so *big* to me, but suddenly he was a boy not much older than I was, and the way he shuddered revealed not only his fear, but his mortality. He could die.

Fallen Gods. He could *die*.

Just then, Gerel and Chenda ran up, sagging backpacks on their shoulders, and noorestones lighting their way. Above, LaLa and Crystal twisted between the trees before they settled on a fat branch.

"What happened?" Gerel removed her backpack and tore it open.

"H—Hurrok." I drew my friend closer and kissed the top of his head. He tasted like dirt and sweat, and everything here—absolutely everything—smelled of blood. "Hurrok found us. Hristo protected me, but—"

"*Seven gods.*" Gerel pulled a medical kit from her bag, finding bandages and ointments. "I need a tourniquet to stop the bleeding. Mira, get his belt. Chenda, hold him steady in case he faints."

Though sweat gleamed over his face, Hristo rasped, "I don't faint." In the light of two noorestones on the ground,

30

it seemed that all the blood had drained from his skin, leaving a washed-out version of my protector.

"Call it passing out or falling unconscious. I don't care." Gerel tore a pad of cotton from its bag and pressed it against the side of his hand. "As long as later you remember to thank me for saving your neck."

When Chenda had Hristo's shoulders, I felt around for his belt, fumbling with the mechanism for a moment before I managed to pull the strip of leather free. Ilina had arrived by then, and while Gerel moved Hurrok's body out of the way, we bored a new hole into the leather.

Within minutes, Gerel had the tourniquet tight around his wrist, and finally, the flow of blood began to slacken. Still, she placed pad after pad over the soft, muscled side of his hand, and he endured the whole thing with teeth-grinding stoicism.

"Put a jacket on him." Gerel glanced at me. "Then we'll need to cauterize the area to make sure it doesn't get infected, otherwise he'll lose the hand."

"Cauterize?" I could barely speak the word.

She nodded. "Get your dragon to heat up a knife blade. Either you or your friend. Then hold him down, because it's going to *hurt*."

The last thing I wanted was to help burn my best friend, but I had to trust her. I *did* trust her.

I stood and clicked for LaLa, who landed on my hand with a *thump*. We'd never taught the dragons to breathe fire on command, but when I showed her the knife, she seemed to understand what I wanted.

Carefully, she turned around so the fire end faced away from me, and when we were clear of everyone, she inhaled into her second lungs. The moment her breath hit her spark gland on the way out, a rush of orange fire followed, licking across the steel blade.

After two more breaths, the metal glowed a dull red.

"That's perfect." Gerel took the knife and approached Hristo, whose eyes were wide with horror. "You're going to live, protector."

"Have you ever done this before?" Ilina knelt at Hristo's right side, keeping his hand aloft.

Gerel peeled off the cotton pads to inspect the wound. "I've had more than adequate training for field medicine."

"That doesn't answer my question," Ilina said. "Have you ever done this before?"

"Do you want to summon a real doctor, then?" Gerel tossed the bloody pads aside. "I would be happy to assist someone with more experience if you can produce them. Until then, I'll do my best to keep your friend alive."

Ilina bit her lip.

"Put a jacket sleeve in his mouth and hold him still."

Chenda did as she was ordered, and braced herself against Hristo's left side. Noorestone light made the maze of her copper tattoos gleam as she whispered something in Hristo's ear.

Then Gerel pressed the flat of the knife on the injury until Hristo's flesh began to sizzle, and he screamed into the sleeve.

LaLa took off toward the trees, while Ilina buried her face in Hristo's shoulder. Chenda never stopped her whispering, though if it brought any comfort, I couldn't see it. My protector cried out again and again, and all I could do was stand there, shaking, as the odor of burning flesh completely enveloped the scent of blood.

My stomach turned, but there was nothing in me to lose. Instead, I reached around and touched the cut on the back of my shoulder. My dress was shredded, and the cut bled freely, but this wasn't the time to bother anyone with it.

::Mira.::

Aaru.

Any other time, someone tapping my arm might have made me jump, but even before the first letter of my name was finished, I knew Aaru was behind me.

I almost turned to face him.

I almost threw my arms around him.

I almost pressed my chest against his and hid my face in the curve where his neck met his shoulder.

But I didn't do any of those things, because this was Aaru, and even an embrace of relief might feel like impropriety.

Plus, I was covered in Hristo's blood.

::Sorry,:: Aaru tapped, and stood at my side as Hristo's muffled screams finally ceased.

My protector slumped, unconscious at last. I hoped he found some relief in dreams.

Gerel tossed the hot knife on the ground and placed a

fresh bandage over the wound. "We need to go now. I saw warriors working through the city, searching for escaped prisoners. In the woods, too. They'll have heard all this noise." She looked up to find Aaru standing beside me. "When did you get here?"

::Moments ago. Didn't want to distract.::

When I interpreted, she just nodded. "Fine. Everyone, carry what you can. I'll get Hristo. We're leaving *now*." She scooped my protector into her arms as though he weighed no more than a kitten, but that was the strength Khulan gave his people. I didn't doubt she could carry all five of us, plus dragons, if she wanted.

Quickly, we gathered up the rest of our supplies and started through the woods once more. It was fully dark by now; only noorestone light and dappled moonslight illuminated our path. Eyes peered at us from dark trees, nocturnal mice and bats, suspicious of a group of clumsy humans tripping through their forest. Bugs whined and night birds called, and the heat of the day was finally fading. Still, the trek wasn't any easier. Gerel instructed everyone where to step, how to cover tracks, and refused to slow when Chenda stumbled over a rock.

Conversation was not permitted; when I tried to ask Ilina if she was all right, Gerel shushed me.

I gritted my teeth against the pain in my shoulder. It wasn't life-threatening, and she was right. We had to get moving. We couldn't slow down for a torn dress.

"No tapping, either." She shot a narrow-eyed look at

34

Aaru and me. "I'm trying to focus on getting Hristo to the safe house and I can't do that when it sounds like you two are auditioning for a spot in the Warriors' Drum Corps."

I glanced at Aaru just in time to catch the way his jaw tightened. It was probably highly insulting to tell an Idrisi they made too much noise.

But we obeyed, because more than anything, we didn't want to go back to the Pit.

CHAPTER FOUR

BY THE TIME WE REACHED THE CABIN, I WAS STICKY
with sweat and blood, and I couldn't stop the shivers
that racked through me every few minutes. My dress
clung to me like an ill-fitting second skin.

We'd been walking for hours—at least it seemed like
hours. My thoughts felt like they were slipping, unable to
gain enough purchase in my head to fully form, and every
piece of my body ached. Especially my shoulder. But how
could I complain when Hristo's hand had been cut wide
open? It seemed amazing he still had all his fingers.

I breathed through the pain. One, two, three, four. It
helped, but I needed to collapse. I needed to *not move*.

Gerel called a halt when we were in sight of the safe
house.

It wasn't much, just a cabin closely surrounded by rain trees and broad-leafed ferns. A small shelter—perhaps an outhouse?—stood off to one side. Our haven almost looked like another part of the forest, except for the two windows. Neither had glass, just tattered curtains half-covering the openings.

"You"—Gerel nodded at Aaru—"go peek inside to make sure no one's there. Be *quiet* about it."

He frowned, but he slipped between the trees without rustling so much as a twig. At the wall, he held absolutely still, his head cocked while he listened. His eyes closed, and his lips parted just so, but after several long moments, he seemed satisfied enough to move the curtain. So carefully I might have thought him mocking Gerel if I didn't know better, he peered inside.

Finally, he waved us into the cabin.

There were two rooms inside. One main area, with a fireplace, fourteen glowing noorestones scattered on the floor, and a pile of rodent-nibbled blankets. No food. The second space was a washroom, and miraculously it had a water pump with a faucet that curved over the lip of a huge iron tub. It was practically a boat, it was so big.

"We could have baths," I whispered.

"And wash our clothes." Chenda plucked at the filthy copper shirt she'd been wearing since arriving in the Pit.

"I wish the facilities were inside." Ilina's tone held just a hint of moping. "Did you see the outhouse?"

"We need to wash Hristo's wound before baths or

complaints." In the main room, Gerel lowered my protector to the floor next to the dark fireplace, arranging his injury so that it was slightly elevated. "We need to boil water."

She was right, of course. Hristo needed everyone's help. "So we need firewood?" I started toward the door, but Gerel's frown stopped me.

"There won't be dry wood out there."

"It will dry off in a fire," I said.

"It will *smoke* in a fire. It'll send a signal out for leagues and we won't be safe here."

Ilina emerged from the washroom. "The water pump doesn't work."

I wanted to slouch to the floor and cry.

Aaru abandoned the backpack he'd been unpacking and went to the washroom. Metal squealed and clanked as he began to dismantle the offending pump.

Vaguely, I wondered if I could use any of these noorestones to heat water, but that would involve knowing how to control my strange gift. Besides, I'd already used it twice today—or maybe that was yesterday now—and I wasn't sure I could stand up for much longer, let alone channel noorestone fire.

"Then we have nothing," Chenda said. "No food, no water, no heat."

"I thought you'd gone to find supplies." The floor seemed like it was slipping, and fog crept around the corners of my vision. This wasn't a panic attack—at least, it

38

didn't feel like one—but it certainly wasn't good. As casually as I could manage, I leaned on a wall. Pain spiked in my shoulder, so I tilted myself to take pressure off the cut.

"We have dragons," Ilina said. "Crystal and LaLa can hunt food."

At the sound of their names, the two *Drakontos raptuses* appeared in the window, their talons digging into the rotting wood. LaLa squawked and rustled her wings.

"How will we cook?" Chenda said. "No dry wood for a fire, remember?"

"Dragons *breathe* fire." Ilina shook her head. "It's not a perfect solution, but we don't have a lot of options. Unless you want all of us to sit around being miserable and useless."

Chenda scowled and crossed her arms. "Go, if that's what you want to do."

"You'll thank us when you have a full stomach." Ilina grabbed a noorestone and the two spare fire-resistant jackets, and then took my arm. "Let's go. Put this on."

Staggering after her, I shrugged on the jacket, struggling to hide my wince as the fabric fell over my injured shoulder. The material wasn't as thick as the hunting gauntlets we wore at the sanctuary, but it would do for now. I clicked for LaLa, who glided over and perched on my forearm, rather than my hand like she normally would.

Inside the cabin, Gerel said, "Chenda, I need you to find a few things. . . ."

There wasn't time to hear what Gerel wanted, or

Chenda's reaction to being given orders, because Ilina led me into the forest and soon we were out of earshot.

It was dark, but that didn't matter to the dragons; they had excellent night vision. The sisters flew into the trees to begin their hunt.

For our part, Ilina and I stepped carefully over roots and around brush, trying to maintain the same level of caution Hristo and Gerel had insisted upon, but my dress snagged on twigs, and sharp leaves scraped my legs. Anyone who knew anything about tracking would be able to tell we'd been through here.

When we reached a small clearing, Ilina and I watched Crystal and LaLa hop from branch to branch, their scales shimmering in the cool noorestone light.

"Your friends were definitely worth coming back here for." As we passed beneath the low branches of a mango tree, she reached up and grabbed a fruit. "One is ready to complain about everything. One thinks she's in charge."

Gerel was good at being in charge, though.

"One betrayed you."

She had a point about Tirta, who'd only pretended to be my friend as part of her assignment from the Luminary Council. Apparently.

"And one won't speak."

"That's not even on the same level as betraying me," I said. "Besides, it's not his fault. Altan did that to him."

"He's not very useful."

"He saved my life." Twice, though I hadn't told her about the second time, when he'd helped keep my

40

noorestone power from exploding. I'd promised Aaru I wouldn't reveal his secret of silence.

She sighed, peeling the skin off the mango. "And I'm grateful he saved you. I just keep thinking about how much trouble we're in now. I wish we'd sneaked out of the inn back in the Shadowed City."

There was nothing I could say to that. Everything would be different if we'd left when they'd come to rescue me: Hristo wouldn't be fighting for his life, and we'd be off doing our best to help save the dragons from a dark fate in the Algotti Empire. But Aaru, Gerel, and Chenda would still be in the Pit, and despite Ilina's criticisms, I liked them. Besides, our gods urged us to think of our neighbors, to be compassionate and helpful. I couldn't have left them in the Pit.

"Here." Ilina cut a slice of mango and offered it to me. "You look like you could use a bite."

"Thanks." The fruit helped, and I considered telling her about the cut on my shoulder, but if I did, she'd take me back into the cabin without letting Crystal and LaLa hunt.

Still, when she offered a few more slices, I didn't refuse them.

Slowly, we walked after the dragons, ready to take their kills. We'd been hunting with these two for years— they were efficient and never let their prey suffer, but they couldn't always carry the game to us. *Drakontos raptuses* were only the size of weasels, and like most dragon species, their bones were hollow. While they could kill prey larger than them—honestly, most prey was larger than *raptuses*—carrying it could be a challenge.

So we followed, watching gold and silver dart down from the trees. Every now and then, a bright flame lit the path ahead: one of the dragons signaling a kill.

"I'm just worried about Hristo." She took a limp-necked quail from Crystal, rewarding the dragon with a mango slice.

"Me too." I scanned the trees for LaLa, then watched as she dived toward the ground, completely silent. A second later, a rabbit screamed. We'd have a good meal tonight—assuming we could light a fire.

I wanted to say something about Hristo's hand. There was no telling when he'd be able to use it again, and it seemed like there must be an incredible sense of loss already building inside of him, haunting his dreams. But I wasn't sure how to vocalize those feelings, or if I even should.

While Hristo had always been more than sensitive to others' feelings, he wasn't fond of talking about his own. If this had happened to Ilina or me, Hristo would have known exactly how to help us.

"I wish we had Doctor Chilikoba," I said at last.

Ilina looked sharply at me. "Do you think Gerel did something wrong?"

I started to shake my head, but the dizziness swarmed in, clouding my sight. "I think Gerel did everything she could. Hristo owes his life to her. Neither of us could have done what she did."

Ilina nodded. "I agree."

"Doctor Chilikoba is a doctor, though. And she would have medicine to help him through the pain, medicine to keep his hand from becoming infected, medicine to help with all the bad feelings he might have." I wished she were here for me, too. For the last eight years, she'd been giving me small amber bottles of twenty pills that numbed the panic. They'd saved me so many times since that first dose.

The pills had been taken from me when I was jailed, so in the Pit, I'd lived on the knife edge of panic. I'd had more attacks in the last two months than I had in the last two years.

"We'll have to be the ones to help him," Ilina said. "Just because his life might change doesn't mean our love for him will. We'll be here for him no matter what."

Together, we gathered up five more kills before summoning LaLa and Crystal to us. They rode on our forearms, talons digging into the heavy wool jackets. "It's too hot to wear these during the day. We'll have to figure out a way to make hunting gauntlets if we're going to do this again," I said.

"I can try cutting the sleeves off these, but then we won't have the jackets."

We didn't have a *Drakontos ignitus* on our hands anymore, so flame-resistant jackets weren't as much of an issue as they had been when I'd taken them from the armory. At that point, I'd been terrified that Kelsine would burn my friends. And me as well. But mostly my friends.

Now Kelsine was gone, and Crystal and LaLa would never hurt us.

Ilina picked more mangoes as we walked back to the cabin, noorestone light guiding us. As glad as I was to be heading indoors again, my thoughts grew sluggish. The cut on my shoulder blade burned, and it was all I could do to keep placing one foot in front of the other.

LaLa trilled and licked my face. I wished I could reassure her, but it was unwise to lie to dragons.

The cabin's bright noorestones drew me the rest of the way in.

Hristo still slept in front of the cold fireplace, wrapped in the third jacket and all the spare blankets. His hand was elevated on a backpack, but sweat poured down his face and his skin was leached of color.

He needed help. Even I, with my fading vision, could see that.

Chenda and Gerel hunched over a pile of plants, organizing them by some system I couldn't discern. The scent of herbs was overpowering, enough to make me stagger.

"We brought dinner," announced Ilina. She transferred Crystal to a window and began showing off the game we'd collected.

From the washroom, the *whoosh* of water gushing into the metal tub made everyone look up. Aaru emerged, his hands dark with soot and rust. A faint smile pulled at his mouth.

It was then I collapsed.

AARU

Five Years Ago

The Book of Silence WAS DECEPTIVELY HEAVY.

Strangers to it often assumed that Idris was quite wordy, considering he was the god of silence, but the truth was that many pages were blank.

Or contained but a few words of wisdom.

These pages allowed the reader time to pause. To reflect. To deeply consider the previous passage.

They were silence incarnate.

In the time it took to turn the page, one might come to a new appreciation for the quiet in their own mind, or a new understanding of the Most Silent.

That, above all, was what Father said we should pray for.

Like a good Idrisi boy, I read *The Book of Silence* every day. And though I was not a fast reader, I usually finished the entire book once a month. I'd lost count of how many times I'd read it.

It was because of my multiple readings that I began to wonder:

Why did the leaders of Grace Community focus on certain pieces of Idris's word every decan? The importance of a few strong voices, bolstered by the righteousness and attentive silence of others. The strength earned by enduring hardships. The superiority of men and the Silent Brothers.

Why were those passages given more weight than others? Such as the duty to consider words carefully. The loveliness of a kind voice. The understanding that silence could be wielded as a weapon—but should not be.

Why did we give more attention to the passages detailing when we should *not* speak, and no attention to those discussing when we should?

I wanted to ask Father, but I already knew what he would say: it was not for me to question wiser men.

And so I buried my questions under layer after layer of silence, as though I could smother them into nonexistence. But still, I wondered:

When could silence become harmful?

CHAPTER FIVE

I DREAMED OF FLYING.

Of great wings and burning stars.

I AWAKENED IN the middle of Gerel stitching my skin back together.

It was an unsettling sensation, but it hurt less than the actual cut, so I clenched my jaw and counted floorboards (seventeen), thumps of a wooden spoon on the sides of a pot (fourteen), and taps of a tree branch against the cabin (twenty-two).

Three long seconds of thunder as it rumbled in the distance. Heralding the storm, the air felt cooler, stiller, and charged with lightning.

"That's it." Gerel clipped the end of the silk thread and

dropped the needle into a bowl of boiling water.

"How many stitches?" My voice was groggy.

"Just five." Gerel took a glob of green slime and smeared it onto the cut, then covered it with a bandage. The paste smelled sharply of anise and several other kinds of herbs I couldn't identify. "This will prevent the wound from getting infected. Chenda and I made it for Hristo, but some people just don't like being left out, do they?"

"Sorry." I sat up, my left shoulder throbbing with the effort. But finally, I got a look around. Ilina was stirring a pot hanging from a hook on the fire. The aroma of cooking rabbit filled the room, lifting my gnawing hunger to a desperate *need* for food.

Hristo was still sleeping, but he looked better now. Less sweaty. Less anguished. They'd probably washed him and given him something for the pain as well. The bandages around his hand looked clean, so the bleeding must have stopped.

On the other side of the room, Chenda and Aaru sorted through the supplies, not speaking but still companionable. And in the windows, LaLa and Crystal spread their wings into the night air as though bathing in the sharp moments before the rain hit. Their necks stretched long and their faces turned up. Sparks danced between LaLa's teeth as somewhere in the distance, lightning flared.

A few seconds later, thunder rumbled through the little cabin, making everyone pause. "Good thing we got here when we did," Ilina said when the quiet returned.

Gerel grunted in the affirmative, then looked at me. "Why didn't you say you were hurt?"

"You said you didn't want to hear about injuries that weren't life-threatening."

She gave a deep sigh and kicked the medical kit toward Chenda. "I'm finished with this." Then she marched into the washroom. The gush of water followed a loud screech from the pump, and when she came back, she was drying her hands on her trousers. "You could have died, Fancy."

"I was trying to follow orders."

Almost invisibly, Aaru slipped into the unoccupied washroom.

"You could have died if that cut had festered more. You lost a good bit of blood, which is probably why you were so dizzy, but you'll get it back in no time. I'll give you a smaller dose of the same things I'm giving Hristo. He lost a *lot* of blood."

"I have more than enough blood." Ilina glanced up from the boiling soup. "Can I give Hristo some of mine? Is that possible?"

"It's been tried." I gazed down at Hristo, wishing there was more we could do for him. Wishing he'd never been in this position to begin with. "Giving blood has saved a few people, but it's killed even more. They get fevers, chills, hives: all kinds of problems. No one's really sure why, because blood is blood, but even attempting transfers is banned on all seven islands, at least until there's better research on how to make it safe."

Firelight shimmered gold over the warm brown of Ilina's face as she dropped her eyes to our sleeping friend. "Let's not try it, then. I can't bear the thought of losing him."

"He's going to live," said Gerel. "At least, I'm reasonably sure. I'm worried about his hand, though. Without a real doctor, he might not be able to use it anymore."

Ilina made a small, anguished noise.

Gerel shook her head. "Sorry. There's not a delicate way to say it. He almost lost the whole thing. He's lucky."

"I doubt he feels that way," Ilina said.

"You can ask him when he wakes up." Gerel gazed at her patient. "If we can get him to a doctor soon, maybe they'll be able to give him better odds."

Then we would get him to a doctor.

Another crash of thunder shuddered through the cabin, making Crystal and LaLa bounce on their perches, trilling happily. Hopefully the approaching storm wouldn't delay us too long.

"At any rate," Gerel went on, "there's no reason to go around offering people your blood. At least not right now."

Chenda raised an eyebrow in my direction. "How do you know these things?"

"My doctor likes to talk," I said, "and I don't forget things that could potentially kill me."

The copper tattoos on her face twisted with her confused frown. "That isn't normal, Mira."

"You aren't the first person to say that about me." I

watched as Aaru emerged from the washroom, his face scrubbed clean of dirt and sweat. When our eyes met, he smiled. Just a little. But when his gaze darted off my cheek, the one with the scar, I couldn't find it in me to smile back.

"I'm sure I won't be the last," Chenda said, just as a log popped in the fire, making shadows leap. They bent strangely around her, like light through a curved glass, but when she caught me noticing, everything snapped back to normal. She winked and touched her lips.

"I see we have a fire." I turned back to Gerel. "What made you change your mind?"

She shrugged. "Now that clouds have covered the moons, the smoke won't be as visible. Warriors might be able to smell it, though, so we can't leave it going for long. But we needed to cook. Chenda looked hungry, and I heard she eats shadows."

Chenda threw a small noorestone at her.

"Speaking of cooking"—Gerel looked pointedly at Ilina—"is the soup ready?"

Ilina nodded and began ladling portions into bowls. "Should we wake Hristo to eat?"

Gerel shook her head and accepted the first bowl. "He needs rest more than he needs soup. After the sedatives I gave him, I'm not sure he could even stay awake for more than a mouthful."

Everyone took the offered bowls. I inhaled the steam from mine, testing the heat before I sipped. It was thin, but someone—Ilina, presumably—had tried to make it interesting by adding wild peppers and ginger. The shredded rabbit was tender, melting on my tongue, and it helped clear the fog from my thoughts.

"We should wash the blood out of our clothes before we leave." I sipped again, another tiny mouthful of returning strength. "I don't want to attract predators."

"Do you even know how to wash clothes?" Ilina smirked, but not in an unfriendly way.

"I do now. Tirta taught me." The thought of her stung; I'd *truly* believed she was a friend, always helping me and showing me how to accomplish simple tasks I'd never learned as a child. But now . . .

"Oh." Ilina frowned.

"We don't have anything to change into," Chenda said. "Gerel and I acquired a few supplies, but not clothes."

"What *did* you get?" Ilina asked.

"Bottles for transporting water. A tent. Arrows. Small packets of rice flour. More backpacks. And shoes."

Shoes would be amazing. The slippers I'd been wearing since Bopha were tattered and torn, and while I didn't know where we were going next, it was clear I'd need real shoes to get me there.

But at that last item, Aaru looked up, and suddenly I realized that he was barefoot. Had been this whole time. Guilt wormed through me. My first concern had been for myself, not my neighbors. Aaru had not only escaped the Pit without shoes, but hiked through the woods for hours—mostly alone—like that.

All this after Altan had tortured him with noorestones altered to flood heat into him. One of those noorestones had shattered, slashing open the bottoms of his feet.

Shame made my throat and cheeks ache, especially when I realized no one—not even I—had included him in the conversation. Aaru was an outsider in our group, made that way by the absence of his voice. I would interpret. Of course I would. But the knowledge of that requirement seemed to force him even more silent than before.

I had to do better.

"Aaru—" Thunder drowned my voice and no one heard me.

"Where did you get all these things?" Ilina drained her bowl.

"Gerel stole them." Chenda smiled at Gerel, whose perpetual glower deepened.

"It's dishonorable to steal," Gerel added, "and Khulan might not forgive me. But I already tried to destroy my people's holiest temple, so stealing a few supplies seems rather inconsequential at this point."

Ilina snorted. "I'd say so."

I finished my soup and climbed to my feet, careful in case the dizziness came back. While the others continued their conversation, I put my bowl next to Ilina's, wandered in and out of the washroom as though I had business in there, then took LaLa from the window. She settled onto my shoulder, mindful of her razor scales near my exposed neck.

When I'd sufficiently moved around the cabin enough

57

so no one would suspect I'd gotten up for one purpose, I sat next to Aaru, careful to keep him on my right side. Opposite the side with the hideous scar—my burning shame.

I stroked LaLa's nose, moving with the scales. "Hello, sweet lizard."

Her tongue flicked out, tasting my skin, and for a moment she held her mouth slightly agape.

"Silly dragon," I whispered. Just being close to her made me feel better.

Aaru's face was dark with shadow, lit only around the edges where noorestone and firelight touched the curves of his forehead and cheek and jaw. He lifted a heavy eyebrow before nodding at LaLa. ::Why?::

"She's holding a scent or taste near her spark gland. Certain odors make the gland tingle, and it must feel good." I petted LaLa's head again. "It looks really silly though, especially on the bigger species. I don't think they realize. They're such proud creatures."

::You know a lot about dragons.::

"I've never loved anything so much." I dropped my eyes, a hot flush pushing up my throat and cheeks. "That's not a very Daminan thing to admit."

::Honest thing.:: He watched LaLa as she nosed through the loose strands of my hair, shaking out noorestone dust that had been trapped there since the explosion. As the cloud of light rose around us, she extended her right wing to catch particles until her scales shimmered.

58

She looked at me questioningly.

"Very pretty," I confirmed. "You're the prettiest dragon I know."

She trilled and hopped onto my lap to lick the noore-stone dust off her wing. Some scholars believed dragons could understand basic human language if they were exposed long enough, like dogs could be taught to come or sit or stay, but skeptics maintained that any appearance of understanding was purely a combination of tone, rewards, and the speaker's imagination.

No one had ever asked me which side I fell on, but if my time with LaLa and Crystal had taught me anything, it was that dragons were far cleverer than humans gave them credit for.

Aaru was still watching LaLa with open amusement and admiration, and on the far side of the room, the others began discussing supplies and how to arrange for everyone to wash their clothes—and themselves.

I switched to the quiet code, tapping against the floor between Aaru and me. ::I was afraid you weren't coming back. Before.::

He looked at me askance. ::Of course I came back.::

Because where else would he go? Right.

I exhaled a deep sigh of relief. ::You were gone longer than I expected.::

::Warriors pursued. Had to follow the stream before I could look for you. Then I was lost.::

We should never have let him go off alone.

::Big forest.:: He lifted his eyes toward the sky. ::Wandered for an hour, maybe more, but your dragon found me. She guided me to you.::

I stroked the top of LaLa's head. ::I'm glad.::

::Me too.:: Tension drained from his muscles as he regarded me with those dark eyes. Neither of us moved, and I allowed myself to study the contours of his face. His heavy eyebrows. His strong cheekbones. His wide nose. His sharp jaw. His full lips that were turned up just so, not in amusement, but in a way that suggested this was just his neutral expression. Pleasant.

Gerel lurched to her feet. "I'm going to set a couple of traps to alert us if anyone's coming," she announced. "Wash off. Clean your clothes. Do all the things you dreamed of doing. Then put out the fire, but keep Hristo warm."

"Do we have soap?" I asked.

::There's a bar.::

"Thank the seven." I couldn't stand the thought of wearing this dress anymore, not when it was covered in Hristo's blood, my own blood, and even Altan's blood. Everything felt sticky and stiff. "I don't think I've felt this gross in my whole life."

"Certainly not since I've known you." Gerel smirked, and with that, she was out the door, her movements strong and easy, as though she hadn't been trapped in a small cell for the last year. Did it feel strange for her? She'd believed she would never leave the Pit, but she'd assumed command as quickly as she'd arrived, saving Hristo's life and getting all of us to this cabin.

Maybe I'd spend my whole life wishing I could be more like Gerel.

Stronger. Braver. Always certain of my actions.

Instead, I was just Mira. And while I was certain trying to free my friends from the Pit had been the right thing, there'd probably been a better way to do it—one that wouldn't have gotten Ilina and Hristo imprisoned as well. One that wouldn't have gotten Hristo hurt.

Thunder boomed, rattling the cabin.

"Do you want to go first?" Ilina took Chenda's bowl and put it aside.

"A cold bath isn't very appealing," said Chenda, but she rolled onto the balls of her feet and drew herself up, because a cold bath was better than no bath.

"I have an idea how to heat the water." Ilina held up her hand and clicked.

Crystal launched herself off the windowsill and landed on Ilina's fingers. She chirruped and bumped Ilina's chin with hers before settling down with her silver wings forming a small tent around her body.

It wasn't long before four humans and two dragons were crowded in the washroom, with LaLa and Crystal perched on the rim of the tub. The dragons blew fire against the metal while Aaru pressed the lever until water gushed out and hit the slope of the tub with a loud hiss.

Ilina and I cheered. The water might not end up *hot*,

but it would be better than the frigid flow coming from the pump.

"Wash your clothes, too," said Ilina. "I'll grab a blanket from the other room for you to wear while your clothes dry."

Because the Daminans or Bophan here might not care so much about nudity in this small group, but the Idrisi definitely would.

We left five noorestones in the washroom for Chenda, then headed into the main room once more. LaLa and Crystal came with us, perched on our shoulders and purring with satisfaction.

::Do they mind?:: Aaru asked. ::Heating the water, I mean. Must make them tired.::

A smile bubbled out of me. "They don't mind. Healthy dragons breathe fire several times a day, and we're just giving them something useful to do with it." But it meant so much that he even considered LaLa and Crystal's feelings. Most people wouldn't. Most people would see them as creatures beneath their notice, because they were only *Drakontos raptuses*, not something more impressive like *titanuses* or *rexes*.

Ilina glanced at Aaru, then me. "What was the question?" When I told her, she nodded. "Different species have different amounts of fire they can safely breathe for long spans, but don't worry about Crystal and LaLa. They're nowhere near their limits."

At the sound of her name, Crystal squawked and

began shoving her face through Ilina's hair.

Aaru smiled at the dragon's display, but when lightning struck and thunder crashed, the expression faltered and he glanced around the cabin. ::**Big storm coming. Need protection.**::

"What do we do?" I had no idea how to prepare the rickety cabin for a storm. My house in Crescent Prominence was always ready, as far as I knew.

::**Windows.**:: He turned to the first window near him and began pinning the curtains in place, just as the night lit up and the first great sheet of rain poured from the sky. I imagined water washing out our footprints. Carrying away small twigs and leaves broken in our passage. Disguising the smoke from our fire. This storm was exactly what we needed.

Ilina dragged me to the window on the other side of the room, and while we worked on that one together, she said, "I've been thinking about our plan. Where to go next. What to do."

"Me too." Now that we were free from the Pit, we could finally find the dragons that had been taken from the Crescent Prominence sanctuary. We could rescue them. "I think we should discuss it with the group first."

"Why?" She lowered her voice and stabbed a pin through the curtain on her side.

"Because they should have a say."

Sensing he wasn't invited to this conversation, Aaru finished his window and began gathering up thin blankets to create a barrier against any water that managed to leak inside.

Ilina bent toward me. "We don't need them anymore. As soon as Hristo is well enough, we should separate."

"What?" I wiped a stream of water off my face. Surely I'd heard her wrong.

She sighed. "Look, we got them out of the Pit. That's what you wanted. Your debt to them is paid." She pushed a long, black curl behind her ear. "We can go anywhere, Mira. Before we found you in Bopha, Hristo and I came up with several places we can hide—you, me, and the dragons—where no one will know us or even care who we are. Three of us can disappear, but six? No."

"I don't want to hide." I pinned the last piece of my curtain in place and stepped back. "And I can't abandon them."

"You wouldn't be. Like I said, your debt is paid."

My heart lurched, and numbers skittered through my head. Ilina and I so rarely disagreed, but here we were at odds. "I promised to get Aaru back to his family, and Chenda will be a useful ally—"

"For *what*?" She took my hand in hers. "You've said that before, and that's why we agreed to free them, too, but the six of us aren't a team, Mira. You, me, and Hristo—yes. We work well together. But the rest of them?" She glanced over my shoulder, her brown eyes darkening with determination. "They're not our responsibility."

"I need them," I whispered. "I need all of you."

She squeezed my hands. "I know you care about people, Mira. And that's one of the best things about you. You truly *care* about others."

I swallowed hard.

"But sometimes I think you care too much, and that can get you in trouble."

I wanted to sink into the ground. She was right that caring got me into trouble, but I'd been born on Damina—in the light of the Lovers. My faith demanded that I care.

How was I to reconcile my beliefs with my desire for self-preservation? And what about all the times my caring got *others* into trouble? Where was the line?

"Sometimes you're so focused on doing the right thing for everyone else that your best friends suffer the consequences."

I felt sick. The last thing I wanted was to hurt my friends. But didn't Gerel, Chenda, and Aaru count now? Maybe they'd never admit it, but . . .

Thunder growled, and rain lashed harder against the cabin, dulling our voices. On the far side of the room, Aaru used his toe to nudge a noorestone away from the wall.

"We have to separate," Ilina said. "Or—"

::Something outside!:: But even before Aaru could finish warning us, a long, low growl vibrated through the cabin, and a *bang* rattled the door with such force that Ilina and I both jumped.

Had Altan found us?

But the next crash against the door came with a roar—a familiar sharp timbre and panicked quaver. LaLa and Crystal squawked and pushed off our shoulders, toward the rafters.

"Open the door!" I lunged for it, too. "Kelsine is outside."

CHAPTER SIX

ILINA REACHED THE DOOR BEFORE I DID, AND WHEN she threw it open, the young *Drakontos ignitus* charged in, slinging mud and water across the floor. She was the height of a large hound, with her shoulder up to my hip and a wingspan wide enough to support her muscular body in flight.

Above, LaLa hissed and spurted fire, but Kelsine ignored her. Instead, the bigger dragon stopped directly in front of me and heaved a sigh as she lowered herself to the floor, exhausted.

Aaru shut the door, muffling the noise of the storm, but he didn't take his eyes off the third dragon in our cabin, while Ilina, predictably, moved around the perimeter of the room to get a better look. She kept her movements slow but deliberate so that when Kelsine noticed her, there'd be no shock or rush to attack. If Ilina knew anything, it was how to approach frightened dragons. That was a lesson learned early in the sanctuary.

But even as Ilina came into Kelsine's line of sight, the dragon didn't seem to care. Slouched at my feet, she blew a smoky breath and lifted her eyes toward me. LaLa squawked again, and Crystal bounced from side to side, little puffs of flame darting between her teeth.

::Is she all right?:: Aaru tapped lightly against the door, just loud enough to be heard over the drive of rain.

"I don't see anything wrong with her." I crouched before the young dragon and offered my fingers for her to sniff. "Besides exhaustion."

"No injuries," Ilina said. "At least that I can see without getting closer."

Cautiously, as though our alliance in the Pit might have been some sort of fluke, Kelsine picked up her head and stretched to meet my fingertips. Her nostrils flared as she inhaled my scent, then dropped her jaw. A breath of smoke tangled over my fingers, then dissipated into the rafters.

LaLa hissed again, hunched over her perch as though ready to stoop toward the larger dragon. A bad idea for all of us.

"Don't be jealous." I kept my voice soft and level as Kelsine butted her head toward my hand. Cautiously, I ran my fingers over warm, slick scales. "Ilina, I think she'll let me pet her while you take a quick look."

::Careful.:: Aaru still hadn't moved from the door. That was probably smart, because Gerel would return soon and the last thing we needed was for her to barge in and frighten Kelsine.

"I'll look." Ilina padded closer while I rubbed Kelsine's snout and up between her eyes.

She was a beautiful creature, all opalescent brown scales, still years from turning red with adulthood. Nubby facial horns scraped my palm as she adjusted herself to force me to pet where she wanted: along her cheeks, under her chin, and down her long throat where the scales glimmered the shade of sun-bleached sand.

Ilina knelt beside Kelsine, resting one hand flat on the dragon's flank while she worked. "No missing scales," she muttered. "There are a few chips, but they're older scales and will be shed soon. The damage wasn't necessarily sustained yesterday or today."

My heart ached for the young dragon as I stroked down the side of her throat. "Poor Kelsine. You've had a hard life."

A deep, grumbling purr rumbled through her body.

"I can't see Altan or the other warriors abusing her." I petted the dragon's cheeks again.

::I can see Altan abusing anyone.::

When I glanced up, Aaru wore a dark mask of emotion—anger or hatred or hurt; it was hard to tell with him. And Aaru had every right to hate Altan, so I didn't say aloud that in spite of all his many faults, Altan cared about dragons. It seemed more likely to me that Kelsine had sustained these injuries when the adult dragons had been taken from the Heart and she'd been hidden.

"Let's see her teeth." Ilina shifted to kneel next to me, her movements confident and competent as she pulled open Kelsine's mouth to peer inside. "Very good," she murmured. "Looks like they're all accounted for, and I don't see any broken or damaged." She released Kelsine's mouth and petted between her forehead horns. "You're a good girl, Kelsine."

Above, Crystal let out an annoyed squawk and flew into a corner. LaLa followed in a flutter of gold wings and disgusted chirping.

"I think they're mad." Ilina smoothed her hand down Kelsine's neck.

::Why?::

"Aaru asked why." I stood and gazed at the small dragons in the corner while I answered his question. "They get jealous quickly, like cats. LaLa and Crystal have watched us work with lots of different dragons in the sanctuary before, but going back and forth with us made them feel special. This is the first time another dragon has come into our collective territory."

Ilina was nodding. "That was my thought, too. They haven't seen us in months, and they believed this was *our* cabin, and *our* time to reconnect. They see Kelsine as an intruder."

Aaru gazed upward, where LaLa and Crystal made small chirps and chatters at each other, having their own private conversation with their backs turned toward us. ::I didn't realize they could feel like that.::

"Of course they can feel like that," Ilina said when I interpreted. "They're very sensitive creatures."

Aaru stepped back, expression falling into blankness.

"He didn't know," I said. "He's never met a dragon before. Have you ever met a dragon?" I glanced at Aaru, suddenly realizing I didn't actually know.

He held up one finger. ::It was not a good meeting.::

I relayed what he said, and Ilina frowned, but nodded. "Our dragons have feelings," she said. "Kelsine, too. And we're going to have to figure out what to do with her."

"I don't want to leave her here where the warriors might find her. We should take her with us."

"Take her with us where?" Ilina shook her head. "And for how long? We can barely care for ourselves at this point, let alone a juvenile *Drakontos ignitus*."

"Then she needs a sanctuary." I held Ilina's gaze, my heart pounding. "You said you wanted to talk about what we do next, and I don't want to hide. I won't."

"You want to help dragons."

I gave a single nod. "You know that's what I want."

She closed her eyes, pulling inward to think. Heartbeats thumped by: seven, eight, nine . . . Thunder crashed outside, and rain slammed ever harder against the cabin. "You've been to the First Harta Dragon Sanctuary, right?"

71

"Twice. The keepers are good people. The sanctuary is well maintained." A knot of tension in my chest eased. "They will take Kelsine, I'm sure of it."

"And the *Chance Encounter* is waiting for us in Lorntah. If we can get to the port, it should only take a day or two to reach Val fa Merce. Of all the ports in the Fallen Isles, that is the one we should head to first, anyway. We'll need new identification, and I hear Val fa Merce is the best place to get that."

"How do you—"

"Which we'll need for getting into other ports, and when we rescue the other dragons, they'll need somewhere to go, and the First Harta Dragon Sanctuary is as good a place as any. But we should warn them."

"They might not have the space to hold that many big dragons long term, but we can contact other sanctuaries too." Already, Ilina was thinking through every keeper she knew and who she could trust to care for the dragons she'd grown up loving. "All right. I'm with you. We'll take Kelsine to Harta, then go after the others."

"How hard can it be?" I laughed, knowing full well it would be next to impossible. But if we didn't make the effort, who would?

"Right." Ilina grinned. "Easy as the moons rising."

"What if—" I hesitated.

Ilina's smile fell. "I know. What if Crescent Prominence wasn't the only one?"

"Right." The word felt hollow. "After all, the dragons in the Heart were removed, but those might have been just because they weren't supposed to have dragons in the first place."

Ilina didn't look convinced. "Maybe."

"Still, we have to try, right?" I offered a brave smile. "It's better to know one way or another. At best, we go to Harta and have a place to take dragons. At worst . . ."

"We know there's no one else we can trust," she finished. "Only ourselves."

I knew she still meant her, Hristo, and me—not the others—but I nodded. Ilina would come around to the others. Hristo would join us wherever we went. And the moment treats were offered, LaLa and Crystal would forgive us for being kind to another dragon.

With dark, thoughtful eyes, Aaru watched from across the room. ::**You want to rescue the dragons taken from your sanctuary?**::

"Yes." My heart caught in my throat. "More than anything."

Aaru lowered his head in a single nod. ::**I understand.**::

I chanced a smile, turning my face as the scar pulled, then I stepped over to the fire. When I called for Kelsine, she crept to me and curled up next to Hristo, falling asleep so quickly it seemed incredible she didn't take us all with her.

"I'm with you," Ilina said again. "We'll take Kelsine to Harta, and then we'll save the other dragons." She clicked and reached for Crystal, who whistled and dived into Ilina's arms.

We were going to be fine.

"YOU WANT TO go to Harta for a dragon?" Gerel had returned from setting traps outside the cabin, and naturally she had questions: where had the third dragon come from, and what did we intend to do with her?

"One of Altan's dragons, at that." Chenda sat near the low fire, opposite the sleeping Kelsine and Hristo. Freshly scrubbed, her deep umber skin practically glowed.

"She's not Altan's dragon anymore." I paused my braiding of Ilina's hair to pet Kelsine. Our baths hadn't been nearly as luxurious as Chenda's, what with the extra dragon needing to be watched, but we'd gotten soap on all the important places, including the tattered remains of our clothes. Unfortunately, all our extra blankets were being used as dams against the encroaching rainwater, so we sat in our damp clothes and hoped the fire helped dry them. "Kelsine is with us," I said. "We're going to take care of her."

Ilina started to nod in agreement, but stopped herself; I still had handfuls of her hair.

"This is a bad idea." Chenda glanced at the sleeping dragon. "Surely there is something more important you could be doing."

"Helping dragons *is* the most important thing I can do." I finished Ilina's second braid and then turned around for her to do mine. We were aiming for fast and simple—just enough to keep our hair out of our faces for a few days—but even so, it felt so wonderful to be (mostly) clean and to let my best friend braid my hair.

"There's still noorestone dust in here." Ilina's tone was a frown. "Did you even try to get it out?"

"What?" I pulled a strand over my shoulder, waiting to hear her laugh and say she'd tricked me, but no. She was right. Tiny particles of noorestone still glowed against the black curls. "I did try to wash it."

Maybe noorestone dust was like cat fur: everywhere, always.

Aaru regarded us with a lifted eyebrow and upturned mouth. ::Cannot understate how much dust there was.::

"That's true." I smiled and wrapped my arms around my knees while Ilina got to work. Noorestone powder in my hair didn't matter. Not here. Not with these people. They weren't Mother, and I wasn't the Hopebearer to them—just Mira.

Just Mira.

Thunder crashed again, shaking the cabin, and wood groaned against a gust of wind.

"Well," Chenda said, "how do you propose to help dragons? We can't even get off the island, let alone to Harta."

Ilina was suspiciously quiet, so I said it: "We have a ship waiting for us."

"A ship." Chenda raised an eyebrow. "Perhaps Kelsine will fit on a ship bound for Harta. Perhaps you can get her *to* the ship. But what about the others? There are far larger dragons you'll want to rescue, correct?"

Heat crawled up my throat and cheeks. "All the species

of dragons taken from our sanctuary were larger—"

"How will you fit three *Drakontos rexes* on a single ship without proper precautions? How will you make the dragons trust you enough, after what they've been through?" Chenda glanced at Gerel for help, but Gerel was hemming a sleeve cut off one of the jackets. The set of her shoulders indicated she was listening, but trying not to get involved. Chenda let out an annoyed breath as she turned back to Ilina and me.

"We'll make it work," Ilina said after a moment. "We could even steal the ship the dragon thieves have been using."

"And sail it with what crew?" Chenda asked.

"Mira is the Hopebearer," Ilina said. "And the Dragonhearted, according to some people. We will find a crew willing to sail for her."

Chenda shook her head. "You are thinking like children playing at a grand adventure, but these plans will get you killed."

"They'll be less likely to get us killed if you're with us," I said.

Ilina tugged my hair in irritation.

Chenda leveled her gaze on me. "Indeed, because I would advise you to seek help from the Luminary Council."

Before she even finished saying the word *luminary*, I was already shaking my head. "The council betrayed me."

"That's what you said before." Gerel looked up, lured into the conversation at last. Whatever she was making was nearly finished, with a long strap that stretched from one end of the sleeve to the other. "But the Great Abandonment—"

"They don't *care*," I said, as Ilina tied off my second braid. "They don't believe it will happen."

Outside, wind screamed through the trees and a loud *crack* signaled a branch breaking free. Everyone stilled, listening for danger, but both *raptuses* were curled up near the fire, and Kelsine hadn't budged from her spot near Hristo.

I dropped my gaze to my hands. "I cannot trust the Luminary Council. They didn't just ignore the problem of dragons being sent to the empire—although that would be bad enough. They might be responsible for it, and that is why they wanted to silence me."

One fact comforted me: as the biggest dragon sanctuary on the Fallen Isles, the Crescent Prominence sanctuary sheltered more than forty large dragons at any given time, including three *Drakontos titanuses*. Not all the large dragons had been taken.

At least not yet.

Ilina touched my arm as wind howled through the forest outside. Water leaked across the floor, still a safe distance from us, but we'd have to create better blanket dams if we didn't want to drown in our sleep later.

"The Mira Treaty is meant to protect dragons." Chenda glanced at Kelsine, LaLa, and Crystal. "And it was signed on Darina, under the light of the Luminary Council."

Again, I was shaking my head before she finished. "I'm afraid the Mira Treaty might be a lie."

Behind me, Ilina gasped. "What? No."

Chenda laced her fingers together and rested her hands on her lap. "The Mira Treaty is one of the most important documents in the Fallen Isles. It's changed *everything*. It cannot be a lie."

"I believed that too," I said, "but Altan told me—"

Ilina hissed. "Altan *lies*."

Gerel bit off the thread she'd been working with and set the strapped sleeve aside. "I agree with Feisty. Altan has a history of lying."

My heart thudded, echoing in my ears as loud as the thunder outside. "Listen to what he told me, and tell me if you don't find it compelling." I counted off the list on my fingers:

"One. The preamble of the treaty claims that we bow to the light of Noore—the one true authority. That's a phrase that supposedly hasn't been used before the treaty, at least not on the Fallen Isles.

"Two. Harta's independence. People didn't suddenly realize that it's wrong to occupy another island. No, we were forced to do the right thing, because in the empire, everything belongs to the empress.

"Three. We're sending dragons and noorestones there. What other reason do we have for giving up the children of the gods, if not as payment for safety?"

Another peal of thunder shook the cabin. Three

seconds. Four. Five. I grabbed one of the nearby noore-stones and squeezed, trying to calm the whirling in my thoughts.

"I don't want it to be true." I turned the noorestone over and over in my hands. Fidgeting was unbecoming, but dawn was close, and I hadn't had even a mediocre night of sleep in two days. Fainting from blood loss earlier probably didn't count as proper rest. "I don't want to believe the Luminary Council would strap us to the empire, but they lied to me about why the dragons were being taken from the sanctuary, and who's to say that lie isn't bigger and more complex than we originally thought? Who's to say the Mira Treaty itself isn't the lie behind everything?"

My throat tightened with those words.

"And if that's true," I added, "then the Algotti Empire has already conquered us."

"Then learning the truth about the Mira Treaty should be our priority," Chenda said. "And through that, we will be able to rescue your dragons."

"If we wait, the dragons will be unreachable." Ilina gazed down at Crystal and LaLa. "We have to go as soon as Hristo can travel. First to Harta, for Kelsine and to make sure they'll take the dragons we rescue. And then we'll figure out where the others have been taken."

"What about your parents, Fancy?" Gerel looked at me. "Can they help?"

"Absolutely not," Ilina said before I had a chance.

"Your father is the architect of the treaty," Chenda said

to me. "It would benefit us to find out what he knows."

"There is no *us*," Ilina said. "We're splitting up. You can go on to Damina and ask Mira's father if he intentionally helped sell us to the Algotti Empire, but Mira, Hristo, and I are going to rescue dragons."

"This is not only about dragons," Chenda said. "This is bigger. This is the safety of the Fallen Isles."

"If the remaining children of the gods are sent away, the gods will abandon us." My jaw hurt from tensing it. "You felt the quake in the Pit. And on Idris two months ago. Even this storm could be part of the Great Abandonment." I gestured around the room as rain beat the walls in an angry staccato, and water crept closer toward us.

Aaru looked down at his hands resting in his lap; I shouldn't have brought up the Idrisi tremor. I didn't know exactly what had happened, but I did know he'd been there, and that something had changed that day.

Lightning flared, illuminating the cabin for a heartbeat.

"Our world is in trouble." I forced my tone even. "We must do what we can to right it."

"Returning four or five dragons will not appease the gods," Chenda said. "We must approach this from another angle, and on a larger scale."

Chenda was a politician. Of course she'd see it like that.

"There's another reason to go after the dragons directly," I said after a moment. "The noorestones."

"What about the noorestones?" Gerel asked.

"The shipment contained ten giant noorestones."

"Why do they matter?" Chenda picked up one of the smaller noorestones scattered on the floor, cupping the blue-white light in her palms. "Even if the crystals are big, Bopha's mines are rich. There are still untouched deposits all over the island."

"Huge noorestones as big as this room." I gestured around. "Do you remember the *Infinity*?"

"She sank and most of the crew was lost." Gerel shrugged. "What does that have to do with noorestones?"

"She didn't just sink." My mind fluttered back to the conversation with Ilina and Hristo when we'd first found the shipping order. "The *Infinity* exploded."

Aaru's eyebrows lifted. Chenda and Gerel exchanged alarmed glances.

"You don't have to tell them everything," Ilina whispered. "We don't need them."

Ilina was wrong. I did need them. I owed them all so much, and Ilina did too. We wouldn't have made it out of the Pit alive without Gerel, Chenda, and Aaru. I just had to make them see things my way, and that was what I was supposed to be good at, right? That was my job as Hopebearer.

"The giant noorestones that power ships like the *Infinity* and *Star-Touched* aren't stable," I said. "Not like these smaller stones." I lifted the one I'd been toying with. "Unfortunately, a dragon being transported on the *Infinity* got loose and something happened between it and one of the noorestones. . . ."

::**Go on,**:: Aaru said.

"It exploded," I said. "Most everyone was killed, including the dragon. I believe it is one of the greatest tragedies of our time, but only a few people know about it. The public would never trust noorestones again if they knew that even a few very rare varieties might be dangerous."

Gerel's expression was dark. "And you know about it because . . ."

"Because she was likely given a speech in case the news got out," Chenda provided. "It's not uncommon."

I nodded. "The shipping order said there were ten giant noorestones going with the dragons. Crystals that size could be used to power ships able to traverse the sea between the Fallen Isles and the mainland. Or—"

"Potential weapons are heading toward the Algotti Empire." Gerel drew a heavy breath. "Altan knows about the dragons. Does he know about this, too?"

"No." I shook my head. "I didn't want him to know."

She lifted an eyebrow.

"When we were little"—I motioned between Ilina and me—"we used to hear stories about the honorable Drakon Warriors and how they protected the Isles. But if Altan could hurt people like he did me, or later Aaru, then I couldn't trust what he'd do with noorestones that could destroy a ship like the *Infinity*." I swallowed hard. "Maybe the Drakon Warriors used to be the good, honorable protectors of the Isles, but they aren't anymore."

Gerel pressed her mouth in a line, hardening her expression like that would disguise the hurt. She'd wanted to be a Drakon Warrior, but she'd believed they'd disbanded, as the Mira Treaty ordered. She hadn't known the elite order had stayed around, just hidden.

"Ten noorestones like that could devastate a city," Chenda said.

"Or several cities, if they knew where to place the noorestones to cause secondary explosions." Gerel closed her eyes and exhaled slowly. "That does change things."

Chenda shot Gerel an annoyed look. "You would think that."

Gerel tilted her head. "Of course I think that we can't let the empire control the most powerful, deadly weapons in the Fallen Isles. You should worry about it, too. If the Mira Treaty is a sham—"

"*If* the treaty is a sham. We need to find proof of that, first of all, and the best way to do that is to visit Crescent Prominence."

"If Mira sets foot in Crescent Prominence, she will be arrested and maybe killed," Ilina said.

"They'd never kill the Hopebearer."

"They don't need me anymore. They found someone else—"

Before I could finish, lightning struck just outside, illuminating the window with blinding electric light. Thunder cracked overhead.

83

Something else cracked too.

A tree.

A wall.

Our screams as wind howled through the main room, and the great gash in the wall as the cabin tore open.

AARU

Ten Years Ago

I FOUND SAFA IN THE RAIN.

It was always raining, at least for half the year, and I
was in charge of the barrels. When they got full, I opened
the taps and let the water flow through hoses, filters, and
into underground cisterns that would hold enough fresh
water to get us through the dry season. At least, the whole
family prayed it lasted. There were four children by then,
a fifth on the way, and we weren't acquiring new cisterns
as quickly.

That night, the noise of rain kept me awake, so I got
up to do chores.

Only my small, fading noorestone illuminated the wet
night, and just as I reached to twist the knob on the last
barrel, I saw her: a tiny, shivering girl tucked between the

barrel and the house. She was maybe three or four years old, wearing a hooded sweater and torn skirts, but no shoes; mud caked her tiny brown feet. At every crash of thunder, she made a low whine.

I led her inside and dried her by the fire, cringing every time she made a sound: a creak in the floor, a shuddering breath, a sneeze. My parents—along with my youngest sister, Hafeez—were in their room, and the other two were in the second bedroom. That left me with a mat near the fireplace.

Or it did, until the girl. I had no idea where I'd sleep now, but she needed the heat more. When she was warm and dry, I gave her my good blanket and tried asking her name. Her eyes followed my fingers tapping on my knees, but she only frowned. Maybe she didn't know the quiet code. Strange.

I eyed the door to my parents' room and kept my voice low. "Can you speak?"

She didn't even look at me.

Another bolt of lightning hit nearby, and thunder broke right over the house, shaking everything.

The girl shrieked and buried herself under the covers.

I checked the bedroom doors—closed—and leaned toward the girl. "Hush," I whispered. "It's only thunder."

She didn't respond. Just whimpered.

Dread welled up inside me. If she didn't stop, we'd both be in trouble. I could already feel the basement steps, the yawning darkness below, and the hours of copying pages from *The Book of Silence* that awaited me.

The thunder faded, and I said, "Hush."

Her cry cut off with a small *meep*.

"Please don't yell again. Thunder can't hurt you." Not like her voice could.

Frantically, she pulled the blankets off her head and leaned toward me, wearing an expression of concentration.

My parents' door opened, and my stomach dropped.

"What are you doing?" Father's voice was both soft and loud at the same time. Beyond him, I heard Korinah and Alya sneak to their bedroom door to listen.

In hurried quiet code, I explained how I'd found the little girl.

Father glanced at Mother; he was always gentler when she was around. "Keep her until morning, but no more screaming or you're both in the basement."

I'd be quiet. We both would.

CHAPTER SEVEN

THE CABIN RIPPED APART, UNLEASHING THE FULL
fury of the storm into our space. LaLa and Crystal
shrieked, diving toward us as though we might be able
to protect them from the weather, and Kelsine lurched
up from her bedding with a surprised roar.

Water lashed across the room in waves, slapping and
stinging exposed skin. Wind grabbed my hair and pulled,
and LaLa trembled in my arms, her wings pressed tight
against her body and her face ducked between us.

"We have to move!" But move where, I didn't know.
In the rain-muted noorestone light, I could just make out
our things sliding across the floor. Packs. Shoes. Bowls.
The blankets we'd been using to dam the tide had already
been lost to the gale.

Aaru tugged my shoulder and pointed toward the washroom.

"Go!" I thrust LaLa into his arms, heedless of her sharp scales. "I'll tell the others."

He opened his mouth as if to argue, but even if sound were able to come out, the roar of wind and driving rain would have drowned his voice.

I pushed him and turned toward Gerel, who was already waking Hristo.

My protector flailed, confused with injury and shock. "What—" Then he saw the gaping hole in the cabin and allowed Gerel to help him to his feet. "What happened? Where are we?" At least, that was what I thought he said; wind whipped away his words.

And when he found me, I pointed toward the washroom where Ilina—carrying Crystal and an armful of random items—vanished through the doorway, with Chenda close behind her. "In there!" I shouted.

Gerel nodded and helped Hristo through the screaming gusts of wind and rain.

The only one left was Kelsine, huddled in the washed-out remains of the fireplace and growling at the storm.

I pushed toward her, straining against the wind as it tried to suck me from the cabin. "Kelsine!" I reached for her, but the dragon just stared at me, wide-eyed and shivering.

The storm keened through the space. Wood groaned and trembled. And under the shriek of wind, I heard Ilina calling me.

"I can't leave her out here!" I shouted over my shoulder, but she couldn't hear me over the howling. I turned back to Kelsine. "Come on." I reached for her again, but she drew backward, deeper into the fireplace, spilling ash and partially burned logs out across the floor.

I couldn't wait. I couldn't persuade her. With all of my might, I grabbed Kelsine at the scruff and around one leg and *pulled*. "Let's go! We can't stay out here!"

Not that I was sure if the washroom would be any better. What if that lost a wall, too?

"Mira!" At the doorway, Ilina grabbed Aaru's arm and hauled him back. He stared at me, eyes wide and mouth making the shape of my name as he reached for me.

Lightning flashed overhead, blinding, and thunder roared, shaking the cabin. The boom startled Kelsine into motion, and at once she and I were racing toward the door. I paused only to scoop up handfuls of anything not taken by the storm, then leaned into the wind to follow.

One last look outside the shredded wall revealed rain falling almost horizontally, trees bending under the strain, and forest debris flying everywhere. The noise of it all sounded like an angry *Drakontos titanus*: huge, powerful, and soul-shuddering. This storm could level a city.

Then I dived into the washroom and threw the door closed—but it bounced back and hit the wall with a *smack*.

Gerel appeared at my side, and together we heaved the door against the violent wind until it shut.

Walls groaned as air whistled through the cracks, and

the door shuddered in its frame. It seemed unlikely the washroom would protect us any more than the main room had.

"What were you thinking?" Gerel nudged me. "Dragging in Kelsine like that. Are you stupid?"

"I couldn't leave her behind. She came to us for help." My hands were shaking, ruddy with scrapes from Kelsine's scales. My jaw ached from clenching. And my heart—my heart beat so hard I could feel it in my temples and throat and wrists. I leaned on the door, gasping for breath around the panicked squeeze in my throat. "Is everyone all right?"

Everyone was soaked, skin slicked with rain and faces ashen from shock. There were but seven noorestones here, and even their light seemed dim under the fury of the storm. Our safe house—the place we'd come to get *away* from trouble—was destroyed.

Just beyond the thin door, wind raged and pushed, trying to get in.

"I think so," Ilina said after a moment of everyone absorbing the idea of being trapped in the washroom. With the tub and the water pump, there wasn't much space for the six of us. Plus the pair of *Drakontos raptuses*, who were perched on the faucet, both of their bodies bent low, worried clicks coming staccato from their throats. And Kelsine, who unsuccessfully tried to press herself between the tub and pump. Dragons usually liked storms.

Not this storm.

Aaru tapped on the tub, not with words, but instruction.

91

"Right." Gerel squeezed away from the tub, putting Chenda in front of her. "Get in."

Chenda scowled. "Why?"

"We need to be inside something solid." Hristo's face was shiny with rain and drawn from exhaustion. He had awakened in a strange location to find his hand wrapped in a thousand bandages and a storm bearing down on us. "This building is not solid."

He was right. The cabin groaned around us, struggling to remain upright against the relentless force of the wind. And the tub was big enough for all of us to fit inside— albeit not comfortably.

"What if lightning strikes again?" In spite of her misgivings, Ilina was already pushing Hristo toward the tub.

"Right now, the wind is more of a danger." In the dim light, Gerel found the sleeve she'd been sewing before. "Protector, I made this for you. Don't laugh, and don't lose it."

He eyed the sleeve. "What is it?"

"A sling to hold your arm still while that heals. Last thing we need is you hitting it and opening the wound again." She nodded at his hand. "Let's put it on first."

Horror slipped over his face, but as the cabin shuddered around us, he stepped toward Gerel. "Show me how to wear it."

Gerel worked quickly, while Chenda climbed into the tub first, sitting on her knees and squeezing to one end. Hristo went next, though he protested, and then Ilina.

LaLa and Crystal folded themselves in with her, covered in a fire-resistant jacket to protect everyone from their razor scales.

Kelsine whined, as though she knew she would not fit with us, and wedged farther between the tub and pump.

I touched the top of her head. "I'm sorry. You'll have to be brave, little firefly."

She whined again and ducked her face.

"Now you." Gerel pointed at Aaru. "In."

He shook his head.

The building trembled. Rain battered the walls—rain and some sort of debris. Was he really going to risk his life because he didn't want to get in with all of us?

"What if you go last?" I had to try. I'd put too much effort into keeping him alive—sneaking food and getting him out of the Pit—to allow him to die in a storm.

Aaru swallowed hard, glancing at the crowded tub, and then me. As the wind keened louder and the cabin gave a long, tortured moan, he acquiesced.

Gerel got in the tub. I got in the tub.

There wasn't much room now, but when everyone repositioned themselves as though we were rowing a boat, there was just enough space for Aaru to squeeze in front of me, his back curved against my chest. Without thinking, I wrapped my arms around him, so my palms were pressed against his thumping heartbeat, and my knuckles pressed against his knees. His body stiffened as blankets fell over us from behind.

"Stay down," Gerel rasped by my ear.

I rested my cheek against the knobs of Aaru's spine. ::We'll be fine,:: I tapped against his ribs. ::The storm will blow over quickly.::

He found my hand and pressed down, acknowledging my comforting lie for what it was.

The space beneath the blanket was dim, lit by the faint glow of noorestone dust trapped in my hair, and the splinters of light that pierced the loose weave of cloth. The air grew stuffy, heavy with all our breathing and too many bodies crammed into a small space.

Wind and thunder shook the building, achingly loud. My ears rang under the onslaught of noise, of tree branches ripping from trunks, of wind and rain and debris hitting the side of the weakening cabin, and of Kelsine keening into the gale. It was impossible to say how much longer the walls would hold up. And what then? The tub was heavy, and the water pump was anchored deep into the ground, but if this storm was actually a hurricane—a god's eye, as *The Book of Love* called them—then we could be here for not just hours, but days.

Thanks to Altan, I could imagine a lot of things I'd never been able to imagine before. I knew what true darkness felt like. I knew the agony of starvation and dehydration. I knew the terror of complete isolation. I knew what it felt like to be tortured, and to watch someone else be tortured.

But this was not Altan's doing. This was nature. Noore. Maybe the gods.

An immense *crack* sounded, like the walls peeling apart, and wind surged into the room. Kelsine shrieked as everyone scrambled to grab hold of the blankets covering us.

"Stay down!" Gerel shouted, tugging the blanket tighter over our heads. The fabric strained, flapping at the edges and corners, but every time someone's grip failed, others kept the cloth in place.

Wood screamed as trees bent and broke, and wind cut itself on the corners and jagged edges of the cabin.

Please, Damyan. Please, Darina. I shouted the prayer in my head. *Please save us from this.* But if my gods were listening, they didn't quell the storm. They didn't lift us out of here. If they heard, they allowed this nightmare to go on and on.

Around us, the whole world rumbled like it was falling apart.

CHAPTER EIGHT

THE STORM DIED OUT, FINALLY DROWNED IN ITS OWN
rage and bluster, leaving behind the soft patter of rain
on wood, the rustle of trees, and the sighing of the cabin's exhausted walls.

I'd long ago lost track of the time, but the ache in my
body suggested we'd been huddled in the same position
for hours. Hunger made my stomach twist, and my throat
was parched with want of water. Muscles cramped and
limbs went numb. I had to relieve myself, too; I probably
wasn't the only one.

"I think it's over." Gerel pushed the wet blankets off
of us, revealing the remains of our safe house. Darkness
softened the destruction, but by the pale light of seven
dust-shrouded noorestones, I could just make out the

walls shredded into a wooden lace. Whole boards had been ripped from the frame, not just in the main room, but in the washroom as well. Immense branches were visible through the holes, the ends ragged where wind had torn them from trunks.

The sharp scent of lightning lingered in the air, but it seemed safe enough for us to come out.

"Can anyone move?" My voice was hoarse with thirst and terror.

"Maybe never again." Ilina groaned as something—maybe her elbow—hit the side of the tub. "I'm trying."

When I looked over my shoulder, I was just in time to see her tumble gracelessly out of the tub and land on the floor with a *thunk*.

She offered a pained smile. "Now the rest of you."

A pair of tiny dragons exploded out of the jacket they'd been wrapped in, and landed on her shoulders. They stretched their wings and necks, then took to higher perches.

Raindrops caught in my lashes as I lifted my eyes. The roof had been ripped off, leaving exposed beams. Clouds smothered the sky, suffocating sunlight. One bright point burned through—the sun moving toward noon—but the day was still very, very dark. In the distance I could hear birds calling, cautious hope in their whistles and chirps.

As Ilina helped Hristo out of the tub, and then Chenda, the pressure of my body against Aaru's eased. Blood rushed back into my legs and feet and toes, a painful stabbing all through my limbs.

I braced myself on the edge of the tub and hauled myself into a standing position, then heaved myself over onto shaking legs. I checked on Kelsine first; she was still wedged between the tub and pump, but at some point she'd fallen asleep. She blinked up at me when I touched the top of her head. "What a brave girl," I whispered to her. And then louder: "Is everyone all right?"

"As all right as we can be," Chenda said. She was already moving around the cabin's remains, picking up anything that looked salvageable. Noorestones. Bags. Blankets.

Aaru began removing himself from the tub last, and he was out before anyone could offer a hand to help. His face was dark with the heat of all of us being pressed together, and softened with shadows.

::Should leave.::

I nodded and told the others.

"Agreed." Gerel followed Chenda into what was left of the main room. "Warriors will be checking the surrounding land for others caught out in the storm. We need to move on immediately."

It seemed like they shouldn't be able to muster more people to search than they already had, but Aaru and Gerel were right: we couldn't linger here.

There wasn't much left over from the storm that we could take, so within minutes, we'd finished our business at the cabin—hiding evidence of our stay—and then we headed east, toward the port city of Lorn-tah.

Even though the rain was down to an annoying drizzle, we didn't talk much for the first hour. My limbs shivered with exhaustion, and every *crack* in the woods put me on edge. Was it the wind? A warrior? I walked close to Hristo, trying to offer a steady hand when his steps shuffled or he stumbled in the mud. He wasn't ready to travel—not at all—but we didn't have a choice.

"I'll be fine," he insisted, as though sweat wasn't pouring down his face, or his complexion ashen with blood loss. "You don't have to help me."

"I know." I tried to smile. "But it makes me feel better to walk with you."

"You don't have to look out for me."

I scoffed. "I'm walking next to you because you're my protector and I trust you to keep me safe."

"Oh." His expression lightened as he wiped rain away from his eyes. "In that case, stay close. Besides, you still have noorestone dust in your hair. You make a nice lantern."

I forced a laugh and bumped my shoulder against his, but my heart wasn't in it. He'd been so hurt, and he hadn't been able to even rest and regroup, to catch his breath before this new tragedy. But I'd give him whatever he needed. Anything to help take his mind off his pain.

Aaru glanced over his shoulder at us, his eyebrows turned inward and his mouth pressed into a straight line. He didn't comment, though, and didn't drop back to walk next to us.

By the time speckles of light broke through the clouds,

slanted golden with late afternoon, I was bone tired and sore; fresh blisters had rubbed into my heels and toes.

"Want to take the dragons hunting?" Ilina asked.

"I'd rather go to sleep right here." I motioned at the muddy path, covered with prickly twigs and leaves. "But I'll go with you."

I instructed Kelsine to guard the others. She huffed fire, but stayed as Ilina and I picked mangoes and moved far enough away from the group that prey wouldn't be scared off. Still, we stayed within earshot, always guiding Crystal and LaLa parallel to the others.

Our game went into a makeshift bag: three quails, two mountain lizards, and one rabbit.

As night settled, we came to an immense obelisk rising through the trees, and Gerel called for a halt.

"What is this?" Chenda dropped her backpack on the lee side of the stone. It was big enough to shield us from the worst of the wind and rain, but we were still shivering and cold. And hungry.

Gerel turned her gaze upward, the tendons on her neck protruding sharply as she scanned the weathered stone face. "This is a monument to the Celestial Warriors, a group of elite men and women who rode against the kingdoms and clans of the mainland during the Sundering two thousand years ago." She hesitated a heartbeat before pressing her palm against the worn carving of small figures on the backs of dragons. "They rode *Drakontos titanuses* across the sea and burned the coasts clear of our enemies. They razed every building, charred the cliffs, and blackened the sand until it ran like molten glass."

"What happened to them?" Ilina whispered.

Gerel let her hand drop to her side. "They took damage, of course. A few poisoned arrows slipped between the scales of a handful of dragons."

"They died there?" Chenda wiped drops of rain off her face.

"They couldn't come home." Gerel glanced at Ilina. "The poison first prevented the dragons from flying, and soon it cast them into a deep sleep. They perished after years of nightmare-filled captivity, but the damage the Celestial Warriors had done—that was enough to prevent new attacks on the Fallen Isles. They sacrificed everything to ensure our freedom."

"Well." Ice nipped Ilina's voice. "Freedom for some. Those born on the right islands."

Hristo didn't respond; the subject of Harta's occupation was one he usually tried to avoid, especially in the company of people he didn't know well. Even Ilina and I barely knew his thoughts, and we were his best friends. But we were also born to Damina, a nation that had controlled his in the past.

"It's a nice monument." I shivered with the rain. "Are we going to camp here or . . ."

Gerel rolled her eyes. "I'll get the fire started. Aaru and Chenda, find water. And more herbs for Hristo's hand, if you see any."

Chenda nodded.

"And you two"—Gerel looked at Ilina and me—"that game won't fix itself."

I almost never prepared my own kills from our hunts in the sanctuary. Hristo usually did, if we were going to keep them for our families, or we gave them whole to homeless shelters. I knew how, though; one of our first hunting lessons had included the gruesome task, although Mother complained that it was beneath me.

Hristo lowered his eyes. "I'll—"

"Sit." Gerel pointed at the base of the obelisk. "Rest and eat a mango. Don't you dare move that hand or I'll cut it off myself."

Reluctantly, he accepted a piece of fruit from Ilina, then slid down the stone face until he sat on the ground with a heavy sigh. His warm brown skin was tinged gray, and shiny with sweat and rain. Hollows hung under his eyes, and he didn't protest as Gerel found what was left of a medical kit and peeled off the bandages to inspect the damage.

"This will heal," she said.

"Will I be able to use it again?" His voice was strong, but still I heard the shiver of uncertainty beneath.

"I don't know." Gerel studied the wound. "Your thumb and forefinger, probably. The others—I'm less certain. But no matter what, you'll figure out how to use what you have."

I glanced at Ilina, wondering if she noticed the way

Gerel cared for Hristo. Surely she would see the value in staying together, all of us.

But she was already bent over her work of cleaning our kills, so I hurried to help.

"I can't fight without my entire hand." His tone flattened, like the full impact of this injury was hitting all at once. Everything he used to do with his right hand—he might lose.

"Nonsense." Gerel tossed a dirty bandage aside and found a clean one. "You might not be able to grip a hilt the same way, but maybe Fancy or Feisty can arrange for a special sword when this is over." She finished applying the fresh bandage, far more a caretaker than she would like to admit. "Anyway, a good warrior knows how to fight with either hand. Are you a good warrior?"

"Yes." The white bandage practically glowed against his skin, a beacon that drew the eye.

"Good." Gerel smirked in his direction, then worked on building up the fire. "Now get back to resting."

Thunder rumbled through the air—through the ground—as I stared at Hristo. His entire life could be forever altered because of this injury.

"Well, if you're done feeling sorry for me, I'd like to eat." He smiled to take the sting from his words.

"Oh. Sorry." I went faster, and by the time Chenda and Aaru returned, we were ready to cook. We worked in silence, listening to the whistle of wind around the obelisk and the patter of rain on stone.

When the soup—as Ilina generously described it—was finished, she offered the first bowl to Hristo. I tried not to hover while he figured out how to eat one-handed; he was proud, and my interference would only make things worse.

"Are we heading to the *Chance Encounter*?" he asked as wind picked up, hissing through trees. In the distance, a dog howled.

Ilina and I glanced at each other. "*We* are," she said. "We have to take Kelsine to safety."

Hristo's gaze settled on the sleeping dragon and he nodded. "Yes. I had noticed she was with us. Where are we taking her?"

"Harta."

If I hadn't been looking for it, I wouldn't have noticed the way Hristo's jaw tightened and his gaze flickered downward. "Very well. And what of you three?" He looked from Gerel to Chenda to Aaru; the latter sat a little ways away from the small fire, his eyes on his clasped hands. "Will you be joining us?"

Ilina's expression darkened. "Can I talk to you over there?" She pointed toward the rain-shrouded woods.

He leveled a glare her way. "Ilina. We owe these people our lives."

She crossed her arms. "We wouldn't if we had just left the Shadowed City when we had the chance, but Mira wouldn't leave them behind."

Gerel and Chenda both frowned, probably irritated by

Ilina's tone, but Aaru lifted his eyes to mine.

I tapped, ::I don't abandon allies.::

"Besides," Ilina went on, "Captain Pentoba agreed to take three of us, not six."

"The captain didn't agree to take a *Drakontos ignitus*, but you know Kelsine will be welcome." Hristo shook his head and sighed. "The *Chance Encounter* will sail for the Hopebearer and her friends. All of them."

"It doesn't even matter," Ilina muttered. "They don't want to save dragons."

Hristo shot a questioning look at Chenda, who said, "Regardless, I would like to leave Khulan."

"I would, too." Gerel's mouth twisted with a sad smile, and a note of grief for her surged through me. She was Khulani. This was her home. Leaving meant muting not only her gift of strength, but closeness to her god as well.

"I think—" I cleared my throat. "I think we should all stay together. But if anyone wants to separate, I think we should wait until we get to Val fa Merce. We all want off this island. Without identification, the *Chance Encounter* is our best opportunity. Then Ilina, Hristo, and I can rescue dragons, and you all can do . . ." I shrugged. "Whatever it is you want to do."

"I wanted to destroy the Heart," Gerel said. "That's done now, albeit a little later than I'd intended."

"What now?" Chenda asked her.

"I hadn't bet on surviving. I suppose I have a lot of free time—and until Harta to decide. Maybe rescue dragons.

Maybe . . ." Her eyes stayed on Chenda. "What are you doing after Harta?"

Chenda touched the tattoos on her cheek, delicate fingers dark against the bright copper. "Bopha needs help. All the Fallen Isles need help. I would like to pursue the truth of the Mira Treaty. Hopefully, I can persuade Mira to see things my way."

Gerel nodded, then turned toward Aaru. "And you?"

He startled, as though he hadn't realized that people could still see him and might not have forgotten about him.

Then our eyes met. His were starless night, deep with sadness and mystery, but also kindness and patience. I wanted him with me, his quiet strength and the soft tap of his code on the back of my hand. I wanted the way he had looked at me for *me*, not for my name.

At last, Aaru sighed and tapped his answer against his knee. ::Home.::

AARU

Ten Years Ago

SAFA WASN'T WELCOME IN HER HOME.

Not really.

By morning, the rain had intensified. Water slammed in silver sheets, obscuring fields and the long, winding road that led to town. My boots sank into the mud as I carried Safa to Nazil's house.

Mother knocked a quick pattern, announcing herself. She was the only one of us who could, though it would have been better if Father were here. But he was at work.

I put Safa down and she took my hand.

We didn't hear anything for several minutes, save the pounding rain as it battered the house and poured into the barrels. Finally, the door opened, and Nazil looked out. He was a tall, wiry man, and dark from working the fields.

His eyes dropped to Safa. He scowled. "You brought her back."

Mother placed her hand on Safa's head. "Aaru found her last night."

Nazil frowned more. He didn't invite us inside, or offer us towels, or a hot drink. "Tell me everything."

Mother looked at me, and I started to tap on my chest—Safa had a strong grip on my other hand—but Nazil grunted.

"Speak out loud."

I shifted with discomfort, but I couldn't disobey. Haltingly, I told him about last night. "I noticed she doesn't know the quiet code."

Mother's glare snapped at me. I tensed. That had been too critical.

"She doesn't know anything about quiet, code or otherwise." Nazil narrowed his eyes. "She won't listen. She's a wild one."

That phrase sent a jolt of terror through me. I'd heard about wild ones before. Parents who could afford it sent their child to a correctional school, and they always returned very silent. Very obedient. But wrong somehow. Broken.

Other children just seemed to vanish.

It was a risk, but I had to try. "Perhaps I could teach her."

Nazil just shook his head and seized Safa's other hand. "Get here. You'll go in the basement."

Safa tightened her grip on my hand and opened her mouth, but she didn't scream. Yet.

"What has she done?" Mother asked, but she didn't intervene.

The man grabbed Safa and threw her over his shoulder. "She was screaming last night, keeping Lina awake. I put her out and told her to stay close, but looks like she ran over to your place."

Horror bloomed in my chest. "You put her outside in a storm. She wanted shelter."

Nazil reached down and slapped me so hard my right eye stopped working for a moment. "Speak when you're spoken to."

Safa started to cry.

"She can't hear!" It was obvious, wasn't it? "She can't hear anything but loud noises, like thunder. She's scared."

His free hand balled into a fist, but he didn't hit me again. He just slammed the door, taking Safa with him.

I wanted to cry, but Father would notice red, swollen eyes later. He'd ask what happened. And then I'd go in the basement, too, for not being a strong enough man. As it was, I might grow a bruise on my right cheek.

"That isn't right." Mother nudged me homeward. "If you're truly willing to teach the girl, perhaps your father will speak to Nazil."

::I am,:: I tapped.

"Then I'll speak to your father for you."

::Thank you.:: I breathed through the tightness in my throat. I wouldn't cry. I wouldn't. ::If we don't help her, no one will.::

"Idris will," Mother said. "Safa will learn strength through silence."

Perhaps. But doubt had already been seeded within me.

CHAPTER NINE

HOME. OF COURSE HE WANTED TO GO HOME. THAT
had been what he'd told me every day, offering stories
of his sisters and their adventures, telling me how he
missed his father and worried for his mother. He loved
his family, and his absence was making life more difficult for them.

He wanted to go home because his family was his life.

Not me.

Of course not me. We barely knew each other.

Before I could move on to the next part of our discussion, though, Chenda yawned so thoroughly that her jaw
popped.

"We should rest," Gerel said. "Before we get going
again."

It wasn't long before everyone settled close together, propping our heads on a rolled-up blanket. Except Gerel, who wasn't going to sleep. And Aaru, who'd moved two steps away to lie down, because he couldn't be this close without also being uncomfortable.

Careful to keep from waking Ilina beside me, I turned my head to look at my silent friend. In the shadow of the Celestial Warriors' obelisk, he was a long and slender shape with finely corded muscle and sharp edges around his cheekbones and jaw.

He was looking at me, too. Studying.

Embarrassment burned up my neck and cheeks. I closed my eyes and pretended to sleep, but I could still feel his attention, and the tension between us, so I sighed and let my gaze flicker down to my chest, where I tapped, ::I promised to help you go home. I will.::

A faint smile tugged at the corners of his mouth. ::Want to go home.:: He tapped on his stomach. ::Want to be with family. See them safe. Want—:: He lifted his eyes to the sky and breathed, his neck stretching and his chest expanding. He moved with such caution, such weariness.

When he'd collected himself, I said, ::It's fine if you're not ready to say it.:: Whatever *it* was.

He breathed again, and his fingers quickly tapped a prayer—::Strength through silence::—before he turned to me once more. ::Want to be with people I love. With people who understand me.::

My heart sank. I wanted to understand him. I'd never

112

wanted to understand someone more. ::What about after that?::

::Someday, I want to get married. Have children. Give them everything my father gave to me.:: His fingers hesitated. ::I'm a simple person, Mira. Only once did I think I could change the world, and that was the moment that led to my imprisonment.::

I nodded slightly.

::Am not a risk taker. A world changer. Sorry.::

::You don't have to explain.::

But apparently he thought he did, because his fingers were a flurry of movement. ::I am Idrisi. Isolated. We don't involve ourselves in others' problems.:: He glanced at my hands, still motionless on my chest. ::Others think that is selfish, but to us it's respectful. Moving into others' spaces all the time, even to offer help—that is rude to us.::

And on Damina, *not* offering help was unforgivably rude. The Lovers demanded we offer, because love didn't hesitate. Love charged forward and shone like a bright star.

For the first, maybe only time ever, I wished for our cells. There'd been a wall between us, yes, and I'd spent an embarrassing amount of time imagining that it was gone, that we were simply next to each other. But now he was just two arm lengths away, and our cultures were more of a barrier than the wall had ever been.

The wall, our small space torn into that stone, had perhaps been the very thing that allowed our friendship to take root. Allowed us to hold hands and offer comfort and reveal secrets.

I missed it. I missed Aaru.

For one hundred heartbeats, I let myself imagine opening my eyes to find his arm outstretched, reaching for me. I'd reach for him, too, and our fingers would bump and twist in wordless knots. We'd stay like that for moment after moment, with sharp yearning growing between us until neither of us could stand it. That was when he'd move closer. He'd take my hands in his, careful not to cage, and kiss my fingers until the deepest parts of me were set on fire. Easily, I could imagine the heat of his body, the stutter of a breath, and the way a touch could say more than words ever dreamed.

When I reached one hundred, I wiped my eyes and tucked that fantasy away. Now was not the time for wishes. I'd indulge it later. Maybe. If the warriors didn't find us. If we got off the island. If we saved the dragons.

Or maybe there would never be a time for fantasies.

MY BODY WAS stiff with restless sleep when Gerel woke everyone and set us east once more.

For five hot days, we walked across the island of Khulan, skirting around a huge lake called Warrior's Depth. There was a bridge, but it was heavily trafficked, with guard stations at regular intervals. We couldn't take the chance that someone would recognize one of us, or ask for papers, so we went around it.

"Armpit Lake," Ilina said, once the decision was made. "That's what we call it at home. Because on a map, it looks like Khulan has one fist on his hip, and the lake is the space between his body and his arm."

"That's rude." But Gerel's tone was cool and she smiled a little.

Twice a day, Ilina and I took Crystal and LaLa hunting. We learned which Khulani game tasted best on a spit or boiled, since we didn't have a lot of cooking options, and which wild herbs would help our sad attempts at a decent meal. The dragons enjoyed the work, at least. Gold and silver scales flashed between the broad-leafed rain trees, and soon palm trees as we descended the mountains toward the sea. At night, we picked up storm-fallen fronds to use as blankets.

A small victory came on the last night, when I found LaLa and Crystal curled up on top of Kelsine, caught in the bends of her legs and curve of her neck. The next day, the two *raptuses* rode on Kelsine's back while she walked alongside us humans.

Evidence of the god's eye was everywhere. Trees were stripped bare of leaves and fronds, and heavy branches sank deep into the mud. We saw dead animals, too: deer drowned in swollen rivers, and rabbits caught in forgotten snares. Brush had been ripped from the ground, leaving gaping holes where roots used to tunnel.

As the towers and monuments of Lorn-tah peeked above the cliffs and treetops, we left the woods and made our way onto the road. There, we found someone's effort to clear the path, but deep ruts and fallen logs still made travel difficult.

"We'll approach the city from the north side," Gerel said. "It's mostly cliffs and rugged terrain unsuitable for farming. There will be fewer people, and fewer patrols. But be on your guard."

"Why?" Ilina asked.

"Cities—even these camps outside—can be dangerous places, and I can't be certain what we'll find when we get there."

That sounded ominous.

"What do you mean *camps*?" Chenda asked. "Are they not part of the city?"

Gerel's jaw tensed as she lengthened her stride. "Hurry. Altan is pursuing us."

"But he wouldn't know to find us here." I dropped my hand to Kelsine's neck. LaLa and Crystal nosed my fingers and wrist, chirruping. "The city is *so* big. Surely we can get lost here."

She met my eyes, her gaze steady and certain. "I put nothing past him."

A reminder that I knew better than to underestimate Altan.

Golden sunlight shot from the western horizon, casting the jagged cliff faces in deep shadow. Ahead, the road split into seven paths; Gerel kept us on the widest. The others wound up and down the cliffs, with sharp switchbacks and steep climbs to the different layers of the camp. Scraggly brush and grass grew over the smaller paths, as though few people traveled that way.

Our path took us toward the largest part of the camp; even from a distance, we could see it was packed with people moving in every direction.

"Put the little dragons somewhere safe," Gerel instructed. "I wish we could hide Kelsine, too."

"She'll stay in the middle of us." I laid a hand on Kelsine's head, feeling her warmth through the slick scales and blunt little horns. Then, I clicked for LaLa, and Ilina and I tucked the small dragons into the packs slung over our shoulders. It wasn't ideal for the dragons, but Gerel was right: it was better to keep them out of sight.

Shortly, we reached the camp. Against the roadside, faded tents and lean-tos huddled in groups of four and five, sharing a single cook pot between them. Some of the thin pallets and flat pillows stuffed inside were occupied, but it didn't look as though anyone was getting actual rest, thanks to the din of chickens squawking in small cages, dirt-covered children playing chase through the street, and men and women grumping over fires.

Everyone was thin, with graying skin and bloodshot eyes. Maybe they were ill. Maybe they were tired. Either way, this was no place to live.

"How could the Warrior Tribunal just let all these people suffer out here?" There were hundreds. Thousands. Far too many to count. This wasn't a part of Lorn-tah I'd ever seen, not on state visits, and not when I'd been shuffled back and forth to the Pit. This was cruelty of the highest order.

Gerel released a long sigh. "These are the dishonored. Would-be warriors who didn't complete their training. And"—her voice hitched—"their children."

I wasn't quick enough to catch what she wasn't saying, but Chenda reached forward and touched Gerel's wrist as though she understood.

"Let's just get through here." Gerel walked faster. "I don't want to talk about it."

We didn't speak for another hundred steps. Two hundred. Three hundred.

Most people paid us little mind as we walked by. They were busy swatting seagulls from scraps of food, or trying to catch the birds. But a few people traced swirls across their faces as they caught sight of the copper tattoos on Chenda's dark skin. Others touched their cheeks, as though mimicking the scar I carried.

"Who are they?" a man whispered. The woman next to him shook her head, and neither of them took their eyes off us. *"They have a dragon."*

"No, three dragons."

Even after everything we'd been through, we stood out on these streets. Partly because we were going somewhere, while everyone else seemed to be settling in as the cliff's shadow stretched toward the sea. But also because there was no way to disguise the elegant way Chenda carried herself, or the strength in Gerel's stride. We couldn't hide the scar on my face, or the protective way Hristo hovered over me. And then there were Ilina and Aaru, who both looked ready to help every family we passed.

"Surely we can spare some of our game." Ilina's hand brushed the sack slung over her shoulder. Crystal made a soft, questioning purr.

In my bag, LaLa echoed; they thought we were going to hunt. "Not right now, little lizard."

"Don't give anything to anyone." Hristo kept his voice low. "We can't risk people getting close enough to recognize Mira or Chenda. And if we feed one family, we'll have to feed them all, and then what will we have to eat?"

Ilina looked at me. She didn't speak.

She didn't need to.

Damina's Law urged us to look to our neighbors and ensure they always had enough. And yes, there were poor people in Crescent Prominence, and in every other major city on Damina, but there was nothing like this. No immense camps filled with thousands of dishonored. No starving children. No pots of soup that were more water than vegetables.

The Book of Love commanded us to be generous, and while my faith in the Luminary Council was forever shaken, my faith in Damyan and Darina was not.

"Mira—" Hristo's tone was warning, but Ilina and I had already decided.

As one, we pulled off our game sacks and offered a

mountain lizard to the man at the nearest cook pot.

His eyes opened wide as he looked from our offering to us. "Why?"

"Damyan and Darina demand it." I turned to a woman with two small boys at her feet, and presented a quail. "It's not much, but maybe it will feed your children."

"I know you." She took the bird and laughed a little. "I've seen you before."

"Mira, let's go." Gerel took my elbow, but she was too late.

"*Hopebearer*," breathed the woman. "You're the Hopebearer. I knew it."

The title rippled outward, on and on until the whole camp seemed to whisper it at once.

"We need to go." Hristo stepped close to me, always the protector. We'd been in situations like this before, with huge crowds converging on me, demanding attention and affection. When I'd been younger, there'd been three incidents when crowds got out of hand. It had been terrifying—people stretching out their hands to touch my hair or clothes, fingernails scraping against my skin, and even lips pressed against my face and arms. Like brushing their bodies against mine could help them, save them, give them some kind of grace, offer prosperity. Each time, Hristo had stepped in to carve a path through the crush of hopeful people.

But this time, no one rushed forward. No one pressed their hands at me. No one begged for anything. Even the way they *looked* at me was different, with eagerness but not expectation. "Hopebearer!"

Hristo's good hand waited on his sword hilt, but the blade remained sheathed. There was no one to attack. There were thousands of people here, but they stayed a respectful distance away. They waited for me to go to them. Even so, Hristo stayed close as I offered red squirrels and rabbits to the gathering strangers.

Gerel leaned toward Chenda. "Why are they excited about Mira but not you?"

"There have been many Ladies of the Eternal Dawn," said Chenda. "And the title means more to Bophans than anyone else. There is but one Hopebearer, and she is for everyone."

Aaru's gaze cut from them to me, his eyes sharp with worry. I couldn't tell whether his frown was for their words or me, and before I could untangle any feelings, a cheer went up.

"Hopebearer!" they cried. Some lifted children onto their shoulders.

The noise went on and on as full darkness settled on the cliffside, with only a handful of campfires to illuminate the crowd. The whites of people's eyes flashed as they stood on their toes to get a better look. Someone held a torch overhead; the orange fire rippled and curled against the night sky.

My heart lifted. This was what I loved about being the Hopebearer—helping people. Seeing their faces. Learning their stories. And maybe, if the gods were with me, giving people a bit of hope.

We couldn't linger here, I knew that. But as the sister moons rose over the sea and I handed out the last of our game, a knot inside me began to tighten. Sharing what we'd caught was something, but it wasn't enough. There were thousands of people here, and I couldn't possibly feed all of them. Not even just the children.

I lifted my eyes to the starry sky and sighed. I wanted to help, but what more could I do?

Then I heard the answer.

Under the thanks and squeals of hungry children, seagulls called to the crashing of the sea. And, as though sensing my thoughts, LaLa stirred in my bag. Her slender body stretched and her wings fluttered, and she waited just long enough for me to open the bag wide before she leaped into the sky. Crystal followed a heartbeat later.

"What are they doing?" Chenda's voice was strained from the way she'd dropped back her head.

She wasn't the only one. When the small dragons took to the air, a haunting quiet followed the rippling path my title had taken. One by one, people pointed at the sky.

Shrieks erupted from above as the *Drakontos raptuses* stirred the flock of seagulls into a wild frenzy. Feathers fell like shredded clouds.

It was hard to tell what was happening in the dark, but against the backdrop of moons and stars, we could see silhouettes of wings and bursts of fire. LaLa and

122

Crystal circled the flock, blowing flame to keep the white-feathered mass from escaping. The dragons took turns darting in to attack.

Then, a man shouted in alarm as a seagull dropped near his head. "What are they doing?"

From the other side of the crowd, someone else said, "They're hunting for us."

More seagulls fell, their necks twisted or their heads burned, and people began calling instructions for how to prepare the birds. "Pull out their entrails," a woman called. "Soak the meat in seawater."

"Seagulls?" Chenda looked at me, her face twisted with disgust. "Really?"

I shrugged. "They're not ideal, but they are edible."

"There's hardly any meat on them," Gerel said.

"Fortunately, there are a lot of seagulls."

"That will feed a few people one meal. They'll still be hungry after this." Gerel glanced over her shoulder, worry plain on her face. She wasn't upset about the seagulls, but something else.

For ten more minutes, we watched as LaLa and Crystal spit fire and seagulls rained from the sky. Arms reached into the air, catching the fallen birds. Family after family cried thanks to the dragons, and then dashed off to their tents, their faces lit with joy; no one took more than their fair share.

The excitement stirred Kelsine, and she darted through the flurry of feathers, playing and setting some on fire.

Most people just watched in wonder, as though they'd never seen a dragon *play* before, but a few of the braver children came toward her, letting her light sticks on fire so they could take them back to their tents and cook pots.

By the time LaLa returned to my shoulder, sounding a pleased trill by my ear, the remaining seagulls had flown off, and people were gathering unburned feathers from the ground. Only nineteen people stayed nearby, all adults with ragged clothes and thin bodies. A middle-aged woman stepped forward. Moonlight gleamed over her dark skin, highlighting a delicate bone structure and kind smile; she had an inner beauty that shone through the grime and hunger of life in northern Lorn-tah.

"Thank you, Hopebearer." Her voice was deep and melodic. Familiar, faintly. "You've done us an incredible service. None here will forget the day you and your friends brought food from the sky."

"I wish I could have done more." That was the truth.

Behind me, Gerel made a soft, shocked noise.

I turned, ready to tell her that I *knew* seagulls didn't taste good, but she was staring at the woman, naked surprise on her face. That was when I saw it. The high cheekbones. The width of her nose. Even the set of her shoulders. And while Gerel's hair was shorn, sharpening her features to knife blades, this woman was a painting of what Gerel might look like with tight curls that fell unbound around her face.

Ilina saw it, too. "Gerel, is this—"

Aaru straightened and cocked his head an instant before I felt thunder in the ground: a regular, rhythmic beating against the earth. Hooves.

"Someone's coming." The woman who might have been Gerel's mother spun to face the dark road behind her, and so did everyone else. The adults in her group. The people picking feathers off the ground. Even those who'd settled in their tents to clean the gulls went quiet.

Voices rode on the air, above the crashing of the ocean below. I couldn't understand what they said, but the tones were hard. Angry. They made my chest tighten with anxiety; my breath squeezed around knots of panic.

A hand brushed against mine. For a heartbeat, I thought it was Ilina's, but the fingers that slid across mine were too rough, too long. I knew this hand from the dark.

Aaru sidestepped close to me, so our shoulders were just a breath apart. ::He's coming,:: he tapped on my knuckles.

"Who?" Even to me, my voice sounded deep with dread.

::Altan.::

CHAPTER TEN

"WE HAVE TO RUN." THE WORDS WERE OUT BEFORE I realized I was speaking. "Altan is coming."

"Seven gods." Gerel drew her knife and started marching *toward* the sound of hooves. "I'll kill him."

Ilina lurched forward and grabbed Gerel by the elbow. "No, we have to run. You might be the best and the strongest of all the warriors, but you haven't slept a full night in nearly a decan. Altan and the others have definitely slept, definitely eaten well, and they have horses and weapons."

Gerel heaved a long breath and narrowed her eyes at Ilina. "Then what do you suggest we do?"

"Come with me." The woman who was probably Gerel's mother looked from Ilina to Gerel, her face twisting with fear and hope. "I'll hide you."

"In a tent?" Hristo shook his head. "They'll check the tents if they think there's even a chance that Mira came through here."

"Not a tent. Somewhere much more secure."

The pounding hooves were growing closer. Altan would be on us within minutes. "Take us there," I said.

And like that, we were off. Running. My lungs protested immediately, and LaLa's talons dug into my shoulder, but the thrum of hooves was closing in and we had only two choices: run, or get caught.

Gerel's (probably) mother guided us through a maze of tents and lean-tos. Fifty-seven strides. Seventy-three. One hundred and twenty. I gulped deep breaths, trying to time my inhales and exhales with my feet hitting the ground, but it was no use. I could hike all day. I could exercise and clean all day. But running for five minutes never failed to make me feel like death.

Kelsine galloped at my side, her wings tented open to give her lift.

Two hundred and five. Three hundred and twenty-six. Four hundred . . .

People stared as we passed by, their faces glowing in the firelight. "Where are you going?" someone asked, but we didn't have time to answer questions.

"You never saw us," Gerel's mother called over her shoulder.

Immediately, people sprang up and began confusing the trail behind us, pressing their footprints into the mud, scattering brush and feathers.

Five hundred and seventeen. Seven hundred and forty-five.

She guided us around outcroppings of rock, pitifully small gardens, and racks of tanning leather. At eight hundred and ninety-three steps, she finally stopped running, and I bent over my knees and gasped for breath. LaLa fluttered and abandoned me to perch on Hristo, while Kelsine leaned against me, almost knocking me over.

Ilina rubbed my shoulders. "Now where?" she asked Gerel's mother.

"Through there." She held aside long strands of moss that shielded a small entrance to a cave. "You'll have to bend over, but you'll fit. It widens out farther in. You'll find several branching tunnels, with noorestones at the entrances."

"Thank you." Gerel went first, with Chenda close behind her. I nudged Kelsine to go before me, then hauled myself straight, even though I hadn't caught my breath (and maybe never would), and went in after her.

Protruding rocks caught my hair and clothes, and I couldn't see much beyond Chenda and Gerel's heads silhouetting a pale glow from ahead. Behind me, Hristo grumbled and struggled to make himself small enough to fit.

But Gerel's mother was right; fifteen steps in, the passage opened into a space wide enough for Kelsine to stretch her wings.

The main tunnel split into seven more, two with wide openings, and five with narrower openings. Ensconced noorestones lit the entryways, revealing just how alone we were down here, in a domed cavern that felt like the belly of a great stone beast.

It felt like the Pit.

The sensation of being underground was overwhelming. The urge to *escape* made my heart thud even harder.

Six people. Three dragons. Eight noorestones.

One exit.

"Which tunnel?" Ilina asked.

"I don't think it matters," Hristo said. "We're trapped here if anyone says anything about this cave, and Altan will send warriors through all the tunnels."

"No one will reveal us, least of all Naran." Gerel stood in the center of the main cavern, her eyes closed and her face lifted to the rocky ceiling. "They're called the dishonored, but there's more honor here than there has ever been in the Heart of the Great Warrior."

"Naran is your mother?" It came out as a question, but it wasn't. Not really.

"My aunt." Gerel marched toward the third tunnel on the right. "Naran and my mother were twins. Together, they became warrior trainees and rose through the ranks quickly."

"None could best them?" I guessed, following her lead through the tunnel. Deeper into the darkness.

Gerel shot an amused glance over her shoulder. "None."

"But Naran ended up here. What happened?"

"My mother got pregnant." Gerel's voice lowered. "Khulan rarely calls warriors to choose between duty and family. To the warrior, they are equal, and pregnancy has never prevented a warrior from going into battle."

Aaru gasped, and I didn't have to ask to know that things were different on Idris.

"But completing warrior training requires certain tests of fitness and endurance. My mother wasn't the first to enter the test so late in a pregnancy, but there were complications. The doctors knew, of course. They told her what might happen if she entered, but she took the risk in spite of that, because the alternative was certain failure."

"They wouldn't let her wait?" Ilina pressed her palms against her stomach. "Couldn't she test later, once the danger had passed?"

Gerel shook her head. "They would not. As a result, she collapsed during the obstacle course, and began bleeding. Naran was also testing at the time. When she saw my mother fall, she abandoned her test and ran to aid her sister. It was too late, though. The doctors pulled me from my mother as she died, and my aunt was dismissed to the dishonored. She took me with her and raised me."

"Here?" I asked.

"Here." Gerel ducked around a low stalactite and into a wide cavern barely tall enough for Chenda and Hristo to walk straight. Five noorestones were placed around the perimeter, letting deep pockets of shadow grow

130

throughout the spaces between. It was empty, besides the lights. No bedding or foodstuffs, no evidence of life. "Well, I lived out there, mostly." Gerel glanced around the darkness. "The dishonored use this old mine for emergencies only: storms, raids, hiding people like us. Last I heard, the warriors don't know about this place. And they never will. The dishonored would die to protect the secret."

"Altan will stop at nothing to capture us." I bit my lip. "Me. I could turn myself in—"

"No." Ilina punched my shoulder softly. "Don't even say those words. It won't happen."

"But like Hristo said, we're trapped here if the warriors find the cave. If they even think we might be here, they'll search every bit of land and they'll kill any dishonored who get in their way. Maybe I can prevent that." The thought of submitting myself to Altan's harsh care once more made my entire body tense with terror, but I tried to shove the fear down deep. I'd sacrifice myself if it meant keeping my friends safe.

"You won't have to do anything like that." Gerel walked to the far wall, where a patch of the blackest shadows gathered. "There's another tunnel back here. The entrance is small, but you can stand up straight on the other side."

"Where does it go?" Chenda asked.

"It leads to a house near the port." Gerel shot a smile over her shoulder. "Over the centuries, the dishonored have secretly expanded the mine to lead to different parts of the city, where sympathizers live, or to the wilderness."

"Did you plan to come through here?" I asked.

She shook her head. "What I said before—about this part of the city being less patrolled—is usually true. On a normal day, we could have walked right into the city without anyone noticing, although the dragons would attract some attention. We'd have needed to hide them in a cart or something. But with the warriors on the lookout for us, I should have anticipated they'd guess our route."

At this point, maybe Gerel was just as tired as the rest of us. That was a frightening thought.

"Lorn-tah isn't the only port city on Khulan," she said, "but it is the biggest."

"How long does it take to get through that tunnel?" I asked.

Gerel pressed her mouth into a line while she thought. "Two hours. Maybe three."

"And we need to assume Altan will find this mine and come after us." Hristo's tone was grave as he adjusted the strap of his sling over his shoulder. "We should leave immediately."

He was right. My breath still rattled through my throat, and my legs felt ready to betray me, but if we left now, then we could *walk*. "Very well. Let's—"

::**Go**.:: Aaru had been leaning against the wall, but abruptly he pushed off. And though I was the only one who understood the quiet code, his alarm was universal.

Everyone scrambled toward the small tunnel at once, just as the evidence of Altan's presence became audible for the rest of us.

"Which way?" His voice was unmistakable, with the power to conjure every fear and feeling of helplessness I'd ever experienced in the Pit. But we weren't in the Pit. Not anymore. I was not the same girl he'd met two months ago.

"I told you, there's no one down here." The voice belonged to a stranger, not Naran.

"You think we haven't been aware of these tunnels for years?" Altan's voice was a sneer. "I know all about this place."

Gerel's expression was a mask of fury. "I'll kill him," she hissed. Behind her, Chenda, then Aaru, crawled through the entryway. I motioned for Hristo to go next.

He crouched onto his elbows and knees and shimmied through the hole, quiet in spite of how uncomfortable it looked.

"Go," I told Gerel.

She rolled her eyes. "I'll go last."

She wouldn't be able to fight all the warriors, though. Not by herself. But there were five noorestones in this chamber, and the moment I became aware of them again, a low hum set in my bones. I could *feel* the energy of the crystals.

"I have another idea." I pushed her toward the tunnel. "Both of you, go. If they come this way, I can use the noorestones."

Ilina shook her head. "Noorestones? What do you—"

I pushed her, too, causing Crystal to flap and jump to my upper arm. "We don't have time to argue. *Go*."

133

Scowls darkened their faces, but Ilina dropped to her hands and knees and began crawling. When she was on the other side, Gerel started to follow, but before she was even halfway in, boots pounded on stone and voices rose: "Through here!"

A mad scramble sounded from the other side of the entryway, where Aaru and the others helped pull Gerel through. "Come on, Mira!" Ilina called, but it was too late.

Seven mace-bearing warriors poured into the room, led by Altan.

His eyes were hooded. Angry. And when he looked at me, with a *Drakontos raptus* on each shoulder and a *Drakontos ignitus* at my side, his expression hardened into granite. "They said you were alive."

They who? But all I said was, "I'm more alive than I've ever been," and I raised my arms to the side, palms up as though I were lifting a heavy weight.

At my beckoning, five noorestones dimmed, and three dragons breathed hot orange flame.

"Capture them!" Altan thrust a finger at me, and six warriors rushed forward. "I want her alive. The dragons, too."

Kelsine growled and charged, while LaLa and Crystal leaped off my shoulders, flew a pair of figure eights, and breathed fire across the warriors' faces. Screams echoed through the room, and as the scent of burning flesh filled the cavern, I caught the forms of Naran and several other dishonored approaching after the warriors. Naran reached for a knife at her hip, but it was too late for them to help us, or for me to help them.

I had to save my group.

With a deep breath, I pulled more energy from the noorestones and cast the room into heavy twilight. Coils of blue illumination twisted around my arms, bright without heat, and for the first time since the Pit, I felt *powerful*. All I needed was for the dragons to get to safety. "Go to Ilina!" I called.

Crystal went immediately, whipping around me so quickly that my dress fluttered in her wake. But LaLa was mid-dive, hurtling toward Altan with flame licking from her jaws. In the dim cavern, she was a brilliant, golden star; her scales shimmered in the light of her own fire. Her wings fanned as she jerked back her head and inhaled, then released a long blaze across his face.

Altan shouted and ducked his head—too late to save himself. But even with his skin withering under dragon fire, he was strong enough to lift his mace and swing it at LaLa.

He missed her body.

But he clipped her wing.

LaLa screamed and went down, and the *thud* of her body hitting the ground was my heart shattering apart.

Light flared from my fingertips, blinding bright as it flooded the room. In that hot glare, I saw warriors with their burned faces hidden in the crooks of their arms. I saw Altan with a twisted grimace or a smile, his mace fallen to

135

the ground near him. And then there was LaLa, my tiny dragon flower, lying prone on the floor. Her injured wing trembled.

Without thinking, I lunged for her.

Altan took up his mace, strong because of his god.

The other warriors gathered their weapons.

But my eyes were for LaLa only. I scooped her into my arms, pressed her small body against my chest, and looked up just in time to see a warrior's mace falling toward me.

I lifted a hand, as if I could push him away, and *light* and *heat* and *rage* surged out of me, knocking him back three steps. The noorestone energy inside me felt ready to explode as I retreated toward the tunnel to follow my friends.

My heart thundered in my ears. A nimbus of fire flickered around me, and a heady, drunk feeling grew within me. It wasn't like before—in the Pit. There weren't as many noorestones. But still, my soul remembered the moments before I exploded—or didn't explode—when I'd screamed for everyone to leave.

I couldn't let myself explode now. Not with my friends just on the other side of a wall. Not with the dishonored so close by. And not with LaLa pressed against me, her injured wing hanging limp across my hand. Her heartbeat fluttered against my fingers; I had to get her to safety.

Faintly, around the rushing in my head, I heard Ilina urging me to hurry.

I spun and dashed toward the tunnel. At the entrance,

I dropped to my knees and scoot-crawled as quickly as I could, given the dragon in my left hand. Kelsine came behind me, a shield she and I both knew the warriors would not strike.

The blue-white light came with me as Ilina and Gerel helped pull me to my feet in a narrow passageway. Kelsine was on my heels, scrambling and clawing through the narrow space.

"Come on," Gerel said. "Move quickly, but pay attention. This way is tricky."

"Good thing Mira is glowing." Chenda glanced over her shoulder, worry in her eyes.

I pressed my mouth in a line and shook my head. "It's fine." Hopefully. But when I looked at Aaru, the same worry reflected in his black gaze. "I'm fine." There had been only five noorestones back there, and the power would fade with distance. I could handle this. I could.

"Walk," Gerel commanded.

We obeyed, careful as we put one foot in front of the other. Five steps. Fifteen. Thirty. This was more tunnel, yes, but it was nothing like the other areas of the cavern; the walls here were ragged, with chisel marks still scarring the stone walls. It was more like the entrance to the mine, with several sharp turns, and drops and rises in the floor, forcing us to walk one at a time.

Fifty shuffling steps.

It was too small, especially with a dragon like Kelsine following. Some of the passages were almost too narrow for her, and we were forced to pause while she squeezed through. We wouldn't be able to outpace the warriors. Not like this.

"Hurry," Ilina whispered. "Hurry, hurry."

Behind us, warriors echoed the sentiment. "Catch them."

We wouldn't make it. And in spite of my reassurances, the hum of noorestone fire under my skin was not diminishing. It was growing.

"What kind of mine was this?" I rasped.

Gerel answered without hesitation: "Noorestone."

"Seven gods." I grabbed Ilina's shoulder, and the moment she turned, I thrust LaLa into her arms. Razor-sharp scales sliced my palm, but I hardly felt it. "Careful of her left wing."

Ilina's mouth dropped open, but I pushed her to continue after the others.

"Now you, little firefly." I pressed myself to the wall to make space for Kelsine to slip by, but she only turned to face the oncoming warriors, her posture low and defensive.

I didn't want her to stay with me, but I *really* didn't have the time to argue with a juvenile *Drakontos ignitus* about who was in charge. Not with the warriors coming. Not with the *power* coming.

Deposits of raw noorestone were scattered throughout the walls. I could feel them even through the stone, tugging at the parts of me that *knew* the crystal. Sensed it.

These noorestones were unilluminated—not yet exposed to the sun, which was what made them glow—but they were still filled with the power of Noore. The inner fire of our world burned within, growing in intensity the longer the stones sat underground.

And that was the power that called to me.

Just as Ilina and the others disappeared around a corner, I spun to face the warriors behind us. I pressed my palms against the ragged tunnel walls, and blood from my cut seeped down the stone, shimmering a deep purple in the light cast from my body.

They were twenty paces away.

Kelsine growled at them.

Fifteen.

Light throbbed from my skin, pulsing as fast as my heartbeat.

Ten.

Altan led the charge, his burned face contorted with pain and rage. Then confusion as he took in my posture, my power, my bared teeth. He paused just four paces away. "What *are* you?"

"Angry," I whispered, and something in me snapped. The tether holding the noorestone power in check. The dam that held back the enormity of my fear and fury.

The earth shook. Just a faint shudder at first, but power thrummed through me, pushing past my fingertips. Fire called to fire as the energy inside me sought the unilluminated noorestones buried in the dark, and pieces of the walls began to break off. Pebbles at first. Then fist-sized chunks. The patter and thud of the tunnel caving in was startlingly loud.

Altan's mouth dropped open as he realized what was happening. At once, he spun away and grabbed the nearest warrior. "Run!"

Then, before I could stop her, Kelsine surged forward—a bolt of brown and fire and teeth—and leaped onto one of the warriors.

"No!" My entire body ached as I tried to pull in the power again, to reverse what was already in motion.

But it was too late. Rubble filled the passage, and plumes of dirt rose with every clap of stone on stone.

Somewhere on the other side of the collapsing tunnel, I heard a man shout about his leg, and someone else call for help. Then, the noise of rocks crashing beat away their cries for aid, and the only thing I could hear was Kelsine screaming for me as she realized the tunnel had collapsed with her on the wrong side.

My heart shattered all over again. "Kelsine!" I scrambled to move rocks out of the way, but they were too heavy, and plumes of dust rose into my face. I coughed.

On the other side of the cave-in, I could hear talons on stone—Kelsine trying to dig her way to me—and the brash voices of warriors as they dragged her away.

"Kelsine!"

As the symphony of destruction died, I dropped to my knees and sucked in a deep breath. There, I finally registered the facts:

1. *Nothing had fallen on me, or behind me; when I reached out to feel the ground around me, there was a clear line where the cave-in stopped.*
2. *Even the dust obeyed that line.*
3. *I'd stopped glowing, and now I was alone in the dark.*
4. *Kelsine was gone.*
5. *I couldn't save her.*

My body felt drained, like the moments after I'd not-exploded in the Pit, but I picked myself up. I needed to get to my friends. But even before I could step away from the destruction, the sound of footfalls came from behind me.

"Mira?" Hristo appeared around the corner, a small noorestone in hand. "Are you all right?"

I nodded, even though I wasn't. But he meant *"Are you hurt?"* or *"Can you walk?"* not *"Is all within you right?"* so I answered the question he'd meant to ask, because the other question was too complicated.

Ilina, Gerel, Chenda, and Aaru came after Hristo, peering over one another's shoulders to see what happened. "Where is Kelsine?" Ilina asked.

The dust had settled unnaturally fast, as though the cave-in had happened three months ago. There was nothing to see but a path blocked by fallen rocks, and my bloody handprint on the wall.

"She's gone," I said. "Altan has her."

PART TWO

THE WORLD'S POWER

CHAPTER ELEVEN

Our escape in numbers:

1. *Seventeen small cuts from LaLa's scales.
   They'd been bleeding before, but now they
   were only faint scabs. Like the scar on my
   face, they'd been healed under noorestone fire.
   The gash on my shoulder, when I felt around
   for that, was better now too.*
2. *Three hours of breathlessly slipping through
   the tunnel, knowing we had to reach the
   docks before Altan or we would be killed.*
3. *Twelve rungs on a ladder that led into a
   secret room in someone's wall. It was stocked
   with food, water, and medical supplies, and*

though Ilina gathered supplies to set LaLa's broken wing, we had no time to help my poor, whimpering dragon.

4. *Two men—one tall and one short—who lived in the house connected to the tunnel. They greeted us with wary eyes, a story about their allegiance to the dishonored, and finally directions to the port. More importantly, they told us of a secret entrance to the port that smugglers used to move a drug called grayhand.*

5. *Fifteen-fifteen—the location where the* Chance Encounter *was docked.*

6. *Ten thousand echoes of Kelsine's cries as we unwillingly left her with my worst enemy.*

GUILT GNAWED AT me as we made our way to the port.

Guilt about Kelsine. Guilt about LaLa. Guilt about being unable to explain what I had done in the tunnel.

But there was no time to let myself steep in it. As quickly as possible, we passed through yards littered with toys or decorated with immaculate hedges trimmed to look like animals. The scent of the sea wove through on the breeze, rustling palm trees and wind chimes made of empty glass bottles. The late hour meant we didn't run into anyone, but still, we needed to be quick.

Altan wouldn't be far behind.

Only when we came within sight of the main gates

did we pause, crouched behind a quiet building, to orient ourselves.

The port was bright, lit with hundreds of noorestones. They shone coolly from iron casings on poles every three paces, and along the docks themselves. Every pile driven into the sea boasted lights; if we could have looked at the port from above, we'd have seen an illuminated outline of every structure.

"The secret entrance should be that way." Gerel pointed south, along a line of warehouses that effectively blocked the way into the port. "Warehouse thirty-nine."

"Then let's go." I picked up my bag—taken from the house at the end of the tunnel and filled with dried fruit and meat—and hiked it over my shoulder. Aaru and Chenda had bags, too, while Ilina carried a lidded basket. Both dragons rode inside, nested in a pile of blankets and the supplies for a wing splint.

I should never have let the dragons help fight the warriors. LaLa had paid for my foolishness with a broken wing—a fractured radius and ulna, Ilina had guessed—and Kelsine had been completely lost to Altan. I could only imagine how frightened she was.

Carefully, we made our way south, passing two other entrances like the first. We hurried past them, trying not to give anyone a chance to wonder about the six dirty people moving through the streets in the middle of the night.

Above, seagulls called and dived for scraps. The roar of the sea was a constant thrum in my heart, with water crashing against hulls and docks and the cliffs on the southern end of the port. Every few minutes, bells rang and workers shouted, but everything was obscured by distance and heavy stone buildings in between.

"This is the one." I paused at warehouse thirty-nine, and within minutes, the six of us slipped through a cleverly disguised door and into a bright space.

Shelves upon shelves, pallets upon pallets: crates of goods rose from floor to ceiling. Where we stood at the back, a dozen crates were labeled as sugarloaves, but a scrawled handprint indicated they were almost definitely grayhand. Just as our benefactors had promised.

Suddenly, I realized we weren't alone in the warehouse. Fourteen workers were moving crates, lifting pallets, and calling out instructions. They hadn't yet noticed us—we stood behind a tall shelving unit with the grayhand—but it wouldn't be long before someone realized they'd heard the door open and shut and came to investigate. Or worse: someone else might open the door to find us here.

We all crouched and moved along the wall, taking care to stay behind the cargo.

Aaru tapped on my arm. ::**What do we do?**::

There were ten rows of shelves, three with clear aisles in between. The workers were mostly focused on the north side of the building, so if we were quick and kept low, we might be able to creep to the huge, open door on the opposite end of the warehouse.

I nudged Gerel and pointed to the empty aisles, praying she understood my intentions.

She nodded, passing it on to Hristo and Ilina.

::Can you make us quiet?:: I asked Aaru. ::Muffle us?::

His eyebrows drew inward, not with a frown, but with focus. ::I can try.::

I leaned toward Gerel and kept my voice as soft as possible. "Let's go."

But before we could get moving, a man came toward us—one I hadn't counted before. A fifteenth worker.

I knew the moment he spotted us, six ragged people hunched next to the crates of grayhand, because his eyes went wide and he opened his lungs to shout. "Thieves!"

And then the warehouse went dark.

"Go," I hissed. "Go, go."

I'd thought I hated running before, but now it was dark. Now, I carried a heavy bag full of food I hadn't had time to eat. Now, I was exhausted from a day of hiking, a run through the dishonored camp, the exertion of using my power over noorestones, and walking another league through a tunnel.

But I ran. We all did.

We raced down one of the empty aisles, and past crates marked as wheat, rice, and sugar. Exhaustion clawed at me, but I kept going toward the glow of the port.

"Stop! Thief!" The workers' footfalls slammed after us, and along parallel aisles.

My head pounded with each impact of my feet on the stone floor, but I kept going, even as the workers behind me gained.

And then I saw them. Five men with crowbars blocked

149

the way to the door, with three more joining them from the other aisles. Plus the seven behind us.

We were surrounded. We couldn't go forward. We couldn't go back.

Breathing hard—except for Gerel—the six of us stood in the center of the aisles and weighed our options. We couldn't run through the line of workers, not without getting hit with an iron bar. But we couldn't stay here.

We needed a third option.

"All right, thieves." One of the workers stepped forward. "Just put down your bags and we'll let you go."

None of us moved, and gradually, the noorestones began to illuminate once more. ::Thanks for trying,:: I tapped to Aaru. He didn't reply.

The lead worker tried again. "Look, I don't want to hurt you, and you're all clearly struggling. But you can't steal. Leave the bags and get out of here."

Ilina glanced at me, just a flicker of a smile before her entire posture shifted. She tilted her head, all sweetness as she pitched her voice slightly higher than normal. "We're not thieves," she said. "We just want to see the ships."

"They're out there." He jerked a thumb over his shoulder. "What'd you do? Come in during the day and hide out back there to steal from us?"

"Oh, no." Ilina shook her head, still speaking with that saccharin-sweet voice. "We came in just now, through the back door."

"There is no back door."

150

"There's the one they sneak the grayhand out of."

His jaw worked, but he couldn't seem to find the words.

And at once, I saw what Ilina was doing. This man—the supervisor of this group, perhaps, if he was speaking for them—didn't know about the grayhand. Or, if he did, he was doing a good job pretending otherwise.

I bit the insides of my lips to keep from smiling.

"We just want to see the ships," she went on. "We heard they were most beautiful at night."

The supervisor turned to one of the other men. "What door is she talking about? There's no grayhand here. Not in *my* building."

"I saw a dozen crates back there," Ilina said. "By the door. They were marked with handprints."

"Go look." The supervisor turned to one of his workers. "Tell me if she's right."

The other man didn't move, and that was enough proof of betrayal for the supervisor. The moment all the men started yelling about tariffs, smuggling, and honor, the six of us darted for the exit.

The controlled chaos of the port welcomed us with squawking gulls, clanging bells, and shouted orders. It was easy to get lost in the crowd, out of sight of any of the warehouse workers who might come after us. Once we were twenty paces outside the huge doors, we slowed and let ourselves get caught up in the current of traffic. Still, we had to stay alert to avoid getting crushed under carts loaded with enormous crates.

Somehow, we reached the long piers that stretched into the water, with ships moored as far as I could see. "It's fifteen-fifteen," I said, scanning the piles for numbers. Seventeen, sixteen . . . "This way!" I headed toward the pier, glancing over my shoulder to make sure everyone was following.

Aaru's expression was tight, pinched almost, as he wove through the crowd. Ilina, Hristo, and Gerel looked all right, but Chenda had her face ducked, as though trying to hide the tattoos over her cheek and neck.

Behind them, the city of Lorn-tah rose on the bluff. Even in the darkness, I caught hints of grandeur: stone obelisks soaring against the sky, multifloor buildings with extravagant balconies, an immense pyramid library that housed tales of every warrior who'd ever lived. Light from the port diminished the stars, but both moons were high tonight, razor-thin crescents.

Something else caught my eye, too: a warrior and a port guard walked side by side, pointing up at ships as they passed.

The warrior was too far away for me to see clearly, though I knew he wasn't Altan. But where there was one warrior, there were others.

And they were clearly searching the ships.

"Hurry." I picked up the pace, even though my legs and arms ached. We'd be safe once we reached the *Chance Encounter*.

Fewer people moved up and down the pier—only people who needed access to these ships. That made our passage easier, but we'd be even more obvious to any of Altan's warriors now.

I counted berths as we passed: one, two, three . . . Ships filled the spaces. Most here were barcs, like the *Chance Encounter*. They were impressive ships, some boasting five masts, but I was looking for a four-masted vessel with red and gold sails.

The regular stomp of boots compelled me to glance over my shoulder again. More warriors and guards, making their way down the pier to the first ship.

Aaru and Gerel had noticed them too. Without speaking, we lengthened our strides, urging the others faster and faster.

Ahead, all I could see were masts and furled sails crowding the night sky. What if the *Chance Encounter* had left? It was possible the berthing fees had become too much, and Captain Pentoba decided to leave on the evening tide.

There would be nowhere to go but back into the port, to search for another ship heading our way. And the warriors were getting closer.

My heart thundered in my ears by the time we reached the berth marked fifteen-fifteen, but the *Chance Encounter* was there, waiting as promised. Her name was painted in curling red letters across the bow.

"Come on!" I darted left down the dock that led to the

gangplank. It was empty, save the crew standing watch and working on the main deck.

Seventeen, eighteen, nineteen . . . I counted steps.

"They're well behind us." Gerel kept her voice low. "They're searching all the ships, and we're only getting on one."

I nodded, but her words didn't soothe the frayed parts of me. "There are more of them than us."

Gerel didn't reply.

We turned up the gangplank, and from the corner of my eye, I caught a troop of warriors swarming down the dock to the barc in fifteen-fourteen.

Closer. Closer.

At the top of the ramp, I forced my shoulders back, my chin up, and my voice steady as I addressed the crewman stationed there. "I need to see Captain Pentoba."

"Who are you to ask about the captain?" asked the crewman, a sun-darkened woman with a slight squint. Her hair was sectioned into eleven neat braids, then pulled up in a ponytail; the ends just brushed the middle of her back. A long knife waited at her hip, not at all hidden by the wrapped vest she wore. Idrisi cotton, if I had to guess. Her trousers, too, were of high quality.

Movement grew on the main deck of the ship across the pier. Warriors called out orders to search the holds.

"Well?" The crewman scowled. "I need a name."

I glanced at Ilina, who nodded. "I'm Mira Minkoba."

At once, the woman's posture changed, and she studied

me with new interest. My dirty clothes. My messy hair. My scarred face. "Hopebearer." She sounded uncertain.

"My companions and I must leave Lorn-tah immediately." I kept my head high, in spite of her scrutiny. In spite of the exposed feeling of standing up here, out in the open. Altan could probably tell I was here just by the scent on the air. "Immediately," I said again.

She looked at me, then at the others. "I know you," she said to Ilina. "All right. Let's go see the captain."

Heart pounding, I stepped onto the deck, pausing just long enough to let my legs adjust to the movement of the ship.

Five more crewmen worked on the deck, and their stares followed us as we hurried after our guide. I didn't see the woman who'd offered a strange salute as I'd disembarked in Bopha, but now I thought I understood what it had been about. Ilina had been in contact with the captain, who might have told some of the crew about me. Certainly, they'd known who I was on my voyage to Bopha; they must have wondered why I'd been on Khulan.

The part where I'd stayed belowdecks for the entirety of the trip hadn't been unusual, though. Elbena—and my parents, because they usually traveled with me—had often kept me out of sight. I'd always assumed that was for my privacy. Now I knew it had been to isolate me.

Our footfalls thumped on the deck as we made our way to the captain's quarters. There, the crewman knocked, waited for a reply, and then ushered us inside.

In spite of being the captain's quarters, it wasn't a large space. The six of us, plus bags and basket, plus the crewman, plus the captain sitting at a desk, made the room hot and crowded. There was a window, the glass panes wide open, but if a breeze managed to find its way into the room, it died upon arrival. The only things coming through were bells ringing and voices calling.

And in my own head, a hum of anxiety began.

"So." Captain Pentoba leaned back in her chair and propped her bare heels on the desk. "You're the Hope-bearer."

I gave a jerky nod, trying not to be too obvious as my breaths turned shaky. But my heart raced inside my chest, and every noise was suddenly louder. Sharper. The creaking of the dragons' basket, the groan of wood, and the clatter of numbers in my head.

Eight people. Five bags. One basket.

Five noorestones, four walls, one desk.

"Took your time." The captain hadn't moved.

"Sorry." The apology was automatic, out before I could recall that we'd spent the last eight days trekking across the island and running for our lives. "Will you still sail for me?"

Those words pulsed through my head, and I tried not to shrink under her glare.

Captain Pentoba was a tiny woman, with smooth black skin even darker than Chenda's, and eyes the color of sand. Her hair and her lips were tinted a deep shade of wine, a

156

magnificent choice that Krasimir would have applauded, but I could only see someone much bolder than I. More confident. Though she wore the same type of wrap vest and trousers as the rest of her crew, everything about her screamed authority.

The anxiety wasn't leaving, and neither were the warriors. I tried again, forcing my words to be more than faint squeaks. "Will you sail for me?"

The captain studied me, then the rest of my friends, before she addressed the crewman who'd brought us here. "Teres, get One in here."

"Yes, Captain." Teres quit the room and let the door fall shut behind her.

The captain looked at Ilina. "You said three people. Now, forgive me if my math skills aren't what I always believed, but there are six of you. That's twice what we agreed upon."

As though she wasn't at all worried about the warriors closing in on us, Ilina let loose one of her dazzling smiles. "I'd rather hoped you wouldn't notice."

"Hard not to notice when that's twice the mouths to feed."

"We brought food." Without waiting for her invitation, I set my bag on her desk and opened the flap. I did it quickly, before she could see the way my hands trembled.

Captain Pentoba slid her feet off the desk and leaned over to peer inside. "I like dates."

I nodded for her to help herself.

"I don't like them dried, though. Only fresh." She curled her lip and leaned back. "But fine. Say I sail for you. What's in it for me?"

Ilina frowned. "We had an arrangement."

"And now the arrangement has cost me a hundred lumes for staying here an extra decan, plus the money I've lost for not delivering the cargo burning a hole through my hull." She shot a pointed look at Ilina, then at me. "And now twice as many people as our arrangement originally stated. Personally, I don't see how this benefits me anymore."

She was right. We were imposing on her. *I* was imposing.

But how would we escape Khulan if she didn't take us?

But why should I expect favors from anyone? She owed me nothing.

But she'd promised Ilina.

Anymore. That word finally caught up with me.

"How did it benefit you to begin with?" My thoughts were a whirlpool and I was helpless to escape.

"I wanted to be on the right side of history, of course." She rolled her eyes. "No, poppet, your friend here indicated there might be monetary benefits to hauling around the Hopebearer, provided everything works out for you."

Aaru's quiet code came against my elbow. ::Thought she would sail because you are Hopebearer.::

I tapped my reply on my leg where only he would notice. ::Me too.::

158

Five noorestones. Five bags. Two paintings.

Please, Damina. Give me peace. Give me grace. But the maelstrom of anxiety caught everything, even prayer. I needed my amber bottle of calming pills. I needed that soothing haze that took over and slowed my thoughts and gave me space to breathe.

I didn't have my medicine. Just this moment. And I had to focus long enough to use it. "And now, Captain, you want something more."

She gave a fluid shrug. "You said it. And I wouldn't say no."

Gerel shoved her bag into Aaru's hands and stomped forward. "Now listen to me—"

I grabbed her arm before she could draw back to hit the captain—or whatever it was that angry former warriors did when they felt betrayed. Violence wouldn't solve this problem. I was already fighting the current of chaos inside me; I'd lose all control if Gerel got into a brawl.

"Captain." I struggled to measure my words. "You waited for us. And you'll have to sail out of here anyway, what with those berthing fees and all that cargo, so you might as well take us with you."

"We have to go now." Ilina's voice was soft. "We're out of time."

I shifted my weight forward, trying to convey the urgency without outright begging. Without letting her see that the walls I'd built around my panic were beginning to collapse. "We'll pay you double."

She sighed and picked a dried date out of the bag, but didn't eat it. She just turned the fruit over in her hands, contemplating.

Everyone went quiet. Through the window, we heard gulls calling and bells ringing and boots thumping on the docks. And voices.

I didn't need Aaru's warning this time. I heard Altan's growling voice all on my own. "Search the ship. Search every hold. I know they're here."

CHAPTER TWELVE

His voice sent a spike of terror through my heart, but before anyone could speak, a large bald man burst into the room, jostling everyone. "Captain, warriors are coming aboard."

"Seven gods." The captain shoved my bag off her desk and into my hands. "One, get these to the bottom. I'll deal with the warriors." She squeezed between us and was out on the main deck within heartbeats. The door slammed shut after her, but I still heard her shout ring out: "What's all this about? What are you doing on my ship?"

"Off the rug." The man called One shooed everyone toward the walls, and when we'd all moved back, he pushed the rug aside to reveal a hidden door. "Get in there."

Another trapdoor. Another small space.

Seven gods, help me.

Gerel hauled open the door and peered inside. "There's not enough room."

I got only a glimpse, but she was right; the compartment was quite small, with enough space for two people if they didn't mind being pressed against a dozen boxes piled up against the walls. Maybe without all the boxes, but how would we move everything in time?

"There's another room below." One took a noorestone from his pocket and gave it to Gerel. "We need to get you in there quickly, so for now leave your belongings up here. They'll be safe."

Ilina hugged the basket with LaLa and Crystal closer. "This one comes with us."

One eyed her askance, but shrugged. "Your choice. Just get down there now."

We'd never make it in time. Through the cabin door, I could hear the thuds and crashes of warriors swarming across the main deck. And I heard Altan shouting: "Where is she?"

Darkness fuzzed in the corners of my vision as Gerel slipped into the first hidden room, then found the second door that was just off-center from the top one. Without hesitation, she dropped to the bottom room and got on her hands and knees to crawl aside. The light went with her, but from the brief look I'd gotten, the second space was not big enough for us, either.

"Go." Hristo dropped his bag in a corner and nudged me. "Go now."

My whole body shook as I lowered myself through the first hatch, accepted the basket of dragons from Ilina, and lowered it into the second space. Gerel took it and slid it away.

"Hurry, Mira." Ilina sounded worried now, too.

In the darkness, in the panic, I could hardly see well enough to find the second door again. But I slipped down and forced each breath to stay long and even.

The captain's voice carried across the ship, even through the closed door. "Get your grunts out of my hold!"

"Come on, Fancy." Gerel took my hands and dragged me toward her. "You're a mess."

"I know." I wanted to cry, but not in front of her. Not in front of anyone except maybe Ilina. And I wanted to be somewhere far away from all this.

"Stay right here." Gerel sat me against a wall next to the dragon basket, and suddenly I realized I was sitting up straight. The space was larger than I'd originally thought.

The first compartment descended partially into this larger one. So while the middle of this area was cramped, the edges were just tall enough for us to stand, and perhaps two paces wide.

This was the "bottom" Captain Pentoba had been talking about. A secret room within a secret room.

A *tiny* room. Like my cell in the Pit.

The others came down one at a time, not nearly fast enough. Ilina put herself on the other side of the dragon basket and took my hands, while Hristo and Chenda dropped in. Then Aaru.

Six people down here. Two dragons. Lots of darkness. No space.

"Stay quiet." One shut the door above us, and something scraped the floor: he'd moved boxes over the door to hide it.

And that was that. We were hidden.

But how well?

Heavy shadows blanketed everything, thanks to the strange shape of our refuge, and then it was all darkness as Gerel tucked the noorestone into her trouser leg and rolled up the cloth to block the light.

Ilina squeezed my hands and let go. A soft scratch of skin on wicker suggested she'd pressed her palms to the basket. For comfort? For reassurance?

Our brave little dragons were being so good.

Or sleeping. I hoped they were sleeping.

Bang.

The noise came from above, and everything inside me tensed again.

Footfalls beat the floor.

Muted voices in angry tones.

An object crashed right over my head.

I bit off a faint whimper. We were going to get caught. We were definitely going to get caught.

Footsteps: three, four, five . . .

"What's this?" Altan's voice rumbled above us. He

was so close. As he flipped back the rug hiding the first hatch, I could almost smell the Pit on him. The stink of unwashed bodies. The bite of blood. The sulfur stench of the washroom.

Dread slithered through me, and the pounding of my heart intensified.

Iron screeched as the first hatch opened, and then wood smacked the floor where he let it fall.

Boots hit wood just in front of me. Someone—Altan— had dropped into the first compartment.

The urge to hide reared inside me, but where could I go? This was the most hidden compartment on the *Chance Encounter*, and there was nowhere else to run. I was cornered. Trapped. This was where I would die.

This was where we would all die.

"What do you keep down here?" Wood muffled Altan's words, but I would forever know the timbre of his voice. The growl. The confidence. The love of suffering.

Faint light shone through the slats of wood, and those threads were just enough to allow me to see Gerel lifting Hristo. He pressed his feet against the interior compartment, and braced himself with his shoulders against the outer wall.

"Private stores, huh?" Altan's tone was a smirk as he opened and closed the lids of boxes.

"Nothing illegal about that." Captain Pentoba's voice came from the main floor of her cabin. "You and I both know it."

Hristo was now holding himself just off the floor. And in the faint threads of illumination, Gerel motioned for the rest of us to do the same. Because she knew.

Altan would find us down here.

Panic surged through my head and seized control of my limbs. How was I supposed to do this? I wasn't strong like them. I couldn't trust my feet to stay where I put them, not while panic controlled my body.

"No, not illegal." Altan's light shifted. "But I imagine your crew wouldn't be happy if they knew what you were hiding from them."

Gerel was already up, the basket of dragons somehow balanced on her stomach. Chenda, too. Ilina wasn't as tall, so she took a little more maneuvering, but she'd quietly braced herself between the walls.

::Hurry.:: Aaru tapped my shoulder.

I couldn't, though. My feet would bang against the inner wall and Altan would know. He'd *know* we were down here and we'd all die.

::Try.::

"What's this?" A box slid off the second door. "Clever, Captain. You are clever."

"What can I say?" The captain didn't sound at all concerned, considering that Altan was about to find us. "I like doors."

::Mira, focus.::

Trembling violently, I lifted one foot—and before it could hit the wall with telltale thumps of our presence,

Aaru took my ankle and pressed the sole of my slipper against the wood. Then he took the other and placed it on the wall. ::Stay.::

Silently, he moved to my shoulders and helped me lift myself up.

::Push.::

I gave a jerky half nod. Holding myself up was difficult, and I kept waiting for the wood to groan or bend under the pressure of all of us pushing against it. But as Aaru scrambled to brace himself, too, the wood held fast.

Within moments, we all held ourselves off the floor—and just in time.

The second door squeaked open and light shone in.

Heat rolled through my body, and sweat formed on my brow. My belly. My legs. All I could hear was my ragged breathing. Noisy. Too noisy. I was going to get us caught.

I held my breath, but then the noise all came from my heart. Pounding. Aching. Slowing because I wasn't breathing.

Time stretched. I wanted to close my eyes, but I couldn't help but watch as Altan's arm reached through and touched the floor. The light extended farther out, and though I couldn't see his head poking into our space, I could imagine him glancing around.

My foot slipped.

Panic thundered through me, and I gasped.

I was going to get us caught. Killed. All because I couldn't control my own body.

Despair clawed at me, forcing a terrified cry up my throat. I swallowed it back. And back. And back. And I squeezed my eyes shut. One. Two. Three.

Four.

Five.

Six.

I counted anything.

Seven.

Eight.

I counted everything.

Nine.

Ten.

As always, my mind resorted to pointless numbers when it needed to plan for the worst. When it needed to be sharp like Gerel's.

Eleven.

Twelve.

Only as the light retreated did I realize we hadn't been caught. Only as the door slammed shut at a normal volume did I realize that every sound had been muted.

Even my breathing. Even the scrape of my foot on the wall. Even my gasp.

"Satisfied?" Captain Pentoba sounded highly annoyed.

"No." Altan's light moved upward as he climbed out of the first compartment. "I'll be satisfied when I apprehend her and her friends."

"Better get to looking elsewhere, then. I heard *Karina's Flag* will be heading to Damina. That's where Mira is likely to go, isn't it?"

The top door slammed shut, followed by the *whap* of the rug as they covered the hatch again. "I'll look into it." Altan didn't sound convinced, but he was leaving.

He was leaving.

I could hardly believe it.

Three, four, five: Altan's footsteps banged on the floor as he left the captain's quarters.

"All right," Gerel whispered. "It's safe to get down."

Carefully, we all lowered ourselves to the floor again, and Gerel brought out the noorestone she'd hidden.

I didn't want to look at anyone. How could I when I was the liability? I rolled onto my elbows and knees and pressed my forehead to the cool floor. Sweat dripped off my face, smelling salty and sour.

"Mira?" Chenda's voice was quiet. "Are you—"

"Just give her space." Hristo knew about the panic, of course. He'd seen me after stressful speeches and the way my hands shook as I opened the bottle of calming pills. He'd seen me after the time Mother had yelled at me for not putting on my cosmetics correctly, and I'd spent hours in front of my mirrors applying and reapplying creams and powders.

I wanted my medicine.

I wanted to melt into the floor.

Ilina's touch was featherlight, just reassurance of her presence. But when she spoke, it wasn't to me. "Chenda, was that you with the shadows?"

"It was." The Dawn Lady sounded cool and calm. Why couldn't I be like her? "Once the light came in, it was easy to call the shadows to obscure us."

"And the sound?" Hristo asked. "Everything was quieter."

No one spoke.

"Thank you." The floor swallowed most of my words. "For hiding us."

"Of course," Chenda said.

::**Always**.:: Aaru's quiet code came against my shoulder. ::**All right?**::

A long groan poured out of me. I was not all right. Adrenaline and terror still surged through me, even though the danger had passed. Even though I knew Altan was leaving the ship, my traitorous mind and body didn't care.

And on top of that, this was humiliating. Here I was, the Hopebearer. The Dragonhearted. *The* Mira Minkoba.

Curled on the floor and crying.

"Hey." Ilina tugged at my forearm. "Come over here with me."

When I sat up, she reached into the dragon basket and took out one of the noorestones. Then, we moved to the opposite side of the room, where we had a small measure of privacy.

She smoothed back my hair and took my face in her hands. "Breathe with me."

I closed my eyes. Her palms were cool on my flushed, sweat- and tear-streaked cheeks, and when I heard her inhale, I breathed in, too.

Together, we breathed out.

Two times.

Three times.

She controlled her breathing, so all I had to do was copy. And with every long, even breath, my heart rate eased and the rush of terror abated. I was safe.

Safe with my best friend. My wingsister.

She released my face. "There. That's better."

I nodded, though it hadn't been a question. We both knew she was right. "I'm sorry." I scrubbed my hands over my cheeks, trying not to cringe at the feel of scar tissue. If I let myself think about Ilina—or anyone—touching it, I'd spiral again.

"Nothing to be sorry about." She scooted until she sat next to me, put one arm around my shoulders, and drew me to her. "When was the last time you had your pills?"

"Before." I leaned my head against hers. "Before the Luminary Council came for me."

"Have you been having attacks this whole time?"

I nodded. The Pit felt like one giant panic attack. Highs and lows, yes, but every moment had held that low-grade terror.

"What have you been doing to get through them?"

"Trying to do what Doctor Chilikoba said. Start with breathing. And—" I'd never told Ilina about the counting, but Aaru knew and he didn't think less of me. Ilina would understand, too. "And I—"

The words wouldn't come out.

"It's all right. You don't have to say." She squeezed me. "You've been really strong, Mira. It's not easy to get through attacks like that without medicine, is it?"

"It feels like I'm dying." I took a shuddering breath. "I thought I was going to get us caught just now."

"But you didn't."

I closed my eyes for a moment. "I feel like I should be stronger than I am."

"What do you mean?"

A pale laugh slipped out of me. "I mean, I've been through so much worse than this."

She touched my shoulder. "No one gets stronger all at once. It happens in pieces, and the hurts with the deepest roots take the longest to heal."

My anxiety, my insecurities—those had roots so deep and dense I'd long ago assumed they were my foundation. But if Ilina was right . . . it just took time. Maybe a lot of time, or maybe they would never fully go away. But I could learn to control them.

"What you did back in the tunnel was brave," she went on. "And don't forget the speech in Bopha: you put others before yourself. Same as when you chose to go back to the Pit to rescue those three. Your selflessness is your strength." The corner of her mouth tipped up in a smile. "You're my wingsister, Mira Minkoba. I see all the ways you've changed since we found those shipping orders, and trust me, you are getting stronger. Stumbling means you aren't standing still."

Love filled up my heart. I didn't deserve her. "Do you practice these speeches in your free time?"

"Every day, just in case."

A screech alerted us to someone coming, and a pair of dragon heads popped up from the basket, curiosity making their eyes wide and round. Seconds later, Captain Pentoba called down, "Everyone all right?"

Gerel answered from the other side of the bottom. "We're going to live."

"Glad to hear it." The captain lowered our bags through the hatch, followed by bladders of water. "You'll have to stay down there a bit longer. The crew will get a cabin made up for you, but until then, I think it's best you stay out of the way. We haven't left Lorn-tah yet, but we will as soon as the tide rises."

I hated the idea of staying in this cramped place any longer, but how could I argue when Captain Pentoba and her crew were helping us?

"So," said the captain. "Where are we going?"

I pulled myself straight and met Ilina's eyes. Then we both glanced toward the dragons sleeping in their basket. "Val fa Merce." My voice shook a little, but the words were out.

"Right. We'll be there tomorrow afternoon. Get comfortable."

Before she could shut the door, I asked, "Do you have a medic on board?"

"Yes."

I looked at Hristo. "Go up. Get your hand looked at."

He glanced at the bandages, then nodded. At the very least, a medic could make sure it wasn't infected.

When Hristo and the captain were gone, Chenda grabbed one of the blankets and a bladder of water. "It seems rude to leave us down here. She could have let us up there to wash ourselves."

But the supplies dropped down had included a few washcloths, which we dampened to scrub the dirt from our faces, necks, hands, and arms. It wasn't perfect, but I felt much better with even part of me clean.

There were no changes of clothes.

"Mira." Ilina opened the dragons' basket. "I need your help with LaLa's wing."

She didn't really—Ilina had done this sort of thing dozens of times without my help—but maybe she just wanted to help me focus my whirling thoughts.

I gathered LaLa into my arms, my sweet little dragon flower. She shivered with pain, but looked up at me as I drew her to my chest. "You're such a brave little lizard," I whispered, and she breathed a puff of smoke at me. Usually it was a sign of affection, but now it felt like her telling me how badly she hurt. How she couldn't move her wing without agony. How she couldn't balance right. How she couldn't *fly*.

I kissed the top of her head and stroked her while Ilina constructed the splint. "We're going to help you, sweet dragon. I promise."

"All right," Ilina said. "I have to set the bones now. It's going to hurt, especially if they've started to fuse already."

Dragon bones were like bird bones: they healed very quickly, and if they weren't set properly right away, LaLa might never fly again. It had only been a few hours, though. LaLa would fly again. She would.

With a few pieces of dried meat and fruit ready to offer as treats, I met Ilina's eyes. "All right. When you're ready."

LATER, I DREAMED of flying.

Of great wings and burning stars.

Of fire and screams.

AARU

❧❧❧

Eight Years Ago

WHEN THE DRAGON ARRIVED, SO DID SAFA'S POWER.

We were walking together through the field, gathering fallen reeds for Mother to weave into mats, when I heard it: a sharp and hollow noise like a strange clap of thunder. But not thunder. The skies, while gray, were filled with the sort of clouds that brought a light, pattering rain; these were not storm clouds.

I used my sleeve to wipe water from my eyes, then looked up. Waiting to hear it again. And Safa, always attentive to my responses to sound, tensed and watched me.

::What?:: Safa's hand slipped into my free one, her question soundless against my knuckles.

::Big noise.:: I scanned the clouds, searching. ::In the sky.::

::Thunder?::

I shook my head. In the two years since Safa and I found each other in the rain, we had tested her hearing. She could sense thunder, screaming, and banging. Loud noises, especially when there was some tactile accompaniment, like vibrations in the ground. Sometimes, she could feel the sounds as much as she could hear them.

But not this time. The sound had been too strange. Too far away. And—

Safa pointed up.

An enormous beast sailed through the sky, shredding clouds with every pump of its wings. It had scales the color of foamy water, and wings so big they could block out the sun.

A dragon.

A big one.

Save in drawings and my limited imagination, I'd never seen a dragon before. Dragons lived in the sanctuaries, and the only one I knew of was near Summerill. Never in my life had I thought I'd actually see one.

I lifted my arms and waved, hoping—in the way only a nine-year-old child could hope—that it would notice me and come to visit us.

Frantically, Safa tugged at my shirt and shook her head.

::It's all right,:: I tapped. ::Dragons are friendly. They live in sanctuaries where humans take care of them.::

She was still shaking her head.

::The Hopebearer has a dragon, you know.:: Everyone

177

knew that, including Safa. Especially Safa, who dreamed of being like the Hopebearer one day; I didn't have the heart to tell her that people like the Hopebearer never came from Idris.

::She has a little dragon.:: Safa had kept her eyes on the sky, and now alarm filled her face. ::It saw you.::

She was right.

When I looked over my shoulder, the dragon had dropped from the sky and was flying toward us—fast. Its belly hissed over stalks, like fiery wind, and all I could see were its strong jaw and long teeth and hard, ember-dark eyes.

I dropped my reeds, grabbed Safa's arm, and ran.

We moved as fast as we could, ducking below the cane as though we might be able to hide from such a creature.

My heart pounded, echoing in my throat and head. We weren't going to make it to safety, not that I even knew where safety was. Not toward Grace Community. Not toward one of the farmhouses. We couldn't put other lives at risk.

Then I tripped, my feet caught on my own haste to escape. "Run," I said to Safa, and though she'd turned when I'd fallen, she wasn't looking at me now.

Her dark eyes were trained on the dragon, which was stomping up behind me, and her mouth fell open as though to scream—

Silence fell out.

Sudden. Complete. Overwhelming.

178

Silence.

It was a bubble around us, as heavy as the air before a storm. But no wind. No patter as rain hit sugar stalks. Even the thudding of my own heartbeat had been taken.

The dragon thrashed its head, as though it could shake away the confusing silence. But the silence persisted, growing and growing, and at last the dragon tore away from us with a soundless snort.

It flew away, and the silence Safa had caused evaporated.

CHAPTER THIRTEEN

QUIET FILLED OUR SPACE WHEN I OPENED MY EYES.

Darkness softened the sharp corners, while noore-stones nestled in the dragons' basket offered just enough light to remind us that we were safe.

Shapes of sleeping people were scattered across the bottom. One, two, three, four . . .

I sat up, looking for Aaru. But the moment I moved, I felt him—a pressure in the air next to me, the sound of his breathing. And so when he touched my arm, I wasn't surprised.

::Here.::

Carefully, I lowered myself once more, and he pulled away.

The worst of my panic attack had worn off, and I was

still tired, but the knowledge of Aaru so close to me—that I could not ignore.

Slowly, I moved my hand toward him, counting the finger-steps between us. Three, four, five . . .

My fingertips brushed the fabric of his blanket, and then warm, rough skin touched the back of my hand. Questioning.

I turned over my hand, tangled my fingers with his, and tried not to imagine that this was more than both of us flat on our backs and a slim connection between us. There might as well have been a wall.

He was leaving.

When we reached Val fa Merce, he'd get a new identity and find a ship bound for Summerill. I might never see him again.

But when I turned my head to look at him, he was looking at me, too. Light from the noorestones touched his face, highlighting the lines of his cheekbone and brow, and the curve of his lips. I wished I could touch him like that light did. Gently. Carefully. All over.

He was not soft like the boys I'd met at charity parties and state dinners. No, he was sharp from hard work, and lean from hunger. He had strength through silence, but it wasn't about the silence. It was his belief. His faith. It was the core of what made him Aaru that also made him strong.

I knew why he had to go, and that it might be safer for him if he did.

181

Just as I realized he'd been rubbing his thumb across mine, he stopped. ::You look worried.::

I nodded.

::I listen when I'm worried.::

::To what?::

His shoulder lifted slightly. ::I just listen.::

I didn't want to listen to anything and everything; I wanted to listen to him. But I couldn't come out and tell him I was already saying good-bye to him in my head, so I closed my eyes. And I listened.

I heard breathing, long and even: the sounds of sleeping. Gerel snored quietly, while Hristo sighed. Ilina mumbled something incoherent, and Chenda just rested peacefully. In a blanket nest, the dragons traded soft meeps as they snuggled closer.

And then I heard the breath of the ship and sea: the creaks of wood above and below; the brush of water against the hull; and the snap of sails as wind caught. The light didn't change down here, and there were no portholes, but I could tell the tide was right and we were getting ready to leave.

Finally, softer than everything, I heard Aaru. From the cadence of his breathing, he was listening, too.

I squeezed his hand. ::I hear.::

::Feel better?::

::Maybe.::

His hand slipped from mine as he rolled onto his side, facing me.

I turned, too. When my knees bumped his, I gasped and pulled back.

Some kind of emotion flickered across his face, gone too quickly for me to read in the dark.

His lips parted, like he wanted to say something out loud. But no sound came, and he sighed.

"Aaru." The floor bit against my shoulder as I moved my hands in front of me, fingers against fingers as though I cupped a ball of light between my palms. He moved, too, and when I slipped my right hand into his, my heart beat like it was on fire. Somehow, our knees bumped again, and this time I didn't pull away.

Seven gods, I wanted to tell him how I felt. I wanted to close the tiny space between us and kiss him. But it wouldn't be fair. He was leaving soon. Within days. And maybe I'd never see him again. In Daminan culture, a kiss might be an appropriate good-bye—an acknowledgment of a relationship that could have been—but for an Idrisi boy, it would be totally inappropriate. Not just rude, but scandalous. Disastrous. It could ruin his entire future if anyone found out, and he'd said before that he wanted to marry someone and have children and give them every-thing.

That was his dream.

I couldn't be the one to take it from him.

::Crying?:: His eyebrows drew inward as he touched my cheek, just above the scar. ::Why?::

"I'll miss you." My voice was so small and tight, it was

a wonder the words came out at all.

His fingertips still rested on my face, as soft as the brush of butterfly wings. His touch was so gentle I almost didn't feel it as he traveled up my cheekbone and then down my jaw—

But I did feel it. Every tiny movement. He was *so* close to the scar.

I cupped my hand over my cheek and turned my head a little.

::Sorry.:: Quickly, he let go of my other hand and tapped on the floor. ::Sorry. Sorry.::

My throat and face heated with humiliation. The places he'd touched ached with wanting more, and a desperate, deep part of me wanted to ask him to do it again.

But the scar. It was huge. There was no ignoring it.

::Sorry,:: he tapped again.

::It's not you.:: My hands were shaking, making my quiet code more fumbling than usual. ::You did nothing wrong.::

::Did I hurt you?::

I shook my head.

::Offend you?::

::No.::

::I don't understand.::

I clenched my jaw as I moved my hand off the scar. "This."

He only glanced at it. ::Don't understand.::

How could I make him understand what the scar was?

What it did to me? How it changed everything?

He studied me for a moment, and then said, ::You hate it.::

"Yes."

::Why?::

"Where do I begin?" The words choked out of me in a strained whisper. "I know I'm not smart or charming or strong. But I was beautiful. My face was the one thing I could count on to make people like me. And now that's gone. Mother is going to be furious when she sees me. She always said my face was perfect, and now it's ruined."

He tilted his head, a line of thought forming between his eyebrows.

And now he knew just how vain I was. Fallen Gods, he deserved better.

::So you hate the scar.::

"Yes." I couldn't speak anymore, not around the lump forming in my throat. ::Don't you?::

I'd asked the question, but suddenly I didn't want to know the answer. I closed my eyes and ducked my face.

One heartbeat. Two. Three. Four.

Cloth shifted as he moved, and he took the hand I'd been using to hide the scar, and he drew my fingers aside. His breath came warm against my skin.

I didn't move.

With such tenderness and care, he pressed his lips against my cheek. Against the scar. The corner of his mouth touched mine. And there, he kissed.

Desperately, I wanted to enjoy this, to feel every scrap of warmth, but my mind betrayed me, as always.

He was *touching* the scar. And he could *feel it*. Wasn't he disgusted? How could he stand to look at it, let alone kiss it?

He was leaving. He was leaving soon, so he was being nice now.

"Mira." My name puffed soundless against my cheek, and tapped against my fingers: ::Mira.:: He pushed himself up and leaned on one hand. Noorestone glow limned his features, and again I envied the light the freedom to touch him as it pleased. ::No one is perfect.::

Especially not me.

He tilted his head, casting his face into shadow so I couldn't read his expression anymore. But when he traced his fingers across my eyebrow, around my temple and jaw, and down my neck, I knew he was studying my face. Maybe the scar.

Then, he took my hand again. ::Imperfections reveal true beauty.::

My heart skipped. I'd heard those words before, from Krasimir. She was the Mistress of Beauty, responsible for many things, including maintaining my body to my mother's high standards. Krasimir had been talking about my counting, though, not the remnant of a giant gash down my cheekbone.

Still. Those words. I hadn't expected to hear—or feel—them again, and definitely not from Aaru. I stared at him, a response lost on my tongue.

He ducked his face. ::Should rest more.::

I nodded.

When he'd settled on the floor again, his hand found mine and there we were, same as we'd been before: both of us on our backs, our hands clasped somewhere in the middle. Then he squeezed, I tried to smile, and silently, he scooted closer to me.

::Good?:: he asked.

"Yes." I threaded my fingers with his, trying not to wish for something closer than this. Trying not to wish I could roll over and rest in the crook of his arm. Trying not to wish for a kiss that would never happen.

::What are you doing?:: he tapped.

"Sleeping."

::Terrible liar.::

I laughed a little, then whispered, "What are you doing?"

::Listening.::

"To what?"

::To you.::

AARU

Eight Years Ago

SILENCE COULD TAKE A THOUSAND FORMS, ACCORD-
ing to Idris's holy book. Reflective and angry and rude
and listening were all different sorts of silence, and a
proper follower of Idris must choose their application
with care. Even someone from another island might
learn Idris's ways, if they desired to be closer to him,
but they would never possess Idris's gift: the ability to
be silent.

That was what Idrisi people were: those of silent language and silent movement and silent *being*. We all had the
gift—some more than others, as on any island.

And then . . . there was the Voice of Idris.

His voice was silence. Pure. Overwhelming. Uncompromising.

True silence was power, Father said, and very few people

possessed it. The boys who did were taken to Summerill, where their talents were honed and they were trained in the laws of the land. Idris smiled upon those boys, and their families as well; if I'd been taken, my parents would have received seventy-five chips a decan. If I'd been taken, my family would have been the second wealthiest in all of Grace Community.

No one knew exactly what happened once the boys finished training and came of age, but there were rumors. Most suggested that when a Silent Brother died, a contest was held among the boys—young men by that point—and the most worthy would take his place as the newest leader in the Idrisi government. But what exactly that contest entailed, no one could say.

Sometimes, I was angry I hadn't been taken. Jealous, honestly. My duty as the eldest son was to help provide for my family, and seventy-five chips a decan would change their lives. Still, being passed over meant I was able to grow up with my family, see my sisters born, and appreciate hard work.

I wasn't silent enough for Idris, but I knew my family needed me, and that alone satisfied my heart.

But Safa . . .

Safa hadn't just been silent, she'd *made* silence. Like the boys taken from their home could. Like the Silent Brothers. Like someone who'd been given the Voice of Idris.

It wasn't supposed to be possible.

• • •

THE NEXT DAY, I mustered the courage to tell Father what Safa had done. In careful quiet code, so that I could not be misunderstood, I explained the dragon, her terror, and the way the silence had expanded from her like a bubble.

But even as I spoke, he was shaking his head. "It isn't possible."

::I was there.:: Although if he hadn't believed me the first time, why did I think he might the second? ::She frightened the dragon away.::

"Girls cannot possess the Voice of Idris." Father glared down at me. "Do not speak of it again or I'll have no choice but to send you to the basement."

With a shiver, I nodded and bowed my head.

But later, against his wishes, I found Mother. When I told her what Safa had done, her eyes grew wide. Round. Frightened.

"Never repeat that." She glanced toward her bedroom door; Father was sleeping beyond. ::If you love Safa, you will never speak of it again, and you will make sure she never does that again. Understand?::

I couldn't comprehend her fear then, but it infected me nonetheless.

CHAPTER FOURTEEN

WHEN THE HATCH SQUEALED OPEN AGAIN, IT WAS One who summoned us above.

"We'll reach Val fa Merce in just over an hour," he said. "The captain said you could all come up and get some fresh air, as long as you stay out of the way."

No one wasted time getting out of the compartment. We climbed up as quickly as we could, then waited in a line outside the captain's quarters; everyone needed to use the facilities.

I leaned against the wall between the open door and Aaru, just absorbing the salt air that tangled through my hair and caressed my skin, the creak of rigging and chants of crewmen, and the beautiful sense of freedom.

Aaru touched my elbow to get my attention. ::Captain Pentoba is a woman.::

"Very observant of you." I smiled so he'd know I was teasing.

::One works for her.::

The first mate, he meant. I nodded.

::Crew is mostly women, too. Is that normal?::

"Of course it's normal."

He drummed his fingers, the quiet code equivalent of *hmm*-ing, and finally said, ::Different on Idris.::

"Does it bother you?" A thread of worry crept through me. I'd known that Idris wasn't always a good place for women—marriages were arranged, women weren't permitted to work, and they were only as useful as their ability to bear children—but I hadn't thought of Aaru in that context. It hadn't occurred to me that seeing Captain Pentoba, a powerful and authoritative woman, might bother him.

But he shook his head, and his expression shifted into thoughtfulness. ::Didn't know it was different. Didn't know another way.:: He sighed and gazed over the deck. ::Will tell Mother and sisters. They'd like to know.::

The urge to hug him was overwhelming, but instead, I slipped one hand into his and squeezed. Words pounded in my heart. They balanced on the tip of my tongue. They almost beat out of my fingertips.

Chenda saved me from humiliating myself. "All yours," she said, and I hurried to do my business.

When I stepped back onto the main deck, Chenda hooked her arm through mine. "Let's get out of the way."

Together, we started toward the bow. It wasn't easy to keep up; she was taller, and her strides were longer than mine, and the sway of the ship certainly didn't help. "How are you doing?" She kept her tone easy, but there was another question in there. Worry.

She was asking about my panic attack without actually asking about it.

"Better." Even after sleeping most of the day, I was still groggy. Attacks always left my head a mess of sludge-like emotion.

But the attacks *had* been less frequent since escaping the Pit. Maybe Ilina had been right.

"Good."

"And you?" I asked as we climbed the stairs to the foredeck. "You were ill in the Pit, but you seem to have recovered."

She gave a single nod. "Shadow sickness, from too much time in the dark. That's why Hurrok screamed every night. He was in incredible pain."

I didn't want to think about Hurrok. Hristo had returned from the medic saying she'd rebroken the bones in his hand to set them properly, and that it was unlikely he'd ever be able to use the last two fingers again. I glanced up at Chenda. "But you're better now?"

"I am. Shadows are resilient things." When we reached the bow, she released my arm and we rested our hands on the rail while we looked out at the rolling sea. Wood cut water, and foam rushed around us as we sped toward a scrape of land on the horizon. "It's beautiful, isn't it?"

The ocean or her shadow: I couldn't tell which she meant, but I nodded anyway.

"I didn't think I'd ever see it again."

Maybe she was talking about both. The sun was falling toward the western horizon, and our shadows extended ahead of us, along with those of lines and sails and crewmen moving about the rigging to slow our approach into the city.

"It's important that you and I are united," she said.

"Why do you think that?"

"Individually, we are strong. But together, we are even stronger. *The Book of Shadow* says, 'A lone shadow may be dark, but many side by side make midnight.'" She looked at me askance and smiled. "When I was young, that used to scare me. In Bopha, there are noorestones everywhere so that we never face true darkness. I couldn't imagine why making midnight would be seen as a good thing."

"And now?"

She traced the copper tattoos on her cheek. "Now I understand that we can make midnight on our enemies. When we stand together, our shadows meld and become indistinguishable, leaving no recourse for those who seek to harm us."

"*The Book of Love* says something like that." I lifted my face to the wind. "It says, 'Hate cannot abide where many stand in love.'"

"We'd all do well to remember that." She gazed forward,

watching as the land grew steadily on the horizon. "The actions of our governments pain me, Mira. We've both been betrayed. We've both been made to believe in these ideals, then been punished for trying to uphold them."

"I don't know how it came to this. The Mira Treaty was meant to make all our islands better places. How did people lose sight of that so quickly?"

"It wasn't quick. It was a little at a time. One compromise after another. And if Altan is right about the Mira Treaty, we were never going to truly achieve those goals. The ambition of darkness does not lead to light."

"Then we must be uncompromising."

"We must."

I stared out at the sea, unsure if I really wanted the answer. I asked anyway. "Why you and me specifically?"

Chenda smiled. "The others follow our lead. Haven't you noticed?"

"Hristo and Ilina are my friends, not my followers." I shook my head. "I'm no leader. I'm not a political mind like you."

"You can be," she said. "If you want to."

"I don't want to. I just want to help dragons."

She gazed down at me, her expression cool and composed. "You cannot help dragons by yourself, Mira. Not at the scale needed to forestall the Great Abandonment. You can, however, inspire others to save dragons for you—if you help them first."

"I don't know how."

"By investigating the Mira Treaty. By ensuring the Fallen Isles do not become just another territory of the Algotti Empire. By rallying an army to fight, if necessary." Chenda touched my shoulder. "You are the Hopebearer. That puts you in a unique and powerful position to create change in our world. But you have to take it."

"Maybe you're right," I said. "But the dragons don't have time to wait for that."

Chenda shifted away from me. "Well, go to the sanctuary here. See what you need to see. But I hope you will reconsider your approach. Look at all the moving pieces of this puzzle, not only what's right in front of you."

Her words echoed in my thoughts, and after a few minutes, the others found us and we all leaned against the rail to watch the sea. Crystal was perched on Ilina's shoulder, and LaLa was cradled in Hristo's right arm—the one still in a sling to protect his bandaged hand. And though she, too, was bandaged together, LaLa had her head thrown back, completely relaxed while Hristo scratched the underside of her chin; her third eyelids were closed, and she chirruped every time he paused.

When Hristo caught me looking, he flashed a weak smile. "We make a pair, don't we?"

"She looks comfortable." I fished a piece of dried papaya and tore off a small bite for LaLa. She just opened her mouth for me to drop the fruit in, then swallowed it and went back to being adored. "She's going to get spoiled."

"Too late." Ilina snatched the rest of the papaya and offered a bite to Crystal.

I leaned my hip against the rail so that I could see everyone. Gerel stood next to Chenda; they shared a smile as they tried to identify something on the water, near the island. And Aaru stood apart, watching them, watching me. His body shifted with the movement of the ship, unconsciously adapting.

He was leaving soon.

A flock of seagulls flew overhead, calling and squawking as their shadows passed over the *Chance Encounter*. The island grew on the horizon, and what had been mere suggestions of buildings grew definitive.

Val fa Merce was a strange city: a mix of old and new, the product of a nation trying to find itself after centuries of occupation. There were remnants from every other island's rule, but from here I could only see the pyramid that loomed over the cove where the port resided. Before the Mira Treaty, there'd been maces carved into the ocean-facing side; they'd been chipped away now, but the evidence was still there. The gold that had once shimmered from every facet, however, had been completely removed.

"It's not a Khulani ship." Gerel shifted closer to Chenda, as though to get a better look. "The shape and sails are all wrong."

"It isn't Bophan, either." Chenda tilted her head. "I did hear that Anahera might be working on a new fleet to protect us from the empire. Perhaps this is one of those ships?"

"It's tiny, though. How can anything so little protect

us?" Gerel scoffed. "Besides, if anyone wanted to protect the Fallen Isles, they'd talk to Khulan's warriors."

"The size of the ship doesn't mean they didn't talk to warriors."

Just west of the port, the ship in question scurried across the water. Its sails stood sharp and black against the rocks, and the hull stretched longer than most ships that size would. It looked sleek, fast, but they were right: it was an unusual ship.

"What makes you so sure it must be from the Fallen Isles?" I asked.

Their smiles faded as they considered the implications. "Do you think it's from the empire?" Chenda faced me.

"I've never seen an Algotti ship." The black vessel drew my eyes again. "I don't know if this is one or not. But if we can't identify it, and there are questions about the legitimacy of the Mira Treaty, then it stands to reason that this ship might not be friendly."

Chenda nodded, but whatever she was about to say was cut short as Captain Pentoba strolled up to the foredeck.

Her hair shone deep crimson in the long sunlight, and she'd shadowed her eyes with the same shade. "Have a good nap?"

In the compartment, she meant. On the floor. We were likely being punished for delaying her departure so much, and now she was rubbing our faces in it. But I'd been so exhausted I wouldn't have cared if she'd made us sleep in a flooded compartment with a flock of angry chickens.

"Yes, thank you." I barely managed not to glance at Aaru, but I'd awakened to find our hands still clasped, and my cheek still feeling the warmth of his kiss.

He was leaving. He was leaving.

Captain Pentoba crossed her arms. "How long do you think you'll spend in Val fa Merce? A day? Two? Do you even have any money to do what you need there?"

"We just escaped from the Pit a decan ago," I said. "We've been running ever since."

"Then you don't have any money?"

"No."

Captain Pentoba sighed, produced a small purse, and tossed it to Gerel. "There's a loan. What about papers?"

Everyone shook their heads, and I said, "We can't use our real names. We've all been in the Pit, and Altan will check with every port in the Fallen Isles to see if we've come through."

"All right." The captain glanced over her shoulder as her crew worked the sails. "I know a forger in Val fa Merce. I'll give you a note stamped with my seal; they'll get on your documents immediately."

Aaru tapped on my arm. ::Is this illegal?::

"On all seven islands," I said.

He frowned. ::Is this a smuggler ship?::

"If this boy wants new residency documents," Captain Pentoba said, "he's going to have to stop looking like he swallowed seagull droppings."

"He wants to know if this is a smuggling ship," I said.

The captain laughed. "Seven gods, no. We're on the right side the law here. Until now, I suppose." She nodded at all of us. "I am smuggling you six."

Aaru's shoulders curled inward.

"But being on the right side of the law doesn't mean I don't know the people who like the wrong side of it. I've got friends everywhere, Hopebearer. Sometimes I do favors—legal favors, mind you—and sometimes I ask for favors. I'll be calling in one of those favors for your new papers, but I expect it'll be worth it."

The question fluttered in my mind again, and then fell off my tongue: "What do you get out of helping us so much?"

"Being on the right side of history." It was the answer she'd given before. That and money. There was something else, though. Something she wasn't ready to say out loud. "Look, I don't want to talk about me. I'm helping you, all right? I'm doing it for my own reasons. And you"—she pointed at Gerel—"I can tell you're worrying about what I'll ask for later. But don't. I expect to be repaid the money I loan you, and I wouldn't say no to a good offer later on, if you have something. But I'm not going to make demands of the Hopebearer and her group."

I bowed my head. "You'll be compensated for your trouble." I had no idea how we'd find the money, but I wouldn't ask Captain Pentoba to risk her life—and the lives of her crew—for nothing.

"Good."

"Captain!" Up on the foremast, a crewman waved and beckoned the captain to join her.

"Three seconds!" called the captain. And then, to us: "I'm thinking we stay here for two nights. I can recommend an inn if you want to sleep in real beds. Get bathed up. Have a few good meals. This is a safe city, and you'll feel better after getting the Pit stink off of you. We'll aim to sail on Ripday morning. Sound good?"

"Very good." I glanced at Aaru, only for a heartbeat. "We'll need one more thing, Captain."

"What's that?"

"Safe passage to Summerill for one. If you know of a ship heading there, someone trustworthy . . ."

She eyed Aaru with distaste. "I'll see who's in port once we arrive and work out some kind of deal."

"Thank you."

"We'll see." With that, she headed toward the foremast to get back to work.

CHAPTER FIFTEEN

GETTING OUR NEW PAPERS WAS REMARKABLY EASY.

As soon as our feet touched solid ground, we walked to the Red Wine Inn—the hotel Captain Pentoba had recommended—and rented a single room with three beds and a privacy screen; Ilina (who'd put herself in charge of the money) said we couldn't afford to separate. We took turns in the washroom, ridding ourselves of travel grime and remnants of the Pit, then slept in real beds for the first time in an age.

In the late morning, we changed into the cheap clothes we'd bought from street vendors, then helped Chenda cover her facial tattoos with an opaque cream. With LaLa and Crystal back into their baskets—we weren't going to leave them behind—we headed to the address the captain had provided. Her note worked wonders with the forger, who called in his assistant to sketch our faces.

It took hours.

While we waited for the papers to be finished, the six of us sat in the front room. Gerel and Chenda had their heads bent together, discussing the strange ship we'd seen yesterday, while Ilina and Hristo talked about where we could go next. I looked at Aaru.

He was rubbing the fabric of his shirt between his fingers. It wasn't anything special, just cheap, stiff cotton, dyed in hues of honey and amber, trimmed in chocolate brown. It brought out the warmth of his skin and the depth of his eyes.

Last night at the hotel, he'd shaved his face and cut his hair, shearing it close to his head, like Gerel and Hristo. For simplicity's sake, perhaps, but the result was striking. It brought more attention to his full lips and heavy eyebrows, making his gaze both intense and thoughtful at the same time.

If only it weren't so impolite to stare.

"How are you?"

::Fine.:: He rubbed his thumb across the hem of his shirt. ::Not fine.::

"Why?" I kept my voice soft.

::Crowded. Loud. Too many voices.::

"Can I help?"

He shrugged.

"What if you take a bed to yourself?" I asked. "Hristo

203

can share with Ilina and me."

::No.:: Aaru cast a wan smile. ::Don't mind Hristo. I like him.::

"He's good." I smiled. "He's been my friend since I was seven years old."

::Long time.::

"What about you? Besides your family, are there any longtime friends you're excited to see when you return to Grace Community?" I didn't want him to go, but I couldn't avoid the subject. And I didn't want him to think I was angry about it.

::Safa. She lives with us sometimes. Like a sister.::

"I remember." By his parents, he had four sisters and one brother, but they often took care of Safa, his neighbor.

He glanced up at me, as though he was surprised I paid attention to every single word he'd ever said or tapped. ::Would like to see work friends, maybe. If any are still alive.::

"Sorry," I whispered. Maybe I shouldn't have asked.

::Can't actually visit them anyway. Will have to hide.:: He pressed the hem of his shirt firmly against his leg, like ordering himself to stop fussing with it. ::Town won't protect me. Only family.::

"How will you work? Even with the new papers, they'll know who you are, won't they?" He wanted to provide for his family, but if he couldn't trust anyone in his town to help . . .

His eyebrows drew together. ::Leave Grace Community, maybe.::

I nodded.

::All I've known, though. Except the Pit.:: Worry touched his brow, and as though to hide his expression, he dropped his gaze to the fabric in his hands, then shook his head. ::I like this. Soft.::

I brushed my fingers against the rough fabric of my own shirt. "Idris produces far finer cotton," I said. "The finest in the Fallen Isles, some say."

He shrugged. ::Never had it.::

My face burned with shame. No, the Idrisi people probably didn't keep much of their fabric. I supposed it was mostly sent to Summerill, or exported to other islands. Wealthier islands.

Like Damina.

Even the simple blue dress I'd been wearing since escaping the Pit was made from Idrisi cotton. That dress was ruined now, of course. It was wadded into a ball in the corner of the hotel washroom, along with the rest of our shredded clothes.

My cheeks burned with shame. This cheap imitation of luxury was the nicest thing Aaru had ever worn, and I'd not only criticized it, but I'd also assumed he'd had access to the same cloth I always had, simply because he'd been born where it was produced.

I was a horrible person.

::No reason to be embarrassed.:: Aaru smiled, and as easily as that, my ignorance was forgiven.

Across the room, Chenda laughed at something Gerel said, and a sweet softness filled the Dawn Lady's gaze.

They seemed to be getting along rather well.

Ilina leaned forward and held a treat near the basket. The lid popped up and silver-scaled nostrils flared, and small teeth appeared to delicately take the bite of fruit. A tiny puff of smoke emitted in thanks as Crystal disappeared back inside. "No smoke," Ilina murmured. "We don't want anyone to notice you."

A soft chortle came from the basket, but that was all.

Finally, the forger strolled into the waiting room, his hands filled with our new identities. "Here we are." One at a time, he offered us the heavy papers, our faces sketched onto the top corner. Mine had the scar, and he'd caught me with my head turned slightly, as though trying to hide it. The scar was also noted in my written description.

Chenda, too, stared at her image; since she'd covered her tattoos, her face probably looked as foreign to her as mine did to me.

"One more thing." The forger offered Aaru a small notebook and pencil. "I asked about you; they said you don't talk. But if you can write . . ."

Aaru nodded, but his eyebrows drew inward with concern as he glanced at Ilina, who was in charge of our money. ::Can't afford?::

When I interpreted, the man pushed the notebook into Aaru's hands. "No charge."

Questions filled Aaru's expression.

"I can see you've got something to say," said the forger. "Maybe writing it down will help you say it."

206

Warmth filled my heart as Aaru took the notebook, letting his thumb caress the front cover. His fingers curled around the pencil. Then, carefully, he offered a small bow in thanks.

Our new papers tucked safely away, the six of us—plus the two dragons in their basket—made our way back onto the busy streets of Val fa Merce.

Harta's capital city spread before us in all its mishmash glory, scented rich and green with all the ivy that crawled up buildings, and the soft grass that pushed between paving stones.

The twisty, narrow roads bustled with thousands of people, all rushing somewhere as though they were late. The noise of the city thrummed in my chest: a cacophony of voices, a clatter of footfalls, and a melody of street musicians. Horsecarres rattled, driving wedges through the crush of people. Folks chatted about the errands they were running, or someone who had a fever, or complained about their children being late for school because they couldn't find their shoes. Strains of all those conversations floated around us, twisting into the controlled chaos of the most populated city on the Fallen Isles.

The sheer number of people made Aaru's shoulders curl inward, and though we let him move into the middle of our group—which meant he was still surrounded, but surrounded by people he knew—the energy of the city was draining to him.

"We're almost back to the hotel," I said.

Aaru didn't respond to my encouragement, just kept marching in Gerel's wake. In the afternoon sun, his face was a hard line of determination.

"I think," said Chenda, "our next order of business should be to find new clothes."

"Why?" Gerel plucked at the peach-colored blouse Chenda had picked out for her yesterday. "What's wrong with this?" Her tone suggested that everything was wrong with it, but the thought of more shopping was even worse.

"We stand out too much." Chenda sighed dramatically. "Even in a city as big as this, we *look* like we got our clothes from people who sell them on the street."

Gerel glanced over her shoulder and frowned. "We did."

"Exactly." Chenda met my eyes. "Help."

"Chenda is right." I scanned the streets to see what others were wearing. There was a lot to choose from. Some wore the wrap-style clothing that was popular on Damina, while others wore straight button-down shirts or tunics, like Aaru had been wearing in the Pit. There were the bright colors of Anaheran fashion, and also the subtler shades the Khulani people liked to wear. This city was filled with every style imaginable, in part because of visitors, but even more because the island had been controlled by every other island in the Fallen Isles at some point. The Hartan people had responded to their independence and search for their own style by claiming *all* the styles. "I think some of us should find clothes, but Ilina and I need to go to the sanctuary."

Gerel's frown deepened. "Even though Kelsine is with *him* now?"

"We still need to make sure the sanctuary is willing to take any dragons we rescue," Ilina said. "More importantly, we need to make sure this sanctuary is safe."

Threads of worry burrowed through me. "Plus," I said, "we need to look at LaLa's wing again, with tools actually meant for dragons."

Ilina glanced at the basket where LaLa and Crystal rode, guilt twisting her expression. But she'd done everything she could for LaLa's wing. If LaLa ever flew again, it would be because of Ilina.

"Very well." Chenda lifted her chin, mouth pinching against the words she really wanted to say; she clearly still believed visiting the sanctuary was a waste of time. "I will lead the expedition for new clothes."

"I'll go with you." Gerel sighed as she tugged on her shirt again. "Upper Gods know what you'll choose for me if I don't."

"I'm going with Mira and Ilina." Hristo kept an eye on the stream of people moving quickly around us. "Aaru, what about you?"

From his pocket, Aaru drew out his notebook and pencil. *Clothes*, he wrote.

His handwriting was careful and deliberate, as clear as though he worked from a copybook. He must have had a lot of practice under a strict teacher.

He switched from writing to the quiet code, which was faster for him. ::**Don't know what clothes they'd get me if I don't go. Might be yellow.**::

Now that was a valid concern. He'd look just fine in yellow, but I couldn't imagine him voluntarily wearing colors that shouted so loudly. "Don't let them get you anything that makes you uncomfortable. Get something blue. Or black. Everyone looks good in black."

He was nodding. ::**Much better than yellow.**::

"We should go now, before it's too late." Ilina nodded toward the crush of people on the street. "It'll take us hours to get there with all these people on the road."

"We can walk for a ways," Hristo said, "then take a horsecarre once we're out of town." He scanned the streets, gaze lingering on the horsecarres trapped in traffic. "I think it will be faster that way."

"I agree. Hold this for a second." Ilina handed the dragon basket to me, then dug out the purse Captain Pentoba had given us. Quickly, she counted the Daminan lumes, took a few to put in her pocket, and gave the rest to Aaru. "You're in charge of the money."

"Why him?" Chenda scowled.

Ilina didn't bother to answer. "Don't let them spend more than twenty lumes per person. That should get several items of clothing for everyone."

"Twenty lumes!" I shook my head. "What can you get with twenty lumes? A sleeve? The toe of a sock?"

"The lume is worth more on Harta." Ilina tucked her

coins into her pocket and looked at Gerel and Chenda. "As for why Aaru is in charge—he's clearly more responsible than either of you."

"You'd let Mira be in charge of the money if she were going with us." Chenda was still frowning, but she didn't mean it; her mouth curled up in one corner.

"Damyan and Darina, no." Ilina shook her head. "I'd trust her even less than I trust you with it. Now go get us new clothes. Shirts. Shoes. One set of trousers each."

We all used Aaru's notepad to write down our measurements, and then Ilina, Hristo, and I pushed our way into the crowd heading south, letting the current carry us. It was slow and annoying, but Ilina walked close and nudged me with her elbow.

"You and Aaru, hmm?" Ilina winked. "I suppose it makes sense. You're both quiet. You both spend a lot of time with your own thoughts."

"He used to speak out loud."

"Often?"

I shook my head. "Not often, but some. Usually for other people. He stopped after Altan—" I didn't want to say the word *torture*. Not here in this city that was so full of hope and life.

Ilina knew what I meant, anyway.

As we pushed onward, Hristo and I pointed out different sites for Ilina, who'd never been here.

"That's the pyramid we saw coming in." Hristo motioned westward, to the immense building rising off the bluff. The sandstone gleamed under the hot sun, blinding. But on the shadowed south side, the stone seemed . . . soft. Like something was growing there now. "The Khulani built it the first time the Warrior Tribunal controlled Harta, and they assigned governors and overseers to live there. When Damina took over after that, they didn't tear down the pyramid—they just moved in."

He said it all matter-of-factly, distanced from the painful history in tone, if not in his heart. Years ago, when I'd first begun to internalize how my ancestors had controlled his, I'd asked if he hated me.

No, he'd said, but he was angry. Angry at the past he couldn't change. Angry at the people who talked as though independence wasn't important. Angry that so many people acted as though the centuries of occupation had never happened at all.

I hadn't understood that anger. Not in him. The Hristo I knew was warm and kind, one of the most wonderful people on all of Noore, and he loved to laugh.

Now I knew there were parts of him that he kept hidden, even from his best friends. And while that knowledge hurt, *The Book of Love* reminded us that we weren't entitled to every raw feeling of others, not even of those closest to us. It said they'd share if they wanted, and love meant we accepted that.

And I loved Hristo. I accepted what parts of him he would share with me, and the parts he chose to keep to himself.

That was how I understood that his detached tone while speaking of his homeland's occupation was a shield. A barrier. A dam against pain that Ilina and I were not allowed to see.

"Bophans added a shadow spire there." He pointed ahead to a slender structure that rose in the center of the city. He and I had gone in there when I was fifteen. I'd been giving a speech to the first class of Hartan students to go through school under the Mira Treaty. It had been a difficult trip for Hristo; we still didn't talk about it.

"The buildings look different in different sections," Ilina said.

She was right. The architecture around the Red Wine Inn was all tall, elegant stonework and large windows, while just a little ways south, there was a cluster of flat buildings made from polished wood.

"Everything from before Harta's occupation was destroyed," Hristo said. "Other islands built Val fa Merce in chunks. A little here, a little there."

"What about that?" Ilina pointed toward a small park dotted with palm trees and metal braziers that could be lit on cold nights. Children raced across the emerald grass, while adults lounged on benches to read or visit with one another. "A park seems like something Hartans would build."

Hristo shook his head. "That one is Anaheran. The previous government had thought to draft Hartans to work on other islands. One person from each family would go. They'd be paid for their work, same as before, but such a law would have torn apart every family in Harta. There were protests for decans, and hundreds of people were jailed for no reason."

Sickness twisted in my stomach. A previous Luminary Council had done that—or tried to.

"At the same time, Anahera was fighting for control of Harta. They won just before the draft could go into effect." Hristo gazed at the park, frowning. "The Fire Ministry had the draft office razed, and they built this park in its place. It was meant to symbolize beauty from ashes, per Anahera's *Book of Destruction*, but one halfway decent act doesn't change the fact that the Fire Ministry was just another government Harta didn't choose."

Ilina pressed her mouth into a tight line. It wasn't necessary to say how horrible the other islands had been to Harta; Hristo knew. And while I'd once believed the Mira Treaty was proof of our growth, the Twilight Senate's deportation decree—and the Luminary Council's support of it—revealed the the truth: people now could be just as horrible as they had been three hundred years ago.

"Hartans haven't had anything to call their own in centuries," Hristo finished, "so they've just embraced everything for now. It's part of their history. Maybe one day it will morph into something new."

He'd said *they*. Like he wasn't Hartan, too.

But he hadn't grown up here; he and his father had come to Damina when he was a baby, and he'd spent his whole life there, or traveling with me.

He'd told me once that he wasn't Hartan. He wasn't Daminan. He wasn't anything.

I'd said that he was Hristo, and that was everything.

I couldn't tell whether he'd believed me.

We continued walking, Hristo pointing out other buildings and monuments—some built since the Mira Treaty came into effect—and I clutched the basket of dragons and watched the crowds.

Finally, we passed through the worst part of the crush, and hailed a horsecarre to take us the rest of the way.

"Where to?" The driver had a deep voice, musical almost, and sunbaked brown skin only partly shaded by a wide-brimmed hat.

"First Harta Dragon Sanctuary." My fingers ached around the basket handles.

"What's your currency?" he asked.

"Lumes." Ilina pulled out one large coin as proof.

"It'll be half a lume there."

"We'll make it two lumes if you wait for us and bring us back to town when we're finished."

"All right." He gave a toothy smile. "Get in."

And though I mourned our chance to bring Kelsine to safety, I hoped this visit would secure a place for her here when we were reunited.

If the gods were with us, this visit would end with aid for a lot of dragons, but I couldn't ignore a sense of dread that tightened inside my gut. Nothing was this easy.

AARU

Eight Years Ago

STEALING WAS WRONG. I KNEW THAT. AND YET, FOR Safa, I took the risk.

Father's dismissal of Safa's power festered like rot within me. And Mother's warning grew into a constant fear that rattled in the back of my head. Safa was a little sister to me, and the thought of anyone coming for her . . .

Idris might frown on my actions, but he was the one who'd given Safa his Voice. If he wouldn't protect her, I would.

After my preparations were complete, I took Safa beyond the fields to where a wide stream fed the river. Rain trees and ferns gathered around the water, providing cover for the small boat that waited on the shore.

::What is this?:: She looked around, frowning.

I listened for anyone nearby, but all I could hear was the breeze against the foliage, water babbling over rocks, and the faint hiss of crops in the fields behind us.

::I told Father what you did,:: I said. ::I told him how you frightened away the dragon.::

Safa lifted an eyebrow. ::Was he impressed?::

::He said it wasn't possible. That girls could not possess the Voice of Idris.::

::But I did it.:: A scowl tugged at her mouth.

I nodded. ::You did. And when I told Mother, she warned me not to tell anyone else. She wanted me to warn you not to do it again.::

::Why?::

I started to shrug, but I knew, didn't I? ::I don't think the Silent Brothers would like it.::

::Why?::

::They believe girls can't have the Voice of Idris.::

::But I do.::

I nodded.

::Then I'm special.::

::You are,:: I agreed. ::But—::

Her expression darkened. ::But what?::

But the Silent Brothers would not reward her special-ness. They would see her as a challenge to their rule, and a contradiction to the customs of our society. ::I think they would hurt you,:: I said at last. ::I think if they knew what you can do, they would hurt you and we'd never see each other again.::

Safa stepped back, alarm plain on her face.

::That's why I did this.:: I gestured toward the boat. ::There's food in sealed containers. Bottles for water. Blankets.::

She just stared at me. ::Why?::

::In case they find out about you. In case you need to run.::

Her round eyes shifted toward the boat, taking in the old wood and the brush half concealing the contents. Then she looked at me again. ::Where would I go?::

::I don't know. Maybe there is somewhere people aren't scared of powerful girls.::

She heaved a deep sigh. ::I won't use the Voice ever again. I'll never tell anyone about it.::

My heart twisted. *The Book of Silence* said to be proud of the gifts our god bestowed, not to hide them in shame. It didn't add "as long as you are a boy," but for some reason, that was how the Silent Brothers interpreted it.

Still, for now, this had to be our secret.

CHAPTER SIXTEEN

An overcast sky, heavy with held-breath pressure and rumbling thunder, greeted us as we finally
approached the immense wall that surrounded the
First Harta Dragon Sanctuary.

"Ever been here before?" The driver turned his head
just slightly, enough to indicate he was talking to us and
not some invisible presence, but not enough to actually
see our faces.

Ilina glanced at me, and I shook my head. I'd visited
the sanctuary both of my previous visits to Harta, but I
didn't need to share that information with a stranger.

"No." Ilina leaned forward, her elbows on her knees, so
she didn't have to shout over the clatter of the horsecarre.
"Have you?"

"Unfortunately not. And if they really do have to move, I probably won't ever get to visit. I hoped to take my children one day."

"I hadn't heard about them moving." Ilina's tone was pitched with just the right amount of curiosity, her shoulders set at just the perfect angle. Even away from our gods, her skills at using Daminan charms were practiced. "Did something happen?"

"A decan ago," he said. "Give or take a few days."

Ilina looked back and caught my eye, worry growing between us. "What was it?"

"Dragon got out." He pointed westward, where the land was completely flat, as though the daughter goddess had swept her hand along the earth to smooth all the wrinkles. "Burned down three farms before the keepers managed to get her back to the sanctuary."

My heart climbed up my throat. What would make a dragon do such a thing? Certainly dragons had burned whatever they liked throughout history, but never within living memory. As intelligent creatures, dragons knew they were endangered, and that humans were struggling to protect them now. Sanctuary dragons in particular seemed keenly aware of this fact.

"Was anyone hurt?" Ilina asked.

The driver shook his head. "Property only. All those harvests were burned, and a house was lost. But people around here are angry enough to start asking officials to have the sanctuary moved."

"Based on one incident?" Ilina was incredulous.

"Dragons are bigger than us," he said. "More dangerous than us."

I wanted to argue that second point, but I kept my mouth shut. We'd reached the sanctuary gate.

"Here we are." The driver reined the horses and we stopped moving. He gestured toward the locked gates. "But they aren't letting anyone in."

Hristo scowled. "Did you know they were closed?"

The driver shrugged. "You said you wanted to come here, and I don't turn down a good fare."

"They'll let us in." Ilina nudged Hristo to exit the horsecarre.

"What makes you think so?" asked the driver. "Plenty of folks have tried."

She flashed a wide smile his way. "I'm Daminan. I'll charm them."

"If you say so. How long do you think you'll be, if your plan works?"

"An hour at most." When we climbed out of the horsecarre, Ilina tossed the driver half a lume—the cost for the ride here.

"Do you think he'll wait for us?" Hristo asked as we walked toward the gate.

Ilina shrugged. "There's another lume and a half for him, and he clearly likes money."

LaLa and Crystal shifted in their basket as we approached the gate, as though they could sense the dragons beyond—and maybe the toys and treats and the oncoming storm. When the lid bounced and a tiny silver face peeked out, Ilina held the basket closed.

"Just a minute."

We paused outside the gates—wrought iron folded into images of Harta tending fields and holding children—and peered through. "Do you see anyone?" I asked.

Between the gates, we had a fractured view of the three facility buildings, and the drakarium beyond. Small dragons flew over and around the delicate arched structure, blowing fire at the clouds, calling and chasing in some endless game I could not fathom.

Most dragons loved storms, letting the taste of lightning tickle the backs of their throats until their spark glands tingled. Scales flashed in the cloud-diffused light, red and yellow and orange. And in the box, LaLa and Crystal strained against the lid, desperate to make new friends and join their games.

"Not until we're inside the sanctuary." Ilina pressed on the lid again, her face twisting up into knots of frustration.

Strangely, when I peered farther, I didn't spot any of the larger species flying in the distance. The land here was flat, a freshly smoothed tablecloth, which was less than ideal for larger species. Knowing this, the sanctuary builders had hauled hundreds—thousands—of boulders and loads of dirt to create mounds a dragon might want to use to build a den. From there, dragons had to build downward, deeper into the ground. I couldn't see the dragon mounds from here, but that in itself wasn't surprising. Nevertheless, there should be at least a couple of big dragons flying. . . .

"There's someone." Hristo nudged me. "Near the offices."

I peered through the gate again, spotting a tall man in a green and tan sanctuary uniform—similar to the uniforms Ilina had always worn at home—but it didn't seem to fit him very well. The sleeves were too short and the jacket too loose.

"Hello!" Ilina called, and waved when he looked over. "Let us in!"

Abruptly, the man strode out of our sight.

"Where are all the other keepers?" Hristo looked at Ilina, like she might have done something with them. "If we don't get in soon, we'll have to go back to the city—"

"I am not letting that driver think he's right. Besides, he could have warned us about the sanctuary being closed if he wanted, but he took our money anyway. Greedy."

"Hello." An older man in a keeper uniform approached the gate. "I heard you yelling, but I'm sorry to say that we aren't taking visitors right now."

He wasn't the same man we'd seen a few moments ago. No, this was a keeper I recognized from my first visit to Harta when I was twelve. He'd been ancient-looking then, and the five years since had only added to the lines and wrinkles and patchy gray hair.

"Keeper Azure." I turned my face slightly, hiding the

scar, and smiled. How lucky to run into a keeper I already knew, someone who would definitely want to help me. It would take no effort at all to persuade him to take refugee dragons into this sanctuary. "I'm sure you don't remember me, but I'm—"

"Mira Minkoba." Though his eyes widened in surprise, he didn't waste any time fishing a set of keys from his pocket. "You've grown."

"It happens to all of us." Thunder growled overhead. "This is my friend Ilina, and you remember my personal guard, Hristo."

The gate screeched open just enough for us to pass through, and I caught Ilina shooting a triumphant smile over her shoulder, toward the horsecarre driver.

"Of course. The Hartan guard with the Daminan name. And you"—he looked at Ilina—"are the daughter of Viktor and Tereza of the Crescent Prominence sanctuary, yes?"

"They are my parents." Ilina bowed her head, hiding every shred of her anger over her parents' betrayal of the Mira Treaty.

"I've heard much about you, Miss Ilina. You're something of a legend in the dragon community."

"That's very generous." Her smile was meant to be demure, but real pride shone through. If Ilina liked anything, it was being good at her job.

Keeper Azure closed the gate behind us and tucked his key into his pocket again. "I'm pleased to have all of you here. Would you like to join me in my office and tell me what you need? I will make tea."

"We'd like to use your medical facilities first, if you don't mind." I reached into the basket on Ilina's arm and pulled LaLa from inside. The golden *Drakontos raptus* perched on my wrist, careful of her talons and my skin. Then she greeted me with a nosebump and throaty purr, her broken wing held carefully aloft.

Then Ilina took Crystal, letting Hristo carry the basket.

Keeper Azure's attention shifted to the dragons. "*Drakontos raptuses*. Superb coloring. Possibly related, if the scales around their eyes are any indication. These must be the famous LaLa and Crystal."

LaLa preened; though (as far as I knew) she couldn't understand his words, his praise-filled tone was clear.

"Broken bones?" He held his hand just near her splinted wing.

"Her radius and ulna were fractured," Ilina provided.

"Dragons do have a remarkable tolerance for pain, don't they? What happened, if you don't mind my asking?"

"An accident," I said, maybe too quickly.

"Ah. Well. Of course you may use the facilities." He glanced at Hristo's right hand, and the scar on my face. "Seems like there's been a lot of accidents lately."

I pressed my mouth into a line.

"You didn't have that the last time I saw you, Mira Minkoba, and I've heard nothing about an injury. Seems like a scar on your face, of all faces, might draw some talk. But that looks old and I've heard nothing about it."

My cheeks burned as I pulled LaLa closer to my chest.

Hristo took a measured step closer to me. "What happened is none of your business. Don't presume."

"My apologies," said Azure. "An old man can't help but feel a bit of curiosity when the Hopebearer, her guard, and her friend show up unannounced. In questionable attire. With a hurt dragon. And evidence of two other major injuries."

Our attire *was* questionable.

"It's fine," I said, even though it felt like undermining Hristo and I actually did appreciate his protectiveness. But we needed Azure on our side.

"This way to the medical facilities." He motioned to a building that was large enough to hold two *Drakontos rexes* for surgery.

"Do you trust him?" Ilina muttered as we walked.

"As much as I trust anyone I don't know well." I petted LaLa, who was sitting alert on my wrist. "He was nice when I met him before."

She nodded. "He never came to Crescent Prominence with Director Bosh and other Hartan keepers. Remember when we held meetings for keepers across the Fallen Isles?"

"I remember." During my first visit here, Azure had told me that for most of his life, he'd traveled the farms of Idris, keeping rice fields fertile, but the moment the Mira

Treaty went into effect, he left for Harta. He'd toured the island for a year before settling in Val fa Merce. "Someone had to stay behind to take care of the dragons, right?" I looked at Hristo. "What about you? Do you trust him?"

"I don't trust anyone," he said. "Except you two. And I suppose Gerel, Chenda, and Aaru. A little."

As we walked, we passed by ten huge carts lined up next to the sanctuary wall. They were covered, with only a few slats in the sides, but the interiors were dark so I couldn't see what they were moving. Boulders for more dragon mounds, perhaps?

The other keeper—the one whose jacket didn't fit properly—slipped between the carts, and when our eyes met for half a moment, he just nodded and edged out of view. Back to work, I supposed.

Still, something was wrong. LaLa shifted back and forth on my hand, and a strange sleepiness nipped at me, as though I'd forgotten to breathe deeply enough.

I shook myself back to alertness and looked at Azure. "What are the carts for?"

He sighed as he pulled open the front door and held it for us. "Sad business. You chose an interesting time to visit."

"Our driver mentioned something about a dragon burning farms," I said when we were all inside.

"Yes. Tiff. Sort of . . ." His hands shook as he motioned us down a long hall with glass windows along the walls. "She left the sanctuary one morning. It's not unusual for our dragons to roam, but they generally stay within the sanctuary. This time, I thought she'd gotten lost and couldn't find her way back."

Dragons were smarter than that, though; surely she knew how to get home. "I remember Tiff from my first visit here," I said. She was a *Drakontos maximus*, huge and sapphire-winged. "She seemed very calm and well behaved."

Azure nodded. "She was calm. Old and powerful, yes, but very calm, at least until this last month. She just seemed more agitated than normal. She snapped at people sometimes. And then she set those farms on fire."

"Our driver said that city officials might force the sanctuary to move farther away from Val fa Merce." I couldn't imagine how that would be possible, though.

He sighed. "Yes, there are people trying to force new legislation through very quickly, without proper research into why this happened. They want a larger minimum distance between the city and the sanctuary."

"Even though the city wasn't harmed?" I frowned.

"Yes. They worry the city will be next. Of course, they also want us to move farther away from the farmland, but Harta, as you may know, is mostly farmland."

Harta was *all* farmland, except for the knots of population collected in cities.

Worry stung inside me. If the city leaders had their way, it wouldn't be possible for the sanctuary to take any dragons we brought them. "What will you do?"

"Perhaps once the farms and buildings are repaired, people will change their minds. A lot of these are the same people who take their children to visit the sanctuary every month. They love having it here, teaching our next generation about the children of the gods and our duty to protect them. But I suppose this is the first time they're seeing that dragons are not docile creatures meant for our amusement."

No, they weren't.

"Most sanctuaries don't allow visitors like that." Ilina managed not to sound judgmental, but I knew she disliked the idea of random people traipsing about dragon sanctuaries. They were *sanctuaries* after all, not menageries.

But Azure was clever enough to hear what she hadn't said. "Most sanctuaries get funding from their governments. When Harta became independent, we couldn't afford a sanctuary, but the people wanted one anyway. We all wanted to do our part to uphold the treaty and protect the children of the gods." A frown flickered across his face. "Visitors pay a fee that helps us recoup the construction and maintenance costs, and only certain parts of the sanctuary are open to the public, and only during certain points of the day. The drakarium, for example, is accessible in the mornings, because that is when the dragons there are most likely to be playing and not care about people staring at them. And visitors are never allowed into the dens of the larger dragons, but occasionally we do have days when we entice big dragons to come to a viewing spot."

I'd heard all of this before, and told Ilina, too, but I got the feeling she didn't care how careful the keepers were—she didn't approve of dragon exhibits.

Now, we walked past dragons in recovery wards. Through glass windows, we saw a *Drakontos aquis* gnawing on a bone, and a *Drakontos quintus* balancing on a wooden ball. Other dragons simply slept inside small, grassy nooks or on rocky perches.

At last, Keeper Azure pushed open a door. "Here you are. Use anything you need."

The room was a fairly standard small-dragon infirmary, with cabinets full of medical supplies, both a perch and a counter, and a large bowl of treats. There was even a tap with running water, and a scale that measured in Hartan stones. Sketches of anatomy covered the walls, beautifully detailed, and focused on the smaller species that would be treated in this room.

Crystal immediately hopped off Ilina's shoulder and went to play with a toy left on the floor—a small rope with knots and frayed ends, and places that looked like they'd caught on fire a few times.

While Ilina rummaged through the cabinets for the supplies she wanted, I took LaLa to the sketch of a *Drakontos raptus* skeleton. "These are the bones we're trying to make better." I pointed at the wing, and dragged my finger over the long bone on the outside.

LaLa wasn't paying attention; the treat bowl had caught her eye and now she stretched her neck as far as it would go, as though she might be able to dive in to steal a slice of dried mango or a sliver of smoked pheasant.

"After Ilina gets your new splint." I kissed her head.

"Impatient little creatures, aren't they?" Azure chuckled. "It's hard to deny them."

LaLa chirruped and gazed at him imploringly, as though hoping he might be gullible enough to fall for her act.

"She senses my weakness." He smiled. "I'll check on the other patients and return in a few minutes."

When the door shut behind him, Ilina said, "It was rude of him to mention your scar." She tucked a packet of padding under her elbow.

"It's hard not to notice, I guess." I placed LaLa on the perch and moved out of Ilina's way. "And he won't be the last one to say something."

"Still." She frowned as she began removing the old splint from LaLa's wing. "It's something to think about. What if other people don't believe you're you because of the scar? He's right that it looks like it's been there for a long time, and people just saw you in Bopha without it."

"No one will talk about what happened in Bopha. Not after that speech." I touched my cheek; that was the speech that earned the scar.

"That's not what I meant." She felt LaLa's wing for the breaks. "I meant what happened on the docks. The people who saw you then weren't the Bophan elite. They were normal people who were excited to see you interact with a *Drakontos rex*."

"Poor Lex." I closed my eyes, seeing the brilliant red

dragon erupt from a galleon, seeing her spit fire and struggle to escape into the clouds. She'd been so beautiful and strong, but the hunger and captivity had been killing her. She'd been wild with rage. "I hope she's still alive."

"I hope so too." Hristo glanced out the window, but the hall was still clear. "The Algotti Empire must want them alive, so I'm sure whoever the Luminary Council has moving the dragons would have helped her."

They hadn't been able to help the other two dragons on that galleon, though. Their screams would haunt my sleep forever.

On the floor, Crystal gnawed fibers free of her rope, then tossed them into the air and blew a puff of flame. The strands fizzled before they hit the floor.

Hopefully she didn't set the building on fire before we were ready to leave.

"There." Ilina finished fixing the splint to LaLa's wing and stepped aside. "All better."

Just as I opened my mouth to ask if they had a strange, gloomy feeling about the sanctuary, a knock sounded on the door and Keeper Azure entered.

"That's very nice work," Azure said, looking at the splint. "Your parents have trained you well."

Ilina glanced at me, and as though she sensed what I'd been about to say, she asked, "Do you need help with Tiff? Perhaps I could look at her."

He shook his head. "I'm afraid that's unnecessary."

"A second opinion never hurts," Hristo said diplomatically.

I offered my hand for LaLa, letting her step onto it. When she was settled, I pulled a small bite of meat from the treat bowl and let her take it.

"That is true," Azure said, "but Tiff is being moved tonight."

The looming sense of wrongness descended fully, and at once I understood the purpose of the carts outside:

The residents of the First Harta Dragon Sanctuary were being taken, just like the others.

CHAPTER SEVENTEEN

"Moved." My throat went raw with the word.

"How many?" Ilina's question was a breath, an echo of my pounding thoughts.

"Ten," Keeper Azure said. "That's most of our larger dragons."

"Why?" I couldn't keep the horror from my voice, even though we'd known this was a possibility. Even though I'd *known* something was wrong here from the minute we stepped up to the gate.

"There have been smaller incidents for a month: dragons flying for hours without hunting, which isn't *so* odd except that three were doing it. One began picking off his scales. Another—" Azure stopped. "I'm sorry. But traveling with Director Bosh, they will be under the best possible care. No one knows more about dragons than he, I assure you. He says they've called other experts as well. They will solve this."

My thoughts spun with the news. If the Crescent Prominence sanctuary wasn't the only one affected, then every sanctuary in the Fallen Isles was at risk.

When I caught Ilina's eyes, I saw my own fear reflected there.

"I hope," Azure went on, "that we'll be able to keep the sanctuary open with the smaller dragons; no one will be able to dispute their continued presence."

Threads of anxiety tugged at me, but I made myself breathe and pull my thoughts together. This wasn't a surprise, just a confirmation. We could deal with it. We could *use* it.

"Where are the dragons being sent?" If he knew the destination, that was where the *Chance Encounter* needed to take us next. First, we would make Keeper Azure see the truth so that he'd fight to keep the dragons here. Then we would rescue the others.

"Director Bosh said they are trying to find a cure for what's making dragons behave so strangely. They need to observe all the dragons in one location." He pressed his mouth into a line. "I don't know exactly where they're going."

All the dragons in one location? That meant dragons in other sanctuaries were behaving strangely, too. *And* Keeper Azure and the director knew theirs wasn't the only sanctuary being plundered. "Let us speak to Director Bosh."

He hesitated, and in that moment, everything was clear: he would deny us, and ten dragons would be taken tonight.

I tucked LaLa against my chest and lurched for the door. "Ilina, Hristo—come on."

"What are you doing?" Azure strode after me, with Hristo, Ilina, and Crystal behind him. "If we don't follow orders, we'll lose the sanctuary. The two hundred dragons living here will have nowhere to go."

"You don't understand." I shifted LaLa to my shoulder and shoved open the facility door. Outside, rain pattered to the ground in heavy drops, and a gray sense of fear flooded the entire sanctuary. I marched toward the carts, my shoes squishing in the mud and grass. "There's more to this than they've told you."

"It doesn't matter," Azure said. "We have to do what's best for the dragons, and not even Mira Minkoba can stop it."

He was wrong. He had to be wrong. What good was my name if it couldn't influence those with the power to do the right thing?

I glanced over my shoulder, but he was hurrying toward the rain-shrouded office building—to find help, probably. "We have to do this fast," I said.

"Are we just going to open the carts?" Ilina peered at me through the veil of rain. "Don't you think there's a

236

better plan? These dragons have been behaving erratically. It's probably not smart to just let them out."

"Probably not," I agreed, "but Keeper Azure will come back any minute, and who knows what will happen then. We open the carts or we let the dragons be taken."

"All right." Ilina didn't hesitate. When we reached the first cart, she turned the latch and let the door swing wide open to reveal a *Drakontos maior*.

Even sleeping, the dragon was magnificent, with closed eyes as big as my splayed-out hand and fangs that dug into the wood of the cart. He had storm-gray scales, which gleamed in the weak, cloud-filtered light, and his breath was short and fast, punctuated with puffs of smoke. He was stressed, even unconscious.

"They've definitely given him some sort of sedative." Ilina stood next to me, with Crystal at sharp attention on her shoulder. LaLa was a mirror upon mine. "I don't know if we can wake him."

"You'll have to do something soon." Hristo was standing watch behind us, the tendons in his neck straining. "There are four keepers now. It won't take them long to get here."

My heart pounded with uncertainty as I touched the gray giant before me. A jolt of anxiety shot through me, bright with flashes of wings pumping and flying straight up to the sun.

But just as quickly as they came, the flashes evaporated, and it was just me standing in the rain, my fingers resting on the *maior* before me. Disoriented, but on solid ground.

The dragon's scales were cool—too cool for a healthy dragon—and rough, as though he'd been rubbing his face on stones or trees. "Poor thing." I turned to Ilina, blinking rain off my eyelashes. "Let's open the other carts. I don't know if we can wake them, but they deserve a chance to escape."

"And if they fly toward the city or set more farms on fire?" Hristo asked.

"I—" My head spun with confusion, anxiety, and anger. I clawed my thoughts together, struggling to focus them through the mess. "I don't know. But we can't let the empire have them."

"All right." Hristo dropped our dragons' basket on the wet grass. "I'll help."

With a firm nod, Ilina was off, running toward the next cart. With one hand on LaLa to help her balance, I went for the one before that. My shoes slipped on the slick grass, but I didn't slow.

Cart by cart, my friends and I pried them open to find ten enormous dragons, all sedated into unconsciousness. How long had they been like this? How could I possibly help them all?

"Step away from the carts!" I knew that voice—he sounded like Director Bosh. Keeper Azure had gone straight to the head of the First Harta Dragon Sanctuary.

I was behind a cart, so I didn't see the director yet as I

hurried back to Ilina and Hristo. Instead, I came face-to-face with the keeper in the ill-fitting jacket; I pulled back just in time to stop from crashing into him and landing us both in the mud.

"Please," I said, just over the rush of rain. "You have to help. These dragons aren't being taken for their health. They're being sent to the Algotti Empire."

He cocked his head. "Are you sure?"

"Yes!" I rested my hand over LaLa again. "Please, we can't let them take our dragons."

"Mira!"

At Ilina's frightened cry, I didn't hesitate—I ran straight for her.

The group of keepers had reached my friends, and one had taken Crystal. His gloved hand was stretched over her back, pinning her wings, and though she could have lashed her head around and blown fire at him, she was too well behaved to defend herself.

She was shaking, though, shining with rain running down her slick scales. The sight of her in the man's grasp stopped me, and I drew my shoulder back as though I could hide LaLa. "Let her go." My voice sounded hollow. Deeper.

Director Bosh—I recognized his face now—shook his head. "I need you to stop what you're doing." He looked at Crystal, a tiny ball of terrified dragon in his hands, and then toward the open carts. "No matter what you do, these dragons will be getting the help they need. You get to decide whether this one"—he held up Crystal—"will be going with them."

My heart skipped, and next to me, a small whimper escaped Ilina.

"You will not take her," I said. "You will not take any of these dragons."

"Oh?" Director Bosh looked from me to Ilina to Hristo. "How will you stop me? How will you even awaken these dragons?"

I wished I had a thousand noorestones. Then he'd learn how I would stop him.

But here, all I had was my voice. "The people of Bopha named me Dragonhearted. Do you want to find out why, or will you *listen* to me when I say that what you're doing is treason?"

"These dragons are ill," he said. "I know you believe something horrible is going to happen to them, but I promise I'm taking them where they can get help."

I shook my head. "No, you're wrong. Fourteen large dragons disappeared from the Crescent Prominence sanctuary, and all the dragons from the Heart of the Great Warrior—"

"The Mira Treaty forbids them from having dragons, anyway. You of all people should know that." Director Bosh jerked his head from the other keepers to the carts. "Close those."

"No!"

At my cry, LaLa shrieked and Crystal whined, but

even more alarming was the jet of smoke that blasted from the nearest dragon—an auburn-scaled *Drakontos rex*. Frightened dragons sometimes awakened with fire, and I had moved directly between the dragon and the director.

"They're being sent to the Algotti Empire. To our enemies." I dared a step forward. Rain drummed harder on the carts, on the ground, and on us. "You know who I am, right?"

The director scoffed. "Of course I know who you are."

"Then you should know that I was sent to the Pit in order to keep this secret. I discovered that dragons had been taken from the sanctuary at Crescent Prominence, and when I told the Luminary Council, they reacted by imprisoning me." My voice shook with cold and anger, and I dragged my finger down the scar. "They did this to me. The Luminary Council. Because of the dragons. Because I wouldn't support the deportation decree. Because I decided not to be their puppet anymore."

Keeper Azure stared hard at the scar, and for a heartbeat I thought he might side with me. But then he looked away.

It didn't matter. I wasn't finished. "This goes above you, Director. If you've been told the dragons will be cared for, or treated for some illness, then you've been lied to."

Another puff of smoke came from the auburn dragon, but I didn't move as the acrid tendrils coiled around me.

One of the keepers started toward the cart. "Director—"

"Yes, give her another shot." But as the keeper pulled

out the syringe, Director Bosh stepped forward. "Wait." He held Crystal toward the keeper.

Ilina let out a strangled scream.

"Sir?" In the driving rain, the keeper stood perfectly still.

All around me, wooden carts groaned and creaked under the weight of shifting dragons. Long huffs sounded as dragons yawned and began to wake. I didn't see them, but I *felt* yellow-green eyes behind me open and blink, struggling to focus through the sedatives already in the dragon's system.

The sedative Director Bosh wanted to put into Crystal.

"You can't," I breathed. "You can't give that to her."

Director Bosh closed the distance between him and the keeper, heedless of the newly awakened *Drakontos rex* at my back. "I don't know where you heard that our dragons are going to the Algotti Empire, but that's a lie. No one in the Fallen Isles would ever let it happen, hear me?"

I clenched my jaw tight.

"I, personally, will be traveling with these dragons to make sure they get the very best care, and I don't like the insinuation that I would let them be harmed."

"You are willing to give a *raptus* a sedative meant for a *rex*." The words shook out of me, too full of fury. Blood pounded through my head, muddying my thoughts, obscuring everything but the needle poised just above a trembling Crystal. "That could kill her." On my shoulder, LaLa gave a low growl and flapped her good wing.

The director leveled his gaze on me. "Mira. Child. My duty is to these dragons, and to this sanctuary." Around us, dragons in the carts grew quiet again, sedated once more. Doors squealed closed as the other keepers finished their work. "If I don't obey the order to take these dragons away, then the First Harta Dragon Sanctuary will be shut down, and every other dragon here will be sent away or abandoned to the wilds. I know Azure has told you as much."

He was putting the needs of the sanctuary above these ten dragons.

Sacrificing these for the sake of the others.

I closed my eyes and exhaled, long and slow. The anger didn't fall out, but I could rein it in now. "Give Crystal back to Ilina."

"Will you leave the sanctuary?" Bosh asked.

I glanced at Ilina, who hadn't looked away from Crystal, and then Hristo. He offered a minute nod.

"Fine," I said. "Give Crystal back."

The keeper with the syringe backed off, his eyes flickering toward the *rex* in the cart behind me. But that dragon was on her way back to sleep, no need for another dose.

Then Director Bosh opened his hands, and Crystal exploded outward in a flurry of squeaks and wingbeats and spraying water. She flew straight for Ilina and buried herself in her person's embrace. And Ilina, for her part, was bent over and shivering, whispering love to her dragon.

I lifted my hand toward LaLa, letting her bump and

243

nuzzle my fingers. "Do you believe in the Great Abandonment, Director? Keepers?" I looked at Azure and the others as they stood together again.

None of them answered.

"I want you to remember this moment," I said. "When you had a choice to do what was right. To see beyond selling ten dragons or giving up the sanctuary. To see a third option."

"There is no third option, Mira. Not this time." Azure looked at me with sad eyes. "Sometimes there are only two bad options, and we have to make the best choice we are able, but I suppose the very young can't always understand that."

I sucked in a heavy breath and pressed my fingertips against the cool scales of the *Drakontos rex*. She was asleep again, captive to the sedatives her keepers had given her. "I'm sorry," I whispered, because I had made my choice, too, and I wasn't proud of it.

AARU

Seven Years Ago

I ALMOST DIED ON MY FIRST DAY OF WORK.

My father repaired important buildings in Grace Community, such as the High House, where the community leader lived. It was the best house in the whole town, with three floors, brick siding, and a wide balcony that overlooked the town square. Father said it walked the line between opulent and acceptable. He'd been all through it to make repairs, of course, and he said it had *five* bedrooms. Kader—the head of Grace Community—and his wife had three children, so no one shared. It was wildly extravagant.

And enviable, but I pushed that feeling aside like a good Idrisi boy. I shouldn't want more than I had.

::Today,:: Father tapped as we made our way through

245

the quiet town square, ::we need to repair a broken tile on the balcony.::

People looked at us as we climbed the steps to the High House, patting out their own conversations, most too fast or too hidden for me to see. But I always felt like they were discussing Safa and how my family had too many girls already. My parents finally had a second boy—Danyal—but he was two, and followed shortly by Essa. Another girl. I was old enough now to realize my parents would have to make marriage arrangements for all of them eventually, and we didn't have anything to offer in the way of dowry. Keeping Safa with us half the time only made us responsible for her, too.

Still, we weren't the worst off in Grace Community. A family down the road had ten children—all girls—who'd never be able to work.

Father took me through a back door into the High House, truly the grandest place I'd ever stepped foot, and showed me all the tools. "This is important," he said. "Our family needs your income."

I knew that.

"You're ten years old. It's time for you to do your part."

Together, we lifted the pieces of broken tile and scraped away the old mud. A sense of pride filled me as we worked; I was needed here.

"Watch while I put in the new tile." He didn't say it out loud, or even tap it, but I heard the words underneath: *It's too important to risk you making a mistake.*

So I observed, standing quietly over him, ugly shame driving its tendrils through the pride from earlier. I wanted to be good. Respected.

When he was finished, I took the initiative to clean up. But then—

I slipped.

A piece of the broken tile slid under my foot and threw me toward the balcony edge. I flailed, teeth clamped on my lips to keep a shout inside, and suddenly—

I was falling.

I DIDN'T REMEMBER hitting the ground. Only waking up in my sisters' room.

"You'll live." Mother crossed her arms.

::Can I keep working?:: I tapped.

"Not with your father. Kader won't have you at the High House again. They cannot risk another delay because of your clumsiness."

Shame burst through me, but there was no indulging it. I'd have to find another job, or my family would starve.

CHAPTER EIGHTEEN

ANGER PROPELLED ME TO THE HORSECARRE, WHERE
the driver still waited, displeasure written plain across
his rain-streaked face; though the retractable roof had
been pulled out, there were no walls to shield him from
the weather, and his canvas raincoat would only protect
him so much.

I was too mad to care. Once the three of us were in the
back of the horsecarre, I slammed the door and hunched
away from the rain leaking through the front window.

Ilina bent over the dragons' basket and fished out a
blanket. Quickly, she wiped off her face and arms, helped
Hristo where his hand limited him, and when they were finished, he offered the blanket to me. "Your hair is frizzing."

"I don't care about my hair." But I snatched the blanket

from him anyway and dried off. The damp linen smelled like smoke and lightning, like our little dragons who'd almost been torn apart forever.

Director Bosh had threatened to *kill* Crystal. He'd have done the same to LaLa, too, if he'd been able to take her.

"We're all angry, Mira." Ilina bent over the basket, one hand inside to pet the dragons. "Now we have to decide what to do next."

I didn't want to talk about our next move. I wanted to go straight back to the sanctuary with handfuls of noorestones, and demand they release the dragons.

Keeper Azure might have believed the story about dragons being removed for medical reasons. Perhaps the dragons *were* behaving strangely. But the dragons could be treated here, in their home, not in some unknown location. And certainly not everyone at the First Harta Dragon Sanctuary believed the excuse Bosh was giving.

He'd been *so* insistent on taking the dragons himself. He'd ignored everything we said.

He was as guilty as Ilina's parents.

A deep, dark part of me raged. I wanted to set him on *fire*.

"You know what this means, right?" I met Ilina's eyes. "If Crescent Prominence, the Heart, and First Harta were all affected—that's a pattern."

She let out a long breath. "It's bigger than we thought."

Every sanctuary in the Fallen Isles was at risk: Summerill Sky Sanctuary on Idris, and the Stardowns on

Bopha, and the Eternal Fire Sanctuary on Anahera. And those were just the big sanctuaries. There were dozens of smaller ones scattered across all seven islands.

"We have to warn them." Even as the words came out, I knew it was pointless. We couldn't *go* to any of the other sanctuaries without losing time at sea; we'd almost been too late for First Harta, and they hadn't even believed us. And we couldn't trust letters to anyone; if they were intercepted . . .

Rain drummed on the horsecarre, cluttering my thoughts with irrelevant numbers.

"How do you propose to do that?" Hristo asked, keeping his voice low so that the driver wouldn't hear.

"I don't know." I dragged my hands down my face, thinking. "Nowhere is safe. None of the sanctuaries."

Which meant that even if we were able to rescue dragons from ships or stops along the way to the empire—and I'd just seen how good I was at rescuing dragons that hadn't even been moved yet—there was nowhere to take them after.

Every dragon in the Fallen Isles would be plundered for the empire's gain.

Unless.

Unless someone with power put a stop to it.

Two decans ago, the people of the Shadowed City named me Dragonhearted, because they thought I'd calmed a dragon to give police time to take control of her. While that hadn't been my intention—I'd wanted her to fly away—the title was still mine.

Dragonhearted.

Mira the Dragonhearted.

"It has to be me," I whispered.

"What?" Ilina cocked her head.

I looked up and made my voice a little stronger. "Chenda was right. I thought if I could only rescue a few dragons, that would be enough. But the problem isn't just that dragons are being taken. It's that Altan may have been right about the treaty and I refused to look into it because I was afraid of going home. But if everyone who signed the Mira Treaty has betrayed us, I need to do something."

Hristo rested his hand on my knee. "Sharing a name with a thing doesn't make you responsible for it."

"Doesn't it?" I'd spent my life defending the treaty; I should be the one to fight it, if it proved false. "Chenda was right," I said again. "We have to go home. I'll ask my parents what they know. I'll ask"—the words choked me—"if they are in fact traitors to the Fallen Isles."

Ilina glanced toward the driver, but if he heard us over the rain and clap of hooves on wet ground, he showed no signs.

I leaned toward Ilina and Hristo and lowered my voice. "Father wrote the treaty. Surely he knows what it did. If he sold the islands to the empire—if he traded our dragons for an illusion of peace—"

Hristo squeezed my arm. "If that's where you think we should go next, I will follow you there."

Unease squirmed within me. I didn't want to go home. I didn't want to see my parents or the Luminary Council.

"I won't let fear stop me," I said. "Not anymore."

The corner of his mouth lifted in a faint smile.

"When we know the truth about the treaty, we'll be able to use that to help the dragons. I'll be the Hopebearer. I'll be the Dragonhearted. I'll be whatever I need to be in order to stop this travesty." Chenda, at least, would be pleased.

Finally, we rolled back into the city. The rain had chased off most pedestrians, and horsecarres dominated the streets, all driven by miserable-looking men and women in waterproofed jackets.

"Busy evening here." Our driver glanced over his shoulder, just loud enough to be heard over the pounding rain. "Are you going to see her?" He straightened and directed the horses around a corner. "She's at the Lexara Theater, so there's probably room if you don't mind standing, but I'd get in line now if you want space to breathe. It's going to be packed, I hear. She hasn't visited in over two years."

Ilina frowned. "Who's here?"

He looked at Ilina as though she were out of her mind. "Mira Minkoba, of course. The Hopebearer."

CHAPTER NINETEEN

I DIDN'T THINK. I JUST REACTED.

As soon as the driver finished saying that *I* was speaking at the Lexara Theater, I pushed open the door and dropped from the horsecarre and into the rain.

"Wait!" Ilina's hands grasped at my shirt, but it was too late; I was already out. "Sorry, so sorry—" She was speaking to the driver now, though I didn't hear the rest.

Instantly drenched but hot with fury, I tore across the street and toward the theater.

Someone was pretending to be me.

Tirta was pretending to be me.

Everywhere, people ducked their heads and hurried to get out of the storm. Street vendors had long since shut up their stalls, and the sheets of rain made strange ghosts of the empty windows and abandoned carts. The clatter of water on wood and stone and steel built a cacophony in my head, but I surged on.

She was pretending to be me.

I'd known it was coming, hadn't I? Tirta had told me the Luminary Council planted her in the Pit to learn how to become me.

And now she had.

My shredded slippers were soaked before I even turned the first corner, but I didn't stop—not until I saw it.

The Lexara Theater rose ahead, an immense stone building that dominated the city center. I knew it from a play my parents had taken me to when we last visited Harta, and its numbers were etched into my mind: seventy-seven stained-glass windows, seven turrets, and seven columns. Inside: three lobbies (one was private), one auditorium with seven thousand seats and seven hundred noorestones, and four private boxes set off from the rest of the seating. And now, seven banners hung down the front face: one for each of the islands.

A line began at the doors, went down the steps, and twisted back and forth across the lawn. Hundreds of people hunched against the storm, many in waterproofed coats, but there were some brave souls who decided to dance between raindrops, while others sang and clapped. Growling thunder provided inconsistent bass.

Someone caught my arm, making me jump and spin, but it was just Hristo. Water dripped down his face, soaking his shirt and sling.

"Mira." He kept his voice low, like someone might overhear such a common name being uttered. Like anyone thought *Mira Minkoba* might be standing out here in the rain, too. "What are you doing?"

My thoughts floated. I could hardly recall running here. I *hated* running, but fury had fast wings. "Tirta is here. She's pretending to be me."

He glanced beyond me, to the lines of people waiting to get into the theater. "You just took off."

Right. Didn't he understand that she was *pretending to be me*? She'd stolen my name. My title. The thing I'd been my entire life.

"This isn't like you."

Even against the thunder, my voice felt low and dangerous. "Maybe it should be." My whole body shook from rain and wind and rage. "I have to see that impostor. I have to . . ."

What? Make her pay? Expose her? Force my way onto the stage and confront her, declaring my identity to all?

Like this, soggy and wearing an ill-fitting shirt and trousers? I would appear as a madwoman to everyone, while Tirta would be wearing *my* clothes. She'd be clean and dry, her face perfectly made up with the finest cosmetics imported from Anahera.

Hristo just watched as reality crushed me once more.

"No one will believe I'm me." The scar on my cheek felt huge, like a range of mountains on the map of my face. "Elbena tried to bleed the Hopebearer right out of me so she could put it into someone else."

He shook his head. "That's not something that can be taken from you, Mira. Not unless you let them."

I closed my eyes. Rain washed down my head and neck and shoulders. "She's probably here."

"Who? Elbena?"

"Yes." A flicker of terror struck me, but it wasn't as though Elbena would peer outside a window and see me here. The theater lawn was filled with people, and the street bore traffic in spite of the rain. I was just another anonymous girl in cheap clothing, and Hristo was another Hartan boy, both of us obscured by the shimmering rain.

But what about my parents? Mother usually traveled with me. Father's company was less frequent, but certainly not unusual.

They might be here. In that theater.

With Tirta?

Would they have agreed to this?

I couldn't make myself look back at the building, too paralyzed by the possibility of seeing Mother's silhouette in a window. "Where's Ilina?" I asked instead.

"She took Crystal and LaLa to the inn."

And Hristo had come chasing me to protect me from myself. "Sorry I ran off." He was right. It wasn't like me.

He studied my face for a moment, searching, and after a moment he sighed. "I understand." Then he adjusted his arm in its sling as he glanced around.

I glanced, too.

1. *People—too many to count.*
2. *Noorestones—fifteen on lampposts around the lawn, and a dozen on the stair rails up to the door.*
3. *Raindrops—infinite.*

"All right. Come with me." He started toward the side of the theater, not bothering to duck or check on whether we were being watched. "I think I know why you came here."

Of course he did. He was Hristo. Half the time, he knew me better than I knew myself.

I lengthened my stride to keep up with him, and soon, we were out of view of the crowd, and the hum of conversation and melody of song were muted. The theater soared above us, imposing in all its glory, and our shoes slurped in the mud and grass.

Hristo kept his voice low. "When you came here before, theater security showed me a secret exit."

"Why?"

He cast a frown over his shoulder. "In case there was a threat against your life."

"In Harta?"

Hristo slowed his steps to let me catch up. "There have been threats against you everywhere we've gone. And you know that even your own home hasn't always been safe."

I bit my lip.

"Your mother wouldn't let me tell you," he went on.

"She wanted you to think that everyone loved you, because you changed after that kidnapping attempt when we were children. She was afraid it broke you, and that anything else would destroy you completely."

My heart sank, pieces of it sloughing off and falling into the abyss. Five steps. Six. Seven. "She said that?"

Hristo nodded. "She said if I ever breathed a word that there were people who'd tried to kill you, she'd have both Father and me removed from Crescent Prominence and I'd never see you again. So I never said anything."

Twelve, thirteen, fourteen . . .

"Before you ask, yes. I thought you deserved to know the truth. But I couldn't take the risk that she'd somehow find out if I told you."

Seventeen, eighteen, nineteen . . . "How many?" I asked.

"How many what?"

"Attempts."

He shook his head. "I don't know. I didn't count them."

Because there were so many? Or because he knew that one day I'd find out and ask, and if I knew the exact number then perhaps Mother's fears would come true?

Hristo didn't know about the counting. No one did, except for Mother, Doctor Chilikoba, and somehow Krasimir and Aaru. At least, if Hristo and Ilina knew about the counting, they'd never said anything.

I sighed. They probably knew.

"I'm sorry my mother put you in that position. That was cruel of her."

He stopped walking and faced me. "She doesn't know as much about people as she thinks she does, but one thing she has never underestimated is how much I love you."

I smiled. "Do you remember when I asked you to marry me?" I'd been all of twelve years old.

He laughed a little. "The answer is still no, Mira Minkoba."

"Well, that's good. I don't want to marry you anymore."

"What?" He pressed his palm against his chest. "I'll never recover from this blow to my ego."

"But I love you, too." I took his hand. Though I'd known him for ten years, we'd hardly ever shown affection with simple touches or embraces, so the shape of his hand was unfamiliar in mine. And yet, it felt just as I'd imagined: strong, rough with calluses from holding weapons and working with his father, but also gentle. "I think we should say that more. All of us. I don't want to wait, saving it for a special moment that might never come, and suddenly it's too late."

"I'll have a decree drawn up."

I smirked and pulled away, face so hot I was surprised the rain didn't steam off my skin. "Show me that secret exit first."

"As you wish."

Together, we crept along the side of the theater. Other buildings rose up next to it, so we tried to move quickly and keep to the shadows, lest anyone glance out a window; the rain would only hide us so much.

The secret exit turned out to be a small back door, like the kind someone might use to dump a bag of trash outside, and that didn't seem *so* secret to me, considering the other hidden passages we'd seen lately. But this one was locked.

"Are you going to break it down?" I asked.

"Of course. You know I always choose brute force." He patted through his pockets, twisting awkwardly when he reached around his bound arm, but finally he pulled out two slender pieces of metal. "I don't suppose you learned to pick locks in prison."

"Where did you get those?" I checked our surroundings, but the buildings around the theater were dark and quiet.

"Captain Pentoba gave them to me." He handed one piece to me—a length of steel with a small flag on one end. "I need your help."

"What do I do?"

He showed me where to insert the tension wrench, how to hold it, and then he slid the lock pick into the keyhole.

It was slow work, because he was used to picking locks with his right hand and I didn't know how at all. But after one hundred and five pounding heartbeats, pressure inside the cylinder gave, and I turned the lock.

"Good work." Hristo put the tools in his pocket and we slipped inside a narrow space, barely big enough for both of us. A small noorestone on the floor illuminated the stone walls and a single wooden door. He rested his hand on the doorknob. "This will open near the servants' washrooms. We can go in and dry off, that way we don't leave a trail of water. There's probably no one in there now, because fake Mira is already here, but we still need to hurry."

"Fake Mira is just Tirta. She was with the Luminary Guards in the Pit, during the tremor."

"If she's masquerading as you," he said, opening the door, "she's fake Mira."

The washrooms were empty, and as soon as we'd scrubbed ourselves dry, we each took a brown theater jacket and slipped it on. I helped Hristo button his closed, and then we headed for the auditorium.

My feet knew the way.

We kept our heads down, offering polite greetings whenever we passed someone in the halls. No one stopped us.

"What's your plan?" Hristo asked as we came to one of the halls with double doors that opened onto the main floor. "Elbena is here. You shouldn't confront anyone."

No need to worry about that. Now that we were here, I wished I wasn't. I wanted to turn around and sneak out through the not-so-secret exit and run all the way to the Red Wine Inn. I'd apologize to Ilina for my abrupt departure. I'd discuss my next move with the others. I'd hold my dragon. I'd pretend like the idea of sending Aaru off to a different ship tomorrow didn't break my heart.

But I was here. And I needed to know.

261

The drone of the audience's conversations drew me through the door and into an enormous shell of polished marble, crafted with such precision that a whisper on the stage would reach even the farthest stretches of the audience.

Seven hundred noorestones illuminated seven thousand seats, distributed across the main floor and three layers of balconies. Statues of all seven gods graced the chamber. Damyan and Darina reached for each other from opposite sides of the stage, while Bopha had been placed to cast the deepest of shadows on a wall. Harta stood by one of the doors, serene and majestic at once, while Khulan held his mace as he glared across the audience. Anahera had both hands covering her face, but one was palm-out; hints of a devious smile suggested she'd laid a trap we were all caught in. And Idris—he was hidden somewhere in the back, present, but often overlooked.

The stage, where Tirta would speak, was dim for now, but the moment she came out, theater workers would adjust mirrors to focus the light of noorestones onto her. She'd stand under that cool blue glow and sparkle, just as I always had, and people would love her.

I thought of the secret exit and Hristo's words; not *everyone* would love her.

No one paid attention to me. Not without my dresses and jewelry and elaborate hairstyles. Here, I was as anonymous as I'd been in the Pit, and I could move about the aisles without arousing suspicion. Hristo followed on my heels.

"You!" An older woman in a theater uniform beckoned me. "Don't dally. There's work to do."

At my glance, Hristo nodded and we hurried over to the woman.

I knew her. She was one of the theater managers. We'd met the last time I'd been here, but if she realized that the "Mira" she was hosting tonight wasn't me, she didn't show it. "You're supposed to be on the upper balcony to work the noorestones when she comes out. Third set to the left."

"Sorry," I said. "I'll go up there right now."

"Good." But before I could move, she grabbed my arm and suddenly *looked* at me.

Thunder rolled in my head, and outside. A breath rasped out as I waited for her to recognize me, to say something about me looking familiar, but it didn't take long for her gaze to flicker to the scar.

She released me.

"Both of you, get to work."

My heart pounded in time with my steps as Hristo and I hurried off the main floor and took the stairs to the upper balcony's lighting room. It was small, and lit with only ambient light, but I'd have a perfect view up here, and no one would question my presence.

"That was close." Hristo closed the door after us. "But I suppose no one expects the Hopebearer to look anything other than exactly as they expect her to appear."

"You're right about that." I looked around our station: twenty-five noorestones, and just as many mirrors and velvet covers. They were the same as those in other theaters and grand halls I'd been in, but I'd never had to *use* them before.

Well, I didn't *have* to use them now. Tirta was stealing *my* identity; I didn't have to do work for her. I was here to watch. If my parents were in Val fa Merce, I could speak to them tonight. I could tell them the truth about the speech on Bopha. And I could learn what they knew about the Mira Treaty.

I shucked off my borrowed theater jacket and went to the edge of the balcony.

We had a perfect view. As workers adjusted their mirrors and filters over the noorestones, a bright beam focused on the center of the stage, where a tall woman stood. The orange dress she wore set off her deep-brown skin, and the thick sash around her waist emphasized her full figure. A matching band held back dark curls, revealing the soft curves of her face.

Eka Delro, the First Matriarch of Harta.

I'd met her both times I'd visited Val fa Merce before, and I'd always thought her wise and kind; did she not know my impostor for what she was?

Applause rose like thunder while Eka stood in the center of the stage, looking as regal as ever. Only when she lifted a hand did the room begin to quiet.

"My dear family." The shape of the theater amplified her voice, and the polished stone made her words echo in just the right places to allow everyone to hear. She gazed out over the crowd, covering every row, every balcony, so that no one would feel left out of her love. "My dear family," she said again, "this evening we have a visitor we all admire, Mira Minkoba, the Hopebearer, the Dragonhearted."

A rush of whispers filled the room: *"Dragonhearted?"*

Eka waited for them, ever patient, and when she could be heard again, she told Elbena's version of what had happened on the docks in the Shadowed City. The way she spoke, I'd bravely put myself between a raging dragon and hundreds of terrified people. I'd lifted my hand and ordered the dragon to halt, and she had. And then I'd gone person to person to help them to their feet and offer a calming word to all.

"Dragons are the children of the gods," Eka said. "We say this, and yet we forget they are fearsome creatures until something like this happens. Or something like the accident from our own sanctuary. We forget that though we are meant to protect the children of the gods, they *are* the children of the gods and they are more powerful than we can understand."

With all the light focused on the stage, it was hard to see the darkened audience. But I caught hints of nodding.

"Calling Mira the Dragonhearted is no light thing." Eka held up her palms as though pleading for her people to understand. "The Dragonhearted must face what we cannot. She must know the children of the gods. She must be incorruptible."

"Seven Fallen Gods." The darkness trapped my whispered curse in the lighting room with only Hristo here to hear it. She was turning me into a legend to convince the audience of the veracity of whatever Tirta was about to say.

"We are beyond happy to welcome her here tonight!"

If the applause before had been a thunder, this was the roar of the ocean crashing against cliffs. This was a shattering of sound as thousands of people poured out their approval.

Mirrors shifted the noorestone light to the ceiling as Eka Delro left the stage, and in the shadows on the stage, another figure moved into the center.

Tirta.

The Luminary Council had said they could replace me—elevate another pretty face—and here she was. Not by declaring another girl special, but turning her into me. She stood before all of us now, waiting between the outstretched hands of Damyan and Darina.

Light moved again. At the back corner of the stage, I could see the shape of Elbena, the Luminary Councilor who'd accompanied me on state visits throughout my life. She'd been a comfort. A friend. A confidant.

I touched the scar on my cheek.

Elbena was a thief. A liar. A traitor. Here, she stood with an impostor.

Tirta wore a long red gown seeded with gemstones that flashed under the bright glow, and her hair had been pressed into loose curls, pulled back with glittering pins. From this far away, she *looked* the part of the Hopebearer. The Dragonhearted. The gown, reminiscent of the red dress I'd worn in the Shadowed City, moved like dragon scales over her slim form.

The applause went on and on. People cheered. Some cried out that they loved her.

Fury pounded through my temples.

In the Pit, when Tirta had befriended me, I'd thought she resembled my sister. It was in her posture. Her delicate features. I hadn't considered that she might have been *studying* me.

She'd come to help me in the end, however, and suggested she wanted to sneak me to safety without the Luminary Guards' knowledge. I'd turned her down.

Now, on the stage, Tirta gazed from one side of the audience to the other. Even from here, I could see the sharp lines of her jaw, the broad strokes of black and gold shading that extended from her eyes to her temple, and the delicate point of her nose.

Hristo touched my arm, his expression dark with worry. "Someone's coming up the stairs."

He was right. The angry *thump thump* of climbing footfalls came toward us.

"The manager?" Twenty-five mirrors and twenty-five covers weren't moving themselves, after all.

The lighting room door flew open, and the manager stood in the doorway, a furious expression darkening her face. "What are you *doing*? Don't you know how to do your job?"

"No."

She glared at me, incredulous. "You're a humiliation. An embarrassment. I want you out of the theater immediately. No pay. I never want to see you again."

Hristo looked to me for instruction.

"We can go." I'd come to look. I'd stayed to see if my parents were here, but if they had come to Val fa Merce with Tirta, they would have been next to Elbena.

Before I could move toward the door, though, Tirta's voice carried across the theater.

"Thank you for having me here tonight." Tirta smiled widely as the crowd finally quieted enough for her to speak. "Seventeen years ago, the Mira Treaty took a stance against discrimination, and against the pillaging of our islands. The treaty states that to truly honor the Fallen Gods, all islands must be equal and independent. Anything less is immoral. Unethical. This truth is indisputable."

Chills ran through me.

I knew those words. I'd spoken them in Bopha two decans ago. But I'd refused to say what came next—that Bophans belonged on Bopha and Hartans belonged on Harta, and that a decree forcing the deportation of hundreds—thousands—of Hartans should be supported.

Chenda had been imprisoned for refusing to encourage that doctrine. I'd been cut across the face.

And here was Tirta, ready to tell a theater full of Hartans that their place was here—that they could not belong anywhere else. She would tell them that hundreds of

Hartans living on Bopha would be sent here, ripped from the land where they'd built lives.

Where did this end? The treaty said equality and freedom, but what if this was only the beginning of the other Isles chipping away at the promises they'd made?

It wouldn't be the first time our governments had betrayed the founding principles of the Mira Treaty.

My heart beat with renewed rage.

Seven hundred noorestones pulsed in response.

Tirta paused in the middle of her line—*"We must show our gratitude by staying loyal to our gods, and to our islands."*—and looked around.

"I told you"—the manager grabbed my arm, her sharp nails scratching me—"you need to leave."

Hristo shoved the manager backward. "Don't touch her!" His voice was deep and dangerous.

Below, Tirta was still going: *"To that end, it is my belief that Bophans belong on Bopha, Hartans belong on Harta—"*

Noorestones pulsed again, faster. How *dare* Tirta speak those words?

"What *are* you?" The manager's face went ashen.

It happened too quickly: she tried to grab me; Hristo tried to intervene; their combined momentum caused me to stumble backward—over the ledge of noorestones.

I fell.

CHAPTER TWENTY

FALLING FELT LIKE FLYING.

I tumbled through the empty expanse between the upper balcony and the main floor, with noorestone fire blazing into my body. Gasps, screams, cries for help: those were inconsequential sounds, buried beneath the heady rush of light and power.

Echoes of misplaced memories cut through me like shrapnel. Something huge, something my soul yearned for but could no longer reach, called to me like a half-forgotten dream that beat with an inferno heart.

I wanted it back. I wanted a thousand stars dripping between my fingers like burning jewels.

Suddenly, I wasn't falling.

I landed on my feet, miraculously unhurt as I stepped off the theater seat hastily evacuated by a young man. He and the others nearby scrambled away, shielding their eyes as though they couldn't bear to look at me.

Maybe they couldn't. When I lifted my gaze, hundreds of threads of cool, blue light bent toward me, surrounding me in a brilliant radiance that must have been terrifying. As though I were a great spider in the center of a web. Or a star with glorious rays of light, but these did not extend from me.

No.

They fed me.

Never had I felt such strength, like noorestone fire flooded my veins and seared through every cell. Like I was vengeance and flame incarnate.

Someone was screaming—maybe lots of someones—but I turned my attention to the impostor and her maker. Everyone else was irrelevant.

My steps were lightning strikes across the theater floor. I ripped chairs from my path with hardly a thought. The people—they just ran. And still, with every breath, with every beat of my inferno heart, more power poured into me. Every noorestone in the theater obeyed my fury.

Tirta stood motionless on the stage, staring, even as Elbena grabbed her arm and shouted something lost in the chaos my descent had caused.

I kept going.

Seven steps.

Eight.

Nine.

Ten.

I was patient. Deliberate. Because behind me, twin tracks of molten marble shone deep and angry red where my wings dragged. The acrid reek of melting stone lifted like a threat.

Fourteen.

Fifteen.

Sixteen.

On the stage, Tirta turned and fled with Elbena, moving swiftly toward the curtains as though they could escape.

No. There *was* no escape. Enraged, I scooped silken ripples of illumination and hurled them at her.

Flame exploded onto the curtains, burning the heavy fabric within seconds. But Tirta and Elbena were gone. I dropped back my head and roared, fury swelling through me. Fire flickered over my skin like scales. My wings extended, setting pieces of the theater ablaze.

I was a dragon and I would burn her.

I would burn every one of my enemies.

Outshine stars.

Swallow galaxies.

I became infinite.

And then—

I staggered, suddenly heavy. Suddenly weighed down by the light of hundreds of noorestones and the things I had just done. I'd tried to *kill* someone.

This wasn't me.

"Stop," I whispered, but the light would not listen. I'd

taken so much, pulling in more and more, believing my appetite was insatiable, and now it controlled me.

The rush of power, which had felt so *good* before, suddenly made me sick. It felt greedy. Gluttonous. My body begged for relief, and I dropped to my knees, struggling to breathe. But it wouldn't stop. Wouldn't relent. I bent over, fingernails digging at the polished floor, and gagged.

This wasn't the same as overeating, though. This was bigger. This was raw energy pouring into me, filling me so full I would burst if I couldn't stop it. Already I could feel it splitting the very seams of my soul.

I wouldn't be able to contain it.

Even when I shut my eyes, intense light squeezed in—too bright.

My skin itched as the light began to shred it apart. Everything inside me was burning up: my tongue, my eyes, my spirit.

Seven hundred noorestones.

Seven hundred.

It was too much too fast too soon.

A scream tore from my throat, and in the farthest reaches of my mind, I recalled the Pit after I'd channeled the power of just thirty-four noorestones:

1. *A valley of black ash around me.*
2. *Cell doors flung wide and broken.*
3. *Powdered noorestone dust floating through the cellblock.*

If I couldn't bite this down—if I couldn't *stop* the fire rushing into me—this would be nothing like the Pit. It would be worse. Complete devastation. A crater where the theater used to be. Maybe the whole block.

Maybe the whole city.

Screams built on screams. Thunder shook the building—or I did—and the evacuation became a stampede. There was no way to get more than seven thousand people safely out of the theater. Not quickly. I had to contain it or they'd all die.

"Give me peace," I prayed. "Give me grace."

The power ebbed.

"Give me peace." I thought the words would have come as a choked sob, but they were bigger. Louder. Deadlier. "Give me grace."

Darina and Damyan were so far away, though. Could they help with such a vast distance between us?

"Give me peace." My voice was a cataclysm, full and huge and heavy. "Give me grace."

My body was ready to burst, but the flow of energy was easing.

"Give me peace," I whispered, if I could even whisper anymore. The theater shuddered in response. "Give me grace."

The world was crumbling apart and I was the hand crushing it.

But the noorestones no longer fed me. The tethers of light were motionless. Waiting.

I breathed. One. Two. Three. Four.

Maybe it was over. Maybe I was safe.

Maybe *everyone* was safe.

Hristo was back there, up the stairs, in the lighting room. Was *he* safe? What had he seen me do? What had I looked like to him?

Just as I pulled myself up to my feet, everything reversed: like blood siphoned from a cut, the energy flew out of me, through the tethers connecting me to the noorestones. Draining. Empty. Destroying.

I dropped to the floor again, screaming as it was all sucked out—or I pushed it out. I couldn't tell anymore. This wasn't me; it was the magic.

::**Give me peace.**:: I pounded the prayer against the floor.

Darkness blanketed the theater.

::**Give me grace.**:: My plea was thunder.

Quiet followed.

::**Give me enough love in my heart.**::

A cool breeze touched my face, followed by someone else's quiet code: ::**Cela, cela.**::

I opened my eyes to find Aaru kneeling before me, worry written across his face. His mouth made the shape of my name, curled at the end with a question.

"I fell." The words stuttered out as I gazed around the theater. It wasn't all dark or all quiet. Just hushed. Dim. The tethers of light still strung me to the noorestones, but rather than expelling all the energy at once, the flow was a trickle.

Aaru helped me sit, and then he cupped my face

275

between his hands. When our eyes met, his were dark and deep and filled with sadness. His fingers curled against my cheeks. ::Are you hurt?::

"No." My whole body began to tremble. "I thought I was going to hurt everyone else."

::But you didn't.::

"Because you stopped it."

He shook his head. ::You stopped it.::

I wanted to slump to the floor and rest, now that the magic was moving back to the noorestones, but I didn't dare. If I closed my eyes, I would sleep for a decan. "Where's Hristo? Is he safe?"

Aaru nodded.

"Did the others come with you?"

::No.:: We sat together for one hundred heartbeats. Two hundred. Then, the quiet began to ease and the light returned, and finally I realized that everything was back to normal. I was a girl again. No scales. No wings. No fanciful delusions that I was something more.

Just a girl.

Aaru's fingertips slid down my neck and shoulders and arms until he took my hands. He stood, then drew me up with him. ::Let's go.::

PART THREE

FOLLOW THE LIGHT

CHAPTER TWENTY-ONE

AARU, HRISTO, AND I FLED THE THEATER WITH THE last of the evacuees.

We just blended in, rushing along with the rest of the people trying to escape my fury, and they had no idea I was the one who'd almost destroyed them, because they hadn't been able to see through the corona of light surrounding me. And when I stumbled, someone took my arm and kept me on my feet. Another person asked if we needed help.

Guilt turned over in me as Hristo and Aaru guided me through the stormy streets. We had to keep to the edges of the crowd to avoid the police pulling people aside for questions, but there were so many others doing the same thing; no one noticed us. When we reached the Red Wine

Inn, I went straight to the washroom and shut the door behind me.

Thunder growled and shook the building.

In the other room, I could hear Hristo as he told the others about Tirta, our attempt to see her, and how I ended up on the main floor and wreathed in fire.

Rain beat against the building, loud enough to drown his words and confuse my mind with irrelevant numbers, but as I sat in the far corner of the washroom floor, I could still hear everything.

"I thought she was going to die," he said. "Falling like that. I thought I was about to see her neck break and that would be the end."

"The end of what?" Gerel's voice darkened.

"The end of everything." Hristo sighed. "She was already glowing when she fell. The noorestone magic was already in her. That's probably why she landed on her feet. That power is what saved her. But then it kept growing until she was too bright to look at. Still, I swear, I saw—"

"What?" That was Chenda.

"Wings?"

Easily, I could imagine Hristo closing his eyes as he tried to sort out the real from the imaginary. As he fought to recall each detail and judge it for accuracy.

"It looked like she had wings made of light," he said. "The floor turned liquid behind her."

"Seven gods."

"What do we do?" Ilina asked. "Can we help her?"

"I don't know."

"What if she gets worse?"

"Remember in the Pit."

"I thought she was going to die in the Pit."

"Me too."

"And then the tunnel."

"That was too close."

"And it was nothing compared to this."

"She should never have rushed in there."

"What's done is done."

"It was impulsive. Dangerous. What if she'd been caught?"

Quiet.

"This was a mistake. All of this."

"Chenda—"

"No. Listen. This mess could have been avoided if you'd listened to me from the start. . . ."

My heart squeezed as the argument escalated, and after a while I didn't even pay attention to who said what. I just pulled my knees to my chest, shivering in my wet clothes, listening to my friends worry about me, about this power, and whether I would accidentally use it to destroy us all.

"Give me peace," I whispered. "Give me grace."

But if Damyan or Darina heard, they refused to give me either.

A MINUTE OR an hour later, the door creaked open and silence walked in.

He'd changed into dry clothes, and he carried a second

pile, which he placed on the counter, and then he stood there. Watching me.

I tucked my face back into the space between my knees and my chest.

Without a sound, he picked up a towel and draped it over my shoulders. ::Dry.::

How could I move, though? How could I do anything but curl myself into a tight ball of misery? I'd endangered my friends so many times. They'd lost so much because of me. And now they were *afraid* of me.

They had every right, too. I'd thought I controlled this power, once it had bent to my will in the tunnel, but when I'd tried to push the overwhelming power away from me—back into the noorestones where it belonged—that had almost caused even *more* damage.

::You must dry.::

I didn't want to move. Even breathing took effort, and the beat of my heart. But if I just sat here, limp and useless, I'd become even more of a burden to my friends.

My limbs felt awkward and heavy, weighed down by water and guilt, but after a moment of fumbling I managed to draw the towel around me and scrub my face, one slow push and pull at a time.

It was too much. I tried to slump over again, but Aaru pressed the towel into my hands again. ::You must.::

I couldn't.

::They don't mean to hurt you.::

I dropped my face into the towel to hide a sob. How

282

could I make him understand that *they* weren't hurting me? Their words of caution and fear didn't hurt me. They weren't betraying me. No, it was I who would betray them.

With my power.

With my name.

With my quest.

I was the problem and I was dragging all of them with me, hurting each of them in terrible ways. Even my dragon hadn't escaped the pain I caused.

But I couldn't scrape up the energy to speak aloud, or the coordination to use the quiet code, and now Aaru would go on believing my hurt feelings were the cause of this inability to even dry off.

He sighed and pried the towel from my fingers. Carefully, he used it to squeeze water out of my braids, then patted the cloth down my back and arms and feet— wherever he could reach. Then he took the folded clothes off the counter and offered them to me. ::**Need to change.**::

I didn't want to. I didn't even want to lift my head. But I couldn't take the risk of him deciding to change my clothes for me. He'd be so embarrassed. Maybe I would be, too, with my skin all prickled with the damp and cold.

So I pulled myself up, bones creaking as I moved, and peeled off my shirt.

Aaru averted his gaze, even as he pulled my towel around to make sure I dried my skin.

My movements were sluggish, but after a moment I managed to pat myself dry, then pull on the fresh shirt he'd brought. We repeated the process with trousers, and he moved away only when I was fully dressed. The wet clothes went into the tub. The towel went over the rim. And he sat next to me.

::Do you want to go out there?::

I shook my head.

::Why?::

How could I explain what I'd become?

He took my hands between his, letting the heat of his body move into mine. Then, he squeezed and tapped on my knuckles. ::Heard your conversation with Ilina on the ship.::

I looked at him.

::When she told you stumbling means you aren't standing still.:: He glanced toward the door, thoughtfulness written across his face. ::This was a stumble, but you will move forward again.::

This had been a *big* stumble, and over something I'd thought was mine to control.

::*The Book of Silence* says progress is a labyrinth. There are obstacles, turns, and sometimes it seems you move opposite the direction you want to go. But the path always takes you home in the end.:: He squeezed my hands. ::Will go to Damina with you.::

My heart caught.

Our eyes met.

"Why?" My voice cracked with chill.

One. Two. Three. I counted breaths of waiting between

us. While he looked at me. While I looked at him. While his heavy eyebrows moved inward. ::If you don't want me to go—::

I leaned toward him. "I want you to come with me." I hadn't meant for my question to sound like anything else. "Why did you change your mind?"

He dropped his gaze to our clasped hands, and for an instant I hoped that meant he wanted to be with me more than he wanted to leave. But that was not our story. That wasn't the way things worked between us.

::I still want to go home. I need to help family. But I need to help you, too.::

Because of what I'd done tonight.

::You saved me from the Pit. Without you, I wouldn't be able to go home ever.::

Oh.

"We'll have to tell Captain Pentoba to cancel any agreement she made to get you to Idris."

::Already did.:: He smiled.

Hesitantly, expecting him to slip away like a cat not wanting to be petted, I leaned my head on his shoulder. When he didn't move, I closed my eyes and counted the heartbeats he let me stay there.

Ninety-three, ninety-four, ninety-five . . .

He didn't displace me.

"Are you afraid of me?" I whispered.

::No.::

"But what I did earlier—I could have killed everyone."

285

He turned his head, breath rustling loose strands of my hair. ::But you didn't.::

"Because you came."

::No. I saw you move the energy back. Hristo said he saw wings. I saw, too.:: Haltingly, awkwardly, he put his arm around my waist and pulled me closer. The side of my body touched his. ::Saw you stagger. Saw you push the magic away. That was you.::

But he'd helped. By muting everything, he'd helped me release the power at a safe rate. "Thank you," I whispered. "For helping."

His hand on my waist tightened, and his thumb rubbed toward my ribs.

I wanted to relish in this closeness, to savor and feel every place we touched and for how long, but despair smothered everything good. It was a fog, making thoughts flat. Suffocating emotions. Dampening the thrill of being held by the boy I'd admired for so long.

"You're getting better at your gift."

::Said I would practice.::

I had said the same thing, but somewhere between then and now, I'd decided I knew enough. Clearly I didn't. "Can I practice with you?"

He nodded. ::Tomorrow.::

"How did you know?"

He drummed his fingers against my knuckles, the quiet-code equivalent of *hmm?*

"How did you know I needed you?" My face warmed;

I'd meant I'd needed his help.

Aaru's shoulder moved up and down with a sigh. His hands both tightened. And then he pulled away to look at me fully. His night-black eyes studied my face down to my throat, and cautiously he pressed the tips of his fingers against my racing heart. ::Heard you. The noorestones.:: He bit his lower lip. ::Felt you.::

I couldn't speak.

::Started to leave, but Ilina came back with dragons. Stayed to hear what she said, then . . .:: He fluttered his fingers away as if to indicate his departure.

"Thank you," I whispered. "For coming to get me."

He glanced downward, toward my mouth, and for a heartbeat I thought he might lean forward. I thought he might touch his lips to mine, even for just a breath.

Instead, he nodded toward the door. ::Ready to go out?::

If the others were still talking about me, I couldn't hear it. Only when I thought about it did I realize there was a bubble of silence around Aaru, preventing us from hearing anything in the other room, but also keeping our conversation private.

"I don't want to go anywhere right now."

I didn't want to stand. To walk. To make an effort to be anything more than a puddle of numb emotion.

::Want me to stay?::

Yes. Yes, I wanted him to stay here with me, even though *here* was the washroom floor and normally that

287

would disgust me beyond measure. Just . . . I couldn't bring myself to care at the moment.

"We can't stay. Neither of us." The mind fog was hard to think through, but a piece of me realized that remaining here would be dangerous. "The girl pretending to be me—it's Tirta. From the Pit."

Aaru scowled and squeezed my hand. ::Did she see you?::

"Not my face, but she saw what I did. And she's seen me affect noorestones before. Not to this level, but she'll figure it out if she hasn't already."

Which meant she knew I was here, and she'd tell Elbena, and they would send the Luminary Guards to search every part of the city. We weren't safe here.

Aaru understood all the words I'd left unsaid. Of course he did. He climbed to his feet and offered a hand.

I took it and let him pull me up.

I followed Aaru into the bedroom.

"We have to leave now."

CHAPTER TWENTY-TWO

Within the hour, we'd left the Red Wine Inn in pairs. Ilina and me. Hristo and Aaru. Gerel and Chenda.

We didn't have much to carry, save our dragons (in their basket), our new clothes, and our forged residency papers, so it didn't look strange for us to leave the inn without telling the owners we were finished with the room; they'd find out in the morning.

Outside, rain pounded on the streets, but we made it back to the port without trouble.

"Look there." Gerel paused and pointed toward a nearby pier.

I squinted through the haze of rain and glowing noore-stones, but I didn't see whatever she was looking at.

"It's the ship," she said. "The black one we saw the other day."

A dark scowl passed over Chenda's face. "The more I consider it, the more I am persuaded the ship belongs to the empire. In all my time as the Dawn Lady, I've never seen a ship like that. Never heard of one."

"Did the Twilight Senate tell you everything, then?" Ilina asked.

Chenda shot her a glare. "More than the Luminary Council told Mira, it seems. I was an actual part of the government, my voice heard and considered, not a puppet with a convenient face."

My heart shattered to a stop.

"You're wrong." Ilina's voice was low and dangerous. "And you'd do well to never say anything like that again."

"Why?" Chenda quirked an eyebrow. "Does it hurt your feelings to hear that? Or does it hurt Mira's feelings? If she wants to say so, she can."

Gerel, Hristo, and Aaru had been quietly looking between Ilina and Chenda. Now, they all looked at me.

"I—" I glanced at the black ship once more. "I'd like to get out of the rain." Without waiting for the others, I turned on my heel and marched down the pier, hunching my shoulders against the cold onslaught from the sky.

Confrontation made my head spin. There had to be a way to ease the tension between Chenda and Ilina. But how could I placate Chenda without also upsetting Ilina? And did I need to apologize to the others for what they'd witnessed? I hadn't actually been part of the argument, except that Chenda had brought my name into it.

290

I climbed up the gangplank, sharply aware of the crackling anger behind me, both Chenda and Ilina biting their tongues. When I glanced over my shoulder, Gerel and Hristo were walking between them, with Aaru in the back.

Teres was watching the gangplank again. If she was surprised to see us in the middle of the night, she didn't show it. She just sent us to Captain Pentoba's office, where Hristo explained the situation, and shortly we were deposited in a small cabin belowdecks. It was the same one I'd shared with Elbena when they'd transported me from Khulan to Bopha, with one small porthole and three small noorestones in lidded sconces.

There'd been two beds before—an upper bunk and a lower bunk—and a large trunk for our belongings. Now, two hammocks were strung over the trunk, and a third between the door and the porthole. They were slightly crooked, but they were clean and had folded blankets in them.

Two beds and three hammocks.

Six people.

"It's not ideal," said the captain.

She wasn't wrong.

"Someone will either have to share or sleep in shifts. I can't do better than this." She glared at each of us in turn. "I could make the crew double up or trade off, but that doesn't seem fair when all of them are working and none of you are."

291

Chenda and Gerel glanced at each other, and then Gerel said, "We'll take the top bunk. Hristo, you take the bottom. I can only imagine you wrestling with a hammock while your arm is bound like that. The rest of you can figure it out."

Aaru pulled out his pad of paper, wrapped in a strip of waterproofed linen. *Will work*, he wrote, and showed it to the captain.

"Very well. Once we're away from the port and any prying eyes to see you on deck, I'll send One down with orders for anyone who wants to be useful." Captain Pentoba started down the corridor, but Gerel stopped her.

"How long has that black ship been docked?" she asked.

"Came in yesterday morning." The captain crossed her arms and tilted her head in thought. "No name painted on her, at least that anyone mentioned. No crew that I could see."

"That's unusual." Hristo shifted his weight toward me.

"It is." The captain glanced at him. "One young man stepped off first thing, but I didn't notice anyone else."

A shiver wove through me. "What did he look like?"

"Normal, I suppose." The captain shrugged and turned away—back to work. "Young, like I said, but I didn't get a good look at him. Now, get some rest, all of you. Since you're back early, we can be off within the hour."

There was no privacy in the small cabin, but there was a washroom down the passageway, just on the other side of the medic's office. Two at a time, we took care of our business and hung our clothes in the washroom, and for about five minutes I hoped we might avoid rekindling the argument from earlier.

When Ilina and I returned to our cabin, she tucked all our bags into one side of the trunk, and in the other side, she made a nest for the dragons. Not that the dragons wanted to be in it. As soon as she opened the basket, LaLa stretched toward me, flapping her good wing pitifully.

I scooped her up and cradled her in my arms, then sat on the closed trunk next to Ilina. She, too, had given in to Crystal's demands for affection.

Guilt wormed itself inside of me. Even now, while we were here safe on the *Chance Encounter*, the ten dragons were being removed from the sanctuary. Drugged to sleep as they were rolled through the gates.

And I hadn't been able to save them.

Then the door creaked open. Gerel and Chenda returned from the washroom, and the boys left for their turn. And that was it.

Chenda cleared her throat. Looked at Ilina askance. Heaved a put-upon sigh.

The silence between them was oppressive, filled with gritted teeth and caught breaths, as though they had just narrowly avoided speaking their minds.

The angry silence between Chenda and Ilina was too much. I broke it.

"Chenda," I started, but my voice caught. I tried again. "You know what happened in the dragon sanctuary today?"

She and Gerel had been leaning against the outer wall, still in damp clothes. Chenda looked up from her whispered conversation with Gerel and frowned. "Yes, I know what happened. And I know what happened in the theater after." She shook her head. "Really, Mira. Running in headfirst didn't go well for you, did it?" Her mouth thinned into a line. "For your sake, I wish you'd just listened to me from the beginning."

My heart thudded in my ears, impossibly loud. She'd told me. She'd told me and I hadn't listened. Now, she had every right to rub that in my face. "You're right. We should have made plans to go to Crescent Prominence and speak to my parents. But I'm ready to go there now."

Ilina glared at me.

Chenda raised an eyebrow. "Why?"

"To talk to them about the Mira Treaty?" Wasn't that what she'd wanted in the first place?

"We don't need their confirmation anymore. The black ship is proof enough of the empire's control of the Fallen Isles." Chenda gazed around the cramped cabin, eyes widening with a sudden thought. "In fact, our enemies are within reach. The empire. The false Mira. Likely Altan, as he will come as soon as he hears what happened in the theater. We shouldn't leave Harta yet. We need to take this opportunity."

"To do what?" Ilina asked.

"To make people listen. We have so few assets, but right here is the real Hopebearer. We can make people hear the truth."

"We can't stop them from hearing the wrong Hopebearer," Gerel said, "unless we do something Hartans wouldn't approve of doing."

My heart knotted up. "Kill her?" I breathed, horror filling the words. No matter that I'd nearly done that myself.

Gerel scoffed. "No. What's wrong with you?"

"You said something Hartans wouldn't approve of."

"I meant kidnapping." Gerel snorted softly. "But we'd have to find her. And then we'd have to be able to keep her safe. And feed her. Honestly, it sounds like a lot of effort."

Ilina made a noise of agreement. "At the very least, she will distract Altan while we go to Damina."

That didn't bring me as much comfort as it should have. I turned to Chenda. "How do you propose we take all this as an opportunity?"

She didn't hesitate. "We should recruit Altan."

"What?" LaLa squawked as I lurched to my feet. "Why would we ally ourselves with Altan?"

"You know what Altan is." Ilina stood, too; Crystal flew up to one of the posts holding up a hammock. "You know what he's done to people in this room."

Just then, the door groaned open and Aaru and Hristo stood there, their expressions dark enough to show they'd both heard Chenda's suggestion.

"What about going to Damina?" I asked.

"We don't need to see your parents anymore," Chenda said. "We know they've betrayed us. Like I said, the ship is proof enough."

"That was Mira's point from the beginning," Ilina said, "but you still wanted to go to Crescent Prominence even though it could get Mira killed." Her voice shook.

Chenda shook her head. "Mira didn't want to go to Crescent Prominence because she was afraid of the truth. She was afraid of what she might learn about her parents. Now she wants to go because she's more afraid of her own power and what she can do with it. That's why she agreed now—"

"No, she said she'd go *before* everything happened in the theater." Ilina's face was dark with anger. "But you weren't there. You don't know."

"I know plenty." Chenda stalked forward, her shoulders thrown back with pride. "You think that because I'm new to your little group that I can't possibly see things clearly. But I do. I see that Mira is afraid and everything she does is a reaction to her fear."

"Her refusal to give the speech in Bopha was incredibly brave. The way she ran to save Lex was brave. Her saving us in the tunnel was brave, too."

My throat and face got hotter the more things Ilina listed.

"And yet," Chenda said, "those were fear and reactions, too."

"They were *selfless*," Ilina said.

Chenda shrugged. "Maybe so, but none of those events were carefully executed plans. And"—she held up a hand—"I am not willing to debate every single one of Mira's actions with you."

"How is recruiting Altan to our side going to help?" Somehow, Gerel kept her tone carefully neutral.

"We wouldn't be recruiting him to our side," Chenda said. "That isn't possible. But Altan wants to help dragons. You all want to help dragons. And Altan wants to protect the Fallen Isles from the empire. We all want that, too. The best way to do that is have an army, and Altan has an army. He cannot be our friend, but he can be our ally."

My hands trembled with anger. "He's *Altan*. He *tortured* us." I glanced at Aaru, meeting his dark eyes for only a breath.

"Then what would you propose?" Chenda asked.

"Go see my parents, like you said before—"

"The situation has changed," Chenda said. "We already have all the information they could give us. No, we must recruit aid where we can and prepare to fight the empire. That means the warriors. That means the dishonored. That means anyone who wants to resist the empire's control and the betrayal of our governments. And if you aren't willing to take risks to save the Fallen Isles, you aren't the Hopebearer after all."

Rain beat against the hull of the ship. Quiet stretched between the six of us.

Hristo looked between Chenda, Ilina, and me, as though wondering whether he should step in. But he was meant to protect me from physical threats, not people I'd thought were friends. Not lists of my inadequacies.

"We need to go after the Algotti Empire," Chenda said, her voice softer.

"We should learn about them first," I said. "Maybe my parents know—"

"They don't." Chenda sighed.

"How do you know?" Ilina asked. "They have connections—"

"Have they *ever* told you anything?" Chenda asked. "Has the Luminary Council ever given you anything other than speeches to recite and a scar on your face?"

I stepped back, heels hitting the trunk, and covered my left cheek.

"That was uncalled-for," Ilina started.

Chenda shook her head. "And you. You need to stop fighting Mira's battles for her." She sucked in a deep breath. "Go to Damina if you want," she said after a moment. "But I will not seek help from the very people who betrayed us—"

"You're allying with *Altan*," I said.

"A monster, yes. But a useful monster." She squeezed between Ilina and me and heaved open the trunk.

"What are you doing?" I asked.

"Whatever is necessary." She found her bag and slipped it over her shoulders. "First, I'm going to look at the black ship. If the man Captain Pentoba saw is really from the empire, then I want to have a chat with him. Gerel? Are you coming?"

The cabin went silent. Three heartbeats. Four. Five.

Gerel looked from Ilina to me, her eyebrows drawn inward with thought. Then: "Of course."

"Good." Chenda grabbed Gerel's bag and slung it toward her.

"Aren't you coming back?" My chest squeezed.

"Not tonight." Chenda strode toward the door, and both boys stepped aside. "The captain said the *Chance Encounter* is leaving within the hour, and if you're intent on going to Damina to see your parents, then I don't want to hold you up. Maybe we'll meet you there in a few days."

Maybe. No guarantees.

Gerel caught my eye as she followed. "Good luck, Fancy."

No promise to try to calm Chenda down, or make her see reason about Altan. No reassurance that the six of us were stronger together.

They were gone.

And I didn't go after them.

DARKNESS WASHED OVER our cabin. The only light came from the porthole, pushed open just enough to let a light breeze whisper through. Rain pounded on the ship's hull, tapping against the glass. Waves crested and crashed below; sometimes they were strong enough that a faint mist of seawater sprayed inside. But no one closed the porthole all the way.

I'd been awake for an hour, running every word of the argument through my head again. Every tone. Every gesture. Not even LaLa—who was sleeping on my chest and meeping softly—could calm the punishing spiral of thoughts. I should have said we'd look at the black ship with them. I should have compromised.

But how could I agree to working with Altan? He was an irredeemable monster who hurt people because it made him feel powerful.

Ilina's voice came from the hammock below mine. "I'm sorry, Mira."

"It's not your fault."

"That's debatable, but nice of you to say anyway."

Lightning flared, illuminating the porthole. A heartbeat later, thunder clapped and the ship shuddered under the assault of sound. LaLa growled in her sleep, readjusting so her good wing covered her head completely.

From the hammock next to mine, Aaru watched her with an amused expression. When he offered a hand to me, I took it. ::How do you feel?::

::Not good.:: I wished I had something better to tell him, but that was the truth. My body still felt heavy and weak from everything that happened in the theater, and now my heart hurt from the fight with Chenda. ::Walk helped. A little.::

300

He nodded. ::When One comes in the morning, tell him you will clean.::

::All right.:: Scrubbing the ship from bow to stern was the last thing I wanted to do, but if the walk had helped, maybe cleaning would, too.

::We will practice with a noorestone, too.::

::Are you sure?:: Given what happened today, practicing tomorrow seemed like a terrible and dangerous idea. Especially since we were on a ship; there was nowhere to escape to if something went wrong.

He nodded. ::One noorestone. Not seven hundred. I will silence if you need.::

::Thank you.::

::Allies help each other.:: He paused, his eyes searching mine in the darkness. ::Friends do too.::

As if helping me learn to use this power was the only thing I was thanking him for. As if he hadn't been my strength through silence these last six decans. ::I wish I could help you like you help me.::

He brushed his thumb over my knuckles, the softest caress, and the sweetest of imaginary kisses. ::You do.::

LATER, I DREAMED of flying.

Of great wings and burning stars.

Of fire and screams.

Of power untold.

AARU

Two Years Ago

THINGS WERE GETTING BETTER. MORE STABLE.

I'd found a job. Not one I liked, but it paid seven chips a decan. For five days, I collected trash off the streets and took it to a sorting point; the other five days, I collected manure from fields and took it to become fertilizer.

Mother said Idris was finished sending her children, so that left us with me, Korinah, Alya, Hafeez, Danyal, and Essa—and Safa, and as far as I knew, there'd been no more bubbles of silence; she was safe. She made our family complete.

Things were better. At least, I thought they were.

"KORINAH NEEDS TO get married."

Father's voice was muffled through his bedroom door.

I'd just gotten home from work—streets today—and was about to change clothes, but those words stopped me by their door. I held myself perfectly still, and silent.

"She's thirteen." Mother said it not like a plea, but a fact.

"I know. It wouldn't be right away, but we need to start making arrangements."

A note of tension edged Mother's voice. "We can't afford a dowry."

"Still, you should begin looking for a strong match. With Aaru's income, we might be able to afford the dowry by the time she's fifteen."

Silence.

I imagined there was tapping—pieces of the conversation I couldn't hear.

"Why not Aaru? He's oldest."

I hated that Mother would give me up so easily, but she was right. I was oldest, and I'd do anything necessary to care for my family.

"We need his income. He won't be able to take a wealthy wife—not with his job—and any dowry her family might be able to pay would be minuscule. It wouldn't make up for the lost income." Father was, of course, practical.

"If only the Silent Brothers had taken him," Mother sighed.

The man who'd come when I was four had returned a few years ago, this time to test Danyal. But he'd left by himself again, which meant the Silent Brothers didn't send

Father seventy-five chips a decan, and my family couldn't do without my income.

"It's marriage for Korinah," Father said, "or Safa needs to return to Nazil. There isn't enough money coming in to feed and clothe all the people in this house."

"You know how Nazil treats Safa."

"I know." He sounded genuinely sad.

If they talked more, it was in quiet code. But I knew what I had to do.

WHEN I WENT to work the next morning, I asked my overseer to double my shifts.

Korinah's arrangements were not spoken of again, and Safa was not sent away.

CHAPTER TWENTY-THREE

THREE DAYS IN NUMBERS:

1. *Three mornings of honey-drizzled biscuits and hot tea for breakfast.*
2. *Twelve (total) hours of scrubbing various parts of the ship: rails and masts and decks and cabins.*
3. *Twenty instances of crewmen hollering for me to get out of their way. (All on day one. After that, I learned better.)*
4. *One three-hour-long discussion in our cabin about our plans and goals in Crescent Prominence, and what we might do after.*
5. *Four hours of learning how to tie seven kinds of knots, as well as their usages. (I wasn't*

clear on why I had to learn this, but Captain
Pentoba said it was imperative.)

6. *Exercise sessions . . . without Gerel. Still,*
   I knew what she would tell me to do: one
   hundred and fifty push-ups, eleven failed
   attempts at handstands, three hundred
   squats, and five different kinds of stretches.
   I performed these every morning and every
   night, with my friends' encouragement and
   my own internal argument with an absent
   ex-warrior.

7. *Two evenings in our cabin with Aaru and*
   me teaching Ilina and Hristo the quiet code.
   Determined to stay with our group and help,
   he thought it might be wise to be able to
   communicate secretly and beyond a notepad
   and pencil.

8. *Six hours alone in a cargo hold with Aaru,*
   at the very bottom of the ship. Just us and a
   single noorestone sitting between our folded
   legs. Just the stillness of our solitude. Just the
   glow of light on his face, his hands resting on
   his knees, and the careful way he sometimes
   touched my fingers for the quiet code—as
   though I couldn't read it just as easily as
   when he tapped the floor.

I liked it, though. That attention. That care. That gentleness.

It was during the last hour of our practice that we came within sight of Crescent Prominence, but I couldn't see it from below.

The practice was going well, at least with a single noore-stone. There was only one thing I wouldn't try—not with Aaru—and that was transferring the noorestone's inner fire to something—or someone—else. Altan had tortured him with three noorestones treated with some sort of liquid, pushing heat into Aaru until the fever almost killed him.

I'd done something similar to Altan when I'd stabbed him that last day in the Pit.

But even without that, there'd been plenty to work on.

I absorbed and expelled sips of power from the noore-stone, making it dim in time with my breath, or with my heartbeat. When I touched the stone, I didn't have to draw power at all; contact was enough to affect its light. I could brighten the stone as well, which would probably shorten its life, but most noorestones lasted for two or three centuries, anyway, and they were plentiful across the Fallen Isles.

When I finished the exercises Aaru had set before me, I placed the stone on the floor and grinned up at him, triumphant.

::Good work.:: His smile was the sun. The stars. His smile was a rare and wondrous treat that sent my heart fluttering. ::Should we go up?::

I didn't want to. Over our three days at sea, the horrible fog that had taken hold of me after the theater was finally beginning to burn off. But it seared away in patches, and I could never tell when I was about to walk into a wall of emptiness. When I got comfortable somewhere, it liked to creep back in.

Mostly, I faced it in the mornings, when rolling out of my hammock was the hardest thing in the world.

But the scrubbing and stretching and strengthening *had* helped. I had more good moments than bad. And even though it was too many noorestones that had caused my lassitude, these moments in the bowels of the ship were among the best.

I forced myself to stand, scooping up the noorestone on my way. Shadows jumped and caught on crates, but these were natural shadows, not like Chenda's.

Aaru touched my arm. ::Mira.::

His expression was soft as he gazed down at me, and when I brought the noorestone between us, light glimmered over the planes of his face, the curve of his lips.

I didn't think.

I let my forefinger brush against the stubble on his jaw. The strong line of his brow. And the swell of his lower lip.

His gasp was sharp. Sudden. And for ten thousand pounding heartbeats, I wondered if I'd broken something.

But when he breathed again, his smile was warm and soft. And when he moved again, his hand slipped down my arm and came to rest on my waist. On my hip.

"May I?" I kept my words below a whisper, just a hint of a question only he would ever hear.

His fingers curled over my hip, and he nodded.

In the soft light of our noorestone, my fingers breezed across his forehead, over his temple and ear, and down the back of his neck. I stayed butterfly light, ready to stop if he asked, but he made no such suggestion. He just closed his eyes and soundlessly breathed my name, his body swaying close to mine.

I loved him.

I *loved* him.

The words would be so easy to say. Hadn't I said them all my life? To family. To friends. To crowds of strangers. So why did my voice refuse to work when it came to Aaru?

Because this would be different—a declaration of something huge, and something I couldn't take back. Something he could not ignore.

Or maybe accept.

He'd delayed his return to Idris—for me, yes—but he would go eventually. Definitely sooner than I wanted. He intended to build a life there. I couldn't steal that future. Love could not be that selfish.

Reluctantly, I stepped back.

His hand fell from my hip.

The noorestone shone between us, illuminating the heavy way he breathed and the confusion in his eyes.

"I'm sorry." My voice was deep with wanting. "I know it's different for you."

A question shone in the tilt of his head, in the posture of his shoulders. His eyebrows moved in and his lips parted, silently asking.

"On Idris." My heart pounded in that anxious way it

did when I knew I'd wronged someone. When I would give anything to make it right, but I didn't know how. And now, my mouth fell open and words dropped out. "You don't touch like that on Idris. Or kiss. Or—" I shook my head, definitely not thinking of anything else. "It's sinful to do any of those things without being married, right? And I want you to know that I respect that, Aaru. I do. Damina says that all our beliefs are different, but showing love—real love—means respecting others' beliefs and not forcing them to change to yours. And yes, there are a lot of reasons I don't trust *people* on Damina right now, but I still trust my gods. I still believe in their wisdom. After all, they're the god and goddess of love. Shouldn't they know about all kinds of love? So I want you to know that. I do respect you and your beliefs, even if what I did just now doesn't show that. I was thoughtless, giving in to what I wanted, and I'm sorry."

Aaru had withdrawn a step, probably at the onslaught of all my words.

Just another way I'd offended him.

Talking too much.

He probably should have left for Idris when he had the chance. Why had he come with me?

He was just being nice. Kind. Thoughtful. He wanted to repay me for helping him out of the Pit, because that's the sort of person he was.

And I was selfish, desperately wanting it to mean something more. Desperately wanting *him*.

His eyes darted toward the noorestone in my fist.

Light leaked between my clutched fingers, pulsing with my heart. My skin was dark and black against the bright glow of the noorestone, and the faceted edges cut against my palm.

I dropped it—the noorestone. I let it bounce across the floor, away from me.

I could still feel it, of course. I could feel *all* the noorestones on the *Chance Encounter*. One large stone—the very heart of the ship—propelling us closer to Crescent Prominence. One hundred and fourteen regular-sized stones in sconces on the three full decks. And another twenty in the captain's quarters and the forecastle bunks. Eight were stashed away in the four lifeboats.

And one in here.

It skidded to a stop just next to Aaru's feet. He bent to retrieve it, cradling the stone rather than gripping it. The light that shone was steady now, illuminating his face and the uncertain expression he wore.

We were standing just next to the main hatch, beside a ladder connecting the floor to the closed door. The main mast drilled through the ship to my left.

Noorestone still cupped in one hand, Aaru stepped to the mast—one, two, three steps—and tapped the quiet code against the wood.

::Is that what you think—::

I started nodding.

::—of me?::

311

I stopped.

::Of::—he hesitated—::us?::

"I don't know what you mean." *Us* as in him and me? Or Idrisi people? Or something else entirely?

But before either of us could clarify, the hatch groaned open and Ilina called in from above. "We're approaching Crescent Prominence."

I managed to squash the shaking in my voice before it showed. "We'll be right up."

"Don't dawdle. I'm leaving the hatch open, so if anyone falls in, it's your fault." Then she was gone, her shoes thumping on the rungs of the ladder that led to the second deck.

Aaru was still looking at me, a mix of emotions playing across his face. They all vanished the moment he realized I was looking back at him, his face as silent as his voice.

"I'm sorry," I said again.

::We should go up.::

Aaru went first, climbing all the way to the main deck without stopping or glancing back. He moved without sound. His steps. His breathing. He was soundless, hiding even from me.

Cool night air brushed my face when I reached the main deck, easing the heat of the humiliation I'd ignited below.

Aaru already stood with Ilina and Hristo on the foredeck. I hurried to join them, making sure to keep out of the way of crewmen working the lines.

312

We'd sailed around the southern reaches of Damyan and Darina—what looked like their feet from a map's view. And now, we approached the capital from the south.

"There's the sanctuary." Ilina pointed westward, where immense mountains rose in stark silhouette against the star-burnished sky. "See the ridge that looks like a dragon wing?"

Aaru nodded.

"That's where a *Drakontos titanus* lives. Lived, rather. Before. She was on the list of dragons to be shipped east. It's a terrible thing for any of the dragons to be taken away, but especially a *Drakontos titanus*. We think there are fewer than three hundred left on the Fallen Isles. Only about half of them live in sanctuaries." Ilina glanced over her shoulder when I reached them. "What's wrong?"

Nothing was obviously a lie, so I just said, "I don't want to talk about it right now," and leaned on the rail next to her.

She frowned, but didn't push. "Well"—she pointed toward the sanctuary again—"you can almost see the ruins. Sometimes the little dragons play around them."

I scanned the foothills and flat land that stretched from the Skyfell Mountains to the sea, squinting until I saw a speck of light in the dark sanctuary.

The empty sky was so strange here. No dragons in flight. No playful calls. No scent of lightning on the breeze.

"There's the old port," Ilina went on, motioning toward

a trio of docks stretching into a small harbor. "It was absorbed into the sanctuary when we began getting more dragons. Most of the structures were removed, but the sanctuary staff maintains a few boats and ships."

She glanced at me, sadness hanging deep in her eyes. That old port was probably where our dragons had been shipped away from Damina.

"Up there is where Mira lives." Ilina's voice was rough as she pointed north, toward the series of high prominences that were splayed out like a seven-fingered hand. The middle was the longest and the highest, with the surrounding fingers growing shorter and lower. "It doesn't look natural at all. Not with the prominences that symmetrical. There are scholars who think that an ancient species of cliff-dwelling dragons spent decades carving the structure before humans arrived on the Fallen Isles."

::Beautiful,:: Aaru tapped, though I couldn't tell if Ilina or Hristo understood.

"When I was little," Ilina went on, "it seemed like there might be something magical hidden in the spaces between them. But it's just water. Sea caves. Birds. Emergency evacuation boats. A few small dragons. *Drakontos raptuses* make their nests in cliffs."

These cliffs were only part of Crescent Prominence; the rest of the city thrived below, with the council house, the temple, and everything else that made the city home. Only the city's elite lived up on the prominences. My family. Most of the Luminary Council. Other public figures wealthy enough to afford the great houses that overlooked the sea.

As the *Chance Encounter* drew past the noorestone-lit buoys, the lighthouses, and alongside the prominences, I tried not to think about the silent boy next to me. That would mean admitting how I'd broken something not with my actions, but my words.

"Is that what you think of me? Of us?" The questions haunted me.

I focused on the city growing ahead of us.

That was what I needed to think about.

Not this.

Not him.

CHAPTER TWENTY-FOUR

THE HARDEST PART OF LEAVING THE SHIP TURNED out to be the dragons. Crystal kept flying onto Ilina's shoulder, while LaLa got on the floor and crawled to me, using her good wing for balance. Both made pitiful chirrup noises, terrible enough to break my heart.

"We'll be back, sweet lizard." I scratched LaLa's chin. "In less than a day."

We couldn't take them. Our belongings would be thoroughly searched at the customs point, and we couldn't risk anyone finding them. If LaLa could have flown, we might have loosed them on the ship and reunited once we were through the gates. But, while LaLa's fractures were nearly healed now (dragon bones healed *quickly*), Ilina didn't want to risk reaggravating the injury.

Ultimately, we tricked them. We brought One and Teres into our cabin, getting them to offer the dragons bites of mango and smoked perch, which distracted the lizards long enough for Ilina and me to escape.

After that, leaving was simple.

Briefly, we'd worried that the dockworkers would recognize me. After all, this was my home port. I'd regularly traveled through here, and most people in Crescent Prominence knew my face.

But:

1. *No one was expecting me.*
2. *I was changed after months in the Pit and on the run.*
3. *My papers had a different name.*
4. *The scar.*

By the time we got through security, it was well after midnight. Weariness tugged at me, but I'd napped before my practice with Aaru because it would be a long walk to Ilina's house.

"Are you nervous about seeing your parents again?" I linked my arm with Ilina's, matching my strides to hers. We walked close behind Hristo, who'd decided to lead the way even though Ilina knew how to get home just fine. Aaru brought up the rear, so quiet I had to turn my head to make sure he was still with us.

Ilina gave a one-shouldered shrug. "They're going to

be angry about the whole running-away-with-Hristo situation." She glanced toward the prominences. "What about you?"

"Your parents love me. I can't wait to see them."

She jogged my elbow. "That's not what I meant."

"I'd rather focus on one step at a time," I said. "Get to your house. Let them take us to my house. Then I'll decide how I feel about seeing my parents."

In truth, I was terrified of seeing Mother. And Father, but I had no idea what to expect from him; he might not have noticed I'd been gone. Zara, reliably, would ignore me.

We'd spent a lot of time arguing about the wisdom of going to Ilina's house, then mine. The more stops we made in Crescent Prominence, the more likely it was that someone would recognize us and word would get back to Altan.

Even going home was a huge risk, but we didn't have a lot of other options. Father worked at the council house, which was definitely unsafe, and Mother moved from place to place as quickly as a butterfly. She always had untold numbers of social engagements that demanded her full attention. Even the scandal of my disappearance— or her efforts to have me returned—would not affect her schedule.

So there was nowhere to "accidentally" bump into my parents and lead them to a safe location where we could talk. And the four of us wouldn't be able to get through the gates without using our real names. The list of people approved to enter was carefully maintained; each family who lived in the prominences had a number of people who were permitted without an escort, which was usually limited to close friends, servants, doctors—trusted people who visited frequently enough that an escort would be needlessly inconvenient.

Which meant that Ilina and Hristo could get in, but not without revealing themselves.

Ilina's parents, however . . . They could get us through the gates.

Crescent Prominence was not a city with a busy night life, so there was no crowd to disappear into. The streets were all but deserted, save the occasional group of people leaving a tavern or party—usually identifiable by the clothes they wore.

And dressed in the simple shirts and trousers the others had bought back on Harta, we fit in with the roving groups of delinquents hoping to sneak home before their parents discovered their absence.

We approached Water Street, one of the major thoroughfares in town. It ran all the way from the tip of the prominences, cut a circle around the council house, continued by the Temple of Damyan and Darina, and went on until it left the city.

This part of Water Street was relatively minor— boasting a bank, an inn whose owner knew every scandal, and the restaurant run by the famous chef who'd trained my family's personal chef. From here, we could see the soaring arches of the temple to our right, and the bell tower of the council house to our left.

A few carriages rolled down the street, but no one paid us any mind. We were anonymous. Harmless. Crescent Prominence was a safe city and no one worried about four reasonably dressed youths.

We were only three blocks from Ilina's house.

Three blocks from safety.

When Hristo waved us across the street, I glanced over my shoulder to make sure Aaru was still with us. Our eyes met.

I looked away first.

"What's wrong?" Ilina kept her voice soft. "You seemed upset earlier."

I *was* upset. I was *still* upset. "Not now." Not where Aaru could overhear us.

There was part of me that wanted to explain my side to Ilina, knowing that Aaru would be able to hear every single word. Like maybe if he knew how deeply I felt for him, and how ardently I wanted to respect that what was proper here was definitely not proper there, he would forgive my gaffe.

But that was cowardly. He deserved something real.

I just had to figure out what that was and how I would ever get up the nerve to speak to him again.

The moons were moving toward the horizon as we closed in on Ilina's neighborhood, casting more than enough light to see by. Still, lampposts with mirror-brightened noorestones stood every twenty paces. When we turned onto Ilina's street, several light posts were decorated with ribbons and flowers.

Though my legs ached from the long walk, seeing Ilina's street made me feel as though I could fly. I'd spent little time here—Mother liked for Ilina to come to me when we weren't in the sanctuary—but I'd burned this street into my memory. The expectations attached to my title always disappeared here, and I was just one of the hundreds of Crescent Prominence girls named Mira.

"Almost home." I squeezed Ilina as we walked.

There wasn't anything terribly special about this neighborhood. The houses were nice, all with granite facing and seven or eight front windows. They had two floors each, and mimicked the arch style of the temple, but the most impressive thing about them was that Ilina lived here. In this ordinary neighborhood. In an ordinary house.

My extraordinary best friend.

Close. So close. Just two houses down.

One house.

When we stopped at Ilina's door and waited for her to find the spare key, I half expected Altan and his warriors to erupt from across the street. Getting through Crescent Prominence unscathed had been too easy, hadn't it? Surely it had all been a trap.

Aaru lingered in the shadows as he took in the surrounding houses, the peak of the temple reaching to the sky, and the view of the prominences that rose above everything. My house stood on the center prominence, windows winking in the moonslight.

::Never seen anything like this.:: He tapped on the gray granite wall—carefully, as though he was afraid to break it. ::So much wealth.::

I didn't know how to answer, but I didn't have to. Ilina found her key and opened the door, and we began to file inside.

Aaru tapped on my shoulder, one eyebrow raised in question. ::At home we take shoes off. Rain.::

Because it rained a lot on Idris, and no one wanted to track in water. "You can leave them on," I said. "It's fine."

A look of deep discomfort passed over his face as he stepped inside. He scrubbed the soles on the front mat before venturing too far in.

"Stay down here." Ilina motioned toward the parlor, where we'd spent hours reading from her parents' home collection of dragon books—not just anatomy and behavioral texts, but stories of individual dragons' lives, various dragon trainers and keepers throughout history, and everything else we could possibly dream of. They had four hundred and eighty-six books here. I'd counted, not because I'd needed to, but because I'd wanted to know how high I should set my goal for my own dragon library.

My feet took me to the first bookcase before Ilina finished directing us.

While Ilina disappeared upstairs, Hristo helped himself

in the kitchen. "Everything is spoiled," he muttered, closing a cupboard.

He was right. Something felt off. Dust had settled over all the books and their shelves, and cards had been left scattered across the table.

Aaru stood in the parlor doorway, his head cocked with listening. Then he met my eyes and tapped against the doorframe. ::No one is here.::

An instant later, Ilina raced down the stairs and ran toward us. "There was a fight," she breathed. "My parents are gone."

AARU

One Decan Before Arrest

SOME PEOPLE SAID IDRIS KILLED MY FATHER.

I'd been promoted to overnight overseer, which left me mostly nocturnal, but in charge of fifteen young men sorting through trash all night. I didn't mind, as it was preferable to the manure and fertilizer jobs, but I didn't like how little I saw my family, or Dema—the eldest daughter of community leader Kader, and my betrothed. Mother and Father had arranged the engagement. I still didn't know how. I was far beneath her.

Still, the job was quiet. None of my workers spoke aloud, and though I could have—I was their superior—I kept my communication limited to quiet code as well. It was just better.

At least until I went home one day and the earth shook.

The earthquake was eerie.

Silent.

I awoke in the basement—where Father and I had built two small beds in the corner and hung strips of old cloth to black out the windows—to find jars of canned fruit walking off the shelves, water sloshing in a cleaning basin, and tools falling from their places on the walls.

But there was no sound.

My heart pounded painfully in my throat, but I couldn't even hear the sound echo in my own head. No crash of glass. No smack of metal. Just pure, unadulterated silence.

The whole earth swirled, trying to knock me off-balance, but I staggered toward the stairs and pulled myself up. What if the house fell on me?

Everyone was running toward the doors. Hafeez glanced at me and opened her mouth, but nothing came out.

We emerged into bright daylight—all of us, except Father, because he was at work. Alya and Safa huddled together, as they always did, tapping and tapping, while Korinah went around to everyone, asking if we were harmed. No one was.

Water sloshed from the rain barrels, and dirt rose in heavy plumes. Then, finally, the shaking subsided. My heartbeat slowed to a normal pace. Sound returned in small measures, first in my own head, and the gasp of others' breathing, and the last rumbles of the ground shuddering.

That was when I noticed it: our family's old noorestone. It was tiny to me now, no bigger than my palm, and its glow had been faint for as long as I could remember. It had rolled out of the house and sat in a corner of shadow now, and I was certain—absolutely certain—it had not been lit before. But now, the soft, deep hum I'd always sensed from the noorestone was back as well.

The earthquake had silenced even the light.

It was unsettling, Idris's silent seizure, but it wasn't the worst thing that happened that day.

An hour later, a cart rolled into our yard and a man jumped out. He strode straight toward Mother and me, tapping out the quiet code:

::The High House collapsed in the earthquake.::

::Dema?:: I asked. We'd been betrothed only a month, but I'd already begun to let myself imagine a life with her. Though how I would make her happy, I could not fathom.

::Kader's family escaped, but none of the workers were able to get out. They're all dead.::

Including my father.

CHAPTER TWENTY-FIVE

HRISTO WENT UP TO LOOK, WHILE I TOOK ILINA BY the shoulders and steered her toward the sofa. "Sit," I said as gently as possible, around the ache of my own pulse in my throat. And, when Ilina didn't move, I tried again. "Sit."

She obeyed, but her hands were shaking and her eyes were wide with horror. She perched on the edge of the seat, as though she was ready to dart away at the slightest noise.

"Tell me what you saw." I hugged her, waiting for her muscles to soften, but she remained tense. Waiting for her cue to flee. "Ilina."

Her voice trembled hard. "Old blood. Not a lot. Some-one tried to clean, but they must have been in a rush because they missed several spots." Her voice caught, twisted, and knotted. "What if it was my mother's blood? Or Father's?"

I squeezed her, because there was nothing to say to that. It probably *was* their blood. "What can I do?"

"I don't know. We have to look for them, but where? Who would hurt my parents? I don't even know where to begin." Ilina dropped her face into her hands. "Gods. Damina. I don't understand."

Suspicion crawled at me.

Aaru looked at me from across the parlor, and in that glance I knew we shared a suspicion.

Dragons.

The answer was always dragons.

Aaru's gaze flickered toward Ilina again, then dropped to his shoes. ::**Strength through silence,**:: he tapped against his fingers.

Bearing witness to others' grief was not something that came easily for most people; they needed tasks to feel useful. Aaru, of all the people in the world, was probably best suited to sit with Ilina, but he edged toward the stairs, as though to give us privacy.

"Upstairs," I said. "Second room on the left. There's a good pack in the wardrobe. Take sanctuary uniforms, boots—practical things."

Aaru nodded and vanished up the stairs.

The moment he left, Ilina released the huge sob she'd been holding in. Her body shook as she buried her face in her forearms and bent over her knees, and all the sadness and frustration and exhaustion seemed to pour out of her at once.

She'd been so strong this whole time, my wingsister. So brave. But even she couldn't keep holding this stress. It would burst free.

I broke away long enough to find a handkerchief for her to wipe her face, and then resumed sitting vigil at her side.

There were no words of comfort I could offer, so I didn't speak. I just petted her shoulders, not acknowledging her tears beyond the handkerchief; Ilina hated crying—Hristo probably didn't even know that Ilina *could* cry—so we sat there until her tears dwindled and she retreated to the downstairs washroom to scrub her face.

By the time Hristo returned, Ilina was sitting up straight, her eyes rimmed with red but dry now.

"Aaru is still packing, but I found this." He offered a scrap of off-white linen. "It's material from a Luminary Guard's uniform."

"My parents were arrested." The words dropped from Ilina like a weight, but she didn't cry again. She wouldn't. "Because of me. Because we ran away." She lurched toward Hristo and took his arms. "We have to find your father. He might have been taken, too."

Fear passed over Hristo's face, but he schooled it away. "We'll see. He's a gardener. The Luminary Council might leave him alone."

"Or they might have decided he's the perfect kind of person to make an example of. You know what they're trying to do to Hartans." Ilina pressed her hands to her mouth. "Darina. Hristo, I'm sorry. That was terrible to even suggest."

Hristo's eyes darkened, but he nodded. "No, you're right. We can't forget that's happening, too. They could say what a dangerous son my father has. Start changing opinions about Hartans living here."

"'Harta hates harm,' though." Ilina shook her head. "People won't believe you're dangerous—or your father."

He just looked at her, his face deadly serious. "To people who want an excuse to be rid of Hartans, anything is believable. Look at Bopha. They want to deport Hartans, so they say Hartans are destroying fields. And when that wasn't enough, they claimed Hartans were burning Bophans. It didn't take long for people to believe it. Now, even people who didn't care suddenly do. That's the nature of fear. It happened on Bopha. Darina isn't immune just because people here think they're the authorities on love."

"Besides," I said. "Hristo is my protector. Everyone knows that. Ten years ago, people couldn't stop talking about how strange it was for a Hartan to be a protector." I wasn't supposed to know about it, but there'd been several incidents of people throwing things at Hristo while he'd been walking home. They usually shouted, "Harta hates harm!" as though they were more of an expert in being Hartan than he was. "People still talk, but they're better at keeping it to themselves."

Ilina's face darkened, but she nodded. "Sorry."

"It's all right." Hristo fidgeted with the strap of his sling. "I know what you meant."

"Regardless, we have to find your father." Ilina started for the door. Hristo took her arm and drew her back.

"We will, but if he's been arrested, it happened days ago. We won't prevent it." He picked up the scrap of Luminary Guard uniform fabric he'd dropped a moment before. "First, we have to figure out where we go next. Our plan was for your parents to take us to Mira's. Who else can do that for us?"

I could think of only two people I trusted enough to ask for help. "Doctor Chilikoba or Krasimir. I don't know where they live, though."

"We can walk to Doctor Chilikoba's house." Ilina's voice was heavy, but she looked stronger.

"I wish we had Chenda's shadows," Hristo said. "We need to be careful."

"You think someone might be watching the house." Ilina gazed toward the windows. "If there is, we've already been seen coming in."

"We'll have to be fast." I looked toward the parlor doorway as Aaru came downstairs, two of Ilina's packs slung over his shoulders. "We'll see what my parents know."

Hristo nodded. "Perhaps they will have information about your parents, Ilina. My father will likely be there."

::And the treaty, of course.:: Aaru offered one of Ilina's packs for inspection.

"And the treaty," I confirmed. "And the dragons." It

331

was possible that Father knew the new route the dragons were being sent on—since I'd compromised the original one. But would the Luminary Council actually tell Father anything if they were worried about his daughter?

Hard to say.

We couldn't count on it. That much I knew.

"Where does the doctor live?" Hristo asked.

"She's close by." Ilina closed her bag and nodded to Aaru, apparently satisfied with his selections. "Thank you for gathering my things."

He smiled, and then we were out the door—without the cloak of shadow, but with a soft bubble of soundlessness to protect us.

ILINA WAS RIGHT: my doctor didn't live far away.

We reached her home only ten minutes later, and since Aaru was the person least likely to be recognized here, he took a hastily scrawled note to the door and knocked. The rest of us lingered several houses down, watching the quiet street and waiting for Aaru to wave us on.

It didn't take long.

My heart jumped at the sight of my doctor, even though she wore a heavy robe over her nightgown, and a blush-colored scarf covered her hair. Pressure marks lined the right side of her brown skin. But she still managed a smile when she saw me, and for the first time in a thousand years, I felt safe.

I'd never been to her home before, but the layout was

similar to Ilina's, with a large staircase that headed up to the second floor, shrouded in darkness with all the noore-stones covered for the night. We turned into the parlor, where she shut the curtains fast and ordered the four of us to sit. "I'll get my bag. Stay here."

Rather than filling her parlor with draconic texts, she'd hung hundreds of drawings. People, mostly. There was a man laughing, a woman praying, and a small girl chasing butterflies.

Aaru left the seat he'd occupied, took three steps across the room, and let his fingers hover over another drawing.

It was me.

I moved next to Aaru. He didn't look away from the drawing.

Careful pencil strokes had captured me as a round-faced child sitting primly on the edge of a large chair. The sketched window in the background suggested it was my house—the sun parlor where the doctor always saw me. My eyes were dark and haunted, trained on the scratches that covered my hands. My face, too, was crisscrossed with cuts.

I'd been seven, and someone had just tried to kid-nap me.

Aaru studied the details, as though committing my child face to memory, then shifted his attention to the next drawing.

It was me again, but this one could have captured any

333

number of moments shortly before my arrest. I was still in the sun parlor, but older here, wearing a sleeveless dress. The artist had caught me looking over my shoulder— as though I'd been gazing out the window and had just turned to see who'd come into the room.

I was pretty in this drawing, with half of my hair bound into a loose bun, while the rest tumbled down my back in tight curls. My body filled out the dress perfectly, and the muscles of my arms were defined but not hard. There was no scar. No evidence of untreated panic attacks. No echoes of torture.

Aaru stared at me. Her. The drawing. A girl who didn't exist anymore.

Doctor Chilikoba came back into the room, a bag slung over her shoulder and a glass pitcher of water clutched in her free hand. "Oh." She tilted her head, seeing what I was looking at. "I hope you don't mind. I draw all my patients. . . ."

"I don't mind." I hurried to take the pitcher from her. "You're a talented artist."

"Thank you. That's sweet of you to say." She nodded toward a sideboard of beautifully carved heartwood. "Set the pitcher there. You can find glasses in the top drawer."

While I followed her orders, she placed her bag on an end table and got to work.

"Do I even want to know what happened to you?" She went to Hristo first, removing his sling. "Seven gods, boy."

"We've run into some trouble." Hristo just watched

while she unwound the bandage. The morning we'd departed Harta, the ship's medic had checked the wound for infection and replaced the bandage. But no one told Doctor Chilikoba she wasn't needed, so Hristo sat still and let her work.

She frowned over the cut, pressing different places to test Hristo's reaction. "Can you move your fingers?"

He wiggled his thumb and forefinger. His middle finger twitched a moment later. Nothing happened with the other two.

"Hm." She studied the healing cut a moment longer, then spread a sharp-smelling salve onto the side of his hand and applied a fresh bandage. "I'm satisfied that you'll live, at least. Whoever treated this probably saved your life."

Gerel would be proud to know that.

"But I'm worried about your last two fingers. Maybe the middle, too. Only time will tell." She sighed and tightened the lid on the jar of salve. "I'll get a new jar for you to take with you, and find a real sling."

Gerel would *not* have liked to hear that; she'd worked hard on this sling.

"Thank you, Doctor." Hristo lowered his eyes to his hand, but if he had any thoughts about using those last two fingers again, he didn't share.

"Now, Mira, perhaps you'd like to tell me why you're here?" The doctor spoke sternly, and I hated that we'd bothered her before dawn, but her eyes were kind when she glanced at me.

335

"We need to see my parents." I finished pouring the water, and one at a time I handed glasses to the others. "We went to Ilina's house first, but no one was there."

"And why can't you go on your own?"

I glanced at Ilina. "We all have forged papers."

"Good Damyan. Do I want to know why?"

"It's complicated." I took a sip from my water and sat on the edge of one of the unclaimed chairs. "I don't know how much we can safely tell you. Not because I don't trust you. I do. But I don't trust the Luminary Council anymore. Or the guards."

"I knew something had happened." She strode toward me. "When I went to your house for our appointment four decans ago, your mother said you were traveling. But she seemed strange. Worried. And she couldn't say when you would return."

"She seemed worried?" My voice felt tight. When Ilina and Hristo had come for me in Bopha, they'd said my mother had been working for my release, but I couldn't imagine her *worried* for me.

Maybe . . . Maybe she was just worried about my face. Same as she'd been the day the man tried to kidnap me.

She was going to be so angry now.

"Of course she was worried. You're her daughter." Doctor Chilikoba crouched in front of me and touched my chin. Carefully, she tilted my left cheek toward the light. "What happened here?"

My throat closed up.

"It looks old, Mira, but I know it's not."

336

I dropped my gaze. "It was Councilor Elbena, just after the new year. But I can't say how it healed so quickly." The noorestone magic was something I couldn't even explain to myself, let alone my doctor.

"It wasn't treated properly. That's why it scarred so badly." She opened her bag wider, but whatever she wanted wasn't in there. "I'll find something for you to put on it. I can't get rid of the scar for you, but we might be able to smooth it down a little."

"Thank you," I whispered. If anyone knew what the scar meant, she did. Then, when she handed me an amber bottle stuffed with my calming pills, I said again, "*Thank you.*" Just the glass under my fingers was a comfort.

Doctor Chilikoba squeezed my knee. "You'll let me know if you need anything else, right?"

"There's something. . . ." I kept my voice low.

"What's that?" She didn't move.

I wasn't sure how to explain the emptiness I'd felt in Val fa Merce without also explaining the noorestone magic. But maybe she wouldn't make me. Maybe she'd just understand that it had been different from the peaceful numb of my calming pills—that it had been something else entirely. Consuming.

"You don't have to say it just right," she murmured. "Tell me what you can."

"I felt scraped hollow." I pressed my palms against my knees to stop the trembling. "Empty. Like there was a fog smothering me."

"Ah." She nodded. "What helped it go away?"

"It's not gone," I whispered. "But it retreats when I'm doing something useful. I've been scrubbing a ship for three days."

Doctor Chilikoba smiled. "All right. I'll get something for that, too."

One at a time, she looked at Ilina and then Aaru, and we did our best to explain what had happened, omitting the parts about dragons, noorestone magic, and the fact that we were all fugitives.

Which probably left her more confused than she'd been before, but she just continued with her work, not asking questions. Cuts and bruises got treated. Sore muscles were soothed. She took care of each of us as though we were all her most precious patients. That was one of the things I liked best about her; she made everyone special.

"All right." She snapped her bag closed. "I'll take you up there. Get something to eat. Rest. I'll call for a ride."

CHAPTER TWENTY-SIX

GETTING THROUGH THE GATES TO THE PROMINENCES was remarkably easy.

My friends and I ducked below the carriage windows. The on-duty guard saw only Doctor Chilikoba, and he waved her through without a second glance. She was a trusted figure, after all. A pillar of the community. No one questioned her goodness.

As we ascended Water Street up to the cliffs, the sky turned shades of violet and deep blue, growing brighter with every passing moment. The approaching sun threaded the wispy clouds pink and orange, and birdsong touched the crisp air. Far below, the waves crashed against the cliffs.

Home.

I could hardly believe I was back here, after everything, but the truth was undeniable. Fresh salt air tangled with the perfume of passionflowers and sea roses, so familiar it hurt. The delicate chime of the guardhouse bell tugged at my sense memory, urging me to feel safe at the knowledge of Luminary Guards patrolling the prominences.

Aaru sat across from me, his gaze darting from tall palm trees, to marble statues of Damyan and Darina, to the long drives that led to foliage-hidden houses; from here, we could only see hints of red brick, or flashes of glass windows. He took in everything, though his expression gave away no feelings even as he tapped on the carriage door.

::Beautiful here.::

I nodded.

::You grew up here.:: Again, his face was as silent as his voice.

And again, I nodded, trying not to wonder what I'd find if I could read his mind. Was he impressed? Scared? Disgusted? I'd thought I knew so much about Idrisi culture, but I'd misjudged too many times now to even guess what his feelings were.

Maybe I wasn't looking hard enough?

By the time we turned into the drive to my house, the sun had crested the horizon. It was hard to see from this vantage point, with hedges and trees and ferns blocking the view, but in hummingbird-quick glimpses, I could see the golden orb sitting on the water, its long rays stretching between clouds and shining into the sky.

Then, my house blocked the view.

The drive circled a large fountain that was set flush into the ground. Lilies floated across the water, while sea roses lined the perimeter. In the spring, butterflies sometimes created huge, colorful clouds above the flowers.

But it wasn't the fountain that drew Aaru's gaze. As the carriage rolled to a stop and we began to file out, he asked, ::How many people live here?::

"Ten."

His eyebrows rose. ::Didn't realize your family was so big.::

"It's not. Hristo and his father live in the servants' quarters. Our chef and maids do, too; they're a family. Otherwise, it's just my parents, Zara, and me." I slid out after him, lifting my eyes to the house as though I might be able to see it as he did.

It *was* large, with three wide stories, each boasting enormous glass windows that glittered in the morning sun. Seventeen of them on this face. The house had been built in a modern style inspired by the First Masters— those who'd designed the temple in the city below—meant to appear elegant and graceful, with decorative touches hand-carved into the pale stones.

For years, it had looked only like home. Now, after the places I'd been, it felt like approaching a palace.

"Do you need me with you?" Doctor Chilikoba asked. "Or was I just the ride?"

She had patients to see, other people who mattered to her. She'd already given me a cream for the scar and a bottle of pills for the emptiness, and we'd tucked everything away in one of Ilina's bags for now.

"Your presence is always welcome," I said. "But I think you should go. See your other patients. Come back in a few hours if you want to make sure we haven't torn one another apart."

She pressed her mouth into a line. "All right, as long as you know I'm worried."

"Noted." The urge to hug her seized me, but I hesitated. I'd been raised in the light of the Lovers, and people here regularly displayed their affection for one another, but that freedom had always paused around me. I was the embodiment of *look, don't touch.*

But Doctor Chilikoba had always read me clearly, and quickly, she wrapped her arms around my shoulders. "I'll check on you later."

"Thank you."

"Let's go." Ilina beckoned everyone forward, one of her packs slung over her shoulder; Hristo had the other.

After waving good-bye to Doctor Chilikoba, I hurried ahead of the others and hesitated only a heartbeat before I stepped inside my house.

Hoping for a moment of relief.

Hoping for the sense of homecoming.

Hoping for something like safety.

But I didn't feel any of that as I moved through the

front hall, elaborately decorated with all the possessions Mother liked to show off.

1. *Two large vases that were three centuries old, if she was to be believed. They were obsidian, shaved so thin that a noorestone placed inside made the black glass glow like a dark lantern.*
2. *Two slender hardwood tables, which bore six bundles of fresh flowers and eleven tiny crystal songbirds.*
3. *Five paintings from a famous artist whose name Mother knew only because it impressed people.*

The front hall opened into the main parlor, a large, airy space with an open design meant to feel light and welcoming. It took up much of the first floor, along with the kitchen, dining room, and a small library. Windows dominated the back wall, crystal-clear glass that faced the cliffs, admitting the morning sunlight as it gleamed across the water.

The windows were two stories tall in the center, where the second floor made a crescent moon of a balcony around the main section of the parlor. From here, I could just see the hallway Zara and I shared, and that her door was shut tight.

In all four corners of the parlor, two columns supported the ceiling, with bookcases pinned between them. None of those books were ever touched; as far as I knew, they were actually hollow, meant only to appear impressive. And finally, a pair of long, curved staircases descended from the balconies at the back, just far enough away from the windows to let the curtains be opened and closed.

::It's so clean.:: Aaru's arms were crossed over his stomach so that he tapped on his elbow. ::And big.::

"You should all sit." I motioned to the sofas and chairs, waiting with soft cushions the colors of the moons.

Ilina and Hristo were already halfway to their favorite seats before I spoke, but Aaru had been waiting for an invitation. He perched on the edge of a chair near Hristo, like he didn't believe he wasn't about to get in trouble.

"I'll find my mother."

Before I could head upstairs, though, Zara's door opened and my sister emerged stomping from her room, her schoolbag slung over one shoulder. But when she reached the balcony and caught sight of us in the parlor below, the bag dropped to the floor.

She opened her mouth. "Mother!"

At the scream, Aaru visibly cringed, while Ilina and Hristo exchanged pained glances. This was, unfortunately, Zara's normal volume.

But it worked. Mother appeared on the opposite balcony, already wearing a sapphire wrap dress and a wrist full of gold bracelets that glowed against her warm brown skin. "Zara, please. You don't—" She spotted everyone in the parlor, and her breath caught. "Mira?"

At once, she was hurrying to the nearest staircase, then taking the steps two at a time. "Zara, send for your father," she said, not looking away from me. Of course, Zara didn't move, and Mother didn't order her again, so Hristo slipped out of the room to find a prominence page.

Mother was still rushing toward me, an unfamiliar expression of joy on her face, and I took one hesitating step forward. Two. Three. For a full moment, I forgot.

Then, Zara said, "Seven gods, Mira. What happened?"

After the scar, I'd started turning my head slightly, hardly ever looking at anyone straight on. It had been conscious at first, trying to hide the mark, but this time I'd been turning my face away from Mother, and toward Zara.

Mother halted just three paces from me, all her maternal concern evaporated as she searched for the source of Zara's alarm. Then, she noticed.

Of course.

She noticed everything, especially about my physical form.

She stalked forward and gripped my chin between her thumb and index finger, and sharply turned my face.

While she inspected the scar, she was so very still, with her mouth pushed into a frown and her chin lifted high so that she could look down on me. Her breathing was long and steady, as though she'd taken all her shock and gathered it deep inside.

Seconds ticked by. I counted them. Five, six, seven . . . Time was passing, I knew it, but somehow it seemed the world would pause its spinning until she gave it permission to continue. Her scrutiny was completely overwhelming.

The amber bottle that held my calming pills was in Ilina's pack, but suddenly I wished I'd taken one before coming here. Home. My heart raced and black vines curled around the edges of my vision. This was what I'd dreaded. Mother confronting the scar.

And I could feel Ilina and Aaru watching us, me with my arms limp at my sides, and Mother with my face pinched between her fingers. What were they thinking? Were they even watching? Maybe it was too much to hope they'd found books and were too engrossed in someone else's struggles to notice.

"What happened?" Mother's tone was sharp and cold and smooth, like ice.

I couldn't speak, because she still had my jaw, but it hadn't truly been a question anyway. Not one I was meant to answer. This was just the illusion of asking, almost touching concern, but not quite reaching it.

What happened? The council happened. Elbena happened.

"It's hideous. Your face is ruined." She released me at last. "Fallen Gods, Mira. What were you thinking?"

As if I'd done this to her. As if I'd *wanted* to be scarred for the rest of my life.

But even if I'd been brave enough to speak those words, I was planted in place, my feet rooted, and my soul sinking deeper into the ground. My mouth couldn't form a defense.

Not that there *was* a real defense. I'd made the choice to speak for Hartans in the Shadowed City. I'd known the cost of such defiance would be high.

I hadn't known it would be this high.

"You'll never be able to speak in front of a crowd again," she murmured. "It's over now."

She was right. Who could bear to look at me?

"Who would be able to pay attention to your words when your face is so distracting?" she went on. "You used to be so beautiful. You commanded the admiration of thousands."

But now I didn't.

"Now you can't," she whispered.

Mother had loved one piece of me, and now it was gone.

"This is what I always warned you about." She caressed my good cheek. "I always told you to be careful, to take care of yourself. Didn't I?"

With the tears pooling in my eyes, obscuring her face, I didn't trust myself to speak. I just nodded.

"And now this." She sighed. "You weren't careful, were you?"

I shook my head, because she was right. I hadn't been careful. I hadn't thought through the consequences of my actions. If I'd just done as Elbena had ordered, everything would be fine.

"I'm sorry." My voice was a tiny squeak, broken under the pressure of a sob struggling to escape.

"I'm just so disappointed," Mother said. "I gave you

the best of everything. I even let you run around the sanctuary with that dragon. All so you would be happy and beautiful and admired by millions. But now, with this"—she gestured at my face—"I don't know what you'll do. Can you even smile anymore?"

Could I?

"Try it." She stepped back. "Let's see your smile."

Rushing filled my ears, my heartbeat a punctuating thunder as I forced a smile onto my face. This was supposed to be something I was good at—something I'd practiced every day as a child, ensuring people melted when I grinned.

But Mother's eyes widened in alarm and disgust. "Oh, Mira."

My false smile fell.

"It's twisted. Your face doesn't move correctly anymore."

A faint whimper worked its way out of my throat.

"I don't know what you'll do," she muttered. "Not anymore. But now I see why you were sent home."

Sent home? "I don't know what you mean."

"And now you're being deliberately stupid." Mother took my face again and glared at the scar. "I can't believe you spoiled your chance to make amends with the Luminary Council. They'll never want anything from you again. Not like this."

She was right. I *had* been given a chance to earn the council's trust again. And I'd turned against them. That was why I'd been cut. Scarred.

"I'm sorry, Mother." I couldn't contain the tears anymore. They spilled down my face, catching on the scar: a shame upon my shame.

"Oh, don't cry. Do you think—"

Ilina surged up from the sofa, fire in her eyes, her hands curled into fists.

It would be so easy to let my best friend stand up for me. I always had, because she was braver than us mere mortals. Scowls did not cow her.

But Ilina couldn't fight my battles for me. Chenda had been right about that. If I wanted to be heard, believed, and followed, I needed to learn when to rely on friends, and when to stand up for myself.

"Stop." My voice. My demand.

Ilina didn't move, but Mother squeezed my face harder. Her glare became steel as I wrenched myself away—out of her grasp.

Speak, I ordered myself. *Speak now.*

"What is *wrong* with you?" The words nearly choked me to death. "You act like I wanted this, but you weren't there. You didn't see what happened."

"Do not use that tone with me, Mira." Mother didn't raise her voice, but she didn't need to. Just the words were enough to make me cringe.

But I fought the urge to wither under her glare, and instead, I said what I knew Ilina would have: "Do you even know who did this to me, Mother?" I dragged my finger down the scar. "Of course you don't. You didn't ask. You just blamed me for this violence."

Mother opened her mouth to respond, but I didn't give her a chance. I couldn't—not if I wanted to finish what I needed to say.

"It was Elbena. The Luminary Councilor. She took a knife and cut me, so if you want to be angry or blame someone, blame her." My tears blurred her shocked expression. "And blame yourself."

She stepped backward. "I did nothing."

"You wanted a perfect daughter to represent the treaty, and you spent years molding me into your puppet. Your doll. My face has always been about your vanity." My voice shook with the truth, with everything I'd ever wanted to say just spilling out of me now. "You care more about my face than you care about my feelings."

Mother's glare hardened into granite. Her anger had never been explosive, but for a moment I wondered if that might change.

Maybe everyone else was wondering, too.

1. *Zara stood on the balcony still, her hands motionless on the rail. Her eyes were wide—a little frightened.*
2. *Hristo was just returning to the parlor. He'd never been able to protect me from Mother, not when she was the one who controlled his job, but now he looked between Mother and me, his expression hopeful, perhaps.*

3. *Ilina leaned forward, as though ready to leap to my rescue, but as the moments ticked on, a faint smile turned up the corners of her mouth.*

4. *And then there was Aaru, watching in complete silence. But I'd warned him, hadn't I? The scar changed everything.*

Mother's eyes narrowed into menacing slits, like she was trying to contain her anger through physical force.

"I came for answers, Mother." My next words were pinched: "I don't need anything else from you."

One.

Two.

Three.

Mother didn't look away. Didn't blink.

Nine.

Ten.

Eleven.

"Fine." Mother spun toward Zara, who was still on the balcony watching. "Didn't you send for your father?"

My sister shook her head. "Hristo went."

"But I told you to do it." Mother stalked toward Zara.

Freed from her scrutiny, my knees buckled a little. I caught myself before I fell, but even if I hadn't, Ilina had crossed the room and reached my side. "Good work," she whispered. "Now maybe sit."

She was right. I did need to sit. My legs felt strangely weak as I reached the nearest chair and dropped to the cushion, but the truth of what had just happened hit harder with every beat of my pounding heart.

I'd stood up to my mother.

And I'd won.

LESS THAN AN hour later, Father arrived and swept me into a hug. For seventeen long heartbeats, his arms were tight around me and I felt like a child again.

But when he pulled away, he was already distant, his mind on more important matters.

It stung. Earlier, I'd watched Hristo and his father embrace, seen the concern over Hristo's hand, and listened to him explain that the ship's medic and Doctor Chilikoba had already looked at it and pronounced it fine. Even now, they sat close together, their heads bent toward each other to keep their conversation private.

I hadn't expected my father to react with that much concern, but he didn't even notice the scar until Mother brought it up to him.

"Hristo's father is safe," Ilina murmured. "So maybe mine weren't taken because of me?"

I squeezed her hand. "I think you're right, but we'll see what my parents know. There's a lot they need to answer for."

While we'd been talking, the rest of the staff had joined us in the parlor. Nadya, who was the family seamstress, came down with her daughters, Sylva and Sofiya (both household and personal maids), and rearranged the

352

room so that everyone could face one another. I positioned myself next to Ilina, and across from Aaru so I could see if he tapped anything.

Our chef came last, bringing trays of pastries, fruit, and pots of tea, and for once, I didn't care what Mother saw me eat. After my first poor choice regarding food in the Pit—throwing away a rotten apple and loaf of chalky bread—I'd vowed never to turn down food again. Aaru had the same idea, and for several minutes after introductions were made, the fugitives among us focused on filling our stomachs.

But once the food was gone and the trays removed, there was no more delaying. I had to ask. Aside from Hristo's father, the rest of the staff had retreated to their respective duties, so it was just the three others in my group, three parents (mine and Hristo's father), and one sister (Zara, hidden on the balcony after our parents had sent her to her room). Eight people total.

I could say it. I could.

"Father," I began, but I didn't know how to finish. I should have practiced this—figured out what I wanted to say and how I wanted to say it, like I would have if I'd been giving a speech. I'd have practiced my tone, my expression, and said the words over and over until I knew them by heart.

But I hadn't thought I'd need all that for this moment—talking to my parents and asking them a question.

Ilina nodded at me, encouraging. And Aaru tapped on

the arm of his chair, ::Strength.::

I lifted an eyebrow in question, knowing I didn't need to say the words. *Strength through silence?*

He shook his head. ::Just strength.::

I took a steadying breath. "Father," I said again. "You know where I've been? Since the Luminary Council had me arrested?"

Father nodded, his gaze darkening as it flickered to the others. "Yes, I know where they sent you."

Of course he'd known. He'd been with me when the Luminary Council had decided my fate, one hand on my shoulder. Mother had sat next to me, trembling with rage.

It hadn't been a real trial, not with an outside judge and witnesses and people to speak on my behalf. No, it had just been another meeting in the council chambers, but this time with more guards, and me having sat in a jail cell for two days.

But my parents had both been there as the Luminary Council decided to send me to the Pit, and Father had squeezed my shoulder while Mother had stood to protest. Not that it had done any good. The squeezing or the protesting.

"One of the guards said something interesting." *Interesting* wasn't the right word; this was the reason I should have practiced. "I mean," I amended, "he told me something I didn't want to believe, but I've had a lot of time to consider it, and now I'm here with you, the architect of the Mira Treaty. So I can just ask."

Father's expression was impassive.

From the corner of my eye, I could see Aaru's head was cocked with listening. I didn't have to turn to know Ilina and Hristo were studying him just as intently.

"What is your question?" Trepidation colored Father's tone, but his posture was relaxed and his expression neutral. Next to him, Mother was frowning.

Give me peace. Give me grace. Give me enough love in my heart. Now that I was on Damina, connected to the god and goddess of love through skin and stone, the prayer whispered through me, warming. I said the words: "Did the Mira Treaty sell the Fallen Isles to the Algotti Empire?"

A faint gasp came from behind me: Hristo's father, I suspected. Mother's expression closed off. And on the balcony, Zara's eyes snapped to Father, shock written plain on her face.

"I don't know what you mean." Aside from a frown and confusion in his tone, my father gave nothing away. His hands were motionless on the arms of his chair, dark brown against the pale cushions, and his breathing seemed even.

Such a lack of reaction to such a bold question . . .

Aaru's quiet code was subtle, so fast against his knee that I almost missed it. ::His heart is racing.::

He could *hear* that?

I focused on my father. "I mean exactly what I said I mean. The guard I spoke with in the Pit—who knew far more about why I was imprisoned than he should have—told me he believes that the Mira Treaty is a sham. That it's a deed of sale, and not a declaration of our greater intent."

Father was shaking his head.

::He's scared,:: tapped Aaru.

I stood, putting on my best Hopebearer expression, my best Hopebearer voice for commanding crowds. And, maybe, the same apparent fearlessness that had earned me the title of Dragonhearted. I put them on like a gown and cosmetics and gemstones around my throat. "Father," I said, "tell me the truth. Did the Mira Treaty sell the Fallen Isles to the Algotti Empire?"

Father replied, "Yes."

AARU

Four Days Before Arrest

THE FALLOUT FROM FATHER'S DEATH WAS IMMEDIATE: Safa was sent back to her parents. All of my sisters cried, because they knew about her father. As I walked Safa down the road, I reminded her about the boat waiting on the bank of the stream. We'd visited it every few months, keeping it stocked and ready, just in case anyone found out about her Voice of Idris. ::**Perhaps we'll be able to take you in again,**:: I said as we walked, ::**but don't forget there's always a third option.**:: She just hugged herself, her shoulders hunched over her narrow frame.

Dema invited me to her uncle's house. We sat in the parlor, under the watchful eyes of chaperones. Using the quiet code, Dema assured me that she would try to keep our engagement, but already her father and uncle wanted to match her with someone else. Someone more suitable. ::**Do what is best for you**,:: I replied, and she gave me a look that said she'd never been told that before.

Then there was Mother. She'd always woven mats and made other small items to trade, but she'd been able to slow down in the last year. Now, she worked in earnest. All the time. She didn't sleep, and sometimes her fingers bled.

Essa asked me if Mother wove because it was easier than crying, and I said yes, because that might have been true—partly. But I knew the rest: weaving and trading was the only kind of work Mother was allowed to do, and we would soon be in desperate need of money.

We were down to one income—mine—but there were seven mouths to feed. Danyal couldn't work for another year. Mother couldn't work ever. Nor could any of my sisters.

Our future loomed uncertain.

WHY, THOUGH?

Why did the law prevent Mother from earning chips? Or my sisters? Korinah, Alya, and Hafeez were all old enough to work . . . but they weren't boys. They spent their days contributing in every way possible: our house was always clean, food always cooked, the garden always tended, blankets always being woven. . . .

And those things helped. They did. But we weren't so self-sufficient that we didn't need chips, and I alone could not provide enough.

My questions had always been there, kept under the surface by Father's certainty and Mother's fear, but now the unfairness seethed within me, gnawing, growing, gaining momentum.

When a few men at work asked how my family would survive, I confessed that we couldn't. Not under the law.

Why?

::It doesn't make sense,:: said one man.

::It's because they're women—not as strong,:: said another.

::My wife has given birth to seven children,:: replied the first. ::That takes strength.::

::Surely Idris would rather a woman work than a family starve,:: said a third man.

::My betrothed wants to work,:: said a fourth. ::She showed me her design for a house. It is masterful. But if we can build it, she can't take credit.::

Why?

The tapped conversations spilled around the floor, and though it was my job to put everyone back to work, I wanted to join them. I hadn't realized that anyone else had these thoughts and ached with the unfairness.

Maybe I should have.

CHAPTER TWENTY-SEVEN

ONE WORD.

Yes.

It would have been the end of my innocence, if that hadn't already been stripped away and smothered in the darkness of the Pit.

Yes.

The Mira Treaty was a lie. Arguably the most important document in the Fallen Isles, and definitely the defining document of my lifetime—it was a lie.

Yes.

It was one thing to suspect such a betrayal, because it might be untrue. From the moment after Altan declared the treaty a lie, to the moment right before Father confirmed it, I hadn't *truly* believed. Even seeing the shipping order for dragons and noorestones, and witnessing the black ship sailing through our waters, there'd been a part of me that clung to denial. But now, I couldn't ignore the truth.

Yes.

One word.

A thousand questions.

"I think you'd better explain." My voice didn't sound like mine. It was too calm. Too focused. I'd locked my knees to keep me upright, but heat pulsed through my body and black fog crept at the corners of my vision.

Carefully, as I'd been trained to do when making speeches, I shifted my weight to one leg, then the other. The black fog retreated.

"It was with the best of intentions," Father said. "It isn't as bad as you think."

Anger kindled inside me. "Oh?" At once, I became aware of exactly how many noorestones were in the house.

I'd known, of course, because I'd counted them hundreds of times. But suddenly, I could feel them all. One hundred and fifty-seven.

There were twenty-five in the parlor alone.

::Mira.:: Aaru's tapping came like warning. ::Let go of them.::

Our eyes met, and I exhaled. The noorestones behind him brightened a hair as I released my awareness of them.

::No one else noticed,:: he said, and I thanked him with a thin smile.

361

"Tell me, Father." I looked at him again. "How bad do I think it is?"

My parents just glanced at each other, as though they were trying to decide how much to admit.

"Well?" I crossed my arms.

"Without the Mira Treaty," Father said, "the empire would have swept across the Fallen Isles."

"That's not an answer to my question."

He leaned forward in his chair, elbows on his knees, palms up in supplication. "It is, though. You think we just gave in without consideration, that we're all somehow enriching ourselves, and that we've betrayed the Fallen Gods. But none of those things are true. We were avoiding *war*, Mira.

"Without the treaty, we'd have resisted the empire, of course, but it would have been a long, bloody war. Expensive in lives and lumes. Hundreds of thousands of our people would have perished. And it would have ended with the empire ruling over the Fallen Isles anyway. Not one of the island governments believed we could win, so the treaty was proposed. It would be bloodless."

"The other governments knew."

Father nodded. "Everyone who signed the document knew what it was."

Every single island was culpable.

Every single government had sold their people to the Algotti Empire.

"With the treaty," he said, "we were able to influence

362

the terms. Most people will never know that the Fallen Isles belong to the Algotti Empire." Again, he whispered, "It was bloodless."

He was trying so hard to justify it—so hard to make *anyone* believe he'd done the right thing, but especially himself. But he was a fool if he thought most people would never know. People would. It was just a matter of time before the empress made herself heard here.

"Bloodless doesn't mean the price wasn't unbearably high." I lowered myself to my chair again, breathing through the anxiety simmering just under the surface of my thoughts. I could feel it in me, writhing, and again I wished I'd taken one of the calming pills, now that I had them. But I didn't want to take one in front of everyone.

No, that wasn't true. I didn't want to take one in front of Mother.

Twenty-five noorestones.

Ten people.

Eight columns.

Twenty-eight steps on two staircases.

Mother narrowed her eyes at me, ever observant. Not even our world crumbling apart could prevent her from judging me. "Stop."

Counting. She meant stop counting.

As though my counting were the most troubling thing happening here.

::Strength through silence.:: I tapped it again and again. They were Idris's holy words, yes, but it was Aaru's wisdom

363

I held to right now: *There is strength*, he'd said months ago, *in knowing when to speak, and when to listen. And when to say nothing at all.*

What I hadn't understood then was that those moments could overlap. Mother was still stinging from earlier, and now she was trying to provoke me again. Maybe to distract from the discussion of the treaty, or maybe because she always did this. But now was the time to use silence against her.

It would bother her more than anything else.

Slowly, deliberately, I looked away from her. Silence for Mother. Questions for Father. "You betrayed the Fallen Isles, Father. You and the rest of the Luminary Council. And the other island governments. Everyone who signed the treaty, everyone who knew what it was, betrayed us." I made my voice into flame. "And you put my name on it."

Panic flickered in his eyes. "That isn't true."

"You put my name on the treaty, knowing it was a false promise to the people of the Fallen Isles."

"Mira—"

"Why was I sent to the Pit, Father?"

He glanced around the room, weighing his words, but I didn't give him a chance to use them.

I used mine instead. "The Luminary Council banished me to the Pit because I'd discovered someone was taking dragons from the Crescent Prominence sanctuary and sending them to the Algotti Empire."

Ilina cleared her throat. "Hristo and I were there,

too. The only reason we weren't imprisoned or worse was because Mira protected us."

Hristo and his father looked at each other, the latter in question. "It's true," Hristo said. "That's why Mira disappeared that day, and why Ilina and I went after her."

"I had no idea." Hristo's father had a soft voice. Kind, I'd always thought. And now it was sad, bearing a heavier burden than I'd ever heard in him.

"You weren't supposed to." Hristo bent toward his father, and whatever he said next, I couldn't hear it.

I just turned back to my own father. "Answer this: Is the Luminary Council sending dragons and noorestones to the Algotti Empire in payment?"

His face was ashen, and Mother looked a little sick. She clearly wanted this line of questioning to end, but if they refused to answer, they wouldn't be able to control *how* I heard the truth.

"It's a necessary part of the bargain," Father said at last. "I don't like it, but better dragons than people, don't you think?"

Beside me, Ilina was shaking with rage, her tone a barely contained fury. "They are the children of the gods."

"It seems to me"—Hristo looked up from his father—"that Mira was imprisoned because of the very treaty you named after her. You enabled the Luminary Council to send dragons to the Algotti Empire, and when we discovered that fact, they sought to silence her in the Pit."

Mother straightened herself. "That—"

"Is true," I said. "Ilina, Hristo, and I noticed dragons missing from the Crescent Prominence sanctuary, but later I found out that dragons had also been taken from the Heart of the Great Warrior. They might even have been the very first victims. And just days ago, we discovered yet more dragons had been taken from the First Harta Dragon Sanctuary, under the pretense of helping them because they're sick."

"They are sick." Father glanced at Ilina. "That's why your parents were taken. Because the dragons began acting strangely, violently, and three people already died trying to contain them."

"So my parents have been kidnapped." Ilina's lips curled in a snarl. "Someone kidnapped dragons, was shocked when those dragons got sick, and kidnapped my parents to try to fix it. Have they *stopped* kidnapping dragons yet?"

Father shook his head. "No. The dragons that have been taken are still in the Fallen Isles, tucked away on Anahera until they're healthy. The empire only wants living dragons."

The blood seemed to drain from Ilina's face. "They're on Anahera?"

I reached for Ilina's hand and squeezed. Anahera. That was good. We could use it. "But they haven't stopped taking dragons in the meantime."

Father's voice was flat now. Defeated. "The Summerill Sky Sanctuary is next. Thirteen large dragons will be taken to Anahera to join the others."

My anger was lightning, lashing out in every direction.

1. At my parents, for hiding the truth for so long.
2. At the Luminary Council, for betraying me
    yet again.
3. At all the island governments, because they'd
    colluded to sell our freedom, our dragons, and
    our noorestones.

"We are so vulnerable," I whispered to no one. Everyone.
Aaru looked at me.

"The Mira Treaty is a lie." My heart pounded at the
thought, aching against my ribs. "The peace we've had
these last seventeen years has been a false peace."

Father shook his head. "The problems of the Mira
Treaty don't negate all the good it does. Remember that
it's united us."

"Another lie." I pressed my fingertips against my temples, trying to squeeze out a headache growing there. "It
united the governments in their conspiracy to sell our
freedom. It claims to protect dragons, while giving them
away to our enemies."

"But Harta—"

I glared at him. "Does one good, loving act nullify the
abhorrent nature of the others? Don't pretend this was
done for Harta and her people. We can't accept multiple atrocities because of the independence our ancestors
should have granted Hartans centuries ago. The fact
that we waited until the Algotti Empire was upon us
before taking that action is just as heinous." My hands
were shaking, so I twisted the hem of my shirt around

them as though my rage might be muffled. "And given that the Twilight Senate is doing everything possible to blame Hartans for the trouble on Bopha, going as far as to deport Hartans who live there legally—well, the argument of *helping* Harta would hold more water if other governments weren't constantly chipping away at those newly granted freedoms."

Father said nothing as golden morning light shone warmer through the windows, creeping across the floor. No one else said anything, either. And my heart was racing, like it was struggling to catch up to all the words I'd said. To my father. To my mother. I'd never been given these kinds of opinions before, so where had they come from?

"The empire technically rules us now," Father said, "but we've hardly felt their influence these last seventeen years. The empress has asked nothing of us—"

"Except for our dragons." Ilina's tone was all steel.

"And our noorestones," I added. "Why would we give up our largest noorestones? We could have used them to power more ships like the *Star-Touched*." Or, like the stones that had exploded the *Infinity* . . .

"That's the empress's way of keeping us contained here," Father said. "Without the giant noorestones, we'll be mostly unable to cross the sea and get to them. But they could come to us."

"They've trapped us here," I whispered.

"What do you mean?" Mother scowled at me, as

though she couldn't see it already. "Why would we *want* to leave?"

Ilina answered for me. "While we were on Khulan, Gerel told me a story. She said that while she was a trainee, she and the others would often go hunting, making a game out of who could catch the most of whatever quarry they were after that day. During one hunt, they'd been told to capture seagulls—alive. So dozens of children jumped after seagulls on the beach. It didn't go well, because seagulls are fast and can fly.

"A few trainees found bits of food, luring the birds to them. They were more successful than those jumping, swinging their arms. But there was another trainee who didn't bother to jump or lure. Instead, she built a small dome out of rocks and driftwood and sea grass, with only a small opening in the top. Inside the dome, she dropped scraps of food.

"By the end of the hunt, she had twenty seagulls trapped. They could get in, but not out. She trapped them by giving them exactly what they wanted, and even making it seem like a protected space, away from other greedy birds. But ultimately, they could not leave to save themselves."

"We're the seagulls," Hristo muttered. "And the empire is the clever trainee."

Ilina nodded. "But that's not the only problem Mira was worried about." She looked at me.

"You're right." I faced my parents again. "Not only has

369

the empire trapped us here to pick off in their own time, but we may soon experience the greatest calamity of all."

"What is that?" Mother asked.

"The Great Abandonment." Fury grew sharp within me, cutting through to the bones of my words. "The treaty solves the short-term problem of a potential war, but you've created a long-term problem for us"—I gestured around at my friends—"in the threat of the Great Abandonment."

"We don't believe in the Great Abandonment," Father said. "You know that."

"The gods don't care what we believe." I twisted my fingers in my shirt. "You've felt the tremors. Heard about the storms. There's even been talk that the fields going fallow on Bopha is another sign of the gods' displeasure with us. Either way," I went on, my voice rising in pitch as anger built upon anger, "what you did with the Mira Treaty was wrong, and you know it. Or you wouldn't have hidden it from everyone."

"That's enough, Mira." Father pushed himself to his feet, and Mother went with him. The two of them. Facing me. "I've listened to enough from you."

I stood, too, and just under the thunder of my heartbeat in my ears, I heard my friends rising to their feet as well. Behind me, Ilina placed her hand on my shoulder.

"You don't have to like what I say, but you can't prevent me from saying it. You ceded control of my voice when you chose to protect that hollow treaty over me."

Surprise gasped through the parlor, and Ilina's

370

fingertips dug into my shoulder. Even I hadn't realized the strength of my hurt until just now, those words falling from my mouth like I'd just expelled poison.

"That's not what happened," Father said.

But it was. Couldn't he see that?

And after everything, the first thing Mother wanted to know, upon my return, was what happened to my face. Not whether I was well, or how I'd escaped the Pit, or if I needed to rest. No, she cared about my face most of all.

I turned to Hristo and his father. "You should go spend time together. And pack whatever you need. We're expected at dusk." It was midmorning now, which gave us just enough time.

"You're leaving again?" his father asked, looking between us.

"It isn't safe for us here." The *Chance Encounter* could stay in the harbor for a few days, waiting for Chenda and Gerel to reach us—if they decided to come, of course— but for me to stay in the city was too much of a risk, no matter how much I wanted to soak up my home. "Go," I said to Hristo again.

My guard studied me, a faint question in his eyes; he wanted to make sure I wouldn't need him.

"I'll be fine." My heart was pounding, but he should get to visit his father. If I needed help, I had Ilina.

Hristo and his father left the parlor, moving toward the servants' quarters.

Mother's tone was warning as she said, "Mira—"

"I have one more question." I faced Mother and Father again. "When the truth about the Mira Treaty becomes public, and the legitimacy of the Luminary Council and every other island government is called into question, will you stand with me?"

Aching quiet followed, and I imagined that we could end this discussion the same way we'd begun it—with a yes—but when my father spoke again, it was with a sigh.

"I will think about it."

CHAPTER TWENTY-EIGHT

HE HADN'T REFUSED ME, EXACTLY.

But he hadn't sided with me, either.

It was strange how much that hurt—worse than if he'd simply said no. At least if he'd said no, I would have understood what that meant. Instead, he had to think about it. He had to weigh his affection for me against his commitment to the treaty and council.

And this—this told me that he'd never thought about it before. He'd never separated me from the treaty.

Ten years ago, when that man had tried to kidnap me from my room, Father had told me there were people who hated the Mira Treaty, and therefore hated me as well. There'd been others who *loved* me without knowing a thing about me. Because to them, I *was* the Mira Treaty.

It just hadn't occurred to me that Father felt the same way.

Mother grabbed Father's forearm, and her tone was all venom. "May I speak with you? Privately?"

It wasn't actually a question. As she began dragging him toward the dining room, Mother held a finger at me, silently instructing me to stay. But the moment my parents closed the door behind them, I motioned Ilina and Aaru upstairs.

"I heard what you said." Zara was on her feet now, her eyes sharp with anger, though I couldn't tell whether it was directed at me or the world in general. "I guess Mother and Father are going to assign five more guards to you."

"You don't know what you're talking about." I brushed past her, leading Ilina and Aaru to my room.

At first, everything seemed the same, light and airy, with pale curtains and a hardwood floor made of golden rain tree wood. A braided rug ran down the center of the room, woven from talopus down, imported from Anahera; the walls held paintings of ships and dragons and mountains, probably created by famous artists, but those had all been Mother's requirements for the room, because as the Hopebearer, I needed culture and class.

The other furnishings were things I'd chosen:

1. *My display case, which held ninety-eight dragon figurines made of glass and stone and metal. Some were worth hundreds of lumes,*

while others were but trinkets for tourists.
Nevertheless, they were all precious to me.

2. *My bookcase: six shelves filled with histories*
   of dragons, texts discussing aspects of The
   Book of Love, *and the latest popular novels.*
   The last section was regularly cleared and
   restocked, unless I was quick enough to pull
   a book aside to save forever. Right now, there
   were thirty books in total, but that number
   fluctuated.

3. *My reading chair, positioned near the cliff-*
   facing window (at the head of my bed), with
   a palm-green blanket thrown over the back in
   casual disarray.

4. *My writing desk, which was clear right now.*
   The pens and inks and papers were tucked
   inside the drawer, always stocked so that I
   could write thank-you notes and letters of
   encouragement.

5. *My framed map of the Fallen Isles,*
   beautifully drawn and detailed, with delicate
   pen strokes I'd always tried (and failed) to
   imitate.

6. *A copy of the Mira Treaty, bordered by chains*
   of lala flowers.

Ilina took the reading chair immediately, wrapping herself in the blanket, but Aaru lingered in the doorway, looking uncertain. He cut a striking figure standing there, dressed in the clothes Chenda had chosen for him back in Val fa Merce. The wrap shirt was deep blue, trimmed with a subtle pattern embroidered in black thread.

But even wearing clothes in the style of my island, there was no mistaking him for anything but Idrisi. His posture said everything; rather than thrown-back shoulders and a lifted chin, he stood straight but not proud, and watchful rather than watched.

Ilina cleared her throat. "I think he's standing there because he'd like you to invite him in. He's not rude like me."

Aaru's cheeks darkened with embarrassment.

I ducked my face. "Sorry. Please come in, Aaru." I motioned to the chair at the writing desk.

Though he probably viewed entering my room as enormously improper, he padded in and took the chair I'd indicated, and gazed around the room to take in every detail.

"Can you understand what they're saying?" I leaned on the dressing room doorway. The hum of muffled voices came from below, but they were too indistinct for me to catch more than angry tones.

Aaru nodded, then stopped, his eyes widening in alarm. ::Your mother is threatening to gut your father.::

Hence Aaru's shock. "It's an empty threat. Probably."

He looked uncertain. ::She thinks your father made a mistake.::

"In what?"

He lifted one shoulder in a faint shrug. ::Just now, I think. Or maybe with the treaty. It's hard to tell.::

That was definitely an accurate description of my mother's anger.

A door slammed down the hall—Zara's door—and Aaru cringed. ::You and your sister don't get along.::

"No," I muttered. "We haven't in a while."

He nodded, thoughtful, but there was a look in his eyes that said he'd give anything to see his sisters again.

"I'm going to pack a few things." I opened the door to my dressing room, letting the morning light fall golden across the hardwood.

"Pack your hunting dresses," Ilina said. "And boots. Don't bring anything that requires its own attendants."

I smirked at her. "You realize I've been managing without silk gowns since Sarai, right? I've more or less figured out what I need to bring in order to survive our new lives as fugitives."

"Thank Damina." She leaned toward Aaru. "Grab some paper. I'm dying to know what you think now that you've seen all this." She swept her hand around the room, but she meant the whole house and everything that had just happened inside it. "One day I'll be good enough at your quiet code, but today is not that day."

I slipped into the dressing room and pulled open the drawer at the bottom of the first wardrobe, where I kept my luggage.

There wasn't much appropriate for this journey—I didn't have backpacks like Ilina—but I did have one large bag with a thick strap I could sling across my body. It was easy to carry and could fit a lot without being bulky.

Just as I unclipped the flap and opened the bag, Mother screamed downstairs, "You didn't bother to ask!"

A door slammed.

Footfalls slammed.

Aaru used a pencil to tap on the desk, ::She's coming.::

Determined to ignore her, I flung open the main doors of the first wardrobe. My clothes were organized by color, rather than use, so I would have to go through all three wardrobes to find what I needed.

There, I discovered what had changed. Or, rather, what was missing. Empty spaces where there should be gowns.

Not all my clothes were missing. The hunting dresses were still here, and several day dresses, but all the silk gowns Ilina had made fun of were gone.

Before I could tell the others, my bedroom door clicked open and Mother walked in; I knew the cadence of her footsteps as well as I knew my own.

"Where is she?" Mother asked.

Through the dressing room door, I saw Ilina point from her perch on my chair. Aaru silently tracked her as she moved through the room and strode into the dressing room with me.

"May I speak with you?"

I didn't want to talk to her any more, but she didn't

378

wait for an answer, just shut the door behind her.

Not wanting to give her the satisfaction of seeing my annoyance, I turned back to the wardrobes, looking at what should be a rainbow of clothes. Twelve dresses in all. That was how many were missing. "What did you do with my gowns?"

"I—" She sat at the vanity, crossing one leg over the other. "We, that is. Your father and I. We got word that the speech in the Shadowed City had gone well. That you'd done exactly as Elbena asked of you, and you'd been restored to your position."

"It must be shocking that they lied to you." I pulled a blue and green hunting dress from the wardrobe and began folding.

"The council said our punishment wasn't over yet, and that you'd be traveling for the foreseeable future. They said we weren't allowed to see you, not for a long time. But they did ask us to send some of your clothes—the gowns you'd wear for speeches." Her voice caught, and for a moment I thought she might cry. But when I glanced at her, she wore a sharp but distant expression.

"They wouldn't let you see me because they'd chosen someone to replace me." I dropped the folded dress into my bag, then rummaged through a drawer for a matching pair of leggings. "There was another girl in the Pit. We became friends, I thought, but she was actually there to study me. To *learn* me. The Luminary Council had her placed there as a contingency."

"Is she the girl who spoke in Val fa Merce?"

I nodded. "Her name is Tirta. She looks enough like me to confuse people who've only seen me from far away. And now she moves like me. Speaks like me."

And knew my noorestone secret.

"I heard there was some kind of explosion at that speech, and the theater was evacuated."

That was certainly not something I wanted to discuss with Mother. "Do you know what the speeches say?" I asked.

She leaned back in her chair. "By your tone, I expect they say something you don't like."

"It's how I got this, Mother." I touched just beneath the scar. "Elbena carved it after the speech in the Shadowed City. After I refused to support a decree that would send all Hartans back to Harta, regardless that such action would separate families and friends, destroy careers, and cause financial chaos. The decree chips away at the freedom and independence granted by the Mira Treaty, yet Elbena—and the Luminary Council—wanted me to support it."

Mother pressed her lips together, as though to hide a frown. She didn't succeed. "Your job isn't to judge how governments work. It never has been. If you want to influence—"

"I know. Campaign for a position." I rolled my eyes. "I'm not going to do that, Mother. I've never wanted to. And I never wanted to be the Hopebearer, either, but in that I was given no choice. For years, you and the council used my voice in support or disapproval, never asking my opinions on matters. But I'm seventeen now, and I've lived through events you can't even imagine."

She just stared at me.

"You and the council gave me a voice," I whispered. "When I found the shipping order for the dragons stolen from our sanctuary, I tried to use that voice to help those dragons. But the council imprisoned me. And in the Shadowed City, when I tried to use my voice to help people being treated unjustly, Elbena cut me."

Mother shifted her weight and dropped her eyes. Discomfort radiated from her.

Good.

"The council that *you* love so much has harmed me twice. When my friends and I go public with the information that the Mira Treaty sold us to our enemies, the council will attempt to silence me again. This time permanently. So I suppose the question is this: will you let them harm me again? Or will you, for once, choose me?"

"Mira . . ."

"Will you choose me, Mother?" My voice caught, but I didn't cry. I wouldn't. There'd been enough tears to last, and Mother didn't deserve them anymore. Not after her part in all this.

She opened her mouth, but before she could form a word—either yes or no—the floor shuddered.

"What was that?"

"I'm not sure," Mother said. "A small tremor?"

I hadn't been asking her; I'd been asking Aaru. Still, I answered her. "It didn't feel like a tremor."

At least, the jolt we'd gotten after the quake on Idris had been different. And it wasn't like the earthquake and aftershocks on Khulan, either.

::Explosion.:: Aaru's taps came as wood against wood: the pencil on my desk. ::In the city.::

I opened the dressing room door and found Ilina already on her way to me. "Get Hristo," I said. "We're leaving now."

She nodded and rerouted herself out of the bedroom.

I looked at Aaru. "Will you help me?"

He nodded and began working as soon as I dropped leggings next to the bag. I tucked in underclothes and socks and boots, then dumped random items from my vanity and other drawers into a smaller pouch. When Aaru put the last of my dresses in the bag, his fingers lingered on the fabric for just a moment. They were just hunting dresses, the sturdiest of my clothes, but they were Idrisi cotton.

"What can I help with?" Mother hadn't moved from the vanity seat.

"We're finished." I pulled the flap over the bag and fastened the clips. "We just need to get out of here."

"Why?" She still hadn't moved. Still wasn't helping. "There was an explosion. The Luminary Guards will tell us if there's any danger to the prominences. We'll be safe here."

"You might be, but my friends and I are not." I hefted my bag over my shoulder and headed out of the room. We had to get back to the ship immediately.

"Mira, wait!" Mother hurried out after me.

I'd already stopped, though. Sunlight glittered off the glass and crystal inside my dragon display case. "I need money, Mother."

She started nodding. "All right. How much?"

"A thousand lumes. More if you can."

Aaru's eyes widened at the thought of so much money, but Mother just nodded and said, "I'll get it for you." She left the room without looking back, happy to have something to do.

I turned to my silent friend. "Will you grab one or two of those?" I pointed to a set of seven ebony boxes, each the size of a loaf of bread. They'd been hand-carved by a renowned woodworker from Anahera, and they all had a different species of dragon etched into the lids.

He nodded.

Hands shaking, I opened the display case of dragons.

"What are you doing?" Ilina's voice came from the doorway. "Mira, you can't."

"We need to pay the captain. And it's hard to say how much money we'll need after this." I removed a midnight-blue dragon whose wings were sprinkled with diamond dust, and another with real sapphires for eyes. When Aaru brought the boxes to me, I lifted the lids and wrapped the dragons in the silk scarves that were folded inside.

Three dragons. Four. Five. Six.

I picked out the most expensive dragons, hands trembling as I wound the lengths of silk to protect their outstretched wings and elegant necks. Then, Aaru nestled them into the boxes, adjusting scarves to pad the delicate creatures.

Ilina looked torn as she tucked them into my bag between the clothes. "You don't have to give them to the captain," she said. "I know they're important to you."

"To get our real dragons back, I'd give up every single one of these."

"What about jewelry? There's that necklace—"

I shook my head. "Gone. Anything of mine that would be worth bringing is with Tirta now. Everything else is in the vault, and we don't have time to wait for that. We have to go now. Did you find Hristo?"

"He's downstairs."

"Good." I pulled the bag's strap across my chest and motioned everyone out.

We moved as quickly as we could, finding Hristo already in the parlor with his backpack on and a sword hanging off his hip.

Mother emerged from her room across the house, a heavy sack in hand. Zara was close on her heels, dispensing questions like birds chirped at morning. "Where are they going?" and "What's the money for?" and "What was that noise earlier?"

Ilina grabbed both of her packs off the sofa where she'd left them. "Let's go."

"Mother," I said. "We need a carriage to the harbor, and we can't be seen."

"I'll call for one." She shoved the sack of coins at me and headed for the front door.

A Luminary Guard was already there, her hand raised to knock.

I scrambled out of sight, but I needn't have worried. She wasn't there for us.

"Stay indoors," said the guard. "The prominence is under lockdown. If you hear the signal, use the cliff stairs."

"What happened?" Mother asked. "What was that sound earlier?"

"The council house." The Luminary Guard's voice shook a little. "It exploded."

"Is—"

"They're all dead." The guard heaved a breath. "Every aide, every cleaner, every guard. And every Luminary Councilor who was inside. They're all dead."

AARU

One Day Before Arrest

My workers' grumbles clattered all around Grace Community. The men were angry. On my behalf. On the behalf of their wives and daughters and sisters and neighbors. On behalf of women they'd never met.

For days, tapped questions spread like sickness as my workers brought up the subject to their loved ones.

Streams of families found their way to my house, and while wives offered Mother packets of rice and seeds and other items to help, husbands asked to speak with me in private.

We met in the basement, ten of us, blasphemously close to Idris with our rebellious whispers.

"It is unfair," said one man.

"Where does *The Book of Silence* say Aaru's family must suffer not just loss, but also hunger because of that loss?"

"It doesn't."

"We will help," said another. "Perhaps between all of us . . ."

Their families were just as poor as mine. They had so little to give; how could we take?

"We must think bigger," I said. "Not just my family, but yours as well."

"What do you propose?"

I lifted my copy of *The Book of Silence* to my chest. "This says, 'Silence which brings harm is unholy.' If we are to be faithful followers of Idris's word, then by his book we are bound to speak."

"Speak?" said one. "To who?"

"I don't know," I admitted.

Quiet rippled throughout the basement as the assembled men bowed their heads in contemplation or prayer.

"Tomorrow," I said, "I will go to the square. If I am alone, then I am alone. If you are with me, we will be stronger."

A man nodded, slowly. "As long as we are respectful," he said. "We all have families to feed and none of us want to anger the leaders."

I gazed around the basement, meeting the other men's eyes. "Strength through silence, brothers. Our presence will be our voice."

AT NOON THE following day, I arrived at the square to find at least five hundred men gathered in silence.

They made a path for me to approach the High House,

already rebuilt after the tremor, and as I stood ahead of them, I caught a glimpse of Dema in one of the windows. She turned away from me, but Kader emerged from within. He stared at us, waiting.

We stood tall and did not make a sound.

"What do you want?" As the community leader, he was permitted to speak aloud to anyone he liked.

Custom dictated that I answer in quiet code, because Kader was my superior, and—perhaps—one day my father-in-law. ::**Freedom**.::

Kader turned and went back through the new door. Because he was the leader, and he did not have to listen to me.

Because he was the leader, and silence was a weapon he wielded against us.

Because he was the leader, and our silence now benefitted him.

Holy are the silent. But that creed had been written by men.

Silence which brings harm is unholy. Those were Idris's words.

If I did not use my voice when it was truly necessary, why have a voice at all? I could be respectful. I could request consideration.

But I would be heard.

"Freedom," I said.

Silence fluttered behind me. Then:

::**Freedom. Freedom. Freedom**.:: The word pattered through the square.

Slowly, Kader turned and a deep scowl etched its way onto his face.

::Freedom. Freedom. Freedom.:: The quiet code went on and on, all five hundred of us tapping in rhythm.

Kader went into his house—demonstrating not only his great wealth, as he could afford to rebuild it quickly, but also his denial of our voice. The silence he wanted from us was oppressive. Angry. Unholy.

::Freedom. Freedom. Freedom.::

Though Kader was gone, we were a single, strong voice, at least until the town guard arrived and tried to make everyone go home.

Someone said no.

Then the riot began.

THE GUARD ARRESTED me the next day, and as I said good-bye to my family, I understood the depth of my mistake.

My anger—my questions—had left them with nothing at all.

CHAPTER TWENTY-NINE

THE LUMINARY COUNCIL WAS GONE.

Not all of them, of course. I'd seen Elbena with Tirta, but she was only one of twenty-seven members, and if even half of them had been in the council house today, their deaths would cripple the Daminan government.

The Luminary Council.

The aides.

The guards.

Even the people who had no connection to the government except for the fact that they cleaned the floors, or worked in the mail room, or had business there today.

Innocent people.

All dead.

"Do we know who's responsible?" Mother asked.

"I'm not at liberty to—"

Long, low tones of a ringing bell cut her off.

"You need to go," said the guard. "To your shelter or to the cliffs. We'll hold them off."

::The cliffs?:: Aaru's eyebrows drew inward.

If Hristo didn't understand the quiet code, he did understand the question on Aaru's face. "The prominence is a prestigious place to live." He motioned everyone to follow him toward the kitchen. "But it's not particularly defendable. The houses up here are just houses, not fortresses."

"They're palaces, not houses," Ilina said, and Aaru nodded in vehement agreement.

We moved through the kitchen quickly, all five of us (Zara included), with Mother and Father and Hristo's father close behind. The back door squealed open and we filed outside one at a time.

Sunlight beamed down on the small path through the back gardens, dazzling where it reflected off the white paving stones and small rocks that divided the lala flowers from the canna lilies from the broad-leafed ferns. This was a constantly evolving space, with different displays of flowers depending on what was in season and the mood of the household, but no matter what was planted here, I'd always loved it. I'd always felt safe.

"Houses or palaces," Hristo was saying, "it's not defendable. There are shelters in the basements of every residence, but we don't want to get trapped. Not if we

391

need to leave." He waved us down a wide path, which ran along a low wooden fence. On the other side, the edge of the cliff waited. A sheer drop into the water. "There's a stair on every prominence. We just have to get to it."

"Hurry," Mother said. She and my father were catching up, Hristo's father right behind them.

The bell continued tolling as the eight of us rushed down the path, joined by other families from this prominence. Servants carried baskets and bags for their employers, while children ran ahead. We'd had drills before, with the Luminary Guards guiding people to the stair, but right now it was only us. Civilians.

Still, the training held. Most of us walked as fast as possible, without pushing, without shouting. We moved quickly but quietly, with only minimal conversation buzzing back and forth.

"What's happening?" someone asked.

"The council house was attacked. Warriors are swarming through the city."

And another: *"Khulan has declared war on us."*

I kept my face down, listening to the wind whistle between slats in the fence, and boots pounding on the paving stones, and the *thump* of my bag against my hip.

::**Do you hear it?**:: Aaru's fingers slid off my shoulder when he finished tapping.

I did hear it then. The clash of metal on metal. The shouts of men and women in battle. The peal of the warning bell . . . and its abrupt stop.

Seventy-five, seventy-six, seventy-seven. I counted steps as the others noticed the sudden silence of the bell, and the crowd moved faster.

We'd always thought ourselves so safe up here, so secure with the guard house at the bottom of the cliffs and all the foliage blocking our homes from the main street. But maybe we were those seagulls from Gerel's story.

"There you are!" As we reached the gate, which led to the cliff stairs, Doctor Chilikoba found us. Dust and sweat streaked her face as she heaved her medical bag along with her.

Aaru took her bag and looped it across his chest.

"You're still here? I thought you'd have gone home by now." I glanced at the doctor, then focused straight ahead again; I didn't want to get left behind.

"I told you I would come back to see you." Doctor Chilikoba bumped my elbow. "I was on my way back to your house, but a guard stopped me. Told me to come here instead."

We stopped walking at the gate, where nearly a hundred people had bottlenecked in order to get through. Though more people arrived every minute, no one shoved or pushed to be first; our drills had taught us to slip through one at a time: one from one group, and then one from another.

Friends couldn't stay together. Nor could families. Only nursing mothers were permitted to remain with their infants, because the infants would be held on the way down. This was to avoid prioritizing one family over another; it seemed to me, though, that it forced families to prioritize their own members. Most families practiced this part, too—who would go first, and who would wait. And for those who were separated, older children and adults would help the very young and the elderly, because in Damyan and Darina's eyes, we were all one family.

"Do you know what's happening?" I asked the doctor as the people ahead of us sorted themselves and we scooted forward little by little.

"I thought it was another earthquake."

My heart thundered in my ears as we moved closer to the gate. Only fifty people stood ahead of me, my group included. Everyone was already shifting themselves into a line, which left my friends positioned evenly between my neighbors.

"It wasn't a quake." I started to explain, but Mother grabbed my shoulder.

"Get in line. You can tell her later." Mother's eyes scanned the crowd, then settled on Zara, who'd fallen behind. Hristo's father had stayed with her, just as protective as his son. "Zara!" Mother called.

Frantically, my sister looked between Mother and the people in front of her; there had to be at least thirty. No one would skip in line, not even Zara, but her fear was obvious. She'd overheard my confrontation with our parents; she knew what was at stake.

There was another unspoken rule about the cliff line:

no trading places. It simply caused too much chaos.

But my parents—still next to each other as the doctor and I squeezed into line ahead of them—glanced at each other, and that was it.

I'd never seen that kind of unspoken communication between them before, that silent understanding, but at once, Mother darted forward and hugged me. "I choose you," she whispered. "Be safe."

Then, she and Father both went to Zara. They hugged her and nudged her to the place in line they'd just occupied. "Mira will protect you." I barely heard Mother's voice under the hum of conversation and the wind that hissed through the gate.

It was done. They'd traded two places for one to make up for the chaos, but even so, people grumbled as Zara sprinted forward. Her hands trembled as she took our parents' place in line.

The crash of the Luminary Guard battling warriors intensified, drawing closer. Someone screamed in pain.

Ahead, Ilina vanished through the gate, and Aaru was only two people behind her, his posture stiff with the number of people surrounding him. Four people ahead of me, Hristo glanced back. Our eyes met.

"You should trade places with me," he said. "Go first."

I shook my head. He was my protector, and it was his duty to think like that, but we had to obey the rules of the stair line; my family had already risked confusing everything.

We crept closer to the gate. Only twenty people stood ahead of me. Fifteen.

I glanced back at my parents; there were thirty-three people between us, everyone anxiously waiting their turn to descend the stairs.

Our drills had always included the stairs, because they were narrow and frightening for many, and that part especially had to be practiced. There was no point in a drill that didn't include the actual escape. But still, most people took the stairs slowly, because the drop into the sea was very long indeed.

::Hurry, hurry,:: I tapped to myself. The prominence had never been under attack during our drills, but now the clash of metal struck closer. In the late-morning sun, the off-white uniforms of the Luminary Guard flashed bright, while the leather uniforms of warriors were duller, but still identifiable as *different*. They didn't belong.

My heart thudded impossibly hard against my ribs, aching with every beat. Even with the warriors here, their god-given strength muted, they were stronger and faster than our guards.

They would cut through the prominence defenses and kill everyone in this line.

::Hurry, hurry,:: I tapped.

"Just breathe," Doctor Chilikoba murmured. She stood right behind me, one hand on my shoulder. "Breathe."

Seven people stood ahead of me, and just before he disappeared, Aaru—still with Doctor Chilikoba's medical bag slung across his body—turned and caught my eye.

There was no smile. No encouragement. No trust that we'd make it through this.

How could there be?

He offered only acknowledgment, and then he was gone through the gate, and the next person shuffled up behind him.

"Look!" Someone pointed toward the street. A Khulani warrior had broken through the trees and was scanning the line. Searching for someone.

Searching for me.

I didn't know this warrior, but he would know me. For my whole life, I'd been one of the most recognizable people on the Isles, and with the scar, I was unmistakable.

I ducked my face as the line shuffled forward. Five people. Four people.

::Hurry, hurry.:: Turning my face away from the warrior, I glanced back at my sister; tears trickled down her cheeks, and she bit down on her lower lip to keep from sobbing out loud.

Beyond her, Mother and Father embraced. Just a moment. Just a sliver of the affection I'd always wondered if they actually held for each other. Then, Mother pulled away.

Two people ahead of me.

Three more warriors appeared through the trees.

It was hard to see, since I was trying to keep my face hidden, but at the edge of my vision, I watched Mother striding away from the line—moving toward them.

The person ahead of me vanished behind the gate.

Though Mother's posture didn't change, something about her did. She became magnetic. Everyone turned to look at her, rather than the warriors or the gate. The air around her felt charged as she approached the warriors, who couldn't take their eyes off her. All four men and women lowered their maces to gaze upon her, as though she were the single most beautiful person they'd ever beheld.

"Go," whispered the doctor behind me.

I wrenched my gaze from my mother and stepped through the gate. Only a small ledge stood between me and the edge of the world. The prominence north of ours looked so far away.

With one step, I began my descent down the stairs carved into the side of the cliff, with only a low guardrail to prevent people from falling.

One thousand, eight hundred and sixty stairs.

At the bottom, we'd find boats we could take to the harbor. To the safety of more Luminary Guards for some. To the *Chance Encounter* for me.

Mother's charm still tugged. It called me, urging me to turn my head and watch her use the gift granted by Damyan and Darina, but I forced myself to focus. On the person ahead of me. On the stairs. On the horizon glittering on the far side of the sea. I needed to take advantage of this crack in the warriors' attention.

Wind hissed across the ledge, tearing at my clothes and braids.

::**Go, go,**:: I tapped, tugging my bag toward my stomach; I needed to center my weight.

Twenty landings had been carved into the cliff, allowing the procession to snake back and forth. I couldn't see the people directly below—the cliffs were slightly concave—but the line ahead of me moved steadily downward. Not rushing. Not pushing.

Ahead of Ilina, a young boy trembled and shook his head at every step, but Ilina touched his shoulder and urged him onward.

I clutched my bag, careful to keep two full steps between myself and the person in front of me. The power of Mother's charm still pulled, but I ignored it and kept moving.

With every step, I leaned left toward the cliff—away from the gaping nothing at my right. Still, there was this awful sensation that the stone might betray me, might somehow shove me over the rail and send me falling to my death.

Twenty-two steps down. When I glanced over my shoulder, the doctor had one hand on the rock wall, and her other on the rail. Two people behind her, Zara was still crying, but she, too, held fast to the rail.

I wished I could clutch the rail, but if I didn't press my bag to my stomach, it hung to the right side of my body— the side with the gaping nothing I so desperately wanted to avoid.

One step at a time.

Twenty-five.

Thirty.

Thirty-five.

Only one thousand, eight hundred and twenty-five steps to go. Gravity had never seemed so sinister.

Slowly, slowly, we descended. No one spoke. The wind did enough of that for us, whistling, trying to snatch us from the precarious steps. All the drills in the world hadn't prepared us for actually making this journey.

Shouts sounded above, people screaming and begging for mercy.

As I finally approached the first landing—ninety-three stairs—I scanned the line behind me. Doctor Chilikoba was at my side, and Zara just two people behind her. Mother and Father had been near thirty people behind, but they should be on the stairs already.

Mother had been using her gift to buy everyone time, and Father might have stayed with her, but surely they'd made it through the gate before the screaming started.

On the landing, Aaru glanced back with fear in his eyes, but he gave no indication as to whether he knew what happened to my parents—if he could hear them through all the wind and shouts and thunder in his mind. Then he turned and vanished from my sight, down the next flight of stairs.

It happened as I reached the landing.

Someone fell.

I was just about to make the same turn Aaru had, and

Hristo shortly after: moving to the next flight of ninety-three stairs. And someone screamed.

Several someones screamed.

The falling person had come from the gate, maybe pushed from people struggling, or perhaps they'd lost their balance—

A Khulani warrior stepped through the gate.

Traffic down the first flight had mostly stopped at the fall, and everyone was looking back, so as the warrior appeared, there was a ripple as people ducked.

The warrior had a bow. So quickly I could barely track her movements, she raised her bow and loosed an arrow.

Even from so far away, she'd spotted me on the first landing, accounted for wind and gravity, and sent her arrow flying straight at me.

Doctor Chilikoba was fast, too.

She pushed me against the cliff.

The arrow pierced her throat.

She staggered away from everyone, even in her last moments thinking of others, and tumbled over the guard-rail.

Gone.

CHAPTER THIRTY

W IND SCREAMED.

I screamed.

Angry black tendrils fluttered on the edge of my sight, and I *wished* for noorestones nearby to give me strength. Power. Something.

But she was gone. My doctor. My confidant.

She'd taken that arrow meant for me, and even in her dying moments, she'd thrown herself off the cliff to prevent her body from tumbling down the stairs, knocking into people, causing more harm than the warrior could have hoped for.

The new person behind me, a man I didn't know, guided me around the corner to the second flight of stairs. "You'll be out of sight," he said. Or, at least, that was what it sounded like he said.

But there was so much screaming.

As I moved down the next set of stairs, my mind dutifully counting steps, another body dropped: the warrior who'd murdered my doctor.

Up and down the evacuation line, people were screaming. It seemed endless. Hopeless. Because even with the assassin dead, we never received word from above—word that the Luminary Guard had defended us and we could climb back up.

We reached the second landing, and then the third.

Everything tunneled: my vision, my breathing, my numbers. I placed one foot in front of the other, following the line, but my mind was far away.

Down, down we went. The last time I'd taken stairs like this, I'd been following warriors into the Pit. But that descent had been nothing. A mere two hundred and fifty-seven steps. And here, there were more than a thousand to go.

Every so often, the man behind me said something my mind was too exhausted to catch, but his tone was kind. Whatever words he used were lost to the shriek of the wind, the haggard sobbing of my sister, and the fears swarming through my head.

Four landings.

Then five.

My legs ached with the strain of stretching, my toes touching the next step, my muscles compensating to find balance. My stomach clenched from holding myself upright, and my head pounded.

Six landings.

Desperately, I wanted to sit down. I wanted to think. I wanted to cry. But the procession continued without pause, because we had no way of knowing if the warriors were coming—if they were following down the stairs. The curve of the cliffs hid us from their sight, but just because they couldn't shoot arrows at us anymore didn't mean they weren't in pursuit. And we had no way of knowing how many there were. I'd seen four. One was dead.

That left three unaccounted for.

As we moved, I kept glancing over my shoulder to check the line behind me, but people were only sobbing, not screaming, and I couldn't tell whether that was a good sign or not.

A thousand years later, we reached the twentieth landing and the boats, which would take us to the harbor. Ten boats sat ten people each.

Like on the stairs, the rule of the boats was that whoever reached them first would take them to the harbor. Then, someone—hopefully Luminary Guards—would bring the boats back to get the others.

The seats filled quickly, everyone in the beginning of the line eager to escape. Two boats loaded. Three. Four.

We crept closer to the loading platform.

Five boats. Six. Seven.

Ilina and Aaru took seats on the ninth boat.

People began loading onto the tenth boat. Hristo swung his backpack onto his lap and sat. The people directly in front of me followed.

"Sit," said the man behind me. "It's your turn."

My whole body shook as I climbed onto the boat and took a seat, then stuffed my bag between my feet.

There was only one seat left.

I spun toward the dock. "Zara!" There wasn't enough room for an eleventh person; she'd have to wait for the boats to return, and Mother had promised I'd protect her. How could I protect her if we weren't on the same boat?

But the man was already helping her into his seat. "Go in the light of the Lovers," he said, and untied the ropes holding us to the dock.

I wanted to thank him, but the words caught in my throat. Before I could shake them free, ten boats all cast into the sea, oars slapping the water in steady rhythms. The numbers ticked in the back of my head as Zara leaned her shoulder against mine.

"Do you think they're still alive?" she whispered. "They have to be, right?"

I didn't know how to answer. Instead, I lifted my eyes to Hristo's, then looked beyond him to the people huddled at the base of the cliff stairs. Though I searched the faces of everyone left waiting, I couldn't see my parents, or Hristo's father.

"I saw Mother use her gift," Zara went on. "They wouldn't have been able to hurt her while she was using it, right? They wouldn't have *wanted* to."

There was nothing to say. It was unfathomable to me

405

that the warriors wouldn't have hurt her, but I didn't want to say that, not to my sister, and not when she was clearly falling apart. I couldn't remember the last time she'd voluntarily talked to me, let alone touched me.

Slap . . . Slap . . . The oars hit the surface of the water. I didn't look down, as though the doctor's body might be floating here, staring up at us with dead eyes while we made our escape and she never left.

Tears flooded my eyes.

They'd killed her. And I had no doubt they'd killed my parents and Hristo's father, too.

Several faint *plops* interrupted the steady sound of the oars. I wiped the tears off my face and looked up.

Three warriors stood on the stairs, just above the dozens of evacuees.

"We have to go back!" I pointed toward the cliffs, but that only made the rower push faster.

"We can't go back," he said. "We can't fit everyone on the boats, and if we try, we'll lose people to their arrows. We have to save as many as possible, and this is what we practiced."

Zara had her knuckles pressed against her mouth, eyes wide as she stared toward the dock we'd just fled. "The man who traded places with me—"

"He knew what he was doing," said a woman across from her. "We all knew there might be warriors on the stairs after us."

That was easy for her to say. She was safe on a boat.

"We have to save them," I said again, just as more

406

arrows landed in the water, splashing short of us.

They weren't even trying to hit us anymore. They simply wanted to make sure we didn't attempt to save the others, warning us away with volleys of arrows as they descended the rest of the way to the docks. If we turned around, some of us would die before we reached the rest of the evacuation line. And before we would be able to load everyone else onto the boats, risking capsizing, we'd all be dead.

When I looked at Hristo and Zara in my boat, and my other friends in the boat ahead of us, I knew I couldn't risk them. Not for a rescue mission that would never succeed.

Still, the fact that none of us would even try . . .

I bent over my legs, linking my hands over the back of my neck, and focused on my breathing. Doctor Chilikoba would tell me to breathe.

Doctor Chilikoba was dead.

Maybe my parents were, too.

Oars hit the water again and again, and seagulls cried, and people screamed on the docks as they died.

At my side, Zara's position mirrored mine as she sobbed openly.

Mother had promised her that I would protect her.

Shaking, I wrapped one arm around my sister and pulled her close.

THE PORT BUSTLED with prominence evacuees rushing to find friends, families scrambling to reconnect, and Luminary Guards struggling to produce order from this chaos.

The moment we disembarked our boat, Hristo found a guard to take it back to the central prominence, but we all knew it was too late for those we'd left behind. The warriors killed indiscriminately.

There was one benefit to the chaos: we found the *Chance Encounter*, her red sails furled against the wind, and we climbed the gangplank without anyone questioning us.

"Another one?" Captain Pentoba frowned as Zara wiped her eyes on her sleeve. "Where am I supposed to put all of you?"

"Chenda and Gerel?" Their names barely squeezed from my throat. "Are they here? Have they come?"

The captain shook her head. "I haven't heard from them."

I wished we hadn't parted ways in such anger. What if I never saw them again?

"What happened over there?" Captain Pentoba motioned toward the city. "We heard an explosion and then people started coming down off those cliffs."

"Attack." The *Chance Encounter* swayed under my feet, familiar and comforting now, but we weren't out of danger yet. Altan's warriors had followed us here. It was likely they'd been the ones to attack the council house. "Have you seen a Khulani ship?"

"Cargo vessels, yes. They're here in port. But if you're asking about something warriors might have come in on—"

I nodded.

"—Then I haven't seen anything. That doesn't mean they're not here, though. There used to be a port just south of the prominences, but it hasn't been in use in decades. Not since this one opened. A company of warriors could defeat the detail stationed there without blinking." Captain Pentoba gave a sharp whistle, and One ran up behind her. "Tell the crew: we sail now."

"We should wait," Zara said. "My parents might be coming. Hristo's father, too."

The captain tested the wind and shook her head. "We'll lose the advantage if we don't go now. One, pay the port fee and let's get moving."

He hurried to obey.

My heart wrenched at the thought of leaving them behind, but she was right. Waiting meant giving the warriors more time to organize against us. Altan would have predicted we'd head straight to the *Chance Encounter*. He was probably on his way out of the old port, not caring if he left warriors behind.

Zara spun to glare at me. "We can't leave without Mother and Father. Don't let the ship leave."

As though it was my decision. "Mother promised you that I would protect you, not follow your orders. She also didn't say anything about waiting for her. You saw what happened on the cliff: we don't know if they're alive."

Zara shoved me, making me stagger back two steps. "Don't say that!"

"Neither Mother nor Father came down the stairs. Not Hristo's father, either."

"That doesn't mean they're dead!" She shoved me again, but this time I was braced for it.

Still, I glanced at Hristo. "Take her somewhere out of the way." Of all the people she might consider listening to, he was the only one on the ship.

He nodded, and a moment later, he had Zara halfway to the forecastle.

"That was insensitive about Hristo's father," Ilina said.

I closed my eyes and breathed. She was right. I should have watched my words. "I'll apologize when we're on the ocean again."

She nodded and grabbed my bag to loop the strap over her shoulders, next to her own belongings. "Good. For now, I'm going to take these to the cabin and check on the dragons. Maybe the captain can leave word for Gerel and Chenda—"

The bags sagged in her grip as she stared over my shoulder.

"Fallen Gods," she breathed.

I turned around, too, as whispers and curses rippled across the deck.

"*Seven gods.*"

"*What is it doing?*"

Wings.

Above the city proper, an immense blue-green *Drakontos titanus* gained height and arched back her neck to let loose an enormous shriek that echoed around the cliffs and over the water. She was thunder. She was lightning. She was *rage*.

Chills crept up my spine as the roar carried across the harbor.

"Dear Damina." Ilina stood at my side. "It's Hush."

::She's beautiful.:: At my other side, Aaru was completely motionless, save his tapping on the back of my hand. ::Where did she come from?::

"I don't—"

Before I could finish, Hush twisted and dived toward the city. Her body cut through the column of smoke coming from the council house remnants, and then she breathed in.

It was always clear when a dragon inhaled into their second lungs: the breath was longer and deeper, and their chest expanded. Hush's did now, her dark scales glistening with a golden shimmer in the midday sun.

When she breathed out, it was with fire.

All around port, the awe shifted into terror as one of the largest dragons in the Fallen Isles set fire to Crescent Prominence.

"No!" The cry came from me, but also from hundreds of others. At once, a stampede of terrified people rushed on and off ships, with several being shoved into the water in the chaos.

"Get to sea!" Captain Pentoba cried. "We're leaving now!"

Flames erupted from the city, with plumes of smoke not far behind. It billowed into the sky, then scattered apart with Hush's heavy wingbeats as she ascended and took another deep gulp of acrid air into her second lungs.

Even from here, the rush and roar of fire was incredibly loud, and the sky over the city glowed orange and black. All around us, people asked why, why, *why*, as though they couldn't tell she was *angry*.

Aaru, Ilina, and I rushed up to the foredeck, keeping out of the way of crewmen running back and forth. We were just in time to see more escape boats reach the harbor, and people leaping out to find their loved ones and stare at the sky. Screaming and crying and begging filled the air as Hush let loose another breath of fire on the city.

I didn't see my parents out there. Or Hristo's father. I didn't see my family's chef or maids or anyone else I knew.

My heart broke.

"We have to go!" the captain shouted from somewhere on the main deck. Rigging groaned and lines hissed. Sails snapped taut, and the *Chance Encounter* began to slip from her berth.

But we were too late.

A long, slender ship was already moving north, her blue sails painted with Khulan's mace and the Drakon Warrior silver claw.

"Faster!" shouted the captain, but it was clear now that there was no way we would escape this harbor without their notice.

Altan was aboard that ship: of that I had no doubt. Worse, he would recognize the *Chance Encounter* from Lorn-tah, and he'd know I was here—trying to escape before his warriors could capture me.

Or kill me.

I had no idea what he wanted anymore. Me, yes, but alive or dead? In the Pit, he'd been angry that I'd stabbed him. He'd been ready to kill me. But in the tunnel by the dishonored camp, he seemed more interested in keeping me alive.

But the arrow that had taken Doctor Chilikoba . . .

Whatever Altan wanted from me, it wasn't good. He didn't mind slaughtering the Luminary Council and everyone else in the building. He didn't care if my neighbors were murdered as they fled their homes. And he didn't care that my sister was on this ship.

He would kill everyone in order to get to me.

Bolts of betrayal and anger struck in the back of my mind; how could Chenda have thought we might work with him?

And if he was here, then where were they?

Before I could worry more, Hristo ran onto the foredeck. "I locked Zara in a cabin. She's furious, but if there's a rampaging dragon—"

"I don't blame you at all." I hugged Hristo. "Thank you for taking care of her."

"Look!" Ilina pointed toward the city again, where Hush screamed into the sky. She was coming toward us,

413

pausing only to set fire to new streets. "Good Damyan and Darina."

My heart pounded as Hush stormed through the sky, blazing over the city as she flew toward us. And at our backs, the warriors' ship prepared to block the harbor entrance and prevent us from leaving.

"You have to do something," said Ilina.

"Me?" But even as Ilina began to nod, I knew what she meant:

1. *Almost a year ago, I'd tripped over a dragon's dinner in the sanctuary. Siff had been ready to gore me, but then I'd reached out for her and she'd stopped.*
2. *On the docks of the Shadowed City, Lex had been scared and angry and hurt, and she'd been ready to set fire to everything around her. But I'd gone to her, and she'd calmed.*
3. *Then there was Kelsine in the Pit.*
4. *And the ghosts of connections with the sedated dragons in Harta.*

"They call you the Dragonhearted for a reason." Ilina squeezed my shoulders. "I don't know how you do it, but every time I think it's impossible, you make them love you."

"All right." I didn't know how I was supposed to do this. Hush was immense. Wild. Just because she was a sanctuary dragon did not mean she was a tame creature. But if I didn't try, everyone here would burn.

Another polyphonic roar echoed across the harbor, closer, louder, hotter. Dark wings spread across the sky, eclipsing the sun. Crewmen dropped back their heads to gaze upon the biggest dragon they'd ever seen.

"Sail!" Captain Pentoba screamed.

Fear pulsed through my heart, and the noorestone powering the ship hummed through me. I could feel it. I could feel *all* the noorestones on the ship—all one hundred and forty-four.

Wind gusted with every beat of Hush's wings as she landed on a huge outcropping of rock. People fled in all directions as she inhaled into her second lungs.

I had to stop her, but I didn't make dragons *do* anything. If my encounters with dragons were different than most people's, it was only because I wanted to understand them. Because I empathized with them.

Something in my heart shifted, and I stepped away from my friends. "Oh, Hush."

Terror slipped through me as the dragon swung her head around, flames dancing between her teeth, but she didn't blow the fire.

In the periphery of my vision, a noorestone glowed brighter; I didn't look away from the *Drakontos titanus*.

Aaru had been right earlier: she was a beautiful creature, with sharp ridges of scales across her face and around her eyes, and horns as long as I was tall. She glimmered golden where light hit, like sun over dark waves.

"You're angry," I whispered, reaching for her. "You have that right."

Her sanctuary had been raided. Other dragons had been stolen. It was a wonder *she* had escaped that fate. How terrifying it must have been for her, coming home to their absence. Hearing the council house explode. Seeing the chaos of people everywhere.

And perhaps she was sick, too, like Tiff and the other large dragons at the First Harta Dragon Sanctuary. This illness, whatever it was, caused dragons to exhibit all sorts of strange—sometimes violent—behavior.

Hush needed our love, not our fear. Our respect, not . . .

Warning bells pealed as police and Luminary Guards swarmed in, bows raised toward the great dragon. Two clangs. Three. Four.

And we were moving farther away. The *Chance Encounter* cut through the water, faster and faster; every noorestone nearby shone with hot blue-white light.

"Hush, fly!"

::The noorestones. We must go faster!:: Aaru spun me and pointed toward the Khulani vessel, positioned to block us in. We'd have to stop or risk ramming into their port side.

Faster, he'd said.

I gripped the rail and closed my eyes, blocking out the tolling bells and rushing water and people shouting and great flaps of wind . . .

I blocked out everything but the noorestone sitting in its cage in the center of the ship. Even from here, I could feel its facets—twenty-one of them—and the fifty-seven places it touched steel bars and copper wires.

And then.

I pushed.

The hum of the giant noorestone intensified as it gave more and more power to the ship. Faintly, I could feel Aaru's hand on my arm, his fingers tapping messages of encouragement. I could feel gusts of wind and the spray of waves caressing my face and tangling through my hair. But those were faraway sensations, growing dimmer against the light pouring from the heart of the *Chance Encounter* and the other hundred and forty-three noorestones ensconced in this ship.

Light erupted from every gap in the wood: a beacon, a promise. I didn't need my eyes to see it, because my heart beat in time with the ship's and I could *feel* it.

Distantly, I heard the dragon roar. The ship scream. My power strained to slip away from me and create its own chaos, as it had in the Pit and the tunnel and the theater, but I held it. And faintly, I felt Ilina, Hristo, and Aaru holding me, giving me confidence and strength.

Power pulsed through my soul and at last broke free.

PART FOUR

DENY THE DARK

CHAPTER THIRTY-ONE

MINUTES MIGHT HAVE PASSED, OR HOURS.

When I opened my eyes and returned to myself, only ocean stretched before us, and the crew sang as they worked the lines. My friends had remained at my side. A wonder, because I could have exploded the ship.

But I hadn't.

I'd used my strange ability with noorestones for something good.

Aaru squeezed my arm and smiled. ::Very good.::

Exhaustion flickered in the corners of my mind, and I knew I needed to rest. The sun angled toward the west, setting over the Daminan mountains.

"That was amazing." Ilina had been looking beyond me, but when I returned to myself, her focus shifted. "The way you spoke to Hush. The way she *listened*." Her voice cracked a little. Worry or weariness or perhaps a bit of jealousy. She was the dragon trainer; if anyone should have this affinity for dragons, it should be her. But she wouldn't show envy beyond that. No. She just wrapped her arms around me and squeezed. "I knew you had it. Hristo and I both knew it."

Hristo nodded.

Before I could ask more, Captain Pentoba strolled across the foredeck. "Well done, Hopebearer. I don't know what you did with my ship, but your friends said it was definitely you. We've outpaced the *Falcon*."

"The *Falcon*?"

"The Khulani ship. I saw her name as we flew past."

"Did you see Altan?" If he'd been on the deck, he'd have seen me standing here, Aaru at my side. The two prisoners he hated most.

Captain Pentoba nodded. "Oh, yes. At the helm and screaming orders. I swear, there was steam coming out of his ears."

The image drew a quick smile from me. I didn't like the idea of missing him that narrowly, but at least we knew where he was.

"We have a few hours' lead," Captain Pentoba said. "But there are some things we need to discuss."

All I wanted was to collapse into my hammock, LaLa curled up on my chest, but I motioned for her to ask her questions.

"What do you want to do about Gerel and Chenda?" The captain squinted south. "We're far from Crescent Prominence now. It's unlikely they'll catch up to us, as fast as we went. And it's unwise to turn back."

"Was anyone able to leave word for them?"

Captain Pentoba shook her head. "I'm afraid not. Between the dragon and the *Falcon*, there was no time."

Ilina glanced down.

"All right," I said after a moment. "Then I guess we go on without them."

The captain nodded. "Which brings me to my next question."

The question of our destination. That made sense. We had to go somewhere, but considering all the disturbing information we'd learned in Crescent Prominence, *everywhere* seemed incredibly dangerous and full of lies.

This side of Darina was the easternmost part of the islands, and we were already going north—toward Anahera. "Let's keep our current heading. It's away from the *Falcon* and we can dock in Flamecrest if we want to get lost in the crowd there."

Ilina's face darkened.

"What's in Flamecrest?" asked the captain.

There were dragons on Anahera, but I'd learned my lesson about trying to rescue them with brute force. We didn't know where they were, or have a good plan to get them, and now we had nowhere to even take them. Ilina's parents were on Anahera, but rescuing them seemed even more impossible. "I don't know if we'll stay there," I said. "But the Flamecrest port is crowded. If we can change our colors and hide for a day, the *Falcon* will pass us by. That will give us some time to discuss everything and come up with a plan."

"I don't want to go to Flamecrest," Ilina said.

"They're not that bad." Wildly extravagant, yes. Over-taxing thieves, no. But for years, rumors about the Isle of Destruction had swirled across Damina, painting the government there as some sort of oppressive regime.

In all my visits to Anahera, I'd seen no evidence of truth in that gossip. The island had its wealthy and its poor, just like any other place, but Aaru told stories of worse poverty on Idris, and I'd seen the dishonored camp with my own eyes. The economic imbalance on Anahera didn't come close.

"I'm surprised to hear you defend them." Captain Pentoba raised an eyebrow. "The High Magistrate was vocally opposed to the Mira Treaty, you know."

"I'm aware." But every time I'd visited the island, the High Magistrate and the Fire Ministry had been nothing but cordial to me, going so far as to throw lavish parties in my honor. When I'd asked the magistrate if his people minded—considering his campaigning against the treaty—he simply said he could not deny the good it had done. "I still think it's worth going. It will give us a safe place to hide and work out what to do next, and if somehow the Anaheran authorities should hear about the explosion of the council house in Crescent Prominence—"

My throat closed at the words. All those innocent people. Slaughtered. Because they'd been in the wrong place at the wrong time.

"We can't ask them for help directly," Hristo muttered, "but if they were to find out the *Falcon* carries the warriors responsible for the explosion, they would feel obligated to seize the ship. For the treaty, and for their god."

Destruction without purpose was an affront to Anahera. Like wildfires making way for fresh growth, or felling a tree to carve something useful from its wood, Anaherans believed in life and death and then new life. They believed destruction should be carefully crafted, with love and understanding, to make a better future. But what happened in Crescent Prominence had been senseless. They would not be able to abide what the warriors had done.

Ilina's gaze was hard as she shook her head. "I can't go there."

"Why?"

"It's personal." She clenched her jaw.

Personal? I'd never heard Ilina talk about a connection to Anahera, not even once. "Then offer a better plan." I frowned, confused and concerned, but we couldn't stand here and debate it. Captain Pentoba needed to know where to go.

Ilina crossed her arms and looked west, her acquiescence spoken only in the set of her shoulders.

I turned back to the captain. "Flamecrest."

"Good." Her gaze flickered beyond me. "And about that dragon . . ."

"Is she all right?" My chest squeezed. "Where is she?"

"Over there." Ilina pointed over my shoulder, toward the jagged peaks of the Skyfell Mountains and the setting sun. "She's been following us."

I shaded my eyes and squinted until I found the dark shape against the golden sky. There she was. *Drakontos titanus*. Her wings outstretched and her body full of air.

"I don't think she's following," I murmured. "I think she's escorting us."

"Whatever she's doing, she makes the crew nervous," Captain Pentoba said.

I watched her for a moment, torn between extremes of understanding. The crew had every right to be afraid: they'd just seen Hush set a city ablaze, and it was impossible to predict what she'd do next.

It had been *my* city she'd set out to destroy, and there was a part of me that was furious with her for that.

But my heart pounded with hers: terrible things were happening to dragons, and humans were to blame. We had started this fight; she intended to finish it. Perhaps I could help direct her fury.

"Captain!" One called up from the main deck. "Another ship coming up."

I was too tired for more disasters, and my legs ached from descending hundreds of stairs, but I followed the captain to the quarterdeck and peered south.

One was right: in the distance, sails stood black against the water, gleaming like oil in the last light of the sun. The ship moved quickly, cutting through the waves as though they were but clouds. In spite of the head start I'd given us, the black ship was gaining on us.

"At least she's not the *Falcon*." Captain Pentoba held a scope to her eye. "If she's not the ship Gerel and Chenda went to investigate, then she's similar."

When she lowered her scope, Hristo took it and peered through. "No one on the deck. At least that I can see."

"I noticed that, too." The captain scowled across the water. "We don't know they're after us. They might also be fleeing Crescent Prominence."

::If they're from the empire, they might be after Mira.::

Fear spiked through my heart as I interpreted Aaru's quiet code. "Why would they be after me?" But I knew, didn't I? No one could ignore what I'd done in the theater. They'd find out. And they'd find me.

Aaru just looked at me, his mouth turned in an unhappy smile.

"If definitely doesn't move like any Fallen Isles ship I've seen. It's so fast." The captain took her scope again, just as the sun slipped beneath the Skyfell Mountains and the black ship vanished against the dark water. "No noore-stones. Only one light, and it's flickering."

"Like fire?" Ilina shook her head. "That seems unnecessarily dangerous."

Aaru pulled out his notepad and wrote, *What do we do?*

I stuffed my shaking hands behind my back and tried to focus on my breathing.

"I think we need to run," said Ilina. "Get away from them as fast as we can."

"And then what?" Hristo asked. "We might escape tonight, but what about tomorrow? Or the next day?"

"We can't run indefinitely," Captain Pentoba reminded them. "Our supplies will only last so long before we need to find a port."

I stared *hard* at the place the black ship had been, but I couldn't see it anymore. Not with the sun set and the moons not yet risen.

There.

A flame.

Panic stirred inside me, and my heart pounded against my chest. Fast. Too fast. And I grasped for my breath, but I'd been awake since midnight. I'd trekked across my city, only to discover that my parents had knowingly betrayed the Fallen Isles and used my name to do it, and now they might be dead. Then I'd been chased down the cliffs, into a trap set by the warriors who'd set off some sort of explosion in the city. And after we'd somehow managed to evade the *Falcon* and calm a raging dragon, we had to deal with the black ship?

Everything was going wrong.

"Hopebearer, can you speed us up again?" Captain Pentoba stuffed her scope back into her pocket.

The idea of touching the ship's noorestone again made

my stomach roil. "Possibly." The word puffed out of me. I didn't want to run anymore—we'd been running every moment since the Pit—but what alternative did we have?

Flame glinted against the water, closer than before.

My heart sped painfully, and at once I remembered my pills. The calming pills Doctor Chilikoba had given me.

Doctor Chilikoba was dead.

Which meant the pills she'd given me today might be the last I'd ever get. Was this attack bad enough to warrant a pill? Could I take one now? What if I took one now but needed it later?

Tears pricked at my eyes, and it felt like everyone was staring at me, watching my descent into panic. I couldn't tell if anyone had said anything. If I was supposed to say something more. Darkness tucked around the corners of my vision.

"I—I can try the noorestone." Did the words even come out loud enough to be heard?

Someone touched my arm; the gentleness suggested Aaru, but I couldn't see him for the black fog tunneling my vision.

"I don't think she can do it again." Ilina's voice sounded far away. "She's having a panic attack. Mira, I'll get a pill."

"No." It was the only word I could find now. The rest—wanting to save the pills for something more serious—was lost in the rush of wind and the shouts of sailors and the bone-shattering cry of a dragon. Her roar bounced off the mountains and pealed across the ocean, echoing and echoing. It was the only thing I could hear: Hush's rage, my panic, and the numbers crowding in my head.

Five of us standing here.

One sister below.

Two friends missing.

One strange black ship.

One angry dragon.

As a strong arm wrapped around my waist, taking some of my weight, Hristo said by my ear, "I have you."

I leaned toward him, letting him help; on the other side of me, Aaru's hand fell off my arm.

But before I had a chance to worry I'd hurt him again, my vision started to come back and I caught sight of a black shadow against the twilight sky: beautiful and deadly.

Captain Pentoba gripped the rail as though to steady herself. "What is she doing?"

There was no need for anyone to answer. Bright blue flame spun from Hush's open jaws, straight toward the black ship.

Its sails caught first, lighting up the ship like a torch. The rush and growl of fire carried across the waves, horrifying.

"Turn about!" Captain Pentoba strode toward her crew. "Prepare to take on survivors! Get Kursha up here!" Her orders rippled across the *Chance Encounter* as the rigging groaned and sails flapped—and slowly the ship began to turn.

Aaru, Hristo, Ilina, and I were pressed against the

railing, watching flames consume the black ship with frightening speed. It had come so much closer in the time we'd been discussing it, so now we had a clear view of its destruction.

Above it all, Hush circled and roared again, ready to finish the ship and any survivors. But this time, I was ready. I leaned on the railing and lifted my face, and although my heart pounded painfully, I called for her.

"Hush!" Her name tore from me like a prayer, because I finally understood what she'd been doing.

She had felt my fear. My panic. She'd responded by attacking the source of my anxiety.

Which meant I needed to focus myself, because Hush couldn't tell the difference between a small panic attack and my imminent death.

One.

Hush pulled up, away from the burning ship.

Two.

Her roar skittered across the water, confused but curious.

Three.

Metal shrieked as something in the black ship ripped apart.

Four.

Screams from the crew rose up as Hush circled both the *Chance Encounter* and the burning black ship.

Five.

Splashes sounded in the water—crewmen leaping in

and swimming toward the wreckage.

Six.

Wood cracked, and a burning mast fell into the ocean.

Seven.

A cry for help.

Eight.

Red and orange raged against the water, illuminating a sheet of black metal with three people clinging to it.

Nine.

The crewmen reached the survivors and began to help them swim toward safety.

Ten.

Wingbeats punctuated the night as Hush—satisfied I was no longer afraid—flew toward land again.

"Do you need a pill?" Amber glass shimmered between Ilina's fingers. My calming pills.

My hands still shook, but from exhaustion, not panic. "I'm all right for now."

She slipped the bottle into my pocket. "Keep that with you. If you feel another panic attack coming, take one. If Hush can sense your anxiety, you need to be able to control it."

The words made my heart twist into a knot, but she was right. I should have considered what this new connection with a *Drakontos titanus* could mean, and what she might do to protect me. If anyone had died . . .

Ilina closed her eyes and exhaled. "I don't mean to make you feel bad. I know it's worse for you. It's just more complicated now."

I let my hand rest over my pocket where the pills waited. "I know. But I think we're going to have to find a way to get more. There are only twenty here."

And my doctor was dead.

Maybe my parents, too.

Possibly Hristo's father.

As well as countless others from Crescent Prominence.

"We'll find something. Maybe Kursha can help." Ilina glanced starboard, where crewmen had a line on a crank and were heaving everyone aboard.

Cautiously, we headed down to the main deck.

"Seven gods," Ilina breathed.

I stood at her side, watching as Teres checked the pulse of the first person pulled onto the deck. He was a young man, with dark-brown skin, but that was all I could see of him. Burns covered half his face and body, leaving his clothes a charred mess of wet fabric. Still, I could tell the jacket was the uniform of a dragon keeper at the First Harta Dragon Sanctuary.

"It's him." I could hardly believe it, although I'd suspected, hadn't I? "It's the man from the sanctuary." I'd nearly run straight into him. And I'd begged him for help. I'd told him that his empire was taking our dragons. Had there been amusement in his tone? Would I even recognize familiar expressions and manners on such a foreign face?

Except his face wasn't strange. He looked normal. He looked like one of us.

Idris is isolated. That was how the song went. But maybe

all of the Fallen Isles were isolated, too. Mother had even asked why we'd ever want to leave.

"I saw him in the theater, too," Hristo said. "Standing near the stage while everyone ran."

My heart clenched up as the man from the empire rolled onto his back and groaned. "Do you think—"

There was no time to finish the question. Two more people lurched onto the deck, their limbs splayed out as they gasped dry air.

Gerel and Chenda.

CHAPTER THIRTY-TWO

THE MAN FROM THE EMPIRE WAS IN NO CONDITION TO speak.

While all three passengers aboard the black ship had suffered burns, Gerel's and Chenda's were small and easily treatable. They protested, but were told to spend the night in the infirmary at the medic's orders. (Plus, Zara had taken the last bed in our cabin, and the infirmary was the only other place they could sleep.)

But the man . . .

The story I'd gotten from Gerel and Chenda had been vague, but the essence was that commandeering a ship was not as hard as I'd expected. At least, if the pair doing the commandeering included a trained warrior and someone who could bend shadows to her will.

They'd ambushed the man and tossed him in his own brig, then set sail the day following our departure from Val fa Merce. But when they arrived in Crescent Prominence, it was just in time to see our frenzied escape from the *Falcon*, as well as the dragon following us. So they'd pushed harder to catch up, only for the dragon to set fire to their new ship.

The sails took the worst of the flames, but when the mast fell, it hit next to the prisoner. So while Gerel was practically ripping off part of the hull for Chenda to float on, the prisoner was inhaling smoke and suffering severe burns. They hadn't known until Gerel went back for him.

The ship's medic was not optimistic about his survival.

But given what else Gerel and Chenda had said about him, we were all hoping he'd make it:

"He is a spy. When he figured out that we know you, he freely admitted his allegiance to the Algotti Empire."

"How did he learn that?" Hristo had asked.

"It's a small ship," Gerel replied. "He overheard. But that's not what's important."

Hristo had looked as dubious as I felt, but we waited for her to finish.

"He said he would gladly tell Mira everything he knows about the treaty, the empire's involvement in it, and the threat to the Fallen Isles—but only Mira." Gerel frowned. "We stayed in Val fa Merce long enough to learn that Altan *had* been there, but left around the same time you did. We debated going after him, but thought we could get more information if we brought the spy to you. When we're ready for him, Altan won't be hard to find." As she spoke Altan's name, her expression tightened.

Maybe, after the fight, she and Chenda were just as reluctant to discuss him again. So I didn't push to find out what they wanted to do about him. I let them focus on the man lying unconscious in the infirmary.

He was a spy from the empire, which made him untrustworthy by default. But he was a spy from the empire who was eager to tell me everything, which meant we needed him.

And he might die.

THINGS I WORRIED about as midnight approached:

1. *The spy and his potential demise. What if he died? Were there more? Could I find them? And if I did, would they be willing to talk to me, too?*
2. *What did it mean that there was even one imperial spy in the Fallen Isles?*
3. *This new bond with Hush was . . . not unwelcome, but potentially a problem if she couldn't tell the difference between an exhaustion-induced panic attack and real, true terror. I could certainly do worse than having a* Drakontos titanus *on my side, but considering how deadly she was, I needed*

about a thousand calming pills.

4. What was I going to do with a huge dragon?
   The little ones were already enough work.

5. Were my parents alive? Dead? I hadn't seen
   them die, so I had to believe they still lived.
   I wouldn't be able to function if I let myself
   believe they might be gone.

6. And what about Hristo's father?

7. Then there were Ilina's parents—somewhere in
   Anahera with dragons waiting to be shipped
   to the Algotti Empire. We would be so close to
   them. It seemed unthinkable that we wouldn't
   mount some sort of rescue, but how? There
   were so few of us and Anahera was such a
   huge island.

8. Zara, of course, hated me more than ever.
   Mother—perhaps as her dying wish—had
   promised I'd protect her, but Zara wanted
   nothing from me. Certainly not my protection.
   I had no idea what to do with her, or how to
   make things right, or if it was even possible.

9. Altan. He'd been on the Falcon, which meant
   he was likely responsible for the destruction
   of the council house. But why? What did that
   accomplish for him?

10. Dragons in general. Were they scared? Ill?
    Worried? The more I imagined all those
    dragons in captivity, the tighter my chest felt.

After trading stories about what happened during our separation, Chenda brought up the giant noorestones from the shipping order. "We cannot forget what the empire could do with noorestones that powerful."

"You're right." I leaned against the wall of the infirmary, cradling LaLa in one arm. She was picking at her splint, either bored or annoyed with it. I couldn't tell. "I've been thinking about what you said before, Chenda."

She raised an eyebrow.

"I think—" I pulled a strip of linen out of LaLa's mouth to give myself a moment to steady my thoughts. "What you said about not looking at the wider scope of what's happening—I think we both fell into that trap."

"I have been concerned about the empire the entire time." There was fight in Chenda's tone, but hesitance as well. Neither one of us wanted to reignite the argument that had driven us apart, but we couldn't ignore it forever.

"You have," I conceded. "You've spoken about the Isles' independence, those who rule, and our obligation to do something about it if our governments won't."

She nodded. "Indeed. Thank you."

"Meanwhile, my focus was on dragons, in part because I don't want our enemies to have them, and the Great Abandonment should terrify us all, but mostly because I love dragons." In the crook of my arm, LaLa looked up at me and blew a puff of smoke at my face. "Even when they're pests." I rubbed the acrid scent from my nose.

From the opposite wall, Aaru cast a faint smile my way.

I looked back at Chenda, sitting motionless on her infirmary bed. "What I mean is that we both have valid concerns. Your nature is to always consider the political problems and try to solve them—"

"While you consider dragons and our duty to care for them, as our gods command." She nodded. "That is true."

I was glad she understood. "What we haven't considered," I said, "is how our focuses intersect. We should have been working together to solve both of these issues, but I resisted because I was afraid." My throat tightened with the words. I was *still* afraid. Of Altan. Of the Luminary Council. Of the Algotti Empire. Of the Great Abandonment. I just couldn't let that fear rule me anymore. "And I think you resisted because you didn't think rescuing dragons was as important."

Her mouth opened, sharp words balanced on her tongue, but then she leaned back, some of the anger leaking out of her. "All right."

"We should have worked together," I said again. "Instead of both of us trying to make our focus everyone else's focus."

Chenda closed her eyes and exhaled slowly. "'A lone shadow may be dark,'" she quoted.

"'But many side by side make midnight,'" I finished.

"When I told you that, I was trying to make you stand by my side." Chenda dropped her gaze in embarrassment. "I didn't think I needed to move closer to yours as well."

I offered my warmest smile. "We won't make that

mistake again. Together we'll be unstoppable."

A beat of quiet pulsed through the room—not Aaru's, but a natural, uncomfortable moment of realizing our friends had been watching our reconciliation.

"How touching," Gerel muttered. "Can we get back to the noorestones? I think one or both of you was about to remind us how terrible everything would be if the empire used the giant noorestones as weapons."

"Something like that." Chenda flashed a smile Gerel's way.

Gerel clapped her hands together. "Then it seems pretty simple. We get more noorestones and we strike first."

"That will be difficult," Chenda said. "Even on Bopha, noorestones of that size are rare." She opened one of the cage-like sconces and plucked a crystal out, then turned it over in her hands, smoothing her fingertips across the facets; shadows jumped across the walls, behaving normally . . . for now. "I've seen only four in my life. Three were on the *Star-Touched*, and one was presented to the Twilight Senate shortly after I became the Lady of Eternal Dawn. Four. In my life. And three of them were in the same place." She glanced down at me, one eyebrow raised in question.

"I've seen three," I confirmed. "The noorestones on the *Star-Touched*. And I've heard about six others: those on the *Great Mace*"—that was the Khulani vessel capable of crossing the sea—"and on the ill-fated *Infinity*."

441

"As I thought." Chenda placed the noorestone back in its sconce and closed the lid.

"All right," Gerel said. "So we find a different weapon. A better one."

"Why strike first?" Hristo asked.

Gerel glared at him. "What would *you* propose, Hartan?"

Harta hates harm.

He lifted an eyebrow. "It seems to me there are two options. One is your idea. Immediate violence. Bigger violence. The second is to find a way to protect ourselves."

"The best way to protect yourself is to be better armed."

He shook his head. "That's not what I mean. You keep reaching for swords. I'm talking about a shield."

"What do you mean?" Ilina asked.

"I don't know exactly." He hesitated, and I could feel everyone struggling to *not* look at me.

And why wouldn't they? I'd demonstrated power over noorestones time and time again. If I could command the energy contained in the giant noorestones, the empire would lose its advantage over us.

Across the room, Aaru shifted his weight. His expression was thoughtful. Inward. He, too, could affect noorestones: he could silence them.

Couldn't *we* be shields?

I would much rather be a shield than a weapon of destruction.

"We're forgetting something," Ilina said, and everyone looked up. "The empire doesn't have our dragons yet. Isn't it possible they don't have our noorestones, either? What if they're on Anahera, with the dragons?"

"Is that where we're heading?" Chenda asked. "Anahera?"

Ilina's eyes darkened, but she didn't protest our destination again. "It's the best chance we have to hide while the *Falcon* is in pursuit. From there, we don't know yet. Maybe it will depend on what he says." She motioned toward the unconscious spy.

His clothes had been cut away, replaced by bandages covering large parts of his body: his arms, his chest, one leg.

"If he wakes up," I whispered.

Just then, the door squealed open and the ship's medic burst into the room.

"What are all of you doing here? This isn't the mess. Get out. All of you." Kursha swung around to look at Gerel and Chenda. "Except for you two. Obviously."

"Sorry." I shouldn't have said anything, though, because she turned her glare on me.

"And you, still awake like this. I heard what you did with the noorestone. That can't be healthy. Get. Some. Rest."

Sufficiently chastised, Aaru, Ilina, Hristo, and I slipped out of the infirmary while LaLa yawned, letting a scrap of linen dangle from her teeth.

Ilina moved Crystal to her shoulder and bent toward LaLa. "She's going to pick the whole splint apart."

"All your hard work."

In our cabin, Zara was already sleeping. Or, rather, pretending to sleep. When Aaru cocked his head, listening, I heard it, too: muffled sniffles and small, gasping breaths.

As Hristo climbed into his bunk, and Ilina into her hammock, I stepped toward my sister to say something. Comfort her. Touch her shoulder maybe. But she tensed, angry energy radiating off her, so I retreated to my side of the cabin and climbed into my hammock.

Before LaLa was finished making herself comfortable over my heart, I was gone—lost to dreams of furious dragons and hot, bright noorestones that devastated the world.

CHAPTER THIRTY-THREE

Spinning thoughts and anxious dreams finally eased into a restless sleep. I awakened at every noise—Zara leaving the cabin, Hristo's unconscious grumbling, and Ilina's quiet snores—and drifted off again. Through the porthole, light shifted brighter as the day crept by in exhausted flashes.

It was LaLa's tugging at her splint that fully jerked me out of sleep. She was perched on my chest, shredding the fabric into neat little piles.

"Stop." Carefully, I pressed the scraps back against her wing, but it was pointless. She just nibbled at my fingers until I moved back, and then she continued her destruction. "Ilina worked hard on that."

"What did I do?" Groggy annoyance filled Ilina's tone, and slowly she reached up toward me, her fingers bent into claws. "Why are you talking so early?" She flexed her fingers out and in, as though demonstrating how she would punish me for waking her.

"It's midafternoon." Hristo turned the page of a book he was reading, still lying in his bunk. "Everyone else is up."

I glanced at Aaru's empty hammock, but before I could ask where he'd gone—if Hristo even knew—LaLa tore off another piece of fabric. "Ilina, she's destroying your splint."

"Still?" My friend scrambled to her feet, transferring Crystal to her shoulder as she moved. "Bad LaLa. That's supposed to keep your wing secure." She reached for my dragon, but LaLa puffed smoke at her, and the last pieces of the splint fell off.

LaLa extended her wing out wide, groaning as though she'd been stiff and it felt good to stretch.

"She can't be healed already, can she?" I asked.

Hristo had abandoned his book and come to watch as Ilina took LaLa and felt along the bones of her wing. "Dragon bones do heal quickly," she muttered. "But two decans quickly. Not eight days quickly."

Perhaps LaLa's bones hadn't gotten the news, though, because when she tested her wings, she caught air and flew a wobbly circle through the cabin while I dropped out of my hammock. When she landed on my shoulder and purred, I stroked the warm scales along her face and neck, then bumped noses with her.

"I'm glad you're feeling better, little dragon flower." My

soul warmed as she pushed off my shoulder, flew at Crystal, tapped her, and raced away. Her flight wasn't perfect yet—she quavered on one side—but it was a small space and she'd *just* recovered. I looked at Ilina. "Should we take them up for fresh air?"

"We'll have to be careful of Hush." But Ilina was already grabbing our hunting equipment—jesses, gauntlets, lines—just in case.

Minutes later, we emerged onto the main deck, our tiny dragons upon our shoulders, stretched as tall and proud as they could be. LaLa strained, eager for flight, but I rested my fingers on her back while I scanned the sky for Hush.

The *Drakontos titanus* was nowhere in sight, though my connection with her still pulled—a gossamer thread from my heart to hers. She was probably eating or resting, since dragons didn't usually travel long distances, but she hadn't left us.

"All right, little lizard." I let go of LaLa and she shot into the sky, Crystal right on her tail.

If a thread connected Hush to my heart, LaLa *was* my heart. She was my soul. Ecstatic joy burst through me as my dragon took flight and played chase with her sister.

Ilina and I grinned at each other as we walked to the foredeck, Hristo in our wake. "It's nice for something to go right for a change." She lifted her eyes to our dragons.

"I'm sorry about Anahera," I started. "I know you don't want to go there."

Her shoulders tensed. "Let's just watch our dragons for now. When the spy wakes up or we get to Flamecrest, we won't have time for anything happy."

I swallowed back more questions. *The Book of Love* reminded us that we were not entitled to explanations. We could ask, but if someone didn't want to share, we had to respect that.

Still, Ilina was my best friend. Shouldn't I know these things about her?

Above, LaLa chased Crystal around the masts, ducking between lines and sliding down sails.

"I hope they don't slice the canvas. Captain Pentoba will kill us." Hristo leaned against the rail, gazing up as LaLa and Crystal zipped past, gliding ahead of the ship. They danced around each other, breathing fire and somersaulting through the air, as though they had no worries at all.

"Don't you wish we could be like them?" Ilina's expression was soft. Wistful. A mask hiding some kind of pain I didn't understand.

The *Chance Encounter* cut through the water, making salt spray fan across my nose and cheeks. Wind and the brilliant afternoon sun dried my skin. Slowly, the light shifted to gold as the day folded in on itself. The mountains were just scrapes of brown against the bright blue sky, but closer in, the forests and fields boasted every shade of green imaginable.

It was the endless ocean east of us that felt like the edge of the world.

Nothing. Nothing. Nothing.

And somewhere beyond that, the Algotti Empire.

Why couldn't they just leave us in peace?

Why had it taken the threat of invasion to unite our islands?

Ahead, the dragons called to each other and slowed their flight, allowing the *Chance Encounter* to catch up before they took off again.

As the sun dipped toward the west, my awareness shifted to the presence behind me. Like a tether snapping into place, or two hearts synchronizing.

I looked across the bustling deck to see Aaru emerging from the hatch. Immediately his dark eyes found mine.

Neither of us moved, but my pulse quickened and all the nearby noorestones flared before I pushed them away.

"Are you all right?" Ilina followed my gaze. "Oh. He looks like he needs to talk."

"I think so." But I couldn't tell whether I was answering her question or agreeing with her statement. Maybe both.

Ilina gave two sharp whistles, and the dragons dived toward her, flaring their wings at the last second as they landed side by side on her outstretched hand. "Come on." She deposited LaLa into Hristo's arms and grabbed the basket off the deck. "Shout if you need me, wingsister." She bumped my shoulder before she and Hristo strode down to the main deck.

Alone, I stood at the bow of the ship and watched

Aaru watching me. He hadn't moved except to shift out of the way of the crew.

Maybe I needed to go to him?

But as I took the first step, he jolted into motion, striding toward me with some unknowable purpose. He was determined; his movements, usually so cautious and measured, were strong and filled with resolve.

I braced myself with one hand on the rail, waiting for him to reach me. Counting heartbeats, and seagull cries, and steps he took.

My mind, tempestuous thing that it was, offered reason after reason for this sudden commitment in him:

1. *He wanted to tell the others about his gift.*
2. *He didn't want to tell the others about his gift.*
3. *On top of everything else, the imperial spy was too much and he was going to catch a ship back to Grace Community the moment we made port in Flamecrest.*
4. *Or maybe my connection with a* Drakontos titanus *was too much.*
5. *Or . . .*

My chest ached. In spite of teaching Ilina and Hristo the quiet code, he'd never indicated that choosing to remain with us after Val fa Merce was anything more than a temporary stay. He'd postponed his return to his home because of me, yes, but because he thought he owed me for rescuing him from the Pit.

After our uncomfortable interaction in the hold, right before Crescent Prominence, maybe he'd changed his mind.

Then he stood before me, a soft bubble of silence around him. Around us. The noise of the ship and sea were softened, though not completely gone.

"Aaru." I almost choked on his name. I didn't want to lose him, but losing him felt inevitable.

His mouth made the shape of my name—*Mira*—but no sound came, and he cringed. He lowered his eyes, letting out a heavy breath. Frustrated. Or upset.

"What is it?" My words came out too airy, and maybe I didn't want to know, but without his pencil and paper, I was the only person he could easily talk to.

My hand trembled as I offered it to him.

And though he could tap on the rail, he took my hand in both of his.

"Is something wrong?" The bubble of his silence caught and trapped my whisper between us.

Sunlight slipped across his face, its glow like honey against the perfect brown of his cheek and neck. And where the light caught his left eye, golden flecks illuminated inside the deep, dark brown. Like stars. I'd never noticed before.

He turned up my hand and tapped against my palm, earnest. ::I understand now. I think.::

I didn't understand anything anymore.

::I assumed you wouldn't hesitate because of where you're from. I thought you would be able to tell.::

"Tell what?"

I needn't have bothered to say anything, because now the words were spilling from his hands into mine, a deluge of thoughts and feelings, more than I could comprehend at once.

::You're from Damina, and people talk about how free Daminans are with—:: He shook his head, and his fingernails scraped my palm like he could take back his unfinished thought. ::I thought what happened meant I misread. Meant you felt different. Meant *no*. But now I think you were trying to be respectful. Thoughtful. And you are. You always have been. I just didn't realize what you were waiting for.::

So many words. From him. To me.

I didn't dare say anything, because I suspected he was talking about my presumptuous behavior in the hold two days ago, but I wasn't certain. He hadn't offered much in the way of context.

But he didn't continue. The space for my response hung heavy between us. His breath came in hard gasps, too, as though he'd said all those words aloud and hadn't bothered to breathe.

My hand still rested between both of his, so I placed my words upward, into his expectant palm. ::What was I waiting for?::

He shifted his weight closer. ::For me to say yes.::

::Yes?::

He lifted both of his hands, letting his fingertips graze my jaw and throat. ::**Yes.**::

Everything inside me spun, and I couldn't keep up with my own thoughts, let alone his. And now that he'd released my hand, it had nothing to do. Nowhere to go except my side or the rail, and neither of those felt right.

He tilted up my chin, and his gaze dropped to my mouth.

Only a moment.

Only a breath.

My heart thundered as the word formed silently on his lips: "Yes?"

I gasped, and both of my wayward hands decided for themselves where they wanted to be: on him. One stole away to rest on his shoulder, while the other explored his jaw and cheek and the back of his neck.

He leaned forward, as though I'd drawn him toward me, and his thumb brushed my lower lip.

Warmth fluttered through me.

::**Yes?**:: He'd taken hold of my waist.

This was him asking. And me asking. Forever asking and asking, orbiting each other with one answer strung between us.

"Yes," I breathed.

I couldn't tell who moved first. Me. Him. Maybe both of us.

His lips were warm, with just the right amount of

softness and strength where they pressed against mine. He was as I'd imagined a thousand times: just right.

Yet, he didn't proceed, like he wasn't completely sure how.

So I showed him.

A tilt of my head. A shift of my body. And when I kissed him, he echoed my every movement with that sweet carefulness he'd always possessed. One kiss was an ask, and the next was an answer: his hand on my waist pressed the pattern of *yes* again and again.

And as his confidence grew and his kiss deepened, he altered his message. ::**I love you.**::

He *loved* me. Like I loved him.

A release. A bond. The knowledge of his love burned inside me like an inferno, fiercer than I'd expected. It sent my soul flying into the sky, blazing through the stars.

For so long, I'd wanted this. His touch. His love. And now we stood together on the bow of the ship, wind rushing past us, water crashing around us, his mouth brushing across mine. His movements were soft. Delicate. As though I were a precious thing. As though he wanted to explore every piece of me, but had no desire to rush the experience. He was the most gentle person in all the world, and I loved him.

"I love you," I whispered against his lips. He tasted like sea salt and thunderstorms.

He drew back, just a breath, and touched his forehead to mine. His heart raced under my fingers, but he was smiling. ::That was . . .:: He didn't finish, as though hoping I would supply him with my opinion first.

::Wonderful.:: I tapped the word against his jaw, around the curve where his neck met his shoulder, and down his collarbone. ::Wonderful, wonderful.::

::Never kissed before.:: His cheeks darkened. ::Wanted to do it right.::

No, he wouldn't have. Not on Idris, where a kiss was a declaration of marriage. ::You were perfect.::

He kissed me again, a touch of his lips to mine. ::Need to practice.::

I liked the way he wasn't in a hurry, the way he didn't try to kiss me to pieces as though I were a strange land to be conquered. For him, this was not step one in his plan to take me to bed so that he could tell his friends he was the first.

::You didn't have to wait so long,:: I said.

He took one measured step back, just enough that we could look at each other comfortably. My hands dropped into his, and he tapped into my palm again. ::That's what I was trying to say before. On Idris, they say Daminans kiss whoever they like, whenever they like.::

Well, that wasn't true, but maybe it seemed like that to outsiders.

::Sometimes I thought you might want to::—his gaze darted to my lips—::but you never did. Thought it must be me.::

::You couldn't tell how I felt?::

::Decided you were being nice to the one who couldn't speak. To the quiet Idrisi. I am the odd one in our group.::

"Oh." I squeezed his hands, our every interaction flickering through my mind. The assumptions I'd made. The assumptions he'd made. Like in the Pit, after he'd stopped me from exploding. I'd wanted to kiss him, but he'd glanced at the scar and I'd assumed he was disgusted; he'd seen my shift in demeanor as a rejection.

Time after time, I'd wanted to kiss him. He'd wanted to kiss me. But we'd both spent those moments making incorrect assumptions about propriety and culture and intention when we should have just talked.

And still, he stayed with me. Even after what seemed like rejection after rejection, he remained a steadfast friend, loving without expectation.

The same missed opportunities haunted his dark eyes. ::I don't understand as much as I thought.::

"Me neither." As the sun set behind the mountains of Damina, I stepped forward and lifted my face toward Aaru's. "Yes?"

Dark and silence washed over us. His hands falling to my hips, he kissed me.

BUT EVEN THE most joyous of dragons could not fly forever.

CHAPTER THIRTY-FOUR

After dinner and my share of the evening chores, I floated down to the infirmary, my heart still pounding with the kiss. Kisses. Aaru *loved* me.

But reality exerted its harsh gravity as I stepped into the room. The spy was still unconscious. Mysterious. Dangerous.

"Any change?" I sat on the corner of Gerel's bed—she and Chenda were supposed to stay here again tonight—and motioned toward the imperial spy.

She shook her head. "He coughed a few times, and Kursha gave him something that smelled foul. She thinks he'll wake up, but it's impossible to tell when."

Guilt gnawed at me once more. I couldn't prevent panic attacks from happening any more than I could prevent the sun from rising. I knew it wasn't actually my fault—if I kept telling myself that, I might actually believe it—but the fact was that if I hadn't had a panic attack at that moment, Hush (probably) wouldn't have attacked the black ship, and Gerel and Chenda would have reached us with their prisoner intact.

"Don't let it eat you up." Gerel leaned forward and squeezed my shoulder. "From what you said about your visit to Crescent Prominence, it sounds like you have enough to keep you up at night without adding this to it."

I looked at her askance. "It's not like you to be so comforting."

"If you even hint about it to anyone, I'll tell them about the time you almost broke your neck doing a handstand and then got lost in your own skirt." She reclined onto her pillow again, ignoring the way my face burned. "So, how was it?"

"The handstand?"

She lifted an eyebrow. "No. I mean you and Aaru."

The way she said it made my insides want to combust with embarrassment. "It was good," I said at last. "It was perfect."

"I'm glad. He seemed nervous."

"How do you know?"

She smiled and produced a folded piece of paper from her pocket. "He asked for help."

That seemed unlike him, but the paper was from his notebook, and filled with his careful handwriting.

Want to kiss her.

Not sure she wants to kiss me.

Followed by single words like *please, I know,* and *thank you,* and other fragments of his end of the conversation.

I traced the letters he'd written. "Why did he ask you?"

She shrugged. "Hristo and Ilina are your best friends. If he'd asked them, then you'd rejected him—"

He couldn't be sure they'd treat him the same after, but Gerel treated everyone with equal disdain.

"Plus," she said, "unless they're really good at hiding it, those two aren't romantically involved. He figured Chenda and I could interpret signals for him."

"Did you?" I glanced at the paper again, and the words *Are you sure?*

"I've never seen two people who want to kiss so badly avoid it so hard." She rolled her eyes and took the paper again, and folded it along the lines from before. "We gave him some advice. I guess he took it, because you seem pleased. We also offered a demonstration, but he ran away."

Now *that* sounded like Aaru.

It also explained his determination. He'd just asked for help, and if he didn't follow through with it, Gerel would tease him about it for the rest of his life.

I smiled. "I'm happy for you and Chenda, too."

"Yes, well." She hesitated, at a loss for words. Maybe Gerel wasn't used to good things happening to her. "All right, go away, please. I'll come get you if anything changes over there." She motioned toward the spy as she handed me the paper.

I tucked it into my pocket. "Thank you."

Just as I stepped into the passageway, though, the man began to cough. It was a violent, wracking sound, like something must be ripping apart inside him.

Gerel leaped off her bed and darted across the infirmary. Holding him down so that he didn't throw himself off the bed, she glanced back at me. "Call for Kursha."

I nodded and slipped into the corridor to ask a passing crewman to fetch the medic. Then, I was right back into the infirmary, watching the spy cough until it seemed like he might fall apart.

But finally he stopped long enough to breathe, and his eyes squinted open.

"Here we go." Gerel helped him sit up on the bed. "You're safe."

Something in the man's chest rattled as he bent over his knees, mindful of the bandages covering half his body—and the cuff fastening him to the bedpost. He swayed with the motion of the ship, unfocused gaze drifting through the infirmary. Then, he found me standing in the doorway and he *looked* at me. Sharply. Knifelike cleverness flashed behind the haze of injury.

"You're Mira Minkoba. The one they call Hopebearer. Dragonhearted." Smoke made his voice terrible—the scratch of bone on bone—and the words came out slowly. His accent was obvious: almost Daminan, but tilted toward a sneer. Still, he knew our language. He looked like us, with brown skin and curly hair and wide-set eyes. He would easily deceive people, in spite of the way he spoke. "I have been looking for you."

I caught Gerel's eye, wishing she knew the quiet code, wishing she and I had the sort of silent understanding I shared with Ilina and Hristo. Because I needed to know:

1. *Was this the best time?*
2. *Was he going to die on us if I asked him questions right now?*
3. *Or did waiting risk him dying without ever sharing his secrets?*
4. *Why did we think he'd tell us the truth, anyway?*

But Gerel couldn't answer any of those questions, even if she could have read them in my eyes. This wasn't something she could give me permission to do. Only I could decide whether I was going to put on the face of a leader, no matter how I felt inside. The fate of the Fallen Isles depended on *someone* doing the work.

I took a fortifying breath and one measured step toward the spy. "Who are you?"

He started to answer, but a wet, hacking cough came out instead. He brought his bandaged arm up to cover his mouth as he rocked forward; Gerel held him upright, and when he stopped coughing, she poured a glass of water and bade him drink.

"Thank you." He took a faint sip. Coughed. Sipped

461

again. Then she set the glass aside while he caught his breath, looking up at me again. "Please forgive me, Hopebearer. There was a fire on my ship. I seem to have inhaled smoke."

Guilt needled me, but I shook it away. "Are you able to answer my questions, or would you like to rest? We've summoned the medic; she'll be here any moment."

He tilted his head, assessing and reassessing me. "Do I have a choice but to answer your questions?"

"You do." I stepped forward again, softening my voice. "Clearly you're our prisoner, but we aren't monsters. You can decide whether you want to speak with me, and you can decide how you want to answer. I suggest honestly, but you'll be treated the same regardless. With respect. With compassion."

"That's very generous of you."

"I have been in your position before," I said. "I would not do to others what was done to me."

One side of his mouth turned up. "I'd heard that about you. It's nice to see that cruelty does not always beget cruelty." He cleared his throat. "I want to talk to you," he said. "Now, if possible. I know I don't have long."

Gerel flashed a worried frown my way as she gave the spy another sip of water.

"All right. Let's start with something easy." I met the spy's gaze. "What's your name?"

"I don't have a name."

Hadn't I *just* asked him to be honest?

"But my designation is Seven. You may call me that if you wish."

"Seven, then."

Behind me, the door crashed open and Kursha burst into the room. She paused long enough to take in our positions—Gerel looming over the spy, while I stood before him with my shoulders thrown back and my hands clasped—and shook her head. "You don't waste time, do you?"

"I assure you, they've been nothing but cordial." The spy followed Kursha's progress as she gathered her supplies: bandages, medicine, and unidentifiable objects. "You must be the medic the Hopebearer spoke of."

Kursha just scowled at him and went to work.

"Seven," I said, and his attention snapped back. "Why have you been looking for me?"

"Because you're the Hopebearer." That half smile turned up again. "How fortunate that your friends decided to kidnap me and bring me straight to you."

Gerel caught my eye and frowned. I didn't like the idea of giving him exactly what he wanted, either, but that didn't change what had happened. I moved on.

"You're a spy for the Algotti Empire?"

He bowed his head in assent. "I serve our empress with every ability the gods have given me."

"How many spies have come to the Fallen Isles?"

"Nine," he said. "A holy number."

Nine. It was hard enough to reconcile one imperial spy

in the Fallen Isles, but nine? But if the Mira Treaty had truly sold us to the empire, then maybe it was a miracle there were *only* nine.

"Why did you come here?"

"We were dispatched after reports of an immense tremor centering here—on an island you call Idris."

As though the name of his home summoned him, I sensed a stillness behind me. Aaru. He slipped soundlessly into the infirmary and paused at my side. Close enough to hear the man's heart over the creak of wood and whisper of waves on the ship, perhaps, because he touched my hand. ::His heartbeat is irregular. His lungs rattle. He is not well.::

Cold shivered through me. Time was running out if I wanted answers.

I tapped my thanks and focused on the spy again. "Why do you care about an earthquake on Idris?"

"Our empress was concerned that the troubles of the Fallen Isles might affect the Algotti Empire. So many tremors. So many storms. She feared for her people, as any ruler would."

"I see." Disappointment festered in me. He intended to lie, to pretend as though the empire hadn't threatened annihilation unless we surrendered. "Tell me, Seven, what does your empress want with the Fallen Isles?" Better to get a sense of his game now, and know how to manipulate him later.

"Cooperation." He tilted his head just slightly and

amended, "To begin with, she wants cooperation."

"And?"

"And what?" He leaned forward as Kursha moved around to inspect one of the burns on his back.

"What of our dragons?" As if he didn't know. I'd seen him in the Hartan sanctuary. Had he been inspecting the dragons? Confirming their number and species? Either way, he and I both knew the dragons were going to the empire. Payment for not destroying us. "Why do you want them?"

"We do not want your dragons." He—Seven—coughed into the crook of his elbow, staining his sleeve with blood.

"What about our noorestones?"

He shook his head. "We have our own resources."

I scowled.

"You're unsatisfied with my answer," he observed.

"Of course," I said. "When my friends said you were willing to share information with me, I'd hoped you would be honest."

He closed his eyes and took a deep breath. "Hope-bearer, though I came here only to investigate the disasters, I found far greater problems for your people. A civil war grows on the horizon, and like it or not, you will be caught in the center of it."

On the main deck, boots thumped hard against the wood. Muffled shouts leaked between the slats, but I couldn't understand what was said.

Aaru touched my hand and stepped away, through the

door again. I watched him go for only a moment, then turned back to Seven. "What do you mean, a civil war?"

"I mean"—he coughed—"without some sort of guidance, your islands will tear one another apart."

"I suppose you think the empire's guidance will help us resolve our differences."

Seven closed his eyes, letting out a short, frustrated breath. "I can understand why you believe that, but I assure you—"

A crash came from above and everyone paused. Looked up. A sharp *thump* sounded right overhead, followed by the quick beats of someone running.

"That doesn't sound good." Kursha frowned at the ceiling.

"It doesn't," I agreed. But Aaru had gone to investigate. I had to trust that if there was something truly wrong, he'd come back to tell me.

"May I speak freely?" Seven asked.

I nodded.

"We have known about your Mira Treaty since its inception. The opposition from within the Fallen Isles has been clear for some time, as I'm sure you know." He lifted an eyebrow at me, as though he needed to remind me of the kidnapping attempt, or Hurrok, or the other unnumbered events Hristo had spoken of—people taking their dislike of the treaty out on me. "The empire has ignored that. It's not our problem. But as storms and tremors became more frequent, as they became stronger, we in the empire did, at last, become worried.

"So my partners and I were dispatched, and soon we discovered attempts to dismantle the Mira Treaty piece by piece. Hartans being sent away from Bopha, though they had lived and worked on the Isle of Shadow their whole lives. Dragons being held in the Heart of the Great Warrior, even though the Drakon Warriors were meant to have disbanded. Civil unrest on Idris. The Hopebearer vanishing from her home on Darina."

"You knew about all of that?" I whispered.

"Of course." He bowed his head. "I would be a poor spy if I had been ignorant of any one of those issues."

"What then?" I asked.

"Then it was decided that we would divide our efforts, and later assemble a complete account of the fragmentation of the Fallen Isles. I began by tracking dragon movement from sanctuaries." He looked up at me. "I didn't recognize you in the First Harta Dragon Sanctuary. Not until later." His eyes shifted to the scar. "No one, as far as I knew at that point, was aware of the change in your appearance."

I braced myself for the crushing embarrassment that came any time someone mentioned the scar, but it didn't come. Not this time. "You chose not to help me free those dragons."

"What could I have done?" He cocked his head. "What would you have had me do, exactly? Attack the keepers?"

"Maybe."

"My purpose is to watch, Hopebearer, not interfere. I am not yours to command."

"Is meeting with me not considered interference?"

"You are getting ahead of me." Though his words were sharp, they did not cut; he offered a pale smile—at least until new thuds sounded from overhead. Then his expression melted into a faint twist of concern.

I was concerned, too, but if I was needed, someone would come to get me. "All right," I said. "You didn't want to interfere. And later, you were at the Lexara Theater. What were you doing there?"

He nodded. "I knew the Hopebearer was scheduled to speak that evening, so I returned to the city to see her. You. But the Mira on stage was a false Hopebearer. The speech she was beginning was the speech you refused to give on Bopha. That was very brave, by the way."

He knew about *that* too?

There were nine spies, but it seemed as though there must be nine hundred. How else could they have so much information? How could everyone at that speech have been so clueless about the presence of an imperial spy?

"But then," Seven went on, "just as the false Hopebearer was ready to taint your name forever, I saw you."

Save the clamor on the main deck, the infirmary was quiet—an anxiously held breath.

The spy coughed again into the crook of his arm, then accepted another sip of water from Gerel. His breath came shallow and rattling. "I saw the fall, the noorestones, the exodus. And I saw how the impostor reacted to you, the real Hopebearer, coming toward her. She was terrified."

A shiver curled around my heart. Tirta *should* have been terrified.

"I followed as she and her minder started to escape the theater. I intended to track them and learn more about why she would impersonate you, but another party intervened and both were taken."

"Taken?"

He nodded. "A team of warriors accosted them. Though I pursued them for a few hours, they managed to elude me." At the memory, a long frown creased his face. "The lead warrior was good. Fearsome. New burns covered half his face, but he behaved as though they didn't bother him at all."

Chills rippled down my spine as I met Gerel's eyes and saw my fear reflected there. Seven had seen Altan abduct Tirta. I was sure of it.

"Do you know where they went?"

Seven shook his head. "Unfortunately not. After I lost them, I went in search of you. The real Mira, I hoped. Seeing you in both the sanctuary and the theater convinced me that you were important enough to find, but you had already left your inn. And, I had assumed, the island."

"Then you returned to your ship," I provided, "and my friends found you."

"Lucky me." He glanced up at Gerel, then doubled over, coughing and coughing. Blood spattered on the floor

469

as both Gerel and Kursha held him steady.

"You should go," Kursha said when the coughing eased. "Let him rest before he answers more questions."

"No," he gasped. "I need to finish now."

Darkness loomed behind his words: he knew he wasn't going to live beyond this conversation. Aaru had heard his shuddering pulse, the liquid in his lungs . . . the early echoes of his death.

"It's a bad idea," Kursha said.

"I'm aware. Your concern is appreciated." He smiled weakly as she got back to work, but before he could continue his story, wood crashed above and a man screamed.

Something was very wrong up there.

I looked at Gerel. "Should one of us check—"

Aaru rushed back into the infirmary and shut the door. His notebook hung out of his pocket, as though he'd needed to write to someone, and his chest heaved with breath.

"What's happening?"

For a moment, I thought he might say that it was nothing, just a few crewmen settling a dispute. Anyone else would have tried to soothe me, tell me to go back to what I'd been doing, but this was Aaru and that was not his way.

::Somehow the *Falcon* caught up. Shrouded noorestones so no one saw. We have been boarded.::

"Seven gods," I whispered. "Are the others—"

::Safe,:: he said. ::Hidden in our cabin. Chenda made shadows.::

470

"What can we do?"

::Finish this.:: Aaru nodded at the spy.

How could I focus on this when our ship had been boarded? This was a cargo ship, not outfitted for battle. The crew shouldn't have to fight for us. That had never been part of the agreement. Maybe I could call Hush. Maybe she—but I couldn't ask her to become a weapon for me. I was supposed to be protecting *her*. And if she used fire, she could hurt one of our own people.

"What is it?" Gerel gripped my arm. "What did he say?"

Before I was finished repeating Aaru's words, Gerel was halfway to the door.

"Where are you going?" I took a step after her.

"To fight. No one else can." She shoved past Aaru and was out the door before anyone could stop her.

A moment later, new screams came from above: Gerel throwing herself into battle against the warriors who'd boarded our ship.

"I should go too," I said, but I didn't move. Seven was waiting, his head full of answers and his heart nearly out of beats.

"What could you do?" Kursha asked.

I didn't know. Something with noorestones. Push the crystals' inner fire into the warriors until they fainted from the heat.

Seven bent over and coughed again. "My time is short, Hopebearer. Allow me to prepare you for what's coming."

"And what is coming?" I spun to face him, adrenaline

471

thrumming into my head. I wouldn't panic. I couldn't. But numbers began ticking in the back of my head: screams, clashes of metal, and the thumps of bodies hitting the deck. "What do you know?"

The spy's expression was neutral; if he was afraid of the warriors above, he didn't show it.

"There's a Drakon Warrior called Altan." His words came wet with blood and exhaustion. "I believe you know him."

"Yes."

"He's one of the people we've been looking for, but while we've intercepted his messages, we haven't been able to get to him. We couldn't get into the Heart of the Great Warrior while he was in there, and now that he's left, we haven't been able to find him."

Then he didn't know the burned warrior he'd encountered in Harta was the very person he'd sought.

"What do you want with him?"

"He claims that your Mira Treaty sells the Fallen Isles to the Algotti Empire."

"Do you deny it?"

"You think you have all the answers, but truth is my life's work." A breath of a laugh escaped him. "I'm telling you what I know: the empire did not purchase the Fallen Isles through your treaty."

Lies.

"Then why are you here? Why are you taking our dragons? Our noorestones?"

Seven closed his eyes, sagging toward his bed; he wouldn't make it much longer. "As I said, I came to observe. And now I'm here to warn you: the Algotti Empire did not conquer your islands with a treaty; that victory went to one of your own."

One of our own? One of the Fallen Isles?

No. He was still lying. He had to be. "That's not possible," I whispered.

It was too horrible to be true. None of the islands would do that to the others, no matter how we fought and bickered among ourselves. We were quarreling siblings, but in the end, we always put our own first.

But that was wrong. Other islands had occupied Harta for hundreds of years. Was it really a stretch to think someone might have decided that wasn't enough, and sought to conquer *all* the others?

"Who?" The cacophony of nearby battle almost smothered my question. "Who would do this?"

"Who do you think?" he asked.

"I don't have time for mysteries," I said. "And neither do you."

"Who might see this world as beyond saving?" Pity filled his eyes, as though he could possibly understand how much it hurt me to suspect one of our own islands. "Who might see a cleansing fire as the only path to redemption?"

My heart dropped into my stomach. My feet. Down through the sea. If he was right, then we were heading straight for the island responsible for the plight of the dragons, the lie of the Mira Treaty, and the coming calamity of the Great Abandonment. "Anahera would never. The Fallen Isles are not beyond saving."

A sad, blood-dotted smile pulled at Seven's mouth. "Perhaps, but you and I both know there are people who will use their gods as excuses to hurt and oppress those they wish to conquer."

"Do you have proof?"

"All my documentation was lost when my ship burned."

"Convenient."

"Not for me."

Not for me, either.

"Hopebearer—" A cough burst out of him. "Know this: the *Infinity* was no accident."

"What?" Someone had *meant* to destroy the *Infinity*? For what purpose?

"A test. It was a test of destructive poten—" Another cough rushed out, and another. He was too weak now to cover his mouth, so blood dripped onto the floor as he took a shuddering breath. "Where are we heading?"

"Anahera." The goddess's name tasted like ashes in my mouth. I'd thought I could not feel any more betrayed by the people of the Fallen Isles, but if Seven was right, the leaders of Anahera were behind everything.

But what if he was lying?

"Good." Seven gasped for air as he listed toward his pillow; Kursha, still frowning, helped make him comfortable. "Nine is in Flamecrest." He didn't open his eyes. "Nine will help you."

Aaru shifted closer to me. ::Fighting has moved down here.::

My heart kicked faster. I had to help. I had to do *something* with all the noorestones aboard this ship—but not until I knew how to find the other spy—and more answers.

"Where in Flamecrest?" I asked.

Seven groaned, but if he tried to respond, I couldn't hear it. Because at that moment, the door crashed open and I whipped around, letting my mind touch all five noorestones in the infirmary. They blazed to life, bathing the room in bright, blue-white light.

But I was too late. Too slow. Four warriors had rushed in, one with healing burns all down the left side of his face. That warrior had Aaru, a knife to his throat.

It was Altan.

CHAPTER THIRTY-FIVE

Dread plunged through my stomach at the sight of steel gleaming over the soft skin of Aaru's throat—bright against brown. A thousand different dark images crashed through my mind—how Altan would kill Aaru. Fast. Slow. Smiling. Apathetic. It was too easy to imagine him in any of those scenarios, because Altan was the cruelest monster I knew.

Three other warriors stood in formation around Altan, their weapons drawn. But they didn't advance. They didn't attack.

Not yet.

"Let him go." The words wrenched out of me. All I could see was the blade and the fear that flashed in Aaru's eyes. It was so hard to believe that just a few hours ago, we'd been tangled up in each other's arms. And now I might lose him—not to his decision to go home, but to the very man we'd been trying to escape.

We should have run farther. Faster.

"I will release him," Altan said. "Once you listen to what I have to say."

"Why should I trust you?"

"Do you have a choice?" Though it must have hurt the burned side of his face terribly, he let loose one of his slow, terrifying smiles. The kind that showed teeth all the way back to the points. A reminder that Altan was a predator, and he could smell terror. He could taste weakness on the air.

Which meant I had to be strong. Bold. If I let him see how much he rattled me, Aaru would surely die.

Five noorestones. Seven people. Four beds. I collected my thoughts, even as my eyes kept drifting toward Aaru. The knife. The pale breath between life and death.

"I know what you did in the Pit," Altan said. "After you escaped, I went back to see the destruction. Truly, it was incredible: twisted metal, mounds of ash. I'd never seen anything like it, at least until I caught up to you in that tunnel." He turned his face slightly, giving me a better view of the black and red burns that bloomed over his golden-brown skin; LaLa had done that—my brave little dragon flower. "It's impressive, Fancy. I didn't know you had it in you."

I pushed strength into my voice. "If you know what I

can do, then you've taken a big risk coming here."

"Have I?" Again, that smile. Like a knife, it pared away my bold words and left me hollow with dread.

Everything inside me screamed to use the noorestones. They were my greatest advantage. My strength. My *power*. But Altan had set the perfect trap.

1. *If I shoved noorestone fire into Altan, it could flood into Aaru. Altan had tortured Aaru like that, back in the Pit, and that was the moment Aaru had stopped using his voice. I couldn't risk hurting him like that again.*
2. *Even if I could be certain Aaru wouldn't feel the noorestone fire, Altan would still be able to kill him. The knife would cut quickly.*
3. *And if I used noorestones against any of the other three warriors, Altan would kill Aaru.*

My shoulders dropped. If Aaru was to survive this, my only option was to let Altan say whatever he'd come to say.

"Good." The warrior's gaze flickered beyond me—to Kursha and Seven. "But before we begin: who are they?"

"She's the ship's medic," I said. "He's a patient."

"What is his name?" Altan's tone grew harder.

"He's just a patient." My heart thundered in my ears, but I wouldn't betray Seven's trust. For all that he was an imperial spy, he seemed like a good man, and there was so much more I needed to talk to him about.

Anahera, Anahera, Anahera . . . How could they?

Behind me, Kursha's rough voice came in quiet monotone. "He's dead."

Aaru and I locked eyes. If Seven was gone, then so were the rest of our answers.

Altan glanced at one of the other warriors—a compact young woman with the Drakon Warrior claw pinned to her jacket. "Confirm it."

She edged around me and felt for Seven's pulse. "Dead."

I swallowed back a wave of unexpected sadness, forcing my expression calm and neutral.

"All right. Put the medic with the rest of them." Altan jerked his head toward the door. Then, to the other two warriors, he said, "Stand guard outside. Make sure no one comes in."

"Sir—"

Altan grinned. "Trust me, I know this girl. She won't take a step while I have him."

Kursha spared me only a worried glance as the warriors escorted her from the room. Where were they taking her? Where were the others? If they were dead, I'd—

Even as the thought struck me, I realized the noise of fighting had gone quiet. Any resistance the crew had mounted was already crushed beneath the boots of Altan's warriors.

The knife on Aaru drew my gaze once more.

Four people: one warrior, one hostage, one dead spy, and one me.

Five noorestones, but zero that I could use.

One honed blade against tender skin.

"All it takes," Altan said, "is a gentle pressure at the right angle and in the right location."

"All what takes?" I asked.

"Cutting." He smiled. "And controlling."

"Is that why you came here? To control me?" I squashed the quaver in my voice. Fear wouldn't save Aaru, nor would it save anyone else on this ship. But there was something terrifying about him ordering the others to leave—as though their presence might have provided me some measure of protection.

"I came here because I think you could be useful."

"Speak, then." I straightened my shoulders, feigning bravery because what else did I have?

"In the Pit," Altan said, "I told you about the Mira Treaty. What it really is." He paused a beat. "Do you recall?"

Anahera, Anahera, Anahera.

Betrayal sliced deep into my bones. When I'd thought it was the empire, I'd been angry. Terrified. But at least it had made *sense*.

Altan had asked a question. I needed to answer—for Aaru's sake. "Of course," I said.

He nodded. "Good."

Aaru's gaze was fixed beyond me—on Seven's body, no doubt. I didn't look to confirm, because the last thing we needed was for Altan to ask more questions about the

480

spy. But when I shifted my weight to one hip, Aaru's eyes flickered over to me.

Slowly, deliberately, I pulled my arms up so my palms cupped my elbows, and there, almost casually, I tapped. ::Hate cannot abide where many stand in love.::

Though Aaru said nothing—not in quiet code and certainly not aloud—when he looked at me again, a deep warmth shone through.

::Courage,:: I told Aaru. And to Altan, I said, "What about the treaty?"

"I didn't come about the treaty. I came about the empire." Altan's eyes narrowed. "Have faith, Hopebearer. The empire will not rule the Fallen Isles without going through the Drakon Warriors. We will fight them."

"Will the tribunal allow your war?" I tilted my head in curiosity. "The leaders of Khulan signed the treaty, same as every other island."

"I will deal with the Warrior Tribunal." His voice was a low growl. A threat and a promise, both.

The question shivered out of me before I could stop it. "Did you deal with the Luminary Council?"

Altan raised an eyebrow. "Do you truly want that answer?"

That was confirmation enough.

"I thought so." His grin pulled at the burn. "The Drakon Warriors have fought the mainland kingdoms before, you know. Two thousand years ago, a group called the Celestial Warriors rode great dragons across the ocean

481

and set fire to their kingdoms until stone ran like water."

Gerel had told that story back on Khulan; it hadn't had a happy ending for the dragons.

"We will be victorious again," Altan said, "but this time we will not stop at the coasts: we will burn the entire Algotti Empire into ash."

"How?" I whispered. "They are bigger than us. Older, some say." Maybe it wasn't wise to question him while his knife still touched Aaru's throat, but I couldn't suck back the words. They were out, and I had to commit to a show of strength. "How do you hope to succeed?"

"With your help."

"Why would I help you?"

"Because you don't want to be ruled by the empire any more than I do, Fancy. And, though the treaty named after you is a lie, you could fight to make it true."

"Your fight will fail." I lowered my hands to my sides, forcing Anahera from my mind. If I wasn't willing to share that information with Altan—and I was *not*, at least until I talked to the others—I needed to pretend as though I still believed the Algotti Empire was responsible. "While in Crescent Prominence, I spoke to my parents about the treaty."

Darkness crept into Altan's eyes, but the knife didn't so much as twitch in his hand. Which meant he understood that if he ever wanted my help, he could not harm Aaru. Not again.

"My father said that all the islands signed the treaty

because they knew there was no possibility of us winning a war. The Warrior Tribunal agreed to that." I shook my head. "Perhaps the Drakon Warriors fought off a few kingdoms two thousand years ago, but that isn't a possibility anymore. They are an empire now. Dragons are disappearing every day. The Great Abandonment is an ever-present threat."

Muscles ticked around Altan's jaw. "If you think my plan is to rush in with a raised mace, then you're not as clever as I believed you were."

"I don't know what your plan is, Altan." I shook my head. "You've tried to kill my friends and me, you might have just slaughtered the Luminary Council and everyone inside their building, and now you've attacked my ship. But you also want my help. Why should I care?"

"Because that plan involves dragons." Anger gleamed on the edges of his voice. "And if there is one thing you and I share, it is our dedication to dragons."

My heart leaped, and five noorestones around the room flared.

Aaru met my eyes.

"I've learned the location of all the dragons that will be shipped to the empire." Altan released a long breath, and some of his rage. "I intend to free them."

"Is that so?" I kept my voice low and careful. "You know where they are?"

"They're on Anahera. We're heading there right now."

A shudder ran deep through me, but I forced my tone

483

calm. "That's a big island."

"And I know *exactly* where they are located—until tomorrow morning." He licked his lips, his tongue scraping over one of the burned places. "You're right that resisting the empire will not be easy. They outnumber us, and even our own governments will not help. But my fellow Drakon Warriors and I don't intend to let this move forward without a fight. First, we prevent these dragons from being sent to the mainland. You and I will do that together."

Would we? There was no trusting Altan. I knew that. But dragons . . .

"Meanwhile, other Drakon Warriors stationed around the islands are working to free dragons from the traitorous sanctuaries."

Free them, he'd said. Not rescue them. Because rescuing dragons implied there was somewhere safe to take them. But there was no true sanctuary for dragons anymore, not with this twisted version of the Mira Treaty in effect.

Even if the spy had been honest and the empire wasn't actually behind the lie of the treaty, dragons were still being taken because of it. But if we freed them . . .

"I've seen what you can do with dragons," Altan went on. "Kelsine. The *titanus*. I heard what you did on the docks of the Shadowed City—how you were given the title of Dragonhearted."

"Then you know that I am more powerful than you."

His glare hardened into granite, and for three

heart-pounding seconds, I thought that might have been too much. But the knife was perfectly still over Aaru's throat. "I know that my chance of success goes up if you are there."

I closed my eyes and listened, just for a heartbeat. I listened to the muttered conversation of the guards posted outside, to the sigh of water against the hull, and to the soft tapping of quiet code.

::I trust you,:: Aaru said.

"My offer won't last forever, Fancy." Sharp annoyance cut Altan's words.

When I caught Aaru's eye, he flashed an encouraging smile.

I knew what I had to do.

"What offer?" I drew myself up tall and took one step toward Altan. Then a second. A third. I stood close enough to feel the heat of Aaru's body, see a fragment of my face in the knife's polished surface, and count the small scars clustered on Altan's temple. "I understand why you need me to free dragons, *warrior*, but why do I need you?"

Alarm shot through Aaru's expression, but he remained motionless.

Altan was a mask of barely contained fury. "I know where the dragons are, *Hopebearer*. I know exactly where they are—right now." He glared down at me. "You could go to Anahera and search, but they'll be moved tomorrow morning and then even I won't be able to find them before they're moved again and again—eventually to the empire."

485

They would never be moved to the empire, if Seven was right. They would stay in the Fallen Isles, growing sicker and sicker in their captivity. And when they died, and the number of dragons fell yet again, we'd be even closer to the Great Abandonment.

"I have something else," Altan said.

I raised an eyebrow.

"Tirta and Elbena."

Noorestones fluttered, not with surprise, but rage. The impostor. The traitor. Without asking permission, my left hand lifted up to touch the scar on my cheek.

"And," Altan went on, "I have Kelsine."

That named softened me. My heart stuttered as echoes of her anguished cries welled up from my memory. I'd hated leaving her, and Altan knew it. "Where is she?"

"Help me free the dragons in Anahera," he said. "Then we'll discuss the others. One thing at a time."

"That's your plan, then?" I pushed strength into my voice, as though that might hide the pounding of my heart. "Hold everything over my head until I agree to help you?"

"If that's what it takes."

A pinprick of sadness stung my heart. While I had grown over the last months, Altan was no different from before. He'd adjusted course and changed tactics as necessary, but only as far as it didn't challenge his belief: that *he* was the hero in this era of the Fallen Isles.

"I'm not the same girl you tortured in the Pit," I said. "I am powerful, not because someone else declared it so, but because I claimed my power. That's why you're here: to borrow my power. Because you saw it in the mess that's left in the Pit. You saw it in the tunnel. And you see it now."

It was easy to touch the nearby noorestones. When I called for just a hint of their fire, a white-blue nimbus flickered around my fingertips.

Altan glanced at my hands.

"Let Aaru go," I said.

His eyes remained on the corona of light dancing between my fingers. "You'll kill me the moment I do."

"If you want to work with me," I said, "then you'll have to trust me. But as you said, time is short. The dragons will be moved in the morning, won't they? You decide if we make it there in time."

He hesitated.

I didn't blink.

Slowly.

Slowly.

The knife lowered.

Aaru slipped out of Altan's grasp, moving to the safety of my side. One hand rested on the small of my back, and it took everything in me to resist wrapping him in my arms. We weren't finished.

"Satisfied?" Altan cocked his head.

"No." I gathered my courage. If I showed any weakness now, I was done. He needed to know that I meant what I said. Slowly, deliberately, I pressed the pads of my fingers to the flat sides of his knife. "I want you to surrender."

Altan's knuckles paled around the hilt. "What?"

"Surrender." Five noorestones flared brighter, and I pushed heat through the steel blade. It didn't burn me, but he would feel it.

"Why should I surrender?" He readjusted his grip on the hilt. "I've already taken the ship."

"And yet you came for my help. You can't free those dragons without me. You can't repel the empire without me." Threads of noorestone fire whispered around my hands, traveling deeper into the blade. "We are not equals, Altan. You know you've done too much to ever win me to your side. How could I ever trust you after all of that? So you will surrender to me, and you will do what *I* want."

"And what do you want?" Though it must have been painfully hot, he didn't release the knife.

"I want to free those dragons," I said. "I want to bring truth to the Mira Treaty. I *can* do it without you, but I will allow you to help."

::Are you sure?:: Aaru tapped against my spine.

No, but an opportunity spread before us. If I didn't seize it, who would?

Back in the safe house, I'd told Ilina I didn't want to hide. But somehow all my running had become a way of hiding. How could I call myself the Hopebearer if I didn't move forward? How could I call myself Dragonhearted if I didn't face my fears?

I was finished running. Finished hiding. And as Altan

searched my face for signs of weakness, I smiled wide enough to show teeth. My scar pulled with the motion, but let him see it. Let him remember what I had survived.

After all, noorestones, the very bones of our world, bent to my will. And dragons, the children of the gods, heard the movements of my soul.

I *was* more powerful than Altan.

And to demonstrate, I released the noorestones. Heat faded from the knife, and something shifted behind Altan's eyes.

"Surrender," I repeated.

"Very well." The Drakon Warrior handed me his weapon. "I surrender."

CHAPTER THIRTY-SIX

THE REST HAPPENED VERY QUICKLY:

1. *Altan ordered his warriors off the* Chance Encounter. *They complained, and he tried to keep a few at his side, but I was not willing to negotiate. So, one by one, they took to the rowboats—likely how they'd gotten to us undetected—and returned to the* Falcon, *carrying Altan's instructions to resume their previous course.*

2. *Miraculously, none of the* Chance Encounter's *people had been killed or even severely wounded. They'd been bound and gagged, and upon release a few said it was almost as though the warriors had been under*

orders not *to kill them. Those with injuries*
visited Kursha while the rest hurried us on our
way to Anahera.

3. *I told Captain Pentoba and One that we*
   needed to get there as quickly as possible—
   tonight, if we wanted a shot at saving the
   dragons—so the first mate immediately
   retreated to his quarters with maps and charts
   and a handful of other tools. He claimed
   that by using the time and distance we'd
   traveled after Crescent Prominence, he could
   calculate how long I'd need to push the ship's
   noorestone tonight.

4. *After relieving Altan of all his remaining*
   weapons, Gerel bound his wrists and ankles
   together, then dropped him into the same
   secret compartment we'd hidden in when he'd
   come looking for us in the port of Lorn-tah.
   It was empty, with not even a blanket to keep
   him warm, but it was the only safe place to
   put him for now.

The six of us—plus two small dragons—were packed
away in the captain's office, perched on and around the
desk. Not only could we monitor the trapdoors that led
down to Altan, but it was bigger than the tiny cabin four
of us had been sharing with my sister. (Plus, she was still
in there, and this wasn't a conversation I wanted to have
in her presence.)

Hugging LaLa close to my heart, I told the others everything that happened after dinner. Gerel and Aaru added their thoughts every so often, but for the most part—in a feat that must have been especially painful for Ilina and Chenda—no one interrupted as I described the discussions with Seven and Altan.

"Anahera?" Ilina's voice was small. Crystal perched on her shoulder, jesses dangling down to Ilina's elbow. With Hush still nearby, we wanted to keep both *raptuses* in their gear. Just the presence of their harnesses made them behave like well-trained hunters, rather than the little delinquents they actually were. "You're *sure* he said Anahera?"

Now that I thought about it, he hadn't said Anahera's name. But he hadn't corrected me when I did. "I am sure," I said carefully, "that he meant Anahera. Whether or not that is true . . ."

My wingsister closed her eyes.

"We should attack them." Gerel beat a pale-knuckled fist on the desk, making everyone jump. "Get the big dragon and set her loose on Flamecrest—"

"No!" I squeezed LaLa so hard she squeaked. "I won't use Hush as a weapon. Besides, we must assume the people of Anahera are innocent. They shouldn't be punished for the actions of their leaders."

Gerel glared. "They elected their leaders."

"Even so"—Ilina spoke softly—"they're not always given a choice."

Chenda's mouth was drawn into a line. "Before we make any sort of judgment against Anahera's leadership or her people, we must find proof. It is one thing to suspect the empire of quietly conquering the Fallen Isles, and the complicity of all our governments to avoid a war. It is another to suspect one of our own."

Hristo nodded. "If it's true, then not only did they use the Mira Treaty against the other islands, they were clever enough to make it look as though the Algotti Empire was responsible."

"That sounds like Anahera," Ilina muttered.

Gerel eyed her. "Why do you hate Anahera so much? Besides this, I mean."

Ilina went rigid. "I—" Her gaze darted around the office. "I don't think it's relevant right now."

Gerel crossed her arms and waited.

"It's all right," I said. "You don't have to say if you don't want to."

"If it gives credit or doubt to the allegations against Anahera," Chenda said, "it is relevant. Don't you think?" Her tone was careful, even, like she understood just how quickly tensions could spike between them.

Ilina licked her lips. "I'm not supposed to talk about it. I made a promise to my parents years ago." She looked up at me. "That's why I never said anything. It's not because I don't trust you. I do. Both of you." Her gaze shifted to Hristo.

He nodded encouragingly.

The office was quiet, save the whisper of water on the hull and the throaty purrs of dragons.

"My father is from Anahera. He escaped to Damina and married my mother so that the Luminary Council would protect him."

No one spoke a word. Because what could we say to that? I desperately wanted to know more—what did she mean, *escaped*?—but considering how reluctant she'd been to tell anyone even this much, questions felt like insensitive prying.

"Ilina." Hristo touched her shoulder, and then wrapped his arms around her when she leaned toward him. If anyone understood the complicated feelings of heritage and home, it was him.

My throat was tight with worry, but I said, "I agree with Chenda that we need to know more before we make any judgments, but right now we do know that the dragons, giant noorestones, and Ilina's parents are all being held on Anahera."

Ilina pulled herself up straight. "My parents said I shouldn't look for them if they were ever captured."

"Oh." My heart twisted painfully.

"But when have I ever done what they've told me?" Her smile trembled, but she was trying to put on a brave face for the others. "Let's rescue them and they can punish me later."

"That's right."

"And Altan?" Hristo asked. "Do you think he was

494

telling the truth about knowing where the dragons are being kept?"

"He's a monster," I said, looking at Chenda. "But maybe—in this case—he can be a useful monster. He does care about dragons. He also cares about protecting the Fallen Isles from outside threats. So yes, I believe he was telling the truth."

Chenda leaned back in the captain's chair; she hadn't hesitated to take it earlier, and it seemed unlikely she'd ever leave. "Still, I don't want to tell him about Seven. Let's keep that to ourselves for now."

"Agreed," I said. "Seven said he has a partner in Flamecrest. A person called Nine. We should find them and look at any documentation they have. If Seven's claim turns out to be true, then we can decide whether or not to tell Altan. But he's not one of us. He doesn't get to know what we know. Not until we're ready to share it."

The others nodded.

LaLa squawked and wiggled away from me to inspect the items on Captain Pentoba's desk. An inkwell, a sheaf of papers, a spare compass: all of it risked becoming LaLa's property.

Chenda watched the *raptus* with an amused smile. "I can't believe that after everything, we're actually going to rescue dragons. Are you happy now?"

I shot a wide smile at her, mostly in jest. "Of course I want to help the dragons. If we have the opportunity, we should. Right?"

"Yes," she conceded. "I'd be a fool to not believe in the Great Abandonment after everything I've seen."

The office door creaked open and the first mate entered. "Made yourselves comfortable, I see." He nodded toward LaLa and Crystal, both on the desk and shredding a piece of paper. "Just make sure they don't touch the logbook and the captain won't care."

"We'll clean up after them." I grinned. "Are the calculations finished?"

He nodded. "We'll be ready for you in a few minutes."

"Thank you, One," I said as he left and closed the door after him.

Aaru tapped on my arm. ::We know a lot of people named after numbers.::

"Do you think One—"

::Don't know.:: Aaru gazed at the door beyond me. ::Strange, isn't it?::

When I interpreted for the others, Ilina said, "I always assumed the captain called him One because he's the first mate. But how can we trust anyone at this point?"

"Surely Captain Pentoba has known him for years. First mate is a trusted position." I reached down to pry the inkwell from LaLa's teeth, but before I touched her, the jar clattered to the desk and rolled, and LaLa let out a long, low whine. Crystal echoed her a moment later.

Ilina petted Crystal's slender neck. "What's wrong, little lizard?"

But instead of coming to us for comfort, the dragons

straightened their spines and made their wings into tents around their bodies. Their whines grew into wails, and within seconds they'd launched themselves into the air— heading directly for the open window.

Everyone scrambled to action, first to close the window and then to block the door. Hristo caught Crystal's jesses and hauled her back to Ilina, but LaLa was wily. She slithered just out of reach and threw herself onto the window, clawing and scraping at the wood.

"LaLa!" Not that she cared about my scolding. Even when I clipped on her tether, she ignored me.

"What's wrong with them?" Chenda asked.

"I don't know." I tugged at LaLa's tether, but she just flapped wildly at me. "They've never done this before."

"They have, though." Ilina had managed to clip on Crystal's tether, but the little dragon exploded from her grasp and shot toward the window. The two small moons strained to escape, their wings arched and ready to steal into the air. "This is the same noise they made the day of the Idrisi tremor. About an hour before we felt it."

Talons shredded the wood as both dragons keened.

"Do you think there will be a quake?" Hristo asked.

Ilina nodded as the draconic howling crescendoed.

::Where?:: Aaru's quiet code came sharp against the desk.

I shook my head and freed a small noorestone from its sconce, hoping to distract the dragons. But they didn't even acknowledge it; LaLa just wailed and thrashed her tail, while Crystal bit at the window. "LaLa, stop! Crystal!"

But they didn't. Maybe couldn't. Our sweet dragons tore at the ship, struggling to escape to the sky. Nothing I did had any effect. Not noorestones, not soothing tones, and when I tried to touch LaLa, she batted my hand away as though I were a stranger.

"I should warn the captain. Hopefully we can reach land before the tremor hits." I'd never been at sea during an earthquake, and I didn't want to find out what it was like.

"Go." Ilina gathered up both tethers. "I'll make sure they don't fly after you."

The moment I opened the door, the dragons abandoned their assault on the window to chase me, but Ilina held fast to their leashes.

Aaru followed me out to the main deck and slammed the door shut behind us. With the little dragons' scratching and wailing muffled, the only noise was the crew chanting, water lapping the hull, and the rush of wind in our sails. We sped north at a fast clip, carried along by air and current and crystal.

Aaru took my hand. ::**Are you all right?**::

My heart pounded, but only some of it was me. The worry for Crystal and LaLa was easy to identify, but there was another terror—deeper and primal—which came through my connection with the dragons. Crystal, LaLa, *and* Hush.

A polyphonic roar cut the night.

498

The crew went quiet and stared west, toward Darina.

The *Drakontos titanus* thrashed through the darkness, pouring fire into the star-strewn sky. Her talons clawed at the air as though to shred it into a thousand pieces.

"What is that?" Captain Pentoba strode across the deck, drawn by the anguished cries of two *raptuses* and one *titanus*. "They won't set my ship on fire, will they?"

I squeezed Aaru's hand and gazed up at Hush. Her flame spun across the sky in great red and orange ribbons, then scattered by the rush from her wings. I could feel it: anger and anticipation pulsed in my temples, hot with terror.

"Ilina said they did this before the tremor on Idris." My jaw ached with tension, and not even the gentle pressure of Aaru's hand around mine could calm the whirling in my thoughts. "What happens if there's a tremor?"

"If the waves looked bad, normally I'd drop anchor to keep from getting carried off course." She frowned up at the sky. "I already know what you're going to say, though."

"Thank you, Captain."

She just shook her head. "Get us there quickly, because if hard waves come before we slow down, we'll be torn apart."

I didn't waste time. The moment One said go, I dropped into my connection with the ship's noorestone and *pushed*.

It was easy now, like breathing. With only a thought, I could make the stones bend to my wishes. I could wrap myself in their power and I could *fly*.

At least, that was what it felt like as the midnight waves split before us. As Darina disappeared behind us. And as the stars moved along their pathways above us.

Aaru stayed at my side, our fingers linked, and when it was time for us to slow, he squeezed. ::**Here. Here. Here.**::

I opened my eyes, tendrils of noorestone shine falling away from me like silk scarves.

::**Incredible.**::

At first, I thought Aaru was talking about Flamecrest. The noorestone-lit city stood between crimson cliffs, a bright fire against the brilliant night sky. From here, it was too far and too dark to see the sandstone-cut buildings or the bright tiles on rooftops, but I'd been here before; though anger and fear now tempered my awe, I knew that Flamecrest had more than earned the title of the Jewel of the Fallen Isles.

But Aaru wasn't looking at the city. He was looking at me.

::**You,**:: he said. ::**You are incredible.**::

My heart leaped, and I couldn't stop my smile. For a moment, it didn't matter that we were about to work with the man who'd tortured both of us, or that we had two shrieking dragons locked with our friends in the captain's quarters, or even that somewhere a tremor was about to begin. For a moment, the only thing was Aaru and the soft way he looked at me.

I listed toward him, letting my lips graze his jaw when

he pulled me close to hug. A shiver worked through him. ::Yes, yes, yes.:: He kissed just above my ear.

But then the captain's door squeaked open and the cacophony of dragons spilled out.

I pulled away, aching with something deep and unfamiliar.

Boots thumped. Voices rumbled. On the quarterdeck, Gerel and Hristo stood on either side of Altan while the warrior told the captain where to go. They'd cuffed his wrists together. The sight of my nemesis as a prisoner should have brought me comfort, but instead it sparked worry in my chest. Altan was here because he wanted to be here. If he'd instructed his warriors only to capture the ship's crew, it was simply because he understood that killing them would prevent him from getting anything from me.

Maybe he should have thought about that before planting an explosion in my city and murdering everyone in the council house. And my *parents*—no, I couldn't think of them now.

"We should help the others." I lifted my eyes to Aaru again. "Before the tremor. Before the little dragons chew a hole in the ship."

He smiled. ::We will have time later.::

Together, we returned to the captain's cabin, where Ilina and Chenda were trying to hold a conversation over the noise of frustrated dragons.

"Where's Hush?" Ilina asked as I relieved Chenda from

her death grip on LaLa's leash.

"She didn't keep up with us." I could feel her in the back of my thoughts—just as frightened and angry as earlier—but the thread was thin.

"Maybe we should let these beasts fly, then." Ilina eyed her dragon, still straining to escape through the door. "Since there's no danger of Hush hurting them."

The other two options were equally bad: we could take them with us—on their leashes—or we could leave a pair of angry dragons on a very flammable ship. We'd already set one ship on fire this decan; it was probably smart to stop there.

"All right." I towed LaLa to me and carried her outside. Her squawks and thrashing only got worse, but I unclipped her. "There you go. Even sweet dragon weasels need to scream sometimes."

As soon as the leashes were off, both dragons launched toward the crescent moons, as brilliant as shooting stars as they streaked upward.

Slowly, the ship turned away from Flamecrest and toward one of the magnificent sandstone cliffs. It was hard to see from here, thanks to distance and all the light billowing up from the city, but I could just make out a familiar structure: broken, soaring arches, ancient and beautiful.

Ruins. I'd seen them before, during my tours of Anahera, but only from afar. No matter how sharp my curiosity, my requests to visit had been denied.

The ruins were sacred, some said. Haunted, said others. Either way, I'd not been permitted to visit the site. To the goddess of destruction, every ruin was a temple.

It was from those ruins that I felt it—the first stirrings of foreign anxiety. Not mine. Not LaLa or Crystal's. And not Hush's.

"That must be it," I breathed.

"What?" Ilina pressed her shoulder against mine as we both looked up.

"That's where the dragons are being held."

CHAPTER THIRTY-SEVEN

Without much time to plan, we had to make
our first decision fast:

Altan would come with us.

We couldn't leave him on the ship—not with my sister
sulking in our cabin, or the crew understandably wary of
any warrior other than Gerel. We considered leaving him
bound and gagged somewhere else, but we couldn't be
sure that he wouldn't escape, or that his warriors wouldn't
come for him.

And because even as my prisoner, Altan knew how
to gain control of a situation. He claimed he could reach
the ruins without alerting Anaheran authorities, and that
he had information regarding the layout and number of
guards stationed there, as well as an idea of how to move

such large creatures out of the building.

Of course, he would not *share* the information. But he would *show* us.

Time was short, leaving us little opportunity for debate, but if we wanted to succeed, then we needed him.

I just hoped this wasn't a mistake.

THERE WAS NOWHERE for the ship to dock—not without going through Flamecrest—so the *Chance Encounter* dropped anchor and the seven of us took a small rowboat to the beach. There, Altan promised we'd find an old trail that led to the elegant, first-century ruins where he claimed the dragons were being held.

Places like this were scattered all over the Fallen Isles. The Crescent Prominence sanctuary even had its own quaint collection of ruins, occupied only by small dragons and dust-smothered memories.

The ruins above Flamecrest were far more impressive. And, according to Anaheran legend, haunted.

As we stepped off the rowboat, I could just see one of the pale towers rising above the edges of the red cliffs. Two thousand years of storms and neglect had left the stone battered and crumbling, but achingly beautiful to behold. Arches, too, reached into the sky, their delicate fingers bent and broken. They vanished from my sight as Altan guided us to a trail, hidden by time and dust and overgrown weeds.

Two by two, with Altan positioned between Gerel and

Hristo, we ascended the trail. Morning haunted us from beyond the horizon, though the sky remained a deep, unending black, studded with stars and softened by hints of distant darkdust. In this predawn hour, I could make out the shapes of Theofania (the Innocent), Lesya (the Weaver), and Suna (the Judge) straight above. Airtor—the Wanderer—was never easy to find, as his stars moved across the sky in unpredictable patterns, but I finally spotted him on the western horizon.

"Do you think the Upper Gods are watching us?" Ilina followed my gaze, the tendons in her neck standing sharp as she lifted her face.

"If they are, they're laughing." We must have seemed so pathetic to them, attempting yet again to help dragons while all the powers around us moved to hasten the Great Abandonment. Perhaps the Upper Gods were just as eager for their Fallen brethren to return as I was to keep them here.

"All right," Gerel said as we walked around a switchback. "We're on our way up. Tell us what to expect when we get there."

"Not yet." Altan rattled the chain between his shackles. "I'll tell you as we reach the top. Otherwise you'll leave me on the side of the trail as soon as you don't need me anymore."

"Don't be ridiculous," Chenda said behind me. "You'd free yourself and run away. We wouldn't risk it."

Altan glanced over his shoulder, his lip curled in

disgust. "Obviously you'd kill me first."

I shook my head. "I know it's difficult for you to understand, but we aren't like you. We value life. Even the lives of monsters."

The warrior's shoulders stiffened; he kept his eyes focused straight ahead.

Maybe calling him a monster to his face—to the back of his head, rather—was too much. I forced my tone even and said, "Tell us what to expect up there. Guards. Layout. Everything. If you want to succeed, we all need to work together."

A slow sigh released the tension from his shoulders. "Very well."

As we moved up the trail, Altan reported all the information he'd been given, clarifying when necessary.

"What about the keepers?" Ilina asked. "Where are they likely to be held?"

"Near the main chamber, I imagine," Altan said. "In one of the towers. The guards will want to ensure the keepers are able to reach the dragons if there's an emergency."

I looped my arm around Ilina's waist and squeezed, just for a moment. "We'll find them," I whispered. "I promise."

A plan began to form around us, and by the time we were halfway up the trail, Hristo, Gerel, and Altan were arguing about contingency plans as well.

Our real plan—the best plan, I thought—was simple: we'd use the gifts of our gods.

We'd hide outside the sea-facing gatehouse at the top of the trail, and under the cover of shadows and silence, I would stretch my senses into the dome and awaken the dragons one at a time. I'd urge them to escape (through the same way they'd come in), and while guards and keepers were distracted trying to figure out why their sedated dragons were suddenly flying away, we would sneak in and look for Ilina's parents.

Straightforward. Nonviolent. Possible even with the impending earthquake.

I just hoped we weren't too late.

And that we could reach the dragons before sunrise.

And that the dragons would be ready to fly free.

And that the coming tremor would be gentle.

We pushed upward; the slope was so gradual it hardly felt like a climb . . . at least until I looked down to see the tops of waves as they gathered up starlight, then crashed onto the dark sand. The *Chance Encounter* stood as a black outline against the luminous sky, her sails furled and noorestones covered to keep her hidden from prying Anaheran eyes.

As we approached the top of the trail, Aaru's hand suddenly shot out. Everyone stopped, listening—and then we scrambled into the scraggly brush lining the path. Shadows bent unnaturally around us just in time.

A man strode by, wearing a flame-blue uniform and a long blade at his hip. The cut of his clothes looked Anaheran, as did the fire emblem on his sleeve.

508

Bile rose in the back of my throat. What did Anahera think of her people twisting her message of benevolent destruction? I could only imagine she felt the same as the other gods—Damyan and Darina's love used to hate, Idris's silence used to harm, Bopha's shadow used to hide misdeeds . . . We—people—were so good at using our beliefs as blunt weapons against one another.

When the guard was out of sight, we continued our ascent at a slower pace, painfully aware of moments slipping toward morning. And with every step I took, pressing my shoes to Anahera's earth, I waited for the telltale tremble of world-shifting movement.

We were *so* close to freeing the dragons.

At last, the trail evened out and the pearlescent expanse of the ruins loomed before us.

The main structure was an immense, egg-shaped dome, its once smooth roof now cracked open and spilling noorestone light into the sky. Seven towers stood sentinel around the dome, broken arches reaching between them. Before time and weather cast this place into ruin, the arches might have been bridges between the upper floors of the towers.

"There," Gerel breathed. "That's where we'll enter."

I followed her gaze toward the gatehouse yawning open before us. How strange that no one had closed it; it was more than big enough for a *Drakontos titanus* to walk through. Perhaps the mechanism no longer worked. I couldn't see anything inside beyond bright light, but the thread of draconic anxiety tightened. They were there. Inside the main chamber. Just beyond the open throat of the seaside gatehouse.

::**Do you hear them?**:: Shadows crossed Aaru's eyes. ::**Noorestones.**::

As he tapped, I became aware of a deep hum in the back of my head. Any other noorestone would have darkened ages ago, but even after twenty-two centuries, these crystals—embedded in the ancient, weather-marked walls—remained lit. It was incredible.

Old.

Powerful.

My fingers found Aaru's. ::**I can feel them.**:: I stretched my senses wider. All the noorestones felt the same, rooted deeply into the red earth of Anahera. The giant noorestones—the potential weapons—were not here.

Given the number of dragons, the coming earthquake, and the instability of those crystals, that was probably a good thing. A reaction between them could level this cliff, Flamecrest, and the entire harbor.

"Hurry." Gerel guided everyone behind a shelf of red rock, putting herself between Altan and the rest of us. "Keep down, and stay sharp for more guards," she whispered. "Remember: stay hidden. No one does anything brave but stupid."

I frowned. "Why are you looking at me?"

"If you feel that warning applies to you . . ." Gerel smirked.

510

"Do you see anything to transport the dragons?" Ilina peered over the rock. "Carts? Wagons?"

Altan shook his head. "They'll be on the other side of the building, toward the road."

"Most of the guards will be over there, then," Hristo said.

"The dragons will be out before the guards even know what's happening." As Chenda gazed up at the structure, noorestone light gleamed off her copper tattoos, making the swirls seem alive. The effect vanished when she looked at me. "Are you ready, Mira?"

Beyond the city's glow, promises of morning hovered on the horizon. Purple just brushed the sky, stripping stars of their nightly reign. I didn't need to be ready: I needed to be fast.

"You can do this," Ilina whispered.

But even before I began, a deep, dark sense of dread gathered in my stomach. Not nerves. Not panic. *Wrongness.*

Earlier, I'd felt a thread of anxiety from the dragons trapped within. Now, as I opened the connection wider, hopelessness and hunger traveled down, capturing me before I could pull back into my own thoughts.

Memory gaped beneath me: isolation.

Three walls.

One grate.

Hundreds of thousands of agonizing seconds of perfect, unobstructed darkness.

A faint *drip drip drip* from the cell next to mine—too far to reach the cup—carved a desperate thirst in my stomach. There'd been no voices but mine, no comforting warmth through the hole in the wall, and no indication as to whether the darkness had made soft the boundaries between itself and my body. I could feather apart.

"Mira?"

I shuddered back into myself, fingers digging into the rock before me while my vision swam back into focus.

Aaru's hand pressed flat against the small of my back.
::What's wrong?::

It was impossible to explain.

Sharing a connection with LaLa made sense; she and I had grown up together, so of course we knew each other's moods and desires.

And though it had taken some time to recognize the way other dragons behaved around me, like Kelsine and Hush, I was beginning to understand how my connections to them worked. I'd sometimes felt their joys and fears, and they'd felt mine.

But this . . .

I did not want strange dragons to be able to unspool my worst memories, especially when the monster responsible knelt only a few paces away.

"They are so, so scared," I whispered.

"Are you going to throw up?" Chenda peered at me.

"No." Hopefully not. "I can do this."

I *had* to do this. For the dragons. For the Fallen Isles.

Already, morning breathed against the sky.

Aaru's hand pressed flat against my back, offering strength as I tried again.

One dragon this time. One sleeping mind to draw free from the sedatives.

Then the next, and the next, and soon they would all do what dragons did best: *burn*.

But even as I reached for one, my stomach clenched, hollowed out with hunger. Two realities collided: me crouched fifty paces away from the gatehouse, pebbles digging into my knees; and me all alone, trapped in whole, unadulterated darkness.

It was the sort of darkness that pressed through my skin, binding to my bones. It was a solid, smothering force that broke everything in its path.

The absence of light.

The absence of hope.

The absence of love.

A groan tumbled out of me, no matter how I tried to bite it off. I didn't want the darkness to have my voice, but I was too late. Everything, everything was swallowed up in this unending darkness.

"Mira!" The darkness consumed Ilina's frantic whisper.

::Mira!:: It made Aaru's quiet code pass right through my body.

But that wasn't right. I'd heard Ilina. I'd felt Aaru. If they were with me, then the darkness was not absolute.

"This isn't real," I whispered. "This isn't *now*."

513

It had been real, yes, but I wasn't in the Pit anymore. Altan was *my* prisoner.

I forced my eyes open and heaved, but the disgust and shame and terror stayed lodged in my chest. These were the dragons' feelings.

Dozens of dragons waited within the ruins, suffering soundlessly, locked within their own bodies. While my isolation had lasted mere days, theirs spanned months.

"What happened?" Ilina hugged me to her. "Seven gods, Mira. You're shivering."

"It's bad." I looked up at the gatehouse, those beautiful, crumbling arches, and the elegant spires piercing the predawn sky. Now I understood why the gate stood open. Not only because it had long ago ceased to close, but because no one here was worried about the dragons escaping.

They couldn't.

They were trapped. Shackled down into their own minds, their bodies filled with lead and rot.

"I don't know if they're being poisoned or if they're sick," I whispered, "but I can't wake them. Every time I try, it feels like I'm getting sucked down with them. Caught in a cage. Left in the darkness." A shudder ran the entire length of my body.

Aaru took my hand and pulled it to his chest. His heartbeat was strong and steady against my curled fingers. ::Not alone.:: His gaze flickered up—beyond me, beyond Ilina, beyond the others. His hands tightened over mine, and I knew he was looking at Altan. I knew he was thinking about the days he and the others had been taken from our cellblock, and by the time the guards had returned him, I'd been delirious with hunger and dehydration.

He'd given me sips of water from his cup that collected drips from the ceiling. He'd talked to me, encouraged me, helped bring me back to life.

My silent friend dropped his eyes to meet mine once more. ::I'm with you.::

I twisted my fingers in his shirt—inadequate when I wanted to fall into his embrace—before sitting all the way up again.

"What do we do, then?" Hristo shifted his weight to one side. "Can we still rescue the dragons?"

"Can we?" Our entire plan—and our contingencies—relied on me being able to wake the dragons so they could fly away. If I couldn't wake them, we had no way to help them. Still, I hadn't come all this way to just give up. "What if we wait for the guards to load the dragons into wagons, then steal the wagons?"

"And do what with them?" Gerel let out a long sigh. "I'm sorry, Mira. If you can't wake them, we need to go. It's too dangerous to stay here."

"Mira went back to the Pit for you," Ilina whispered.

A sour, sick feeling festered in my stomach. From the dragons. From this failure. From coming all this way and daring to have hope. And from working with Altan—of all people.

"My parents could be in there," Ilina went on. "We can at least rescue them."

"How?" Chenda glanced up at the bruising sky. "I'm not saying we can't. But we need a plan. We can't just go charging in. There are guards."

Despair clawed at me. All those dragons. Ilina's parents.

Aaru closed his eyes. Listening, his expression said. But whatever he heard must have displeased him, because a frown settled around his mouth.

Then, slowly, he nodded.

And chaos broke loose.

It began with Altan. He bolted from our cover, a knife shining in one hand, and headed top speed toward one of the western towers—away from this gatehouse.

Gerel swore and felt at her boot, but it was too late: Altan had stolen not only her knife, but the key to his cuffs as well.

A lone alarm bell rang from one of the towers, echoing across the weather-worn stone.

"He'll get us all killed." Chenda's words dripped venom. "I knew bringing him was a mistake."

But while we'd been crouched here, half a dozen guards exited the gatehouse and ran after Altan . . . clearing the way for the rest of us. Moments after the blue-jacketed guards ran by, a man cried out for help—and was cut off. There was a solid thump: a body hitting the ground.

"Chenda, we need shadows." I grabbed Ilina's hand and

lurched to my feet. "Come on. We're saving your parents."
Maybe there was no chance for the dragons—although it
hurt to even think that—but my friend deserved to see her
mother and father again.

We didn't wait for anyone else. Shadows or no shadows, my wingsister and I ran straight for the looming
ruins, its gatehouse jaw hanging wide open.

Five steps. Six. Seven. The noise of our footfalls
vanished under Aaru's silence as he caught up with us.
Shadows folded around us, but there was only so much
Chenda could do when the very walls shone bright with
noorestones.

Twelve, thirteen, fourteen. A sense of deep discomfort
welled up within my soul, humming from the gossamer
strand that connected me to the dragons trapped inside.
Every step I took toward them strengthened that thread,
spinning it tighter and hotter.

Twenty-five, twenty-six, twenty-seven. My breath
puffed out in short gasps, in time with my steps.

The white ruins dominated my view. They were
immense. Imposing. A cage for dragons—and us, if we
were caught. But I wouldn't let fear stop me anymore.

Fifty strides from our hiding spot, we finally reached
the gatehouse. Ilina and I passed through the mouth, into
a long tunnel that shone with noorestones. Silence and
shadows fell away, pointless in this passage.

Muffled sounds of violence chased us into the building:
Gerel and Hristo had weapons drawn and were guarding

the entrance from a pair of men in Anaheran blue.

"Hurry." The word came out in a flat huff of air as I picked up my pace, shedding the last shambles of our plan. There'd be no sneaking out now that the guards knew we were here. Even if we somehow managed to avoid being overwhelmed, Gerel and Hristo would have to incapacitate anyone in our way. And then we'd have to escape with Ilina's parents, leaving behind dozens of frightened dragons.

Another rush of their anguish caused me to stumble, but Ilina reached for me. We kept going together.

We ran past halls that led to towers, past hollows carved out for statuary, looted long ago, and past column after column that stretched toward the high ceiling. A bright, indistinct glow shone ahead, but Altan had already explained what awaited us.

Most people believed this building had been used for blood sports or performances, because the center held a deep depression with tiered levels toward the perimeter, like an arena with seating for thousands. That was where the dragons would be: in a place once reserved for public murder.

My head pounded in time with my steps as we thundered into the main space, and my eyes watered and struggled to adjust to the bright glow of noorestones on alabaster walls. Enormous, dark mounds covered the floor. I blinked away tears and the shapes finally resolved into dragons.

Dozens of them.

I dropped to my knees and stared across the arena. Dragons huddled close to columns and walls, barely alive. A fog-like quiet pressed over the space. To some, it might have seemed peaceful—all these big, territorial dragons together—but anyone who knew dragons knew this was wrong. And I . . . I could *feel* them.

The walls.

The darkness clouding their minds.

The sluggish pulse of blood through their bodies.

Just before me, a russet *Drakontos maximus* lay on her side, gasping for breath. Her wings drooped across the floor, and her hazel eyes were glazed over. She stared at nothing. One of her facial horns had cracked, leaving a sharp, jagged edge.

Another *maximus* lay nearby, his condition just as awful. Dull scales. Shallow breathing. Glazed eyes. Beyond him were a *titanus*, a *rex*, and then a dragon I knew.

"Lex." Her name tore from my throat. Ragged. Painful. "Oh, Darina. Damyan."

"All the gods." Chenda pressed her hands to her heart, breathing hard after our run. "This is abhorrent."

And yet, our own governments had enabled this torment. Whether they'd believed the dragons were being sent to the Algotti Empire or staying here on Anahera, the governments she and I had spent our lives serving had willingly given up the children of the gods.

"I see Tower." Ilina pressed her hands to her mouth. "And Astrid."

I couldn't look away from Lex.

The *Drakontos rex* had been one of the first dragons to go missing from the Crescent Prominence sanctuary, and the dragon I'd tried to save in the Shadowed City. Once, her scales had been as bright and deep as rubies; now, they were faded and scraped, missing in several places as though they'd fallen off or she'd picked at them.

I'd tried to save her, and still she'd ended up here. And come the dawn, her captors would take her somewhere else.

"We can't leave them."

Aaru placed his hands on my shoulders and squeezed, but I couldn't look away from the dragons. Magnificent, wild creatures that belonged in the sky.

For a dark moment, I was glad LaLa and Crystal and Hush weren't here. They shouldn't have to see this. *Feel* this.

Misery and hopelessness festered within me—not mine, but the dragons'. Every one of them fluttered around the edges of my thoughts, beckoning me toward the abyss.

A moan shuddered out of me. I dropped back my head, bumping Aaru's leg. His fingers curled against my shoulders. There I saw it: a great split ran the length of the ceiling, like a giant child had cracked open the dome to peer inside.

Altan—who'd likely abandoned us the moment he'd ran off—had mentioned the gash, but I'd been unprepared for how *big* it was. And through it, beyond the glare of the noorestone glow, deep purple and red washed out the

stars. Morning encroached. We had to find Ilina's parents.
We had to help these dragons.

"Ilina, we—"

"I know." Tears crowded her voice. "I know. Maybe we can find a way—"

"Who's there?" A woman's voice came from the far side of the chamber.

Ilina looked up, sudden hope lighting her eyes. "Mother?"

And then:

1. A wave of absolute desolation rushed toward me: emptiness in its purest form.
2. Aaru caught me as I wilted to the floor.
3. Brash, angry voices carried through the tunnel as guards broke through Hristo and Gerel's blockade.
4. The entire world shuddered as the earthquake finally hit.

CHAPTER THIRTY-EIGHT

At first, it was just like any other tremor.

The world shook.

Someone screamed.

Aaru pressed his body against mine, keeping his arms tight around my shoulders. Steadying.

And then it passed. The great rumble traveled beneath us and was gone, rippling farther away from its center. To the others, it must have seemed like such a small thing. All that raving and fire from the *raptuses* and Hush—and we'd gotten nothing more than a few shifting moments.

But none of them could feel the dragons. The worst was yet to come.

Hearts fluttered and not one dragon moved, but inside, they were maelstroms of unending torment. Of walls and hunger and starless night. This sickness had plunged its tendrils into dozens of dragons, and it refused to release its grip.

Now I was caught in it, too. Breathing the same air as the dragons, sharing the same space, a great wave of misery kicked me sideways of my own emotions. I was caught in the undertow of draconic feeling: immense and perfect grief for the world as it began to fall apart.

This tremor wasn't over. Not nearly.

But as I opened my mouth to warn the others, a low, anguished groan fell out. Not my voice. Not any human's voice.

"What happened?" Ilina rushed for me, and I felt Aaru shaking his head in confusion.

I tried again to warn them, but it seemed sharp needles stitched my voice silent. Bright flares cast unfamiliar shapes across my eyes. A cage fell around my thoughts, trying to cast me back in the darkness of the Pit.

Stolen into captivity, separated from the sun and sky: one dragon had gone wild with fear and hunger. He'd cried out for others to help, stretching his mind to theirs, and that was when the sickness spread, beginning with his own species. Sickness of the body, sickness of the mind: it was all the same to the children of the gods.

And now my connection to dragons made me just as susceptible.

I would slouch to the floor, hissing air through tight lungs as my skin turned loose and gray. I would become like these dragons. Dying.

No.

No, I would not let myself become trapped in my own mind. Nor would I leave the dragons to suffer alone.

With a soft bellow, I wrested open my eyes. Understanding flashed as I took in the situation around me:

Ilina held her palm to my forehead, her skin cool against my burning.

Aaru cradled me in his arms. His heart beat hummingbird-quick against my cheek as he gazed down at me, concern written across his face.

Chenda stood above us, her eyes darting from the tunnel to the small figure rushing through the maze of dragons. Ilina's mother. Tereza.

"Go see her," I told Ilina. "We'll need her help if we want to free these dragons."

My wingsister hesitated, but I hid the throbbing in my head behind a clenched jaw and steady glare. Then she nodded and pushed away from us—toward her mother.

I wanted to take a moment to breathe, but I pulled myself up straight, blinking to clear the last echoes of dark walls from my mind.

Aaru bit his lip. ::Thought you were dying.::

"I'll be all right." I forced a smile. "Thank you for catching me."

He squeezed my shoulder.

"We should consider running." Chenda offered her hands, and I let her pull me to my feet. "We're outnumbered."

As Aaru stood and took my hand, I looked toward the tunnel. Chenda was right: eight Anaheran guards in flame-blue jackets rushed toward us, with Gerel and Hristo on their heels. My friends must have been knocked away during the tremor because they didn't appear hurt—thank all the Fallen Gods—but even if I could wake up every single dragon right now, we'd still be in trouble.

The lead guard's eyes fell on me as he ran into the arena. "Surrender!"

I would do no such thing.

Hundreds—maybe thousands—of ancient noore-stones hummed against the back of my thoughts. I started to reach for them, but the

world

wrenched

sideways.

An immense roar ripped through the ground, throwing two of the guards to their knees. The others shouted and braced themselves as a crack opened across one of the gleaming white walls, and a broken column crashed to the ground. Stone shattered. Shards shot out, slicing into unconscious dragons who could not react. Shrouds of dust shivered through the air, dimming the noorestone-lit arena into a trembling gloom.

This.

This was the earthquake the dragons had tried to warn us about.

Aaru took my hand and moved toward the exit—but even with debris clouding the air, we'd be easy targets for the guards.

I dug in my heels and pulled him back, but it didn't

seem any safer here. The dome shuddered all around, its rumble deep and dangerous and growing. Maybe I could still use the noorestones' power to defend us, but these crystals were so, so old, and connected to Noore in a way I couldn't understand. An attempt to tap into the power here could be perilous. And during a bone-trembling earthquake? I didn't dare.

Aaru's eyes were wide, dark with memories of past tremors. He lifted his gaze to the slashed-open ceiling, the terror on his face as clear as any spoken words.

Staying here could get us crushed, but we couldn't escape through the wall of guards.

And I would not leave without the dragons.

From beyond a *Drakontos rex*, Tereza beckoned us deeper into the chamber. "This way!"

Aaru's jaw clenched, but when I tugged, he followed, keeping his fingers laced tightly with mine as chaos built throughout the shuddering arena.

A man screamed in the tunnel. I looked over my shoulder just in time to see Gerel driving her sword through his side. Bile crept up my throat as Aaru pulled me faster after Tereza, around motionless dragons and over their splayed limbs. With the ground shifting beneath us and the world roaring around us, it was hard to move quickly, carefully, but the sounds of battle in the tunnel spurred us onward.

Another tunnel, bigger than the first, gaped across the arena. More guards poured through, accompanying dozens of men drawing metal carts, each big enough to bear a full-grown *Drakontos titanus*.

Rage shifted inside of me. Even with the earthquake, this evidence of our gods' fury, these people intended to carry out their plans for these dragons.

But if they weren't going to the empire, then what was the purpose of all this?

"Down!" Tereza ducked into the curve of an emerald *Drakontos maior*'s forelegs and belly, dragging Ilina with her. Aaru and I followed, with Chenda just after. A blanket of shadow fell over the space, thin thanks to the light coming from all around, but better than nothing.

Dirt-heavy air squeezed into my lungs, aching as the earthquake rolled beneath us. Stone screamed as it was hewn apart, with entire columns beginning to crumble.

Never had I felt an earthquake so strong, or one that continued for such a long time. Wherever this quake was centered, it must have been close. Maybe Anahera herself.

Abruptly, the noise of the fighting and the earthquake went quiet. Not muted, but muffled. Relief set over Aaru's face, in spite of the focus needed to maintain this bubble.

Chenda sent a small nod Aaru's way, acknowledgment and thanks.

Tereza turned on Ilina, like the magic and tremor and fighting meant nothing to her. "Explain. Now."

"Where's Father?" Ilina scanned our surroundings, unaffected by her mother's glare.

"Flamecrest." Tereza's voice cracked. "The High Magistrate sent for him."

"Can we get him back?"

"Can we not change the subject?"

"We came to help—"

Tereza's expression darkened. "I told you if they ever came for us, you were to stay away. Was I not clear?"

Ilina tilted her chin. "The dragons. We came to help the dragons."

Her mother's glower deepened, but it was a mask. Beneath it, real terror filled her eyes.

"It doesn't matter anymore, does it?" Ilina said. "We're here and that's not going to change because you're mad."

"You are pushing me." The sharp words and tone were a show, though; Tereza's expression softened as she pulled Ilina into a fierce embrace. "Oh, Ilina. I missed you so much."

I lowered my eyes, chest aching with the opposing ways our mothers greeted us after an absence—and stinging with the knowledge that mine might not even be alive now.

Aaru watched them, naked longing in his expression. I reached for his hand and squeezed; I would get him back to his family. I would.

"I'm going to help Gerel." Chenda stood, taking her shadow with her. "Figure out what you need to do and do it, if you still can." As the floor gave a wild jerk, she reached out to steady herself—but stopped short of touching the dragon. Respect? Fear? It was hard to say.

As Ilina explained our original plan to her mother, I watched Chenda stagger between the dragons, her shadow leaping ahead of her. Light from all directions made her shadow pale, weaker than in the Pit, but still it served to confuse and distract a pair of guards attacking Hristo and Gerel.

"We thought if Mira could wake them, they'd just fly away," Ilina said, "but there's something wrong. Every time she tries, they take her down, too."

"You thought Mira could wake them." Tereza shifted her gaze toward me, her eyes a deep, warm brown, steady, even as the world trembled. "Did you think you could?"

"Yes," I whispered, pressing my palm against the emerald dragon's scales. They were cooler than they should be, with ragged, chipped edges. Even so, a faint, shivering connection spun between us. He knew I was here to help. He wanted me to help. I climbed to my feet, bracing myself against the dragon as the floor shuddered. From this angle, I could just see the way his back pressed against a broken column; his spine ridges scraped one of the embedded noorestones with every labored breath. "I can feel his pain and fear."

"Mira, is that wise?" Ilina started to shift toward me, but the world gave a heavy jolt and she had to catch herself. "What if you can't break free this time?"

"I know how to help them." I pulled myself straight. A strange joy bubbled in my chest. "Look up."

Above us, a roar shattered the sky, followed by thundering wingbeats.

One.

Two.

Three.

An immense, blue-green shape passed over the break in the ceiling.

::Hush?:: Aaru stood next to me, his eyes trained above.

"Yes." I lifted both hands into the air just as two small moons streaked into the arena, cutting through the dusty gloom. LaLa thumped onto my fingers, talons squeezing as fire burst against her spark gland. The back of my throat tingled with hers. "Hello, my precious dragon flower." I kissed her nose.

Ilina caught Crystal just as the silver dragon spread her wings to slow. "What are you doing here?" She pulled Crystal close, but the pair had other ideas.

Both dragons pushed off, zipping toward a team of blue-jacketed guards and ignoring Ilina's protest.

Dragons, even little dragons, did not like to be told no.

"They want to protect the others." I smiled at her. "We're their trainers, not their mothers, and we've trained them to be brave."

Before Ilina could argue that, a great thud crashed above us, and talons curled in through the tear in the ceiling. Chunks of stone cracked and crumbled under Hush's grip.

"We need to get out of here." Ilina peered around the arena—at the men struggling to load dragons onto carts, at the guards fighting Gerel and Hristo and Chenda, and the entire building still shuddering under the onslaught of the earthquake. "The dome will fall in."

"Go." I took Ilina's shoulders. "Get the others and lead

them out. Everyone needs to get clear, because I'm going to wake the dragons."

Worry filled her eyes. "Are you sure you can do it?"

I nodded. "I know what to do now."

She bit her lip, then rushed forward to hug me. "I trust you." Then, she took her mother and they hurried between the unconscious dragons.

I turned to Aaru.

::**Not leaving you.**:: A smile tugged at one corner of his mouth.

"Good."

::**How will you help the dragons?**::

"Watch," I breathed. Suddenly, it was so clear.

1. *The cut on my cheek.*
2. *The gash on my shoulder.*
3. *LaLa's wing.*
4. *And every dragon I'd ever known hoarded the glowing crystals in their dens.*

I didn't stop to second-guess myself.

One step back. One deep breath. I closed my eyes and opened my mind to the ruin's noorestones.

They were two thousand and thirteen blazing stars scattered across the sky of my thoughts. No need to count their number; I simply knew.

All across the shuddering building, light pulsed and breathed, shining from the arena, the towers, and the

531

forgotten corners of these ruins. I reached, and the power stretched toward me as ghostly filaments of blue-white light, soft and hesitant and warm. They hung around me like a lace gown made of shining silk threads. Beads of hot white illumination hung suspended for a mere breath, then slid toward my heart.

The world shivered. The dragons slumbered. The power of Noore filled me.

My light reflected in Aaru's midnight eyes, but he wore no worry, no fear, no waiting with his silence. He understood, as well as I did, that this was nothing like the Pit, or the tunnel, or the theater. Now, I knew how to contain the energy. I knew how to control it.

Power wrapped around my arms and chest and legs. I breathed it all in until it filled my heart and pumped through my veins. Muscles rippled down my back, and noorestone fire spread around me like plasmic wings.

The dawn-scraped sky beckoned, but I had work here on the ground.

I began with the emerald dragon, pressing my palms against his flank, opening my thoughts wide to his.

Dark threads of anguish twisted through his mind. I could feel it all: the walls, the hunger, the desperation. He'd suffered so much at the hands of humans.

No longer.

I burned away the walls caging his mind. I fed him the power of noorestones, sip after hot sip, strengthening his body. And I whispered a prayer because he could not:

"Give him peace. Give him grace. Give him enough hope in his heart."

The emerald dragon's scales warmed under my fingers, and all around us, others began to stir; my light traveled throughout the arena, healing the same way the sickness had spread.

Above, Hush released a mighty roar, orange and white flames dragging from between her teeth. She spit fire toward the road where more carts and wagons waited to steal her brethren away. Through her eyes, the guards were insignificant rodents, a dozen of them fighting one man in a warrior uniform, wielding only a knife.

Hush released another bellow of flame, setting the last of the wagons ablaze before she swung her head back around and peered into the arena, catching sight of Gerel attacking a guard, and Hristo blocking a blow meant for Chenda, whose shadow was away. LaLa and Crystal—tiny to Hush's great eyes—flittered about, blowing streaks of fire to discourage guards from closing in.

Then there was Ilina with her mother, both of them tearing out of the building as fast as two humans possibly could. They stumbled around fracturing columns, over fresh cracks in the floor, and past debris falling from the ever-widening gash in the ceiling. When the others noticed their escape, they followed without hesitation, abandoning battles. Guards exchanged confused looks, but as a chunk of stone slammed to the floor nearby, they took off at a run.

I pulled back to my own eyes, urgency pressing against

the back of my thoughts. The tremor was beginning to ease, but Hush intended to finish its work by ripping open the ruins—her sisters' and brothers' prison.

The noorestone light would spread between the dragons and burn away their sickness, but not before Hush tore down the building. I could try to calm her, but after all she and the others had been through, who was I to rein in her anger?

"We have to hurry." I turned to Aaru, who was gazing at me with something like awe. "Stay close." Now that the dragons were awakening, they needed to see him as my friend.

He nodded, but kept a safe distance from the nimbus of light surrounding me. That was probably wise; neither of us could know what would happen if he touched it.

My chest. My limbs. My very blood was hot with power as I found Lex, my ruby-scaled *Drakontos rex*. I placed my hands on her wide cheek and throat so that my noorestone fire flowed directly into her. "I've come for you," I whispered. "It's time to go home."

Under my fingers, Lex warmed and rumbled, stirring from the floor where she'd lain prone for so long. Her wings rustled and her teeth ground as she tested her body, and then one huge eye opened to focus on me.

"Hello, sweet Lex." I leaned forward and kissed one of her ragged scales. Heat bloomed beneath my lips, and everywhere I stroked along her neck. When she started to pull herself up, I took two long steps backward. "You're free now."

As Hush continued her assault on the roof, dropping huge chunks of stone into the arena, I moved from dragon to dragon and pushed noorestone fire into them, burning away the last traces of illness.

With wind and sky and morning sun pouring through the widening hole in the roof, the other dragons drew themselves to all fours and tested their strength against the remaining columns and walls. Structures cracked apart, and noorestones scattered across the fragmented floor like dying stars.

More and more dragons found their feet and wings, and even as the earthquake eased and ended, the building was lost.

::Run?:: Aaru tapped against his own hand.

I lifted my face. Chunks of the dome rained in, shattering where they hit what was left of the floor. The ruins crumbled around us as dragons took flight, breaking off jagged pieces of walls and towers. Flame spun from Hush's open jaws as she roared in triumph, then pushed off into the sky.

The remaining dragons followed, spreading their wings to take flight through the open ceiling.

It was too late to run, but I could protect us.

As the ruins screamed and cracked, and immense slabs plummeted toward us, I reached for Aaru.

His eyes flickered to the noorestone glow shimmering between my arms.

Under the roar of the dome crumbling in, I whispered, "Do you trust me?"

His jaw tightened.

He stepped into my arms.

I ducked his head to my chest, letting my fire wings spread wide around us as the ruins collapsed in plumes of pale stone and dust. An incredible crash sounded as a broken arch dropped, and noorestone after noorestone winked out—finally darkened after all this time.

As tunnels buckled, and walls sloughed apart, and towers crumbled inward, I drew the last remnants of fire from the ruin noorestones before they, too, were gone.

One thousand noorestones.

Four hundred.

Twenty.

One.

The noorestone fire died. My wings disappeared. I was just a girl again, my arms wrapped tight around Aaru as the last of the stones fell, and dust whispered away in the morning breeze.

The ruins were completely destroyed, this once-glorious arena reduced to chunks of rock and darkened noorestones that glittered dimly in the rising light. I stepped back from Aaru, coughing against the swirling dust, but when my heel kicked a drift of shattered stone, I noticed a perfect circle cut around us.

Aaru lifted his eyes and smiled. His hands stayed clasped with mine. ::**You changed the prayer for the dragons. You said hope instead of love.**::

I squeezed his hands and ducked my face, hardly

536

able to contain the relieved smile blooming out of me. ::It seemed to me they needed hope more than anything. I could heal them; they needed to believe it.::

He stepped close to kiss me, just a soft brush of his mouth on mine. ::You are a true Hopebearer.::

"Mira!" Across a white field of shattered stone, Ilina stood with the rest of our friends, her mother, and Altan. The warrior was back in cuffs, held in place between Hristo and Gerel. I couldn't believe he hadn't escaped once he'd distracted the guards, but maybe his honor wouldn't have allowed it. He still owed me Tirta, Elbena, and Kelsine.

We couldn't stay here. Anaheran authorities would arrive any minute. But before I could lead everyone back down the trail—to the rowboat and the *Chance Encounter*—Ilina waved and pointed up. "Look!"

Aaru and I both obeyed.

Dozens of dragons wove through the dawn, their wings outstretched to create a brilliant tapestry that glittered in the hot morning sun. They circled into a tower of color—ruby and topaz and emerald and sapphire—spiraling around one another, shooting fire as they climbed higher into the sky. They roared and stretched, finally—*finally*—free to go where they wanted.

There was Lex, her red scales shining. And Tower and Astrid, the other two I'd known from the Crescent Prominence sanctuary. The emerald dragon I'd first healed thrashed his head around, twisting his body through the blue sky. And ahead of all the dragons flew Hush.

She didn't land to say good-bye. She didn't even turn to look at me. But my heart pounded with a joy like fire, and I knew it was hers.

::Where are they going?:: Aaru asked.

"Somewhere far away." A piece of my soul ached to go with them. "Somewhere humans can't hurt them anymore."

Wingbeats faded. The pull in my chest eased. The dragons disappeared into the sky. Gone, but safe.

Ilina picked her way through the rubble, coming toward me. Both *raptuses* were perched on her shoulders, hunched low where Ilina rested her fingertips over them to keep them still. "I don't think we'll ever see anything like that again. All those dragons together."

"It's hard to imagine." I turned to my best friend. "I can't believe we did it. At last."

She grinned and released LaLa, who dived into my arms, clicking and humming.

"And you, little dragon weasel, were very brave." I bumped my nose against hers. "The bravest gold dragon I've ever met."

"She wanted to fly back in when the building started to fall." Ilina pulled Crystal into her arms and hugged her close. "Seven gods, I wanted to fly back in after you, but—"

Next to me, Aaru gasped. No voice, just a sharp, indrawn breath filled with alarm. Ilina and I followed his gaze to where a new shape snagged my sight.

An enormous mountain rose in the distance, gleaming

like molten gold in the morning light. Though it was too far to notice details, the fact that we could see it from this great distance meant it had to be huge.

Immense. Bigger than anything I'd ever seen before. "It's incredible," I breathed. "What do you think it is?"

Aaru's hand trembled as he touched my arm and tapped in his quiet code. ::Idris.::

CHAPTER THIRTY-NINE

IDRIS. THE GOD OF SILENCE.

The mountain was shaped like a giant man. He was kneeling, his head hung so his chin pointed at his chest. Not in shame or humiliation, but in deep, contemplative thought. He glistened in the hot sunlight, though whether the glow came from his skin or the water rushing down his form, I couldn't be sure. Distance obscured detail.

And Idris was *so* far away. That we could see him from here, on the opposite end of the Fallen Isles, spoke to his immense size.

I couldn't stop staring.

Or my heart from tumbling over itself.

Or the way horror clawed up my throat and got stuck.

This was it. This was the Great Abandonment.
A Fallen God had risen.

FOUR THINGS:

1. *He was magnetic, drawing everyone's eyes.
   None could look away from the titanic god
   on the horizon.*
2. *Did anything matter now? We'd come all this
   way and freed over two dozen dragons, but
   still, Idris had pulled himself from the ocean
   floor to abandon his people. We had been too
   late.*
3. *The Mira Treaty. The inevitable war between
   every Fallen Isle. The location of spies. All
   paled beneath the shadow of the risen god.
   Except . . .*
4. *Aaru's family was dead. His friends. His
   community. No one could have survived the
   violence of a god rising up from the sea.*

There was nothing for Aaru to return to.

SOUND VANISHED AS Aaru dropped to his knees, hopelessness washed across his face like a shroud.

I heard nothing—no gulls, no waves, no screams, no
wind, no breathing. Aaru's sorrow smothered everything
with silence.

The silence spilled beyond our sphere, rolling down the cliff and hill and running into the city, where it crashed like a wave. Streetlights went out. Buildings went dark. And the hum of civilization vanished.

Silence. Darkness. A risen god.

Anyone in the path of Aaru's silence must have tried to scream, but they wouldn't have been able to hear it. It must have been chaos down there in the city, but I couldn't feel anything for them now. In this moment, everything went to one person.

At my feet, Aaru was an aching mirror of his god.

I knelt before him and took his shoulders, but he wouldn't look at me. He didn't seem to be present at all, as though the grief had ripped the essence of Aaru right out of his body. He just stayed there, not moving, not even blinking.

Then his eyes focused, first on me, then the great mountain of his god behind me. His mouth opened in a silent cry of anguish. Despair. At once, he bent over and sobbed, his chest heaving with each soundless howl.

Our world was collapsing. His world was already gone.

I shifted around and sat on my feet so that he could rest his forehead on my knees, and it was there, as I stroked his back—as if there was any way to smooth away the horror—that sound began to return.

Wind whispered through the grass.

Noorestones flickered and resumed their normal glow.

Murmuring voices came from the far side of the hill.

"Oh, Aaru," I breathed, and when I bent over him, LaLa slipped from my arms and curled up with my silent friend. She gave a faint, sorrowful purr, and licked his cheek. "Aaru, I'm sorry." The word felt too weak for what I wanted to show. Too little against the magnitude of what he'd lost.

Everything.

AARU

First Day in the Pit

WATER DRIPPED FROM THE CEILING.

Slowly.

Evenly.

Maddeningly.

A wooden cup under the leak captured the water; it had been full when I'd arrived, so I'd drunk it all, not thinking I needed to save it. Not thinking the guards would be so cruel as to give us food and water only once a day.

But water continued its unrelenting drip, and the quality of the drops hitting the wood shifted from flat to full. Other sounds skittered throughout the cellblock: voices, groans, and muted movements. Across the hall and over, a young woman with shorn hair exercised; I listened to the hitch of her breath as she pulled herself up on the door, stood on her hands and pushed up, did a thousand other things.

Darkness came.

Screams came.

I retreated beneath the bench meant to double as a bed. There, I wrapped my thin blanket around my head to muffle the cacophony, but there was no blocking out the echoes in my mind.

The riot. The expressions my family wore as I was taken. The question of their survival.

I tried tapping *The Book of Silence* against my chest, but each letter stabbed me in the heart. Nowhere did the god of silence instruct that families should starve rather than allow a mother to work. Nowhere did the Most Silent say that girls could never possess the Voice of Idris. Nowhere did *The Book of Silence* insist that it was forbidden to speak against injustice.

Wasn't all that just as important as what the book *did* say?

Who, then, had decided my mother was not as strong or as wise as my father? Who, then, had decided that cruel little boys could possess the Voice of Idris, but not sweet Safa? And who, then, had decided that people should endure injustice in silence?

The few who benefited from our suffering.

The few who had turned silence into a weapon.

The few who had twisted Idris's holy words to benefit themselves.

· · ·

Sometime after the noorestones illuminated again and food was distributed, guards came through the hall a second time.

They had a girl my age.

She was tall, clad in a long dress that flowed around her legs like water, but her hands were bound and dirt smudged her warm brown skin. Another prisoner.

I stayed under my bed, watching as her sad eyes scanned my cell for signs of life, and then she was gone—waiting while the guards opened the cell next to mine.

When they left, her breath tightened and squeezed, and soon she began to cry. I listened, but there was nothing I could do for her. Not when my own heart was still shattering.

Later, I listened to her tell herself to stop crying, and attempt to introduce herself to the other prisoners. It seemed she was even more unsuited to prison than I.

Then darkness came.

Screams came.

And when quiet followed later, I could hear her on the other side, breaths rasping and catching in fitful sleep. Like me, she'd retreated to the quietest place she could find. She wasn't Idrisi, not with all those unnecessary words and the extravagant way she dressed, but perhaps we weren't all that different: her grief and fear matched my own.

I found my wooden cup, full now, and took it to a hole between my cell and hers.

::Strength through silence,:: I prayed, because even if my leaders had betrayed me, my god had not. Then, I found my voice and spoke the name she'd given.

"MIRA."

CHAPTER FORTY

LATER, I DREAMED OF FLYING.

Of great wings and burning stars.

Of fire and screams.

Of power untold.

And when I opened my eyes, I wasn't dreaming.

ACKNOWLEDGMENTS

Sequels are tricky creatures, and it seemed impossible that I would ever finish this one. But I was never alone on this journey. As always, many people helped me through the endless drafts to make this book the best it could be.

First, I must thank Lauren MacLeod, my fearless agent. Every time I complained I'd never finish this book, she reminded me of the last fifty times I said the same thing but made it through alive.

Maria Barbo and Stephanie Guerdan, my incredible editors who worked hard to make sure this book has sparkles . . . and more dragons.

The entire team at Katherine Tegen Books, including Bess Braswell, Sabrina Abballe, Rosanne Romanello, Joel Tippie, Emily Rader, and Katherine Tegen.

As with *Before She Ignites*, I must acknowledge and thank an incredible group of critique partners, sensitivity readers, brainstormers, and cheerleaders: Brodi Ashton, Martina Boone, Erin Bowman, Valerie Cole, Julie Daly, Cynthia Hand, Deborah Hawkins, Suna Jung, Sarah Kershaw, Stacey Lee, Sarah Glenn Marsh, Myra McEntire, Mary E. Pearson, Kathryn Purdie, C. J. Redwine, Aminah Mae Safi, Alexa Santiago, Francina Simone, Erin Summerill, Laurel Symonds, Christina Termini, Tiffie van Bordeveld, Alana Whitman, Fran Wilde, the entire OQ Support Group, and anyone I've shamefully forgotten in my eleventh-hour acknowledgment writing.

Thanks to the teams at OwlCrate and the Bookie Box, for including *Before She Ignites* in such wonderful boxes, and to all the readers who subscribe to them.

Of course, thanks to my mom, sister, and husband, who put up with more book talk than anyone should have to endure.

And, as always, thank you, readers.

Don't miss the fiery conclusion to the
FALLEN ISLES TRILOGY!

WHEN
SHE
REIGNS

Coming soon!